About the Author

Ruby Slipperjack was born and raised at her father's trapline at Whitewater Lake, Ontario. She is fluent in her Ojibwe Native language and has retained the Indigenous knowledge and culture of her Anishinawbe people. She is a member of the Eabametoong First Nation. Her formal education includes a B.A. in History, B.Ed., M.Ed., and a Ph.D. in Educational Studies from the University of Western Ontario. She is a tenured, full professor in the Indigenous Learning department at Lakehead University. Ruby lives in Thunder Bay with her husband and spends summers at her ancestral home at Whitewater Lake, which is still the source of much of her creative inspiration. They have three adult children. Ruby's previous novels include *Honour the Sun* (1987), *Silent Words* (Fifth House, 1992), *Little Voice* (2001), and *Weesquachak* (2005).

BEAR CREEK FIRST NATION

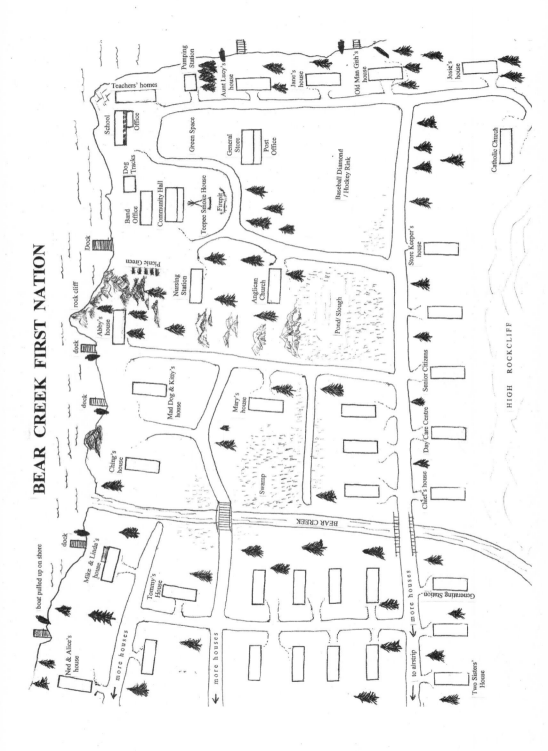

To my girls, Rosanna, Lindsay, and Amy.

*Special thanks to Lindsay for her inspiration
and our brainstorming sessions in a hospital
room, where the story first took shape.*

Dog Tracks

a novel by
Ruby Slipperjack

FIFTH
HOUSE

Cover design by Jacquie Morris and Delta Embree, Liverpool, Nova Scotia
Interior design by John Luckhurst
Copyedited by Kirsten Craven
Proofread by Ann Sullivan

The type in this book is set in Minion 11 on 14 point

The publisher gratefully acknowledges the support of
The Canada Council for the Arts and the Department of Canadian Heritage.

THE CANADA COUNCIL | LE CONSEIL DES ARTS
FOR THE ARTS | DU CANADA
SINCE 1957 | DEPUIS 1957

We acknowledge the financial support of the Government of Canada through the Book Publishing Industry Development Program (BPIDP) for our publishing activities.

Printed in Canada on Forest Stewardship Council (FSC) approved paper.

Recycled
Supporting responsible use
of forest resources
FSC   www.fsc.org Cert no. SW-COC-1271
© 1996 Forest Stewardship Council

2008 / 1

First published in the United States in 2009 by
Fitzhenry & Whiteside
311 Washington Street
Brighton, Massachusetts, 02135

Library and Archives Canada National Cataloguing in Publication

Slipperjack, Ruby, 1952-   Dog tracks / Ruby Slipperjack.

ISBN 978-1-897252-29-1

1. Ojibwa Indians—Juvenile fiction. I. Title.

PS8587.L53D63 2008   jC813'.54   C2008-904175-5

Fifth House Ltd.
A Fitzhenry & Whiteside Company
1511, 1800-4 St. SW
Calgary, Alberta T2S 2S5
1-800-387-9776
www.fitzhenry.ca

Contents

CHAPTER ONE
A New Home – 1

CHAPTER TWO
The Real Anishinawbe Experience – 17

CHAPTER THREE
Ki-Moot and Chief Paulie – 34

CHAPTER FOUR
The Pine Beetle Goes Blueberry Picking – 48

CHAPTER FIVE
Summer Camping – 70

CHAPTER SIX
Fall Hunting – 87

CHAPTER SEVEN
Mad Dog – 100

CHAPTER EIGHT
Holidays – 124

CHAPTER NINE
My Second Spring – 138

CHAPTER TEN
Family Time – 148

CHAPTER ELEVEN
Back to the Blueberries – 159

CHAPTER TWELVE
A New Arrival Amidst Chaos – 178

CHAPTER THIRTEEN
Work at Camp – 194

CHAPTER FOURTEEN
Dog Tracks – 214

CHAPTER ONE

A New Home

I awoke to the sound of howling wind outside my attic window. The smell of toast and coffee was already in the air, and it wafted up the stairs to my bedroom. I always left the door open so that I could listen to Grandma and Grandpa talking downstairs. I call my grandma Goom and my grandpa Choom. That's my short form in Ojibwe.

I smiled at the sound of Goom's laughter coming from the kitchen below. Stretching and yawning, I threw back my sheets and glanced at the window. Pulling the pink ruffled comforter around me, I went to the window and drew the white lace curtains aside and saw snowflakes blowing across the windowpane. I loved my curtains. They had little pink flowers on them. Goom got them for me at Christmas and we decorated my room too. Now, it was all pink and white. I looked down the street. Our small white house was the last on the block, and as always, it seemed, I saw an old man cross the street with his little black dog.

Dressing quickly, I went down the stairs just in time to see Choom coming into the kitchen with his walker. His rasping breath turned into a chuckle as he said, "Well, look who's up before she is called this morning."

I giggled, replying, "My name is not 'This Morning'!" Every time I came down without being called, we would have that same exchange. I went into the bathroom to brush my teeth, and I heard him shuffling into the kitchen.

It was going to be another cold morning to run to school. I usually took a shortcut across a small field behind our house that opened out into the schoolyard. It wasn't that far but it got very cold on windy days.

I was sitting at the table crunching on my favourite dry cereal with lots of milk in it when the phone rang. I couldn't hear what Goom was saying because of my crunching. Choom winked at me and nodded his white head toward the phone. There was only a bit of black hair left on the top of his head but it was still thick. Just as I swallowed, I heard Goom saying, "Is Blair going to school today? Better make him stay home if he still has that bad cold." It was my mom! I dropped my spoon, ran to the phone, and hugged Goom around her waist while she talked. My head came up almost level to hers. I remembered when I was much shorter than that.

I had been with Goom and Choom since I was seven years old. I was going to be thirteen in May. Thirteen! Finally, Goom handed the phone to me and I sat down on the chair beside the telephone stand. I heard my mother saying, "Hello, Abby. How are you? Make sure you dress warm going to school today, alright? Is it snowing there yet? We had a lot of snow last night. It has cleared a bit, but it is really cold." After responding with a series of yes and no answers, I brought the phone over to Choom who went into long sentences in Ojibwe.

I sat down and resumed my chewing of the cereal that was now very soggy and thick. I dropped the spoon and faced Goom, who had now set down her egg on toast on the table and sat in front of me. The oval table was pushed against the kitchen wall and our three chairs were placed around it. "What's the matter?" she asked. Her blond hair had slowly turned white at the top and sides of her head, but her blue eyes twinkled with humour as they always had. Choom always said she had a happy soul and that all you had to do was look into her eyes and you would suddenly feel better.

I sighed and asked, "How come Mom always talks about the weather, or about Blink, John, Maggie, or the Band office?"

She smiled and said, "What do you talk to her about?" I pulled over the jar of kiddy pops from the centre of the table. Goom always brought back my favourite butterscotch lollipops whenever she went into Thunder Bay for something. I stuck it into my pocket. I usually ate the pops at recess or on the way home for lunch.

I answered, "Can't talk to her about anything because she doesn't ask about stuff I do. If I tell her about my favourite music or TV show, or even my homework, she doesn't say much about it."

Goom swallowed her first bite of toast and said, "Well, maybe you should go to the reserve more often than just on holidays."

I sat back on the chair. "There's nothing to do there! Maggie never pays any attention to me either. I only saw her once the last time we were there! She always hangs around with her other friends."

Our attention turned to Choom, who was talking about moose hunting. Mom must have handed the phone over to my stepfather, John. Goom grinned at me when Choom began laughing, telling a story in his rasping breath about one particularly funny hunting trip.

Goom was quite fluent in Ojibwe, but we always spoke English. Most of the time, Choom spoke to me in Ojibwe, but I'd often forget and answer in English. I think that was because I came home one day with a note from the teacher saying that my English was bad. After that, Goom always spoke English with me, and soon my Ojibwe started including English words. My Ojibwe friend at school always laughed at me when I said something in a mix of English and Ojibwe words. I'd say something like, "*peesh candy api school eshayun*," instead of saying "bring some candy for school." I guess it did sound pretty funny. Choom never stopped talking to me in Ojibwe, though; he always said that someone had to.

When Choom finally put the phone down, Goom set a plate of breakfast in front of him. He liked his egg on toast too. I glanced at the clock and ran up the stairs to my room. I grabbed my backpack from the couch and placed the remote on top of the television that sat at the corner of my room. After hastily fixing my bed, I ran back down the stairs. Goom was ready with my hairbrush and she brushed my hair back and snapped a clip into it. After a quick kiss on Choom's forehead, I was out in the porch pulling on my boots and Goom was there with my winter coat, toque, scarf, and mitts. She kissed the top of my head, and I dashed out the door.

No matter how early I got up, I was always running late. It was the phone call that did it that morning! The day before, it was Goom insisting that I wear those thick gloves, one of which I couldn't find. The day before that, I couldn't find a book that had my homework in it. It had fallen down behind the television. Oh, well.

I had lost count of the steps. I always counted my steps when I ran from my door to the school. Sometimes I didn't even really pay attention to how many steps it took, I just counted.

I got to the school just as the clanging bell rang out into the windswept space across the schoolyard. There was no one hanging around outside. I ran inside to the chaos in the boot room. We had to take off our boots and line them up on benches and shelves. Well, that was supposed to be the idea, but boots were strewn around everywhere, and I had to kick several of them aside in order to reach my boot corner. I remembered one fall morning, one of the boys had kicked a dead skunk on the road and his shoe stank up the boot room so badly that it took the janitor some time before he finally figured out which was the stinking shoe and threw it outside. The teachers laughed about that, saying that it was the first time a shoe got expelled from school.

Sliding on the shiny tiled hallway in my soft fuzzy socks, I hurried to the grade seven room on the right. The bell rang the second time just as I pushed the door open. I stuffed my toque, scarf, and mitts into the sleeves of my coat, hung it up, and hurried to my seat. Mr. B. was already at the board writing down the day's date as if we didn't already know. That date was to appear on the top page of everything we wrote. I picked up my pen and wrote Wednesday, February 20, 2008, and signed my name, Abby S. beneath it.

A rolled-up piece of paper landed on my desk as Mr. B. wrote down the subjects for the day. I quickly grabbed it before the teacher glanced my way. As I wrote down the first topic, I opened the paper and read, "Sally." With a sigh of relief, I threw the paper on the desk of the person in front of me and it promptly disappeared. So, Sally was to be "it" that day. That was twice for her that month already. I glanced at her, two rows away, hunched over her desk. Her black hair always looked like it had been slicked with oil, it was so shiny and pure black. Meanwhile, her skin was just the opposite— it was porcelain white. She was an Asian girl from the family who owned the only restaurant in town, besides the restaurant at the gas station.

The building had been renovated since Goom worked there, and it looked brand new now. The wood was made to look like bamboo at the front and it had beautiful Chinese art on all the walls inside. It was a very busy place because the Nibika Hotel, the only hotel in town, was right across the street. The food was wonderful there, and that was the place Goom used to work as a waitress when it was run by the original owner, who had long since passed away.

As Choom's story goes, one night Goom was coming back from Thunder Bay when she had a flat tire. She had an old car that was always breaking down, so she had gone to the city to get it fixed. Anyway, she was just coming into town when she had the flat tire. She was getting the spare tire out when a truck pulled up and out jumped a tall, handsome Ojibwe man, who changed the tire for her. While they talked, she told him where she worked and every day after that he came into the restaurant and soon they got married. He worked as a section man on the Canadian National Railway. Then, my aunty Gilda was born and then after that, my mom was born.

I became aware of sudden silence and giggles broke out when I realized that all eyes were on me. Mr. B.'s dark face bore no expression as his deep brown eyes remained on me. Mr. B. was from South Africa. He had a jar of sand on his desk that he said was the soil of his homeland in Africa. I used to put my hand in the large pickle jar and let the sand filter between my fingers in awe until Joey said that it was sand from the pit behind Mr. Johnson's warehouse.

Mr. B. said, "Abby, I will repeat the question and please do listen carefully." Before he could repeat the question, Sally let out an awful scream that startled everyone. Someone had dropped a large crawling silverfish on top of her writing paper. I quickly located the culprit with a glance. It was Jimmy, sitting beside her, who had done it while she had her head turned. But Jimmy sat there quietly, looking innocently at me. Mr. B. removed the bug, put it into a jar, and paused to comfort Sally.

I turned to watch P. H. giggling with a pencil dangling from his mouth. He was the new boy who joined us in September. Although they were his initials, we actually called him P. H. because he had brown hair and the ends were dyed purple. So, we called him Purple Head, P. H. for short. Right from the first week, Joey said P. H. had a box in his room with all our names written on little pieces of paper and every day he would draw a name and drop the name back into the box. If your name came up, you were "it" for the day. Everyone in the class could ask you to do anything and they could play tricks on you too.

My name was drawn just before Christmas, and I was the cloak girl for the day. It was more like they just threw their coats and stuff at me before I could take them to hang them up. As a result, there was a large heap of mitts and scarves on the floor that the students ended up sorting themselves if they wanted to get home warm. I also discovered that someone had put a big glob of glue inside my toque.

What? Oh, the question. I had missed it again. Mr. B. said that I now had to write a paragraph about the question and hand it in before I could go out for recess. I immediately thought about the kiddy pop in my pocket that I'd planned to have at recess. Now that I had my paragraph to write, how was I going to have enough time to finish it before the bell rang?

About a quarter of the twenty-six students in my class were Anishinawbe children of parents who worked in town. The nearby reserve had its own school and it had mostly Anishinawbe teachers. Autumn, the Anishinawbe girl beside me, was one of my best friends. She was the one who used to make fun of my mixed language of Ojibwe and English. My other two friends were Alexa, the redhead with fuzzy curly hair at the front, and Jalene, the girl with the straight long blond hair who sat at the back beside P. H. All four of us hung out together. Mr. B. separated our seats in October because he said we were disrupting the class too much. Of course, it wasn't us at all who did it most of the time. At recess, I wrote the paragraph for Mr. B. and he took it without comment. After throwing on my coat and pulling on my boots, I raced out to the swings, where I saw the girls waiting for me. I wanted to see what kinds of candy they had brought because sometimes we traded.

We got to go to the library before lunch, so Autumn, Alexa, Jalene, and I found a corner of the library where we exchanged titles and summaries of the books that we'd read so we could add them to our list of books read for that month. The list had to be handed in at the end of each month. When our assignments were done, we usually hung out together outside of school. We'd go for pop at the restaurant, and sometimes we'd drop by Aunty Gilda's place.

Gilda sold cosmetics door-to-door and she always had bottles and jars of stuff left over from her samples. Sometimes she would practice putting makeup on our faces and we always had different tiny lipstick samples to pick from. Gilda was like a woman from the cosmetics section of a department store. She had long fingernails and her light brown hair was always professionally styled. Her light complexion matched her blue eyes, and sometimes when she laughed, you could see that she was Goom's daughter, alright. She wore tailored suits and other outfits that fitted her slim body. She also carried a tote bag with her samples and a briefcase for her appointments and orders and went about the community in her little white car. She always went to the reserve on Wednesdays and would stay there all day. Sometimes she would drop by at Goom and Choom's place on her way home to tell Choom all about the happenings on the reserve where he had been born and raised. Her red-haired husband was called Captain Ron by his buddies and, like Choom, he had worked as a section man on the Canadian National Railway that ran through town. He always packed a lunch and left home at the same time every morning and came home at the same time every evening. Gilda and Captain Ron had no children.

Instead of going over to Gilda's on this day, however, I ran all the way home and bounded into the porch, kicking off my boots before pushing open the door that led to the area between the dining room and the living room. Choom was sitting at the kitchen table with one of my kiddy pops sticking out of the corner of his mouth, snoring away, fast asleep.

I quietly deposited my bag and tiptoed to his chair. Just as I reached out to take the lollipop from his mouth, he suddenly grabbed my hand, saying, "I got ya!" Laughing, I let him warm my cheeks with his hands. I knew he wasn't asleep. He did this all the time and I still always pretended that he surprised me, although I did notice that his quick grab was now a lot slower than it used to be.

"Where's Goom?" I asked.

He replied, "Not back from your Aunty Gilda's. They're cutting up quilt patterns or something for the church bazaar."

It was always Aunty Gilda and the church! Goom helped her bake cookies and desserts for after-church service on Sundays too. But Goom never went to church with her. Choom was not a particularly religious man, although we used to go with Gilda as a family on special occasions and holidays. It was only since Choom came down with his heart condition that he and Goom stayed home most of the time, and that was okay with me because I had no patience for church services. I knew that Choom was more into traditional Anishinawbe ways of doing things, anyway. His relatives often came to pick him up for their traditional ceremonies at the reserve. Goom went with him only on rare occasions and sometimes all of us went to the powwow there or a traditional feast. But most of the time he'd go by himself to visit.

Choom tried to get up from the table several times but sank back down. I brought his walker to him and held it as he finally stood up and steadied himself before I stepped aside and watched him slowly shuffle into the living room. I followed him and turned the television on as he sank down into the soft cushions of the couch. He decided he wanted to lie down, so I lifted his legs onto the couch and fixed the cushions under his head until he seemed comfortable. The television was on the news channel he liked, and I asked him, "You okay, Choom? Can I get you anything else?" He smiled and shook his head, so I left him lying there and ran up with my school bag to my room, where I threw it on the couch. It was always cooler up there when the wind was blowing against my window.

I sat down at the dresser beside the window. I studied my reflection in the dresser mirror. My cheeks were still red from the biting cold, but my dark eyes were clear and I made a face, sticking out my lips, imitating Aunty Gilda's full red lips. My black eyebrows drew together. I didn't like her taking up Goom's time and leaving Choom to sit by himself at the table. My black hair was long and straight. My bangs hung perfectly curved at the top of my eyebrows. I did several more big red lip imitations, whispering, "Would you care for some cookies and tea, my dear?" and thought that Choom had probably gone to sleep. Best that I should stay up here and do my homework so as not to wake him until Goom came home.

I turned on my television and flipped the channels for a bit before I settled on a kids' show that I liked to watch when no one else was around. After arranging my homework in piles of priority, I began with an assignment that was due the next day. Some time went by until I noticed that there was a noise downstairs. Goom had probably just come through the door. I continued with my homework and then totally lost track of time. I was into the hardest question when I heard Goom's panicked voice at the bottom of the stairs.

"Abby! Come down here, quick!" I practically flew down the stairs in time to see Goom on the phone calling 911. Choom was lying on the floor! I ran to him and was relieved that he was still breathing. I grabbed a couch cushion and propped it under his head, and then Goom was beside me, saying, "Go call Gilda before she leaves her house."

I ran to the phone and stood there trying to remember her number. Goom, seeing my hesitation, called out the number to me. Oh, yes, of course, how could I have forgotten! I quickly dialled the number and thankfully Aunty Gilda picked up the phone. Afterward, I couldn't remember exactly what I'd said to her, but she was at the house just as the ambulance pulled into our driveway.

We waited at the small Nibika Hospital for a long time until it was decided that Choom would have to go to the Thunder Bay Regional Hospital right away. Aunty Gilda drove me home to pack some overnight stuff for Goom, and we rushed back to the hospital in time to give Goom her overnight bag before she got into the ambulance with Choom. When the ambulance pulled away, I remained standing there in the middle of the road. For the first time in my life, I felt totally alone. I heard Aunty Gilda's steps behind me and then she took my arm, saying, "Come, let's go get your things and you can stay at my place until they get back, okay?" I wanted to cry so badly, but Choom always said: "Big girls don't cry." I nodded and sat looking out the window as we drove silently back to the little white house.

Gilda stayed in the car and I went in rather slowly and didn't bother kicking off my boots as I trudged up the stairs to my room. I flicked on the light and saw my papers and textbooks on the table where I'd dropped them. I methodically stuffed them all into my backpack, threw in my toothbrush and the clothes that Goom had hung in my closet, ready for tomorrow, and turned off the television. I glanced back at my neat and bright room before I shut off the light and closed my door. It was getting dark now and I realized I was hungry. I grabbed a kiddy pop off the kitchen table before I locked the door behind me. I pressed the door key to my palm as I slid back into the front seat of the car. Aunty Gilda blew her nose and sniffled before I realized that she'd been crying. I turned to her and said, "Choom will be alright. You'll see. He'll be okay." I don't know why I said that. Maybe it was just something I was supposed to say. I certainly didn't take any comfort from it and Aunty Gilda didn't say anything as she drove home.

Early Saturday morning I listened to the phone ringing in the kitchen for awhile before I heard Aunty Gilda come running from the bathroom. I normally didn't answer her phone since it was always women calling for their orders or placing orders for the cosmetics that she sold. I rolled over and covered my head with the quilt. I had been sleeping on the couch in the living room and I was just about to go back to sleep after Captain Ron had packed a lunch and left to go ice fishing with his buddies. Then Aunty Gilda was beside me, saying, "Abby, we're going into the city to pick up Grandma. Hurry! We can get there by lunchtime and be back in time for supper. Grandpa is fine but he'll have to stay there for awhile yet." I was up and running into the bathroom before she finished speaking.

It only took ten minutes to drive to the Trans-Canada Highway from our little town of Nibika, and then it was almost two hours to the city. The drive there was quiet and uneventful. I stared out the window and Gilda drove in silence. We drove directly to the hospital and parked the car. We hurried through the lobby and up the flight of stairs. Soon, we saw Goom standing by a hallway window looking outside. I slowed my step to match Aunty Gilda's. Then she stopped and stood there looking at Goom. I was about to ask why when she said, just under her breath, "She looks so frail.

So old . . . " I gazed back at Goom and took Aunty Gilda's hand, saying, "She's just tired, that's all. She looks tired. She'll be okay." She looked down at me and squeezed my hand and gave a tight smile. I realized then that I was just trying to reassure myself by speaking those words out loud. Things would be alright. Everything was going to be okay. It's what Choom would say.

Goom's face lit up when she saw us. After she gave both of us a big hug, she led us to Choom's room. I walked slowly to the side of the bed and saw that he was asleep. He looked pale and I took his hand, but he didn't move. He had tubes coming and going from his body and the little box beside him blinked and hummed as it sent a series of lines scrolling across a screen. I suddenly felt sick, and I flopped down on a chair that sat close by. Goom was talking to Gilda as she flicked the pages of a chart that lay at the foot of Choom's bed.

A nurse came in and asked if I would like to wait in the waiting room across the hall, then I saw that the doctor was right behind her. I left Goom and Aunty Gilda to talk to the doctor and I went into the waiting room. I sat down and reached for the remote when I saw the television in the corner. I flicked the channels until I found a cartoon that I liked. Soon, Goom and Aunty Gilda came in, still talking. Goom had had enough of hospital cafeteria food and wanted to eat at a restaurant before we all headed home together. After a quick lunch at a fast-food place, we took the expressway heading out of town. I sat in the back seat, slowly sipping on the pop I had brought with me from the lunch stop. I wasn't interested in looking around or getting excited about the city; I just wanted to go back home to the little white house with Goom.

Just like the drive to the hospital, the drive home was quiet, both Aunty Gilda and Goom lost in thought. I certainly didn't feel like chatting about this or that either. Aunty Gilda came in with us when we got back home. I hadn't been back to the house since Wednesday and the familiar comforting smell enveloped me when I stepped inside. After hanging up my coat and kicking off my boots, I ran up the stairs and sat down on my bed. I could hear them talking in the kitchen and heard the rattle of pots and pans. Goom would be making supper.

When I heard the back door close, I went to the window to see Aunty Gilda driving off. It suddenly became very quiet in the house and as I turned, I caught my reflection in my dresser mirror. I saw furrowed dark eyebrows, messy hair, and there was a big bubble on my lip. I had been chewing on the pop straw on the way home and began sucking my lip into the straw to see how far it would go in. I made the Aunty Gilda big lips imitation again, whispering, "You shouldn't have done that, my dear. Now you have an ugly bubbly mole on your lip!"

I heard Goom calling from the bottom of the stairs, "Are you going to come down to join me at supper?" At the table, Goom tried to be cheery, but I could tell she was worried and nothing seemed right without Choom sitting at the side of the table between us. We sat facing each other and then she said in Ojibwe, "What's with the big bubbly mole on your lip?" That brought a giggle up from my throat and then we sat there laughing for a bit, and then, our eyes back on the plates, it became quiet again.

As the days came and went, we began a sort of routine that seemed to work. On Mondays, Wednesdays, and Fridays, I would run from school to Aunty Gilda's place for lunch because that was where Goom would be. School went on as usual, and because everyone knew each other in this small town, people were very supportive and always asked me how my grandpa was doing. The one thing that never changed was that every morning I'd get up and go to the window of my bedroom, and as always, I'd see that old man crossing the street with his little black dog.

I came home one day in the first week of March to find Aunty Gilda and Goom sitting at the kitchen table, apparently waiting for me to get home. Aunty Gilda told me to sit down, and Goom placed some cookies and milk in front of me. I knew something was up. It was Aunty Gilda who did most of the talking. Choom was ready to come home, but he was going to need full-time care until he got better, which was going to take a longer bit of time. Goom wasn't going to be able to do that by herself, so they'd decided to move Goom and Choom over to Aunty Gilda's place and use her office area as a bedroom for them. The little white house would be sold and a small apartment would be found for them when Choom got better.

I'd taken a bite of the cookie but found that I couldn't swallow. I took a sip of the milk and noticed that my hand shook. My heart was pounding so fast I could feel it closing up my throat. I managed to ask, almost in a whisper, "What about me?"

Goom said with as much reassurance as she could muster in her voice, "I'll take you to your mother and family up north. I won't just send you there by yourself. But we have to do it next week on Wednesday because the hospital just called us this morning to tell us that Choom will be home on Friday next week."

I sat stunned for a few minutes until I fully realized that I was being sent away and that I was going to lose everything I knew and loved—Goom, Choom, my bedroom, my home! My eyes landed on the cupful of kiddy pops and I pulled one out and stuck it in my mouth. I tasted butterscotch, and I began to calm down. Choom's voice inside my head repeated, "Big girls don't cry." Finally, I looked back at Goom. Her pain-filled eyes held steady on me and I pushed the candy to the side of my mouth where it bulged out on my cheek before I said, "You'll visit me, right?"

She smiled and tears filled her eyes as she said, "Of course, I will! Try holding me back. I'll visit you very often, my little one. Don't you worry!"

I nodded and squared my shoulders. I had to get out of there quick! After swallowing a mouthful of butterscotch saliva from the kiddy pop, I smiled and left the table and raced up the stairs. For the first time ever, I slammed the door shut behind me with my foot and threw myself on the bed and stuffed my face into my pillow. I bawled as I'd never done before. I cried and mourned the life and love that I'd known in this little white house. I'd hoped that Choom would be back to normal and come home just as he was before. Now I knew things would never be the same again.

It was some time later, after I'd slobbered up my pillow, that I sat up and went to the dresser mirror and saw how awful my reflection looked. My eyes were all puffed up and my nose was even puffy and red. I wondered how I was going to go to school looking like that the next day and I hoped I wouldn't be so puffy in the morning. Then I heard the phone ring downstairs.

I knew Aunty Gilda was still down there so it had to be someone else. I was beginning to feel very angry. I felt like they were getting rid of me. Then I heard Goom yelling, "Abby, your mother wants to talk to you!" No! Tears flooded my eyes again and a painful squeeze started from my chest up to my throat, but then, as I grew angrier, the tears disappeared. No! I couldn't talk to her right now! But Goom was yelling up the stairs again, "Abby? Your mother is waiting, come down now, baby. Everything is all right." I knew there was no way of getting around this, so I wiped my sleeve across my eyes and marched down the stairs.

I pulled my sweater over my head to hide my face and grabbed the phone off the telephone stand, "Yeah?"

I heard my mother's voice saying, "Abby, it's okay. If you don't like it here, you can go back to Goom wherever she may be living. We just want you to try living here for awhile. We're just trying to make things easier for Goom right now because Goom and Gilda will have to look after Choom around the clock for awhile. He won't be able to do anything for himself for a long time. Would you come and live with me? It's the best I can do to help them because I can't come down there. Would you please come home to me?"

I found myself calming down and replied, "Yeah, I guess so. It's not like I have any choice, do I?"

Goom came and put her arms around me from behind and when I hung up the phone, I wasn't angry anymore. Actually, I wasn't feeling anything at all. Then Goom kissed my forehead and said, "It's okay, everything will be all right."

We packed and hauled stuff to Aunty Gilda's place and, finally, Goom and I were at the airport waiting for the scheduled plane heading up north. I was feeling sorry for Goom because she often got motion sickness, but she'd taken a pill that was supposed to prevent that. I had a suitcase and two boxes with me, and Goom carried two more. She would be sending me the rest of my stuff later on when she'd finished unpacking.

The plane had two rows of seats on each side with a narrow aisle running in between. It was full, but no one bothered to try to talk above the noise. Goom and I didn't have seats together, so we each settled into our spot and prepared for takeoff. I watched the trees and lakes pass by below for quite awhile before we approached the first community. When the plane's tires hit the runway, I noticed that the trees looked shorter than the ones at Nibika, and there was a berm on each side of the runway from the land that they had pushed back to clear the runway.

When the plane took off again, I looked at the old lady across from me. She had on a pair of running shoes. I also noticed that she had white socks and black slacks tucked inside them. Then on top of that she had a bright blue and red flowered print skirt on. She was wearing a blue windbreaker jacket and a black and red flowered scarf over her head that was securely tied under her chin. At that point, her weathered face broke into a big smile and I locked eyes with her. She'd caught me looking at her and I smiled in embarrassment. I felt I had to say something, so I leaned over and said in Ojibwe as loud as I could, "Your skirt and kerchief are really beautiful!"

She giggled shyly in response to my compliment, and then she leaned over and yelled back, "They were gifts from my children! For times when I go to town!" We smiled at each other off and on for the rest of the trip.

At the second stop there were no trees on the runway. It was like a field or a muskeg. At the third stop, the last of the people got off, including the old lady across from me. However, as she got up to leave, she put a hand on my shoulder and said, "It is so nice to hear one so young as you speaking the language. Never, ever, forget your language." With that, she slowly made her way down the aisle.

Before the airplane moved, Goom came and sat down in the vacated seat across the aisle from me. The engines roared as the plane got set to take off again. I leaned over to Goom and yelled, "Are you okay?" She smiled and nodded her head, "I'm okay, so far!" The last stop was our destination, Bear Creek First Nation. There were more rocks, trees, and lakes below and finally, we were on the short runway with thick bush on either side. My heart began to pound when the plane slowly taxied to the buildings. When would I be leaving this place? Goom smiled at me, saying, "Look, there's John waiting for us!"

When the plane came to a stop at the little shack that served as the ticket office, we got off the plane. My stepfather, John, was there to help Goom down the steps, and he gave each of us a hug and picked up our bags and boxes. We followed him away from the plane toward a fence, behind which sat his old snow machine with a large sled tied behind it. His old truck didn't run in the wintertime as the battery tended to freeze. He loaded up the sled and I sat down on the end box and watched him criss-cross a rope to tie the load down. He then laid the rope over my lap, too, so I had that to hang on to as Goom got on the machine behind him. It was a clear sunny day but the wind was still cold as we took off down the side of the airport road.

Finally, we turned off the road toward the lake and there was the house. Smoke slowly wafted up from the chimney, and the snow-covered lake beyond shimmered in the sun. There were piles of wood along the side of the house that led up to the small porch.

We pulled up and Goom stomped her feet before she helped me up from the box. John unloaded our stuff, and I still remember the sudden total quietness of the place. Then the door opened and Mom came out, pulling on a coat. She ran down the steps as Goom said, "Sophie! It's so good to see you!" Mom came over and gave Goom a hug and then she had her arms around me. She always smelled of woodsmoke and coffee. They laughed and talked, but I had a strange feeling knowing I wasn't there for a short visit this time. This was to be my home now. I stood, slowly turning around. There was a path to the right that led to the Band office. That was Mom's shortcut to and from her work as the secretary there. There was a big pile of wood beneath a shelter that stood against the house. Beside the wood was the sawhorse and a big block of wood that John used as a chopping block.

John had disappeared inside the house with our stuff and I turned my attention to Mom and Goom. My mom was taller than Aunty Gilda and her long brown hair hung loose down her back that day. Her eyes were light brown with golden specks and her skin was the same shade as mine. Her smile, however, was the same as Goom's. I followed them up the three wooden steps to the plywood-enclosed porch. There was a large freezer against the back wall with shelves above it. The heat welcomed us as we entered the living room/kitchen area. A couch was pushed up against the right wall and the woodstove sat mid-right of the room with an upholstered bench behind it. Lines of wire criss-crossed between the stovepipe and the wall. That was where the wet socks and mitts were usually hung. To the left was the propane cookstove and a cupboard that held the dishes and the pots and pans. Below the window was a counter that had a black telephone and other stuff on it. Across the room was a large dining room table with six chairs around it. Four more chairs stood against the wall below the large window that overlooked the lake. To the right was the hallway, from which a freckle-faced boy with bushy dark haired emerged. That was six-year-old Blink, my half-brother. He blinked at me and then ran to Goom and she gave him a big hug, laughing and swinging him around.

I stood surveying this place that I would now call home. For some reason, I was taking it all in as if I was seeing it for the first time. I noticed that Blink was ignoring me. I could tell that I was going to have trouble with him. I never liked him very much, the spoiled little brat! I continued my survey of the house. There was a bathroom to the right of the hallway. The white metal medicine cabinet held the only mirror in the place, other than Mom's dresser mirror in her and John's bedroom. To the left was the bedroom where I would be staying, to the right was Blink's room, and beyond that was the back of the house with Mom's small sewing room to the left and their larger bedroom to the right. Goom and I had always stayed in the first bedroom. It had two twin beds. So, the deal was that after Goom left they would move the other single bed to the sewing room, so that I could use the sewing table in there to do my homework on. My eyes settled on the old linoleum floor that had lost all trace of its brown squares with the yellow flowers in the middle, on the high-traffic areas between the stove and kitchen table.

After lunch, everyone went off to work and school and Goom and I lay on one of the single beds and talked. With all the stuff that had happened since the day she found Choom on the floor when she got home, we hadn't had time to sit down and talk. Each night since then, I had taken to crying into my pillow until I fell asleep. Meanwhile, Goom had spent every spare minute with Aunty Gilda, making plans and visiting lawyers and real estate people. As if giving me last instructions, Goom told me that I must be nice and stay happy and be helpful. I was not to be upset by things that Blink or any of the other kids might say or do, and I must not answer back or make comments that might cause tension in the house. I was to start school on Monday.

Thinking about a new school made me nervous. Of course, I'd seen the children in the community when we'd come to visit, but since we'd always just come to visit, I'd never made any effort to make friends with any of them. Most times, they just stood and stared at us when we went to the Band office or the store. I had a very hard job in front of me.

I was really going to miss Autumn, Alexa, and Jalene. Before I'd left, we'd sworn that we'd stay in touch. We'd even exchanged e-mail addresses. I was feeling uneasy, though. I didn't even know if I'd have access to a computer around here. I knew there wasn't one in the house, not even a television. Maybe there was one at school. I guess I'd find out soon enough. Failing that, there was always the post office.

"Goom? We were planning to go to Winnipeg on my birthday, remember?"

Goom stroked my hair and said, "I told your mom about that and she said that they would take you to Winnipeg. All of you will be going. Won't that be nice? I can't believe that you'll be thirteen years old!"

I smiled, thinking that I would have had a big birthday party at Nibika with my friends around me. We always had fun on birthdays. Once, Alexa's mom and dad drove the four of us to Thunder Bay to see a movie matinee at the big theatre. Then we had supper at a fancy restaurant. That was wonderful! Goom asked in Ojibwe, "What are you smiling about?" I turned and faced her, "About my wonderful birthdays in Nibika." I saw tears welling in her eyes, but she smiled back at me.

CHAPTER TWO

The Real Anishinawbe Experience

It was early spring and the ice had just melted. I was with John down by the shore beside the overturned canoe. I could see around the curve of the bay to where Mike's house stood. Farther down was Ned's house. They were the last of the houses before the shoreline broke into a high rock cliff. Dad had decided to cut my hair that morning. I was just now beginning to get comfortable with calling John Dad, too, since that was all I heard from Blink all day long. It was Dad this and Dad that.

I thought I was doing pretty good at keeping my mouth shut around Blink, just like Goom had asked. Goom and I spoke on the phone often. Choom was still the same, meaning that his health hadn't improved and he still couldn't talk. Mom had to talk to me several times when I'd get mad at Blink. Like that one time Goom sent me a bag of kiddy pops. They were all butterscotch too. The little rat had sniffed them out and the next thing I knew, he came running into the Band office where I was waiting for Mom with one sticking out of his mouth. I screamed at him and smacked him on the back of the head with my notebook when I discovered that he'd not only taken one, but that the whole bag was gone! Apparently, he'd passed them around to his friends before he got to the Band office.

I was furious! Mom told me that candy was candy and that it would have been gone anyway. But, she said, the hurt and anger I'd caused would be hanging around like skunk stink between me and Blink for a long time.

Skunk stink? Since then, I'd look at Blink and think, "S.S.! Skunk Stink." Mom did tell Blink not to touch my things again. I also heard John talking to Blink outside once when I happened to be at the open kitchen window. It made me feel good when I overheard John saying that I was Blink's sister and that he should treat me like one, and that I was his daughter too. I think that was when I decided that he was my dad.

John was a certified mechanic and he could fix any kind of engine, including the school furnace, the daycare furnace, and the church's oil stoves, whenever he was needed. He was a Band councillor and he also earned his living by guiding for the Bear Creek Tourist Lodge in the summer and trapping in the winter. He was a rather skinny man, and he looked even skinnier with his checkered shirt tucked into his jeans. He always wore his long black hair in braids that hung down on each side of his chest. Mom usually wore her straight long brown hair braided and hanging down her back. And mine? Well, Goom used to brush my hair every morning. Now, I just brushed it as best I could and left it like that. I still did have my bangs, though they were very long now.

That morning I could tell it was going to be a very hot, muggy day. The plastic garbage bag draped over my shoulders was already sticking to my neck. I sat on an overturned wooden box and listened to the "crunch, crunch, crunch" as Dad's scissors gnawed their way across the back of my neck. "Hey, not too short! I don't want to look like a boy, you know."

His voice sounded above my head,. "You won't look like a boy. I'm just cutting straight across below your neckline. How did you get the glue in your hair anyway?"

I sighed. "I was at Tommy's this morning, when I went to get Blink, and David was behind me with a tube of superglue and the top was dried shut so they started hitting it on the table with something. Anyway, I guess they broke a hole in the tube and it sprayed into my hair every time they hit it. I didn't know it until I came out. My hair kept pulling cause it was glued to my jacket."

Sounding like he was really concentrating on the haircut, he said, "Mom's still mad at you, you know. That jacket cost lots of money."

I replied, "Well, it wasn't my fault. That was the best jacket I ever had too!" I wondered where I'd find another one like it. I liked the bright pink jacket with the blue sleeves, and the embroidered feathers at the back were really beautiful! Mom said she bought the jacket from some guy who brought the jackets to sell at the Band office, but he was gone now. I'd asked her if the guy came to the office often, but she'd just shrugged and said she'd only seen him the one time.

I saw Dad's feet come around my chair and he said, "Okay. Bangs. Want me to trim your bangs up a bit? They're starting to fall over your eyes."

I bit down on my lip and said, "Okay, but I want my hair cut right along my eyebrows. Right *on* the eyebrows, and not on top."

He planted his feet on each side of mine. "Okay, no higher than the top of the eyebrows. Hold still."

I held my breath and sat very still. Then he said, "We could go see Old Man Gish's dog's puppies today." Gish was an old man who Dad and his friend Mike hung out with. Apparently, he was teaching them all the cultural things he knew and showing them how things were done long ago. Dad was working on a long piece of birch wood the day before that he said was the beginning of a snowshoe.

I raised my eyebrows to look straight up at his face without moving my head as he continued. "There's a black and white female puppy . . . hold still."

I held my head straight in line with his chest as I continued looking up at his face. "Really? We're going to get a puppy?"

His hand brushed my nose as he said, "Well, they're only a few weeks old now. You'd have to wait until we come back from Winnipeg. It should be able to eat by itself by then."

I could hardly contain my excitement as the scissors chewed their way across my forehead.

I kept my eyes on his face as he snipped the corners of my bangs. He looked like he was performing an operation or something. I glanced down to shake off the hair that was raining down on my hands. "Are you done now?" I asked.

"Yeah . . . " his voice faded and he suddenly drew in his breath and stood perfectly still, looking down at me. This wasn't a good sign at all!

I was all ready to jump up, but he remained in front of me, so I demanded, "What? What's wrong?"

He backed away from me, took a deep breath, and dropped the scissors on top of the overturned canoe. "What?" I asked. He turned and looked out at the lake but still didn't say anything. Suddenly my hands flew to my head. I felt the back and scurried them over to the front, where, to my horror, my hands became still. I could feel my bangs and the ends came almost to the top of my hairline!

"You cut my bangs too short! Now I have a big bald forehead!"

I jumped off the wooden box and ran up the hill to the house. I stomped across the porch and flung the door open and ran smack into Blink, the S.S. All I saw was a blur as he crashed inside the wood box beside the stove. I ran on, blinded with tears and pent-up anger. I banged my bedroom door shut and plopped myself on the edge of the bed. I crunched through a fold on the wrist of my sweater sleeve, thinking, "What am I going to do now? I can't be seen like this!" The crunch, crunch of my corner tooth slicing through the fabric gave me some comfort. I'd recently taken to chewing on fabric when I was upset. I think the first time it happened was when I'd shoved a pillow over my mouth and let out a huge howl of a scream when S.S. got home from school first one day and ate all the cake left over in the kitchen and didn't leave me a piece. It was rather a comforting sound, chewing on fabric, and now I found myself biting on my sleeves because they were handy.

I lay down, shaking with anger, and surveyed my bedroom for the gizzilienth time. The faded flower-designed curtains over the window were held up by a string; the unpainted plywood walls had nails sticking out for hanging stuff; the closet had no door; and my grey army blanket was topped with a faded quilt. There was unpainted plywood on the floor too. Goom had sent me my pink and white ruffled bedspread and shams, but I didn't want to put them on my unpainted plywood bed. Somehow, they just seemed very out of place. So, I'd stuck them back in the box and shoved it in the corner of the closet. No matter what my bedroom looked like, it was my space and I never allowed S.S. into it.

I could hear Blink howling, my mother screeching, and then John's booming voice joining in the fray. Suddenly, Mom was at the door, knocking. "What's the matter? Are you alright?"

I ran to the door and put my back to it saying, "Go away! I don't want to come out right now!"

I could hear her desperate voice beseeching Dad. "What happened? Why is she so upset?"

Then I heard Dad's voice, lower than normal, saying, "I didn't realize she was looking up at me and wrinkling up her forehead. All I measured was the top of her eyebrows, just like she told me, and I cut straight across. Well, when she looked down, her forehead dropped and her bangs are now ... kinda hanging way up in the air, sort of."

I could tell by the tremor in his voice that he was trying hard not to laugh. Laughing at me! I couldn't hear anything from my mom. I bet she was laughing too! What was I going to do? I sat down on the edge of my bed. I didn't have a mirror there; it was in the bathroom. I knew everybody was going to laugh at me the next day at school.

There was one boy who always sat at the back of the classroom, and he'd always whisper to whoever was sitting beside him, and then they would laugh at me. His name was Abraham. Sometimes I wished I could throw a mud ball right in his face! My homeroom was with the Native language teacher, and we usually went to that class first thing in the morning. Then we moved to another class after recess. The kids were nice during my first week of school, but after that, they started picking on me. They teased me about what I wore and how I spoke. I never saw my sister Maggie at school, either. The older kids were in another wing of the school, and they had their own entrance at the back. I couldn't wait for school to be over!

Dad's voice seeped through my door. "I'm sorry, Abby. I didn't know you were looking up at me. I was just trying to be so careful, I forgot to look down at you. Anyway, I can't put back the hair I cut. So, please, let's just go. Let's go see those puppies. I promise, you can have one just for yourself. Okay?"

The puppy! I supposed I could put a scarf over my head. I slowly approached the door, then yanked it open. Dad was apparently about to say something else and he grabbed the door frame for balance when I stepped in front of him. He moved aside and Mom looked straight at me. She was standing at the kitchen table and she said, "Turn around, let's see your hair. Oh, the back looks nice, and the front, well, that will take a few weeks to grow in and in another one or two weeks, it will be perfect. By then, do you know what that time will be?"

"One and a half to two weeks? That's our trip to Winnipeg!" I smiled half-heartedly and continued, "Oh, yeah, my birthday!"

Mom held out her hand. "Come now, it'll be your thirteenth birthday and it will be very special. It will be your special trip to Winnipeg. Won't that be nice?"

"Yeah," I nodded my head.

She pulled me to their bedroom, where I stood in front of the dresser mirror. For the first time, I witnessed the butchery on my forehead! Mom's hand flattened my bangs against my forehead and they came within an inch of the top of my eyebrows. However, when she removed her hand, they popped back up and I looked like I had a bald forehead!

Mom pulled out a drawer from the dresser and held out a package of stretchy headbands that Dad had bought her. I had only seen her wear a black one, but now I watched her pull out a red one. The package came in colours of red, blue, white, green, purple, and black. She slipped the red one over my head, saying, "Here, this will match the little red flowers on your shirt."

She pulled the headband over my forehead and my short bangs disappeared underneath. My hair was neatly tucked beneath the headband and there was no reason to suspect that there was anything wrong. Mom had fixed it! I laughed and threw my arms around her. She gave me the package, saying, "Here, use these until your hair grows back. And go tell your dad that it's all right. He feels really bad, you know."

I pushed her back, saying, "Feels bad! I heard him laughing!"

Mom smiled. "Well, that was later. Right after he cut it, he said he nearly puked when he saw what he'd done."

Blink dashed in. "Come on, come on! Let's go!" He didn't glance at me at all.

I looked at Mom and she shook her head as he disappeared out the door.

"Blink didn't see my hair?"

Mom laughed out loud. "How could he have? He was coming out with the old fuzzy blanket for the puppies when you ran into him. He fell into the wood box and got wedged in there. He couldn't get up. That's why he was yelling and hollering for help! So, you just saved yourself some teasing for today. He's going to see your hair at some point, though."

We reached the truck and S.S. was already sitting in the back seat. Dad's battered old blue truck was running again, but most of the time it sat in the backyard, dead like his old snow machine. Dad liked to say the truck went on a sit-down strike when he didn't get exactly what it needed, and the snow machine died when he got too much of the stuff that it wasn't designed for. I took that to mean the parts that I'd seen attached to the snow machine, like parts of a kid's skipping rope, ladies' nylons, large hairpins, springs from pens, large rubber bands, key chain links, and any number of odds and ends that you could find around the place.

I scrambled up to the front seat of the truck and pretended to click on the missing seat belt clip. One day, Dad had automatically strapped the seat belt on Old Gish when they had to go down a winter road to the nearest town, but then he had to run into the Band office first to get some papers.

After Dad had been gone awhile, Gish decided he didn't want to sit there waiting any longer but couldn't figure out how to take the clip off. So he pulled out the hunting knife that he always had hanging from his belt, cut the belt, threw it off him, and went into the Band office to see what was taking Dad so long.

I turned to look back and noticed Blink sitting there in the back seat, bobbing his head like a little partridge. I turned to Dad and asked, "Why is he doing that?" He smiled and shrugged.

Suddenly, Blink turned his attention to me and said, "That's Mom's." His lips indicated my headband.

I said, "I know. She gave it to me."

He blinked several more times at me before he turned his attention to the road ahead as the truck pulled away from our house. I looked back at Mom. She was sitting well inside the truck's tailgate. She had all kinds of stuff back there that she insisted had to be kept watch over in case the rough ride to Gish's place got them banged around.

When I glanced back at Blink he was looking out the window and had resumed his partridge head bob.

"Why are you doing that?" I asked him.

He looked at me, made a face, and said, "I was listening to music in my head. Wanna hear it?"

I giggled. Weird kid. When he was a baby, he shut his eyes for a long time when he blinked, so that's why he's called Blink. He didn't like me coming home, I think. But I didn't care. I figured I had as much right to be here as he did. Besides, I also had a sister here. Although, I still didn't see Maggie all that much. Huh! Blink didn't talk to me for several days after Goom left, which was actually kinda nice, until he realized I was never going to go away again.

I'd stayed with Choom and Goom since I was six or seven and Maggie, my older sister who's fifteen now, stayed with Mom. I don't know how it was decided who went with whom. Our own dad left us when I was a baby and Maggie was two years old. He never came back, so we never knew him. When I was about four years old, his parents notified Mom that he'd died in a car accident. I used to wonder what his parents were like and where they lived. It would have been nice to have another set of grandparents. But Mom didn't want to have any contact with them since they never wanted to know anything about us. Mom worked in the office at the college in Thunder Bay back then, which was where she met John, and then they got married. They moved here with Maggie to his reserve. Then they had a baby, Blair, that's Blink. Maggie now lives at Aunt Lucy's place—that's John's youngest sister. Aunt Lucy just had her first baby, so Maggie and her friend Jane moved in there to help her. Aunt Lucy's husband, Joe, worked over at the post office.

Over the years, Goom and Choom had always brought me up here two times a year. Once for a visit in the summertime and then at Christmas. Life can change pretty quickly, though. The letters from my friends Alexa and Jalene stopped coming. We'd all promised to stay friends forever and that we'd stay in touch. At first they wrote a letter to me from all of them during library hour, but after that I only received short letters from Alexa and Autumn, and now only Autumn kept writing to me. I guess I had more time up here for letter writing than Jalene and Alexa had down in Nibika.

We got to the intersection by the swamp where the right turn leads to the airstrip and the left turn takes us past the turnoff to the Band office and the community hall. We drove past that intersection and past the generating station on the right, then past Chief Paulie's house. She had just come out when we came by and she waved like she hadn't seen us in a long time.

I liked Chief Paulie. She could be very businesslike, but she could also roll around in the snow with you if she felt like it. She had no husband and no kids. She had apparently been gone a long time from the reserve, but her family had always lived here. Her family was, in fact, one of the founding members of this community. It was funny, though, the way she arrived home. Her widowed father had died. He'd been the Chief for so many years on the reserve. His wife had died ten years or so before and they had no sons, but everyone knew they had one daughter somewhere in Winnipeg. Then there she was. Mom said she stepped off the airplane like she'd just left the day before. After two years, she was still here and was now the Chief of the community.

I remember when I was here with Goom and Choom one time, just before the election of the new Chief and Council, when Paulie came to the door to talk to Mom and Dad. With her in the kitchen, it sounded like there was a party inside our house. She laughed a lot and Dad said, "She speaks how she sees things." I didn't quite understand what he meant when he said that.

"Abby, Abby! Man, when you get to daydreaming, you don't hear anything! I was asking if you saw Ned and his old lady this morning."

If they were going somewhere, they would have had to pass by Tommy's house, where I was this morning. "No, I didn't notice them. Why?"

Dad had shoved a black baseball cap over his head that said *pish-ish-igaw* at the front. It meant "empty" in English. The cap had been a Christmas present from his buddy Mike. He replied, "They were supposed to go talk to Paulie this morning. See if she'd agree to them joining our little venture."

The "little venture" was a plan that Dad and some of his friends had dreamt up two winters ago. They'd convinced Chief Paulie that it was a good business to get into because nobody in the North had started one up yet. That plan was to start a business called "The Real Anishinawbe Experience." They would take tourists out into the wilderness to experience the winter life of the Anishinawbe as it was back in the 1800s. I remembered my history textbooks that showed the voyageurs and Indians in leather clothes and teepees. I was already feeling like I'd gone back in time since I'd moved back in with Mom. No traffic, no department stores, no restaurants, nowhere to go and nothing to do. Bringing tourists up to experience life in this place was a pretty cool idea, I thought. But to actually go back in time? Now that would be a real experience, for sure.

One night Dad's friend Mike and Old Man Gish were over at our place talking about dogs and dog teams. I learned that Gish's female dog had been bred with Mike's dog, Bingo, who was one of the sled dogs. Her name was Daish and she turned out to be a natural lead dog. After asking Mike and Old Gish a lot of questions, I found out that a lead dog in a sled team would have to know the dangers of thin ice and how to avoid it, and know where the trail was even under thick overblown snow. A lead dog was also expected to find his or her way home if the hunter got lost somewhere. Just when I was about to ask another question, Mom had caught my eye and shook her head, and I realized that I was interrupting the conversation again. She'd had to remind me about that several times already, that I was not to interrupt until the elders had finished speaking. I would have to wait until later to ask Mom or Dad after the others had gone.

I rolled down the truck window, sniffed the air and said, "I think it's going to rain, I can smell it."

Dad glanced at me. "Oh, yeah?" I nodded. I was really looking forward to seeing the first litter of puppies that were to be groomed for a dog team.

We pulled off to the shoulder of the road at Gish's house. He had boards laid down on the walkway from the side of his house right up to the road. Daish barked from the stand of trees beside the house, where he had her tied up. Her doghouse under the tree was in the shade and she was standing there wagging her tail as we all walked up the walkway. Gish came around the corner of the house saying, "Eh, look what just come up over the top of the trees. It will pour, it will pour!" Dad smiled at me. Gish's voice faded as he turned to look at his most prized possession, or rather, his friend and companion—Daish. Gish always wore a solid green baseball cap on the top of his head that made his longish grey hair look like it was gushing out from around the sides.

Blink rushed forward and was now on his hands and knees in front of the doghouse, looking in. Gish said, "They're not in there. I've got the puppies in a box around the back. Giving Daish a break." *Daish* just meant "my dog" in Ojibwe. Mom put her hand on my shoulder as we made our way around the corner of the house. When I think about it now, I realize she was trying to hold me back from rushing around the house the way Blink did. Beside Gish's firepit stood the box of puppies with Blink's butt sticking out of it. He held up a black puppy as we approached. Dad and Gish stood side by side as they looked down at the four puppies in the box. It was a large paper box lined with a thick bed of field grass. Gish was saying " . . . put down three females, kept one female, and those other three are all males."

I saw Dad looking at something behind me and I noticed that Gish's woodshed behind the firepit was almost empty. Somehow, I could tell when Dad was thinking about something he must do. He was always filling up our woodshed beside the house and keeping a pile of split wood handy for Mom to use. Gish was saying, "With Mike's two dogs, Ching's big one, and Ned's two dogs, we should be able to start training these little ones by November. Too bad Willy moved away. Those were two good dogs he had."

I whispered to Mom as she kneeled to pick up the black and white female, "Why did he kill the other three females?"

She glanced at me and said, "Ask your dad when we get home."

Blink had a beige puppy with a black head and black tail wriggling in his arms. He yelled, "I want this one! I want this one!"

Dad was holding the all-black puppy and Mom was softly running her hand over the one surviving female, who was rapidly falling asleep. I too ran my finger over her smooth head. Mom whispered to me, "Do you want this one?" She smiled.

I smiled back, "Yeah, I want this one."

Mom and Dad looked at each other as Gish put the black puppy back into the box and said, "Well, Blink, you can't have that one. That puppy you're holding is from one of Mike's dogs. He's already claimed that one." Gish continued, "You can have that female there because she's special. Do you know why?"

Blink was kicking at the ground with his boot. "Why?"

Gish put his hands in his pockets and rocked back and forth on his heels before he said, "Because when she's all grown up, she'll be mated with Mike's other dog and then she'll have puppies!"

Dad added, "You'll have to look after her puppies until they're all taken and you could also keep one of her puppies if you want."

Blink blinked several times before he grinned and said, "Okay."

Gish turned to Dad. "You know John, in about three years we'll have the best dog team in the North!"

Dad grinned at him and said, "Who's raising the black one?"

Gish hiked up his pants from the pockets again as he said, "Oh, Ching's taking the white one, and I think Chief Paulie is taking the black one. Since it was her idea to start breeding sled dogs, I gave her first pick."

Their voices faded as they entered the back door of Gish's house.

"Can we take her home now?" Blink asked Mom.

"No, she'll have to be fully weaned first. They're still nursing." She turned to me and said, "Go get the box I put in the back of the truck."

I ran back to the truck as Mom entered the house with her freshly baked bannock in one hand and a pot of stew in the other. I pulled the box to the tailgate, where I could lift it up. It had canned milk and Pablum in it. Baby food! I lugged the box into the house and put it on the table, saying to Gish, "You're going to feed the puppies baby food?"

Gish chuckled as he came over to the box and looked inside it. "Oh, that's good! No, I'm going to fill a bottle and I'm going to go lie down on my bed and suck on it myself!"

Blink laughed. "And you're going to eat the Pablum too?"

Gish put a bowl on the table and said, "No, I'm going to pour milk in here when I start taking them off their mama's milk, and then I'm going to make fish broth and put a little bit of the Pablum in it to thicken it, see?"

Suddenly, Maggie came running in with her friend Jane, yelling, "Mom! Are we getting one of the puppies?"

I asked, "How did you know we were here?"

She glanced at me and laughed, "We could see the truck on the road, silly!" I'd forgotten that Jane's house was next door to Gish's and on the other side of Jane's house was Aunt Lucy's house.

In a flash, Blink was out the door pulling her behind him. I turned to Mom. "Did you see her hair? It's red!"

Mom's mouth was hanging open. Dad said, "Sophie, close your mouth before a fly goes in."

Gish let out the rasping laugh he normally gets when he's really laughing hard.

Dad looked at me and asked, "Is that what you're going to be like when you're fifteen years old too?"

I laughed. "No way! I'm not as crazy and Jane and Maggie. Mary told me at school that she saw them at Josie's place on Sunday and they were gluing long fake nails on their fingers and then they painted them red!" Jane and Maggie spent a lot of time together, and I'd figured out by now that Jane liked it that Maggie spent more time with her than me.

Mom began putting cups on the table as Gish shut off the flames of the propane gas stove and brought the teapot to the table. Just then, there was a tremendous crash that shook the house. I heard a scream outside and I ran to the door just in time to see the girls and Blink scrambling into the woodshed with the box of puppies. Then came the blinding flash of lightning followed by more thunder. Just as the girls came running into the house with the box of puppies, the rain came down. The door remained open as sheets of water poured off the overhanging roof.

During a lull between the thunder, the girls had run out, heading for Jane's house. I sat down in the living room, where the window faced the road, the puppy on my lap. Mom spoke from the table. "If the puppy starts moving around, better put it back in the box because it will pee on you." As if on cue, the puppy poked its head up from the crook of my arm and struggled to turn around. I had no sooner dropped her back in the box when she piddled in it. I noticed then that there was plastic under the grass in the box. I glanced at Gish. He was making a big production of lighting his pipe and he held it out in all four directions and took huge puffs of his tobacco.

I whispered to Mom, "What's he doing?"

He heard me and answered, "Well, it's just to let the Thunderbirds know that they're the most powerful and to acknowledge their existence. Like, well, it's like we're bowing to them. We don't want to get them angry at us, do we?"

He smiled at me as another booming clap of thunder shook the house.

Blink came over to the box and dropped the black puppy he'd been holding into it, and we watched all the puppies huddle, crawling on top of each other until they settled into a pile in one corner. They went to sleep.

The sun was shining between the clouds just as Mike's red truck pulled up on the other side of the road. The rain was just spitting lightly when the big man came in through the back door. "Did you order this rain, old man?" he asked as he stomped his feet on the sheets of cardboard paper at the door.

Mike wasn't just Dad's friend, he was Dad's best friend. They'd been friends from the time they were boys. He was a big tall man with muscular legs and arms. His belly stretched the button holes of his shirt, and his long black hair was also in braids that hung down on each side of his chest. His jeans kind of sagged at the butt and he always had a big grin on his face. Mike was also a Band councillor. The Band had three councillors. The other one was a woman from the other end of the community.

Gish pulled up another chair to the table and Mom poured a cup of tea for Mike. Blink, who was still sitting beside the puppy box, found a dog harness from the closet beside him. He was trying to clip it around his waist just as a flash of lightning lit up the living room and the sun disappeared and another deafening boom shook the house. Gish said that the Thunderbirds usually check along the ridge of the rock cliff that flanked our village. They would be looking for their food. Before I realized it, I interrupted the conversation and found out that Thunderbirds fed on snakes and frogs.

The high rock cliffs ran the length of the back of the village and the ground sloped down toward the lake. From between the largest rock cliffs flowed a creek that ran through the village. That was called Bear Creek. Every household or tent was expected to light a candle or leave the lights on in the dark if the Thunderbirds were going by overhead. This was done to let them know that people were down below and then they'd be careful not to accidentally hit anyone. I'd never heard that before. I didn't remember Choom ever saying anything about Thunderbirds. He never said anything about the ceremonies he attended either. For some reason, I'd never thought to ask questions about that. It seemed that I was just a little kid and didn't have to know those things when I was with Goom and Choom. But now that I was back with Mom, I felt like an ignorant kid who didn't know anything.

More rain came as I sat down at the end of a bench beside the oil stove. The ends of my kerchief gave a very satisfying crunch, crunch as I bit into the fabric. There was no divider between the living room and the kitchen, and now I turned my attention to the conversation around the table. Mike was saying, "Paulie said she's got some money coming that would pay the two sisters Minnie and Lizzy to work on two moose skins."

The two sisters were the women who lived down the road from us. They were the only ones who knew how or took the time to make their leather the traditional way. People were always after them to sell their hand-processed moosehides. Mom said it was hardly worth their while, though, for the amount of hard work that went into making the traditional hand-processed hide when compared to the price they got for it. People just normally bought split cowhide from the store.

Gish said, "How is the wood for the sled taking shape?"

Dad replied after sipping his tea. "The trees I cut last spring had perfect grain and the beams are quite straight. I've still got them on the mould racks."

Mike piped in, "We'll kill two moose on the first hunting weekend in the fall and the women can start on the hides.

"What?" Mom started to laugh.

Mike continued, "What's this? She's laughing at me! John, she's laughing at me. You think we can't kill two moose?"

Mom said, "Well, there may not happen to be two moose around when you decide to go hunting. So you'd better give yourself more time before that."

Dad said, "Oh, Gish can tell us where the moose are, eh?"

Gish winked at me and said, "Well, I'll have to ask the raven if he's seen any." Gish saw my raised eyebrows, and he winked at me again, saying, "When it's time for Mike and your dad to go hunting, I'll hold a moose shoulder blade over hot embers and the first brown spot to show will tell me where the moose is. Oh, but then the moose will have to decide if it's a good day to die or not."

"What do you mean?" I asked. I felt quite alarmed at the thought.

Gish smiled. "Oh, don't worry. If the hunters are worthy, the moose will give up their lives to them."

I was still concerned. Did the moose really give itself up to the hunters? Why would it ever want to do that? Gish continued, "When you see two baby moose in the spring, that will be them, eh? Born again!"

I hadn't thought of it like that. Hmm, then maybe it wasn't too bad after all. I wanted to find out more about Gish's ideas about reincarnation, but I looked at Mom and she was smiling back at me as if she were, willing me, please, not to ask any more questions.

Dad and Mike were still talking and Mike was saying, "We'll collect the hair when the women cut it off the moose skin. We'll dry it and we'll use that to fill the dog collars."

"That I am going to make," Dad finished.

"What was that about the moose hair?" I asked. Despite the look Mom was giving me, I'd decided that Gish was in the mood for answering questions. He liked an audience, as I had discovered at school. The teachers would call him in to talk about some cultural stuff in the Native language class once in a while.

Gish answered, "Well, it's for the dog harness collars. The collars are made of the soft processed moosehide, just like the thick hide used on the bottom of the foot piece of a mukluk. Now, Mike here will have the moose hair all cleaned and dried out. Then your father is going to cut the hide into pieces that he will then stuff with hair to keep its shape and sew into a long sausage circle. Much like garlic sausage sewn together at the ends, see? That will fit over the dogs' heads and around their collars. Your dad will make them fit perfectly for each dog."

"What are you going to make, Mom?" I asked.

They all turned to her and she smiled. "I'm going to make the little booties for the dogs' feet!"

I giggled, "No way!"

She said, "Oh, yes. In the spring they have to wear boots so they don't cut their feet on the sharp ice."

Gish nodded, smiling. "She's right."

"What can I do to help?" I asked before I realized I was volunteering to get involved in this crazy idea of creating an old Indian winter camp.

Dad looked at me and raised his eyebrows. "Why, you're going to look after the puppy, of course. Blink is too small and not too responsible right now, so that will be your job!"

"I am too! I am too!" came Blink's response from the living room.

Mike said, "Hey, what are you going to do, Gish?"

Gish slapped his knees and said, "Why, I'll be the boss, of course! When you're done with the moose hair, you can start on the harnesses. See if you can find a very sharp knife and you'll also have to remind me to tell the sisters to leave the bottom half of one hide raw so you can make *babiche* out of it."

Blink was at the table now, beside Dad. "What's *babiche*, Gish?"

Gish drew in a big breath and took a long sip of his tea before he said, "Well, *babiche* is what Mike will end up with after he cuts the raw hide into thin strips for the mesh work on the snowshoes and wider strips for the sleigh laces."

Gish was really getting into answering our questions, but I'd decided to take my cue from Mom if the time was right to ask any more.

"Who will make the snowshoes?" I asked.

Dad said, "Oh, you know we already have snowshoes, but we'll need extra ones." Turning to Mike and Gish, he said, "I've also got four moulds in place that I need to split in half and . . . " he smiled and finished, "That's going to be one big job!"

Mom cut in. "I'll do the mesh work on the snowshoes. I'm pretty sure I remember how it's done, but just to make sure, I'll do the first one at the sisters' place."

I asked, "What are you actually going to do with the two dog teams?"

Gish laughed and slapped his knee again, saying, "That's the question to ask! Well, Paulie says we can have a tourist business going with a real dog team taking people to a real live Anishinawbe camp with a large, warm wigwam to tell stories in, sleep, and have hearty meals in."

"What are the people going to do when they get there?" I asked. I found myself getting drawn into the planning and I was actually getting excited. Somehow, it was becoming real and it would be wonderful to find something to do in this place. It was like making those history textbook pictures come alive. Even more exciting was the thought of having a dog. I'd never had a pet in my whole life!

Mike answered, "Well, we'll take them ice fishing, rabbit snaring, and snowshoeing—that's what the snowshoes are for! They can go there for one, two, or three days, at first, and then maybe later they can go longer if we have enough people to look after them there."

Mom turned to Dad. "Did Paulie and the others ever decide if the camp was going to be on the island or way over by the river?"

Dad answered, "It's going to be on the island the last I heard. They were afraid we might lose tourists through the ice at the river."

I'd never even been on lake ice before. The thought that a person could fall through the ice was alarming. The island would definitely be a lot safer.

I thought I'd like to be out there, too, at the camp. I knew I'd especially like dressing up in traditional Indian clothing. Oh, that was something else I had to remember—never say "Indian." That's what the Native language teacher said to me the very first day in class. "We are Anishinawbe and not Indians from India."

Later that evening as we got ready for bed, Blink emerged from the bathroom in his pyjamas and stopped short, staring at me. Then he blurted out, "Who balded your forehead?" With all of the excitement of the day, I'd totally forgotten about my short bangs and I couldn't think of a thing to say back to him. Mom turned Blink around and pushed him into his bedroom. I was at the kitchen counter muttering under my breath, "S.S. will probably have everyone pointing at me at school tomorrow!" when I heard Mom ask, "Who's S.S.?" I turned and smiled, whispering, "Skunk Stink." She stifled a laugh and went down the hall to her bedroom. I was in bed when I heard Dad coming in and then the house became quiet.

The storm had now passed over us, leaving echoes of rumbling thunder beyond the hills. I thought, the mosquitoes will be out now. They always were after the rain.

CHAPTER THREE

Ki-Moot and Chief Paulie

The day after we got back from Winnipeg, we brought the puppy home. We were wondering what name to call her so Dad said that we'd just have to watch her and see which name she'd pick for herself.

Right after we got her home, she was on Blink's bed pulling out a package of gum from Blink's pocket and had already sunk her sharp little teeth into it before he saw what she was up to. Then, while Dad was sitting at the table after supper, he picked her up in his arms and she stuck her head under his arm and managed to reach his plate on the table and lick it clean. After that, socks and small things went missing. She'd drag things away and gnaw on everything she could sink her little teeth into. One morning she came into the kitchen area dragging Dad's underwear. That was it! I began hanging up my laundry bag behind the door of my bedroom. Finally, things had to be moved out of her reach from the floor because she'd get into them. That's how she came to be known as Ki-Moot, the thief.

Mom said it was like having a baby in the house. We were always having to clean up after her. She got into everything and she'd always step into her water bowl and spill it. There was also the "piddling" as Mom called it. Ki-Moot was, however, very good at going outside when she was taken out. I liked her better when she was asleep, though. Mom said it would be better when she was house-trained. I didn't know it would take so long!

I came in through the back door of our house after a rainy school day and kicked off my boots. It was very muddy outside. Mmm, something smelled good in the kitchen. Mom was making supper. It made me feel better right away when I came in the door and I walked up to Mom and put my arms around her. She stroked my back and asked, "Had a bad day? Who was it this time?"

I shrugged. "Everything. Everyone. I just hate the place!"

She patted my back and said, "What exactly is bad and what can we do about it?"

I replied with a sigh, "I don't know. It was the girls again and the boys at the back. No one even comes to talk to me at recess. I stayed by the swings by myself and someone threw mud at my back. I don't know which one of them did it, but they were all laughing. Our Native language teacher, Miss Mitig, said I could stay inside and help her tomorrow morning."

Mom took a deep breath then let it out. "Well, I'll talk to her tomorrow and see if she has any suggestions."

I went to the table and sat down. She set some hot bannock on the table and I sat munching on a fresh slice with butter melting on top. I'd better not think of calling Goom again. Mom said the telephone bill was really high last month. Mmm, the bannock was good. Choom always made the bannock at home but not very often. Goom said she'd never got the hang of it and Choom's bannock was always better than hers. But what I really missed the most was a cold glass of milk! Fresh milk was very expensive here. Now I mostly drank powdered fruit-flavoured drink mixes or hot water with a tablespoon of cocoa, sugar, and canned milk in it.

The door suddenly flew open and Blink and his friend David ran inside with muddy boots flying against the wall, and Mom yelled, "Whoa! Boots off in the porch! What's going on anyway?"

Before she even finished, Blink yelled, "Mike and Ned are coming. We were trying to see if we could run through the shortcut path and beat them to the door and we did it!"

I saw Mike's truck pull in with Dad and Ned inside. They all came in while Blink was still blabbing about their race to the house. The men sat down at the table and Mom was there pouring coffee for them. Ned lived across the creek on the other side of Mike's place. There was just him and his old lady there. That's what Choom used to say, "someone and his old lady." They'd just moved back to the reserve about the same time I arrived. Before that they'd been living in Ned's wife's community for about five years. Now they were back. Ned was a trapper and his wife, Alice, hardly ever came out of their house.

"Hi, Abby, got any homework?" Dad asked.

"Nope, nothing at all." I took my mud-smeared jacket off the bench and hung it up behind the oil stove.

"Come over here then, and see what you think." Dad had a sheet of paper in front of him. I looked at the sheet as I pulled a chair up beside him. Dots and triangles. "What is it?" I asked.

Mike answered, "Destination points. We're figuring out the places to take the tourists!"

"Humph," I replied.

Dad nudged me with his elbow. "What do you mean, humph? We're just telling Ned here about the Real Anishinawbe Experience."

Ned winked at me. "Yep, Paulie says I'm a good man for the job and I've got a dog, and my brother says we can use his dog for the winter too."

Then Ned turned his attention to Dad and Mike. "Okay, what happened last winter? I thought you said you had the places all figured out."

"Oh." Mike made a face and Dad laughed as Mom came over to sit down with us.

Dad said, "After we trained the dog team, we figured we'd do a trial run into Ashiganish and back again."

I smiled as I translated Ashiganish in my head, meaning "old stocking" in Ojibwe. I was getting better at Ojibwe. Part of the reason why the kids were making fun of me at school was that my Ojibwe sentences were mixed in with English words. Adding to that was the fact that Choom's Ojibwe dialect was different from how they spoke it here.

Mike was saying, "I was there with Fred and we were going to organize an ice fishing trip from there and then John would bring the tourists back here again for the night."

Ned asked, "You had tourists?"

Dad laughed. "No, no, not real tourists. Our pretend tourists were Rev. Roberts; the nurse, Sara Jones; Gish; and Paulie. But we found out we could only take two at a time on the dog sled."

Mom joined in, "That's a three-hour ride just to get to Ashiganish—on a good day!"

Mike started chuckling, saying, "Well, right off the bat, Ching's dog got free."

Dad told his story to Ned. "Ozit wasn't part of the dog team yet, but he used to howl and create such a ruckus, he wanted to go so badly. Especially when our dog team whizzed past Ching's place on the way to Mike's house or back here. Anyway, so off we went, on our way to Ashiganish. Our pretend tourists that day were Gish and Paulie. After about half an hour out, I looked back and there was Ozit trotting along right behind us. When we got to the shoreline, we decided to strap him in with the rest of the team, right behind Bannock, and after giving himself a big shake, he stood ready to go! I couldn't believe that dog. Ching said there was no way he'd ever even been near a sleigh, let alone pulled one! So there we were, plus one more dog, and off we went into the bush road. The snow machines, about six of them, had packed the road hard the day before. So we got through the next couple of hours pretty fast. Then we came out onto the ice on the other side and there were four machines sitting there waiting for us."

Mike now added, "That was me, Fred, and two other guys. 'What are you doing here?' John says. Well, after Sophie called to tell us they were coming, we got to talking about what would happen when the dog team arrived with all those loose dogs they have there at Ashiganish. So we decided to go and give them an escort to the community hall."

Dad took up the story again. "Well, that's exactly what happened. As soon as we came around the big island in front of the community, little dots appeared in a long line and started closing in on us. I'm telling you, I was quite nervous when the dogs came at us full speed. Then the snow machines spread out, two on each side of the sleigh, and headed the dogs off and kept them at bay. There was one big black dog that kept trying to get at us from the back, then he'd dart to the front. Man, could that dog run! He was vicious, too, eh, Mike?"

Mike nodded. "Oh, yeah! That dog kept wanting to sneak up and take a nip at our dogs. He was especially interested in Bingo. Oh, he took an instant dislike to Bingo like he was a dog from hell! We had to bring the dogs into the porch area of the community hall just to keep them from getting ripped apart because they were all still leashed together."

My heart was pounding at this point in the story. I was terrified of the dogs that ran loose on the streets. I'd taken to using Mom's shortcut to the Band office. I always ran from the school to the Band office and then home. There were always dogs running loose on the streets and they always hung around doorways in all the buildings, even at school. Sometimes they would fight each other by the doorways too. I was especially scared of the dogs that came charging at you from some houses when you walked by on the street.

Dad ended the story by saying, "We managed to get them cooled off, fed, and watered. After a few hours' rest, we came back home. By then, it was around ten at night, eh?" He turned to Mom.

Mom turned from the stove and put another pot of coffee on the table. She had stew in the thick cook pot simmering slowly. That's what I'd smelled when I came in. I noticed there was now only half the bannock left on the table. The men were buttering the hot bannock as they talked and sipped their coffee. Everyone ate bannock here. Even at school some of the teachers brought bannock for their coffee breaks. Mom said that bread was very expensive at the store. I remembered my first morning here, I'd started looking for the toaster before I realized there was no bread in the house.

Mom said, "Yeah, everyone agreed that Ashiganish wasn't a good place to go. I like Paulie's idea of using the summer tourist fishing lodge. It's only an hour's ride away up the river."

Mike sat back in his chair. "Yep, don't know why we never thought of it before."

Dad said, "That's because of the antifreeze waterlines and sump pumps and all that work to winterize the place. I just didn't like the idea of waking up that beast in the middle of winter."

Mom said, "Well, Gish suggested that all he'd need would be that big teaching wigwam at the back of the lodge and someone to get the central fireplace going and light up the fireplaces in each of the sleeping compartments or bedrooms and that would be it. Oh, yes, the kitchen propane stove would need to be relit and the tank filled up. The tourists could use the outhouse and just rough it. We could line the path to the toilet with pine branches and cover the outhouse with more pine branches and we could leave a candle lantern going inside to generate some heat until they all went to bed." I sat listening quietly to the discussion. It was beginning to sound very complicated. I'd never even heard of antifreeze lines and sump pumps!

Ned asked, "Who's going to sleep over there with the tourists?"

Mike answered, "Well, we don't know yet. We'll have to have a meeting about that. Gish for sure, because he'd not be coming back at night after his late wigwam stories with the tourists."

Dad asked, "Who have we got? We'd need a couple to cook and keep the fires going. How about you, Ned? Alice can cook for the tourists and you'd just shovel the walkways and keep the fires going."

Ned leaned back in his chair, which forced his shirt to stretch over his belly before he said, "Well, I've got a trapline to run, but then, if I'm getting paid to lend you my dogs and keep fires going, I might consider it."

I'd never met a real traditional Indian trapper, oops, an Anishinawbe trapper before. His hair was tied in a ponytail at the back of his neck and his Ojibwe accent was very thick. I would have found Ned scary if I'd met him in Nibika, but here he seemed comfortable and homey. I turned to him and asked, "What's your brother's dog's name?"

Ned smiled at me. "His name is Samson and he's a big dog, bigger than Mike's Bingo. He's very strong, but you know something about that dog? He's so friendly and loving, he'd just jump up at you to lick your face, even if he's never seen you before!" I thought Ned had just described himself pretty well too.

Then I said, "Your dog Chippy, he's hard and tough. I like the way his tail curls right around and he has small ears. He doesn't look like the other dogs, and he's smaller too. Do you think he'll pick a fight with Bingo or Bannock? Or what if Chippy and Ozit decide to have a fight instead of pulling the sled?" I'd been thinking about the dogs fighting around the buildings in town and it seemed logical to me that these dogs would fight too.

The men stopped and looked at each other. Mom started laughing and Ned said, "Trust a woman to come up with something we never even thought about!"

A woman? My face went red and I was thankful for the distraction when the door opened and Ned's wife, Alice, came in. She was a portly woman with a scarf secured tightly around her head. She had on a green raincoat, and her thick dark skirt hung low over her stockings. She pulled off her boots and took off her coat, saying, "Oh, I had to stay and watch the end of that show. I got Ned to get me a satellite dish back home and now I'm hooked on some of the television programs."

Ned snorted from where he sat. "That was the first thing I had to set up for her at the house when we got here. She's even got games that she likes to play on the television."

She wrinkled her nose at him, saying, "Well, I'll have to borrow Blink and David sometime. I do miss the kids from back home. I used to bake cookies and babysit my neighbour's kids all the time."

Mom took her coat and went to get another chair for her at the table when Mike stood up, "Oh, boy, I'd better get home before the phone rings. David! Let's go home!"

His son David and S.S. emerged from Blink's small bedroom. As Mike and David headed out the door, S.S. pulled up a chair at the table and made faces at me. When I came home at lunch, I'd caught him in my bedroom with his feet sticking out from under my bed. Without thinking, I'd grabbed his feet and dragged him out of there and into the hallway, with him screaming that he was trying to reach Ki-Moot, who had disappeared under my bed with his pencil. I felt bad but I couldn't get myself to apologize, even though I knew I should have.

I ignored him, and Mom put the plates down in front of the people around the table. Alice and Ned had supper with us and the conversation continued about the plans for the coming winter.

At one point, Ned asked his wife, "How did you get here so quickly?" Alice bit her lip and winked at him. "I'd just left the house when Ching came by and I got a ride from him on that ATV machine!"

Ned raised his eyebrows. "You, on an ATV? You don't like those things!"

She half-whispered, leaning over to Mom, "I threw my leg over the seat and sat behind him and hugged him real tight when we came around the corner!" That had everyone sputtering with laughter. I discovered then that Alice had a great sense of humour that got everyone laughing at the table. I really liked her.

Alice also turned out to be very good at sewing. Since the Anishinawbe staff working at the winter camp were supposed to be living life from long ago, they would need to be dressed up like they would have been long ago. Alice said a rabbit-skin hood and jacket to fit me would take about eighty rabbits! I wondered to myself how rabbit skins become clothing. There were so many things I didn't understand that I didn't even know what questions to ask.

By the time supper was over, Mike's two moose had grown to six moose to clothe everyone in authentic period clothing. I dished out another ladleful of moose stew and set about dunking the bannock into the broth when Ned asked, "What kind of food are you going to cook for breakfast for those tourists, Alice?"

Alice sat there chewing before she replied, "Well, bannock for sure and maybe wild blueberry jam and what else?"

She looked at Mom. Mom popped a broth-soaked piece of bannock into her mouth before she said, "I hear popped wild rice tastes like puffed wheat. We could have milk to make it a cereal breakfast."

Ned asked, "Was there milk back then, John?"

Dad looked into Mom's eyes and said, "No, but they had honey and maple syrup, and I image the wild rice could have been made into rice flour, and, there you go, pancakes!"

Alice said, "Ah, that's too much work! No tourist is worth that much time and work!"

After supper, Dad drove Alice and Ned back to their house. I helped Mom with the dishes while Blink went to soak in the tub. Mom had discovered a can of water filled with tadpoles in Blink's room and she freaked out when she found out Blink and David had been playing with them on his bed. She made S.S. go and return them to where he'd got them. While he was out, he slipped and fell into the muddy slough beside the road. When he came back, he was covered with mud up to his waist. I laughed so hard that he began to cry, which was a big mistake because Mom then made me clean up his room after I was finished doing the dishes.

Mom said that Dad probably stopped by at Mike's place to talk about the next meeting about the Real Anishinawbe Experience.

"How many people are actually going to be involved in this Experience?" I asked slowly. I still hadn't a clue where I would fit into any of the things that apparently needed to be done. Mom filled a cup of tea and sat down at the table.

"Well, let's see. There's Gish, Mike and Linda, Ned and Alice, John and I, and Ching. John says we need one more person to drive the teams."

"What does Ching do?" I asked. I knew only a few things about Ching. He was a funny character. Dad said he was called Ching because when he first got a credit card, he always said he was going into town and then he'd say, "ching-ching." After that, people just started calling him Ching. He didn't seem to mind. I think his real name was Charlie. He was a tall, skinny man about thirty years old. He lived alone with his dog, Ozit. That's "foot" in Ojibwe. He said he kept stepping on the puppy's foot when he first brought it home, so he just called him Ozit. Ozit was beige and appeared to be a very quiet, thoughtful dog. You know, one of those kinds of dogs that seem to be sitting there thinking about something or maybe just zoning out into nothingness.

Ching also took one of the new pups from Gish. His puppy's name was Shingoos. That's "weasel" in Ojibwe. He named him that because Shingoos was white with a black tip on his tail. Shingoos was just crazy! He was very hyper and noisy, and he was always getting into trouble and always managing to get off his leash. Houdini would have been a better name for that dog. I thought about the puppies' names. Mike's puppy's name was Wiener because he loved eating them so much. I thought about my Ki-Moot. She was the best of the bunch! We didn't see Chief Paulie's pup very often. She named him Mucko, "bear" in Ojibwe, because he was all black.

Mom was saying, "Well, Ching has never driven a dog team, but he's the camp cook during forest fire season and he runs the Band's ATV in summer and the snow machines in the winter, getting firewood for the offices. Dad says he's volunteered to feed and care for the dogs. Cool them down and harness and unharness them. Thank goodness we have the two sisters to do all the sewing, and Alice doing the cooking."

Our talk was interrupted by the sound of Dad's truck pulling into the driveway. Well, it was time to do some reading. Goom had just sent me another batch of books that I was bursting to get into. I didn't really miss the television as much as I thought I would, and I had no access to a computer so I was doing a lot of reading lately.

As I pulled out my books from the desk drawer in my bedroom, my photo album fell out. Mom had bought me the album after Dad developed the pictures that I took of our trip to Winnipeg.

I flipped the cover and saw a photo of my beaming face at the restaurant where we ate our first meal. Then there was a picture of me and Dad, one with Mom and Dad, one with all of us in the hotel lobby. The girl behind the counter took that one. Then there was Blink by the escalator at a mall. He was so terrified of the moving stairs that he refused to step on it to go up and absolutely refused to go down. So we had to use the elevator.

Then there were the pictures taken at the zoo. There was me in front of the grizzly bear pen. There were two bears there, one was swimming and the other was sprawled over a large flat rock. We saw snakes, llamas, flamingos, a huge fish pond, and then there's one of Blink with the kangaroo behind the fence. Blink had insisted on riding around on a zoo baby cart because he was too lazy to walk! I flipped through some more pages and then I laughed out loud. There was the picture of the camel at the zoo that had come up beside Blink, and it sent a spray of spit that landed—splat!—right on his lap! That was the best part of my trip to Winnipeg!

Several days later I hurried down the road to Gish's place. The smell of sweet flowers filled my nose as I went down the street. There were lots of wild raspberry bushes along the road that were filled with pink flowers. There was something wrong with my puppy. She hadn't eaten anything since the night before and now it was almost noon again. I held Ki-Moot in the nook of my arm and she didn't move as I walked with hurried footsteps. Her nose was very dry and she was breathing in very small, shallow breaths. As I came up the wooden walkway to Gish's place, Daish came up to meet me with her tail wagging. She seemed very interested in what I held in my arms. I talked to her as I came around the cabin to the door. I sat by the door and put the puppy down on the ground beside the female dog. She sniffed at it and the puppy lifted its head. She licked the puppy on the mouth and then the door opened behind me.

"What's the matter with your puppy?" Gish asked. He was behind me with his sleeves rolled up and a dish towel in his hand. His baggy pants were strapped to his shoulders by a pair of dirty suspenders that lay over his old checkered shirt. The smell of food wafted through the doorway. It appeared that he'd just finished his meal and was washing his dishes. Even without his cap on, its imprint left his hair sticking out on all sides.

I shrugged. "I don't know, she threw up after supper yesterday and she hasn't eaten anything yet today."

Gish said, "Bring her in here."

I took the puppy and went into the dim room. Gish very rarely put the light on, even when it was a dark, dismal day. He took the puppy and pried its mouth open with one big finger and ran his hands down the puppy's body. Then he put it down on the floor and picked up a cup from the corner of the shelf by the door. He poured out some broth from whatever he had in the cook pot on the counter. The broth contained what looked like a piece of meat of some kind. He picked up the puppy again and sat by the stove and periodically dipped his finger into the cup and ran it over the puppy's lips. After several attempts, the puppy still wasn't interested, but then suddenly it lifted its head and licked his finger. After that, he wanted more of the stuff. I giggled as Gish talked to the puppy. He made it sound like it was the puppy doing the talking. When the puppy had lapped up the contents of the cup, Gish put her down on the floor.

"She'll be alright now. What did she eat the last time she ate?"

I thought awhile. "I think Blink gave her some spaghetti from his plate at supper yesterday."

Gish sighed. "Yeah, that would do it. Tell that little brother of yours not to give her stuff like that. The puppy is to have only meat or fish, broth, and whatever other stuff is in a cooking pot. No fried stuff, no ducks, and no canned stuff. Okay?"

I nodded, so happy that Ki-Moot was going to live. I thought she was going to die! I grabbed her and hurried out the door to tell Mom exactly what Gish had said. The puppy's ears flopped up and down on her head as I ran down the street toward our house. Just as I came to the intersection, I whispered, "Oh, no!" as my heart leapt to my throat. Two dogs came running toward me and started sniffing up at the puppy. They wouldn't go away and one dog began jumping up at my side as I started turning around, holding the puppy away from them. I started yelling for them to go away when a truck came down the road. The dogs took off and the truck went by. My heart was still thumping as I came to our street. Ki-Moot was almost falling asleep in my arms by the time I ran up our driveway.

I had just come up the porch steps when Dad's truck pulled up into the driveway behind me. I sat down and waited for them. Mom and Dad got out of the truck with Blink. I waited and Dad came up to me, saying, "Where have you been?"

I said, "I took little Ki-Moot to Gish. She was really sick. I thought she was going to die and two dogs tried to pull her out of my arms on the way home."

Mom turned from the truck. "What do you mean, really sick?"

I replied, "Remember yesterday, Blink gave her spaghetti from his plate and then she threw up on the floor after that? Well, she didn't eat this morning and she wouldn't eat at lunch, and when I got home, she still wouldn't eat, so I took her to Gish." I followed them into the house and sat down on the couch with Ki-Moot on my lap while they put their grocery bags on the table. "Gish gave her some broth from his pot and he said to tell you guys and especially you, Blink, that you cannot give Ki-Moot any canned stuff and ducks."

I asked, "Why did he say ducks, Mom? Are ducks poisonous for dogs? What about chickens?"

Mom turned and smiled at me as she began unpacking some cans onto the shelf. "No, ducks aren't poisonous. It's just that ducks aren't fed to the dogs because dogs are normally used to fetch the ducks when the ducks are shot down by hunters in the spring and fall. So they grow up thinking that ducks aren't food for them to eat. As for chickens, they're included as other meat of all kinds, including partridge, that dogs can eat."

The next day, I was coming home from school when I heard Chief Paulie calling my name from her house. I turned to see her waving at me to come over. I turned and had to step off the road to avoid a truck that was coming a bit too fast. I ran down the slope to her walkway and she held the door open for me as I came into the porch, shaking off my rubber boots. It had been raining again all day and it was muddy everywhere. I heard Miss Tracy, the English teacher, say that she was at least two inches taller by the time she reached the school that morning, meaning that was how much mud had accumulated on her boots.

Chief Paulie hurried into the living room, where she had stacks of empty shoe boxes of all sizes and a pile of leather and fur mitts, mukluks, and moccasins scattered on the floor. She stopped and beamed at me from across the coffee table and handed me a notepad. She had a round face framed by tightly permed, short curly black hair. Her dark eyes surveyed the room before she said, "Here, I'll pay you something if you'll be my stock girl. I need someone to sort this stuff and keep an inventory of all the things we have so far, and I also need you to mark the sizes on the footwear and mitts, label them with these stickers and mark each box accordingly for each pair."

I took the pad and looked at the rows and columns and slowly asked, "Ah, right now? What about my homework?" This had taken me quite by surprise and I didn't really know what to say.

She broke into one of her peals of laughter, saying, "No, no! I don't mean right this minute. Take that pad home and after your homework, you can figure out how you'd like to arrange the items, sizes, colours, descriptions, or whatever. I'll leave that up to you, okay?"

I nodded and then asked, "Why me?"

She smiled and sat down on the couch, saying, "Your mom says you're spending too much time by yourself and that she can't help you with your math problems. So I told her you could join me in my lonesome house doing that stuff and I could help you if you get stuck with your homework. I'm glad to hear your higher grade-level work is working out well with the new math teacher and Miss Tracy."

Right. That was another reason the rest of the kids at school teased me. I'd already been taught all the stuff they were working on two years ago, and I'd get very impatient and sigh, listening to the other kids struggling with the math and English. That was when Mr. Toms, the math teacher, finally had a chat with the principal about me. Miss Tracy also volunteered to teach me at a higher level. So now I was working on stuff separately from what was actually going on in the classroom.

I still hadn't moved and as the realization sank in that all these adults had been talking about me, I looked down at her upturned face and repeated, "Why me?" I didn't understand why she would take an interest in me. Chief Paulie cleared a space on the couch for me to sit, so I sat down.

She said, "Why you? Well, you remind me of myself when I first came back here. Both my parents were gone and I'd been going to university in Winnipeg, but when I came back here to visit, I saw what I could do and decided to stay. Even though I knew the people, they still acted strange around me until I realized that I was the one who'd changed. I asked an Elder about that once and he said that it was like moving a rock from the side of a creek and putting it down in the middle. It's the same rock and the same creek but now the water had to flow in a different way around it, that's all. With you, you were always sitting on top of a rock on the creek and then someone nudged you over and you fell—plop— into the creek and now the water is having to go around you. Understand?"

Totally baffled, I nodded my head and said, "Yes, I understand. I understand that there's absolutely no way I'm going to understand what you've just said until I ask Gish or another elder."

She laughed and leaned back on the couch, saying, "I'm just saying people need to get used to going by you now where you never used to be. And the math? I have university level math, so I'll be able to help you with that if you're willing to help me with this." She spread her arms to indicate the overflowing couch, chairs, and floor and ended by saying, "I had a nightmare last night where I was up to my ears and drowning in this stuff!" I laughed and began to relax. I guessed it was okay. I didn't mind her and it would certainly keep me busy.

I bit my lip and said almost shyly, "I've been wondering what I can possibly do to get involved in this old Anishinawbe Experience. This, I can do! Thanks. I'll ask Mom and Dad."

She smiled, "I already did. John said I'd have to pay you, though. So, I'll give you, what? Five bucks an hour?" I'd never earned any kind of money before, so this sounded pretty good to me.

I nodded. "Okay, it's a deal!"

As it turned out, I never remembered to keep the time I spent at Chief Paulie's and neither did she since she wasn't home all the time. So she just gave me fifty dollars a week, even if I did more or less time in that week. She also gave me her house key so I could get in there to work when she wasn't home. I felt kind of important when I opened the door to her house and sometimes I'd sit on her living room couch and pretend it was my home. I liked the feeling of being in my own space, in my room, and thought it must be wonderful to have your own house! I cleaned her kitchen, bathroom, and living room, too, when she was gone. Only, I never went into her bedroom. That was private.

One day after I started going to Chief Paulie's house, Dad brought the Medicine Man over to our place for lunch. I'd heard that he wasn't one for staying up later than sunset, so if you wanted to talk to him about something, it would have to be just after sunrise and noon. I didn't know why Dad brought him to our house at lunchtime but there he was. He had a good smile and he even stopped to talk to Ki-Moot in the porch. He came in, saying, "You have a very happy dog. It says a lot about the people who are looking after her."

He sat down at the table and Mom was scrambling because some government people had arrived at the Band office and Dad also had to fix something at the church. Anyway, we all made it to the lunch table. The conversation had to do with me joining my family here at the reserve and that I was in the process of getting officially recognized as a member of the Anishinawbe community. I didn't quite understand what that meant just yet. The old man took his time eating and seemed to do things rather slowly. My Ojibwe was getting better and better, and I told him a story about the mice in the school and that Blink wanted to know if they were learning English too. I didn't realize that my Ojibwe wasn't that good until I had to speak it every day. I had just stopped mixing in Ojibwe words in my English sentences with Goom and Choom back in Nibika before I left there. Here, I was asked to repeat the sentence if it had an English word in it.

When lunch was over, the Medicine Man put his hand on my shoulder as he was heading out the door and said, "You are a good girl. Listen to your parents and learn from those around you." I nodded and smiled. They went out the door and Dad drove him home, and I ran back to school.

CHAPTER FOUR

The Pine Beetle
Goes Blueberry Picking

I walked slowly, shuffling my feet along the hot gravel road. I'd just talked to Goom on the phone. She'd called to tell me that Mom had told her that she had to keep rolling up my sleeves because I had the cuffs all chewed up into many tiny little holes. I'd taken to wearing a kerchief around my neck, but it wasn't long until that, too, looked like it had been eaten up by moths. Goom said I had to promise Mom that I'd stop chewing my sleeves. She said she'd send me some very nice, expensive silk kerchiefs that would discourage me from chewing on them.

When Goom was talking to me, my chest began to hurt and I felt like bawling my eyes out. I didn't like it that Mom made Goom give me heck, although she'd done it in a nice way. I wiped the tears off my face with my sleeve. I was so excited when I picked up the ringing phone and heard her voice. I thought I'd have a long chat with her because after that first long-distance phone bill, I hadn't talked to her unless she called. Then it turned out she was calling only to give me heck. I felt another rush of tears flowing over my cheeks.

The sun was heating up my head, and the truck that went by kicked up a cloud of dust around me. I covered my mouth with my kerchief and I immediately heard the comforting sound of crunch, crunch, crunch. I hurried to the Band office to tell Mom that Goom had called. Dogs were barking by the playground across from the community centre. The kids there were screaming and laughing, cheering on their baseball players. I made a face, thinking that they sounded so happy and here I was, miserable as could be.

I came into our homeroom classroom one day and the kids were giggling and calling me a name. It sounded like "cheap spit," so I asked them, "Who's Cheap Spit?" They all laughed and the name stuck. Miss Mitig, our homeroom and Native language teacher, told me they were calling me "Chief's Pet" until I said "cheap spit." So I guess it was my fault. I thought it was strange, though, that they didn't make fun of me for helping Miss Mitig in class instead of sitting out on the swings. Oh yes, they always made sure there wasn't one empty swing at recess. Was I ever glad yesterday was the last day of school.

Sticking my hand into my pocket, I felt the crinkled paper of the letter I'd received last week from Autumn. I stopped and read the short note again.

Hello, Abby. Hope you are having a great time at the reserve. My friends at the reserve always come to visit me at my house on weekends when their parents come to town. Do you have friends over to visit at your house? Did Jalene tell you they were moving? Well, she's gone now and Alexa has a new friend too. She's a new girl at school and I don't know her very well, but her name is Nikki. I don't know what happened, but as soon as you left, we just kinda fell apart too. Anyway, I will always write to you and please call me or come and see me if you ever come back to Nibika. I have to go now, my dad is taking me with him to Thunder Bay today. Bye, Autumn.

I stuck the letter back in my pocket. How could she ask me about even having any friends? I'd already told her about the totally rotten kids and school here! I even told her I was going to try to come back to Nibika one way or another as soon as I could. She sounded like she'd never even got that letter. Maybe she didn't get it before she wrote this one. I didn't know how long it took to get a letter from Bear Creek to Nibika.

A dog came running as I neared the Band office. It was the dog that always hung around the school door. I think she was Miss Tracy's dog. None of the loose dogs were exactly owned by any of the teachers; they just hung out at the teachers' houses because they always fed them. Most of the teachers had left that morning to head home for the summer, to wherever they were from.

The Band office was one of the few buildings in the community that was made of logs. It was a chalet-style log building that sat sideways to the lake. It fronted the road to the dock and the green picnic area beside the road. People usually sat around the picnic tables watching the float planes that came in from other communities that didn't have airstrips.

I ran up the steps and the door was pulled open just as I pushed it. I stepped aside as Alice stood there with the door open and asked, "Abby, are you looking for your mom?"

I nodded and she said as she came out, "Come, sit with me on the steps here a moment. There's no one in there right now. Just Chief Paulie, talking on the phone. I just came from the community centre. Your mom is still there. We finished counting all the stuff that's in the freezers. We'll have to work hard to make sure there's enough food for the ceremonial feasts to get through the summer. Then we'll have to start all over again for another whole year." She settled down on the top step.

I flopped down beside her. I looked down at our feet. Alice had black cotton running shoes on over white socks, which were pulled up over beige cotton stockings. I wore white running shoes that Mom had bought for me in Winnipeg. Alice had on a blue print dress with tiny pink flowers on it and she wore a green sweater that was buttoned only at the first three top buttons. Her greying hair was pulled into one braid down her back, and her brown, wrinkled face was shining with sweat from the hot afternoon. Her dark eyes glanced at me as I asked the first question that came to mind. I was sure she could tell I'd been crying and I wanted to distract her from asking me any questions. "How many feasts are there?"

"Oh, about eight or maybe more. Depends on what the elders decide is needed. It's not how many feasts we have, it's the number of people we would expect to feed that determines how much food we must store. The spring powwow drew in more people from neighbouring communities than we expected and we ended up cooking more ducks than we planned, so we have to get a lot more in the fall."

I looked at her, "The powwow? I don't remember a powwow. When was that?"

She looked down the lake before she replied, "It was at the end of May this year." I began crunching on my scarf again as I sat there thinking. That was when we went to Winnipeg! Mom and Dad never told me they had to miss the powwow because I wanted to go to Winnipeg for my birthday.

Alice smiled at me and said, "Do you ever hear that bug in an old dry tree or in piles of wood that goes 'crunch, crunch, crunch' as it chews through the wood?" I blinked, not knowing how that had anything to do with a powwow. She laughed and said, "That's what you sound like!" I immediately felt defensive, but then I started to smile because I actually did know what that sounded like.

"What's that bug called?" I asked.

She smiled. "A pine beetle, I think." I hid a smile with the corner of my kerchief, just as Mom came around the corner. She smiled and sat down beside me.

Alice said, "I put the freezer content list on the bulletin board in the meeting room."

With a sigh, she stood up, saying, "I'd best get on home or Ned will wonder where I've gone to." She went down the steps one at a time and glanced back with a smile as she walked around the corner.

I looked up at Mom. "Why did Alice say 'freezer content list' in English?"

She laughed. "Well, that's what it says on the top of the sheet, and Alice sat there practicing it the whole time we were repacking the freezers."

Then she glanced at me and said in a softer voice, "You've been crying. What's the matter?"

I sat and crunched through another layer of my kerchief before I replied. "Goom called. She said you didn't like me ruining all my sweaters because I bite holes in the sleeves."

Mom said softly, "I've asked you to stop that many times. The sweaters are expensive and you can't keep rolling up your sleeves until they hit your elbows. People will begin to think you're rolling up your sleeves for a fight."

When I said nothing, she continued. "When you're not wearing your sweaters, you're chewing through your kerchiefs. I asked Goom if she knew how to discourage you from ruining your things, that was all. So did she have any suggestions?"

I glanced up at her. "Goom says she'll send me a box of really expensive silk kerchiefs."

She sighed and said below her breath, "Oh, Mom!" I took another snip of what was left at the corner of my kerchief. She turned to me, saying, "That doesn't explain why you were crying."

I sat looking down at my running shoes and crunched through another layer of fabric and said, "I was hurt because you told her something I was doing wrong. It was like you told on me or complained about me. Why don't you just send me back? I want to go back to Goom and Choom!"

I could feel the warm tears rolling down my cheeks again. Her arm came around me and she held me in a big hug for the longest time before she said, "You're my baby and I'll never ever leave you behind again. I'll certainly never ever send you away from me! When I first moved here, Maggie was old enough to go to school, but they only had half-day school for children your age. I couldn't bring you up here because I had to work and I didn't want to leave you to be babysat by a stranger. Besides, Goom and Choom wouldn't let me bring you up here because you had a heart murmur that they wanted to monitor with the specialist in Thunder Bay. Did they ever tell you that? Anyway, you outgrew the heart condition and by then, they said they wouldn't know what to do without you, so I said I would come and get you later when it was the right time. Well, when Choom got sick, it was the right time for you to come home to me, and here you'll stay until it's time for you to go to high school somewhere and then on to university."

After some time, when I stopped sniffling, she said, "I asked my own mama what I should do. I always ask my mama when I don't know what else to do. You are to do the same thing too, you understand? Tell me what's bothering you and ask me questions about things that you don't under-stand. If I can't answer you, we'll ask my mama, okay?"

She kissed my forehead and I nodded. She pulled back and asked, "What did Alice say?"

I smiled and replied, "She said I sounded like a pine beetle." Mom laughed out loud and I giggled just as a bunch of people came around the corner of the building. Dad was at the back of the line. He was sweating hot and laughing with the other guys. Then I noticed the baseball gloves. They were the ones playing baseball. I thought it was the kids. I could have gone to watch if I hadn't been so busy feeling sorry for myself!

Dad sat down beside me and Mom went in to get her things. He looked at me and said, "You okay?" I nodded just as Blink came tearing around the corner, going "klink, klink" on pop cans clamped to the bottom of his shoe heels. Dad jumped down, lifted him up by the arms, and kicked his klink-ing cans off his feet. They went flying off into the bush as he squealed in protest. Mom came out and we held hands on the way home, with Mom beside me and Blink between Mom and Dad.

Mom said, "Blueberry Festival is at the end of the month. Why don't we call Goom and tell her to come up here? Aunty Gilda can look after Choom while she's here. Would you like that?" She linked her arms around my elbow and I smiled, saying, "Yeah, we can take her blueberry picking and she can stay for the festival!"

By the time we reached home, we'd planned the blueberry-picking trip and then we had to see how long Goom would stay, if she could come. Mom called Goom as soon as we came in the door and when she hung up, she said with a beaming smile, "Yes! Yes! She's coming on Monday!"

Next, Mom called Chief Paulie and she began laughing on the phone about whatever Paulie was saying. When she hung up, she said, "She always says the same thing every time I ask her for some time off. She says, 'Oh, just go. Take as much time as you'd like. Enjoy the summer and the great outdoors!' Now she said, 'Mucko is rather an excellent secretary, don't you know? You should hear how he answers the telephone!'"

I sputtered into my cup of fruit juice. That was my joke that I shared with Paulie! I'd told her about the kids' TV show that featured little talking animals that I used to like watching at Nibika. She'd walked in one evening when I was in her living room. I'd been cataloguing all the stuff she'd dumped into big boxes in one of the bedrooms. I had things made out of rabbit, mink, martin, skunk, beaver, bear, muskrat, and weasel pelts, all arranged in piles. So, when she came in, I used my voice in different tones to have a rabbit hat let out a squeal, "Hurry! Hurry! Run for your lives!" A beaver mitt jumped up, "What? What? Where?" Mink and martin pelts crashed into each other and knocked themselves out. Then a right bear mitt stood up, facing her with her left-hand mate at her side and demanded, "Who has entered this land of the animals?"

Chief Paulie had doubled over and let out a high-pitched wail before she went into peals of laughter. That was the only way you could describe her laugh. It was actually quite awful if you had to listen to it for any length of time.

Since that time, though, whenever there was an opportunity during the evening, we would look out her living room window and if we saw any wandering dogs on the street, we'd have them carry on conversations, sharing gossip about each other or planning what to do about a particularly nasty dog that occasionally showed up at this end of the community. Or, they just made comments as they sniffed and passed each other with stiff-legged steps. It was definitely better than television!

Like last night, I'd just finished with a bag of stuff that Minnie and

Lizzy had dropped off when Paulie came in. I looked out the window and saw Mucko come running down the street at full speed, and I said in the voice that I used for Mucko, "Wait! Wait! Paulie! Don't close the door! Please, don't close the door! Crooked Skunk is coming after me!" Behind Mucko, I saw the big black dog with the two white stripes that came from his white neck. He was a bully and he sure could fight! We'd seen him beat any dog that dared to challenge him. Paulie quickly whirled around and pulled the door open and Mucko sailed right into the house without a pause. We'd laughed when Crooked Skunk stopped in the road, looking rather disappointed. Paulie used the low voice we'd given Crooked Skunk and said, "Aw, shucks! I was really going to give it to him this time! Mucko, huh? He's no bear, I can tell you that!" Without another glance back, Crooked Skunk turned and trotted up the road toward the Band office.

After supper, Ned and Alice dropped by and the rest of the blueberry-picking trip was finalized. Ching and Gish would be coming too to get as many partridge and fish as they could, and Mike and his wife, Linda, would also be there. Blink was happy that David would be there to play with. By the time Sunday came around, everyone was ready to leave the next day. Goom would arrive when the plane came in the morning.

I moved my things out of my bedroom so Goom could just leave her bags there when she came in. That way she would have a place to sleep all ready for her when we returned from the blueberry-picking trip. I was so excited, I couldn't get to sleep that night. I had never gone camping before and I couldn't wait to see Goom. I started imagining what we would do when we got to the campground. What would it look like?

It was very late in the night when I became aware of a noise in the porch. I heard Ki-Moot growling and then she started barking frantically. I was at the door pulling it open when Dad came up behind me. Ki-Moot ran into the house while Dad turned the light on and stepped out. Suddenly he whirled around, hurried back in, and slammed the door. By then, Mom was standing beside me. Dad, who had his back to the door, said, "I just came face to face with a big bear!" He was standing there with just his shorts on when he dashed past us and into the bedroom, from where he emerged a minute later with his clothes on and grabbed the flashlight by the door.

We hadn't even moved and Mom said, "Why are you going out? It will go away."

Dad turned as he cautiously stepped into the porch. "I put the fishnet inside the boat and my gun is already out there too . . . along with the box of groceries I got from the store yesterday."

Mom rolled her eyes as he disappeared outside. We went to the window and we could see his flashlight bobbing toward the lake. Suddenly, Ki-Moot was at the door barking again. There was a crash inside the porch! That was Ki-Moot's food bowl! Mom stood there looking at the door and I was over at the window trying to pull it open. I finally managed to slide it open and I yelled out the screen window as loud as I could, "Dad! Dad! The bear's inside the porch! The bear's inside the porch!"

I saw him stop at the boat and shine his flashlight back at the house. He'd heard me. There was another bang in the porch and Ki-Moot was going nuts, barking beside Mom. I yelled at Dad again, "The bear is still inside the porch!" I saw him lift a box out of the boat and start walking back, shining the flashlight back and forth.

He yelled back, "There he goes! He just ran across the driveway heading down the road."

Dad came in, saying, "Ned had his lights on. He never stays up this late. Maybe the bear came along the shoreline and came upon his house first. The question is, did the bear swim across the creek or did he walk up the creek and cross the old wooden bridge? We're just lucky the bear didn't realize I had lard and butter in here."

He set the box down beside the door, kicked off his shoes, and said to Ki-Moot, "Well, the bear ate your food and put a hole in your bowl too!"

Ki-Moot closed her eyes as Dad ran his hand over her head. "You turned out to be a good watchdog, didn't you?"

Mom took my arm and said, "Come, off to bed with you. Why were you up, or did Ki-Moot wake you up too?"

I replied, "I was just lying there. I couldn't go to sleep thinking about Goom and our camping trip."

I went back to bed and snuggled in. I could hear Dad saying, "I don't ever remember a bear coming around, do you? Not since I was a kid anyway." I could hear them talking a while longer in the bedroom before I drifted off to sleep.

By the time I got up on Monday morning, there were boxes at the door that held our kitchen stuff, bedding, and food. I scrambled to catch up as I'd really, really slept in! I ate fast and rolled up my pillow and bedding and stuffed them into the bag that lay at the foot of my bed. It was a good thing I'd packed my clothes before I went to bed the night before. Gish and Ching would bring the tents and stoves. Four boats would be used to take us to the island where the blueberries grew.

Alice and Ned pulled their boat up beside our dock. Dad was loading the stuff into our boat when they came up the path. Alice came into the house laughing. "I heard a deep, raspy breathing above my head by the open window last night. Ned was snoring beside me, so I reached for the big flashlight beside my bed and got up on my elbow and shone the light—right into a huge bear's eyes! He whirled around and crashed into my rainwater barrel at the corner of the house."

Ned came into the house behind Alice and said, "That was when I awoke to the racket. She probably blinded it with the flashlight. That thing is very bright, you know. The bear knocked the barrel over and I could hear the water rushing out and then some loud crashing through the bush, and then it was very quiet. I got my gun ready and waited for it to come back. I was going to blast it. If it got anything to eat, it'll be back."

I noticed Blink sitting at the table with his mouth open, holding a cup in his hand. I realized then that no one had thought to tell him about the bear. How could he have slept through the noise in the house last night anyway? I watched his eyes widen when Mom began her story about Ki-Moot waking up the house and just then, Dad came up behind Ned and added his story of having to go out and rescue the food box from the boat. That was when Blink suddenly slid off the kitchen chair, crashed his cup down on the table, and demanded, "Why didn't anyone wake me up? I missed the whole most exciting thing ever to happen around here and no one woke me up!"

We glanced at each other. Frankly, I never even thought to wake Blink last night. I turned around and went back into my bedroom and giggled. That made me feel so great! Blink had missed the whole thing and nobody remembered him!

I grabbed my raincoat off the hanger. I might need that too. There was still commotion in the kitchen when I saw Alice and Ned heading back down to their boat by the shore. They were going to the grocery store by boat. I guess that made sense, since they wouldn't have to unload the groceries from the boat until they got to the island.

Blink had finished his tantrum when I came back into the kitchen. He sat at the table sulking and casting dagger eyes at me. Finally, Dad had finished loading up the boat and came in to get his keys. Blink perked up when Dad said, "Blink, want to come with me to pick up Grandma from the airport?" Without a word, he was out the door.

Mom made some tea, chicken noodle soup, and fresh bannock while we sat at the table waiting for them to return for lunch. I asked when Maggie was going to show up or if she was coming. Mom said she wasn't coming because she and Jane were making a quilt or something for the baby that they wanted to finish. I wasn't surprised. The only time we saw her was if she had to come here to get some things or have Mom make something for her or alter some of her clothes. She always came with Jane too, so I never had any chance to spend time with her alone. Jane always giggled and whispered things to Maggie that I couldn't hear, and they would laugh together, always leaving me out of their secrets.

Ching and Gish had already gone to the island to make sure everything was all set up for our arrival. That would mean the tents would be up, stoves in place inside each tent, and a stack of firewood ready.

I asked Mom, "How many baskets of berries do we have to pick?"

She filled her cup with fresh tea and sat back with a sigh. "I hope it's not too hot while we're out there. I packed a lot of mosquito repellent. I also hope the rain doesn't hang around too long when it comes, and that the winds let us cross the lake when we need to."

I smiled and said, "The baskets?"

She laughed. "Oh. Well, we'll have six large coolers. When four are filled, someone will have to come back and put the berries into freezer bags and get them into the freezer and bring back the empty coolers. The two that are left at camp should be filled by then and then the whole process begins again . . . unless the weather doesn't want to cooperate."

Mom continued, "There are also ceremonies and feasts at the end of the first week out on the island. There's a ceremonial area where they conduct weddings or whatever the community requires. Sometimes the ceremonies run two full days, Saturday and Sunday of that weekend. What we normally do is we come back here on Friday evening. We get cleaned up and do a lot of cooking."

I was really excited about this. I'd never been to a ceremony or feast like that. Mom smiled at a memory as she said, "Then, early Saturday morning, we head back out to the island in our best dress-up clothes and with lots of food. There's a feast in the morning, at noon, and in the evening. The powwow is usually held right at the end. Then we head back Saturday night. I remember one time, it was a clear moonlit night and we came back across the lake after midnight. Oh, it was so beautiful!" She made a face and added,

"That's when things go right! You just never know what's going to happen because we all do whatever the weather allows us to do."

I smiled in excitement. "What about last summer? Did you go to the ceremonies last summer too?"

She laughed. "No, we got rained out. They had to do the ceremonies at the community centre. So many people had arrived that they had to put up a big tent outside on the field. Oh, and remember, we have the blueberry festival at the end of July."

I'd just dished out some chicken noodle soup to cool off when Dad's truck pulled up in the driveway. I dashed to the door and ran down the steps. Dad was opening the passenger door and out stepped an old white woman. I didn't remember Goom looking that old! Her blond hair was now all white and it was pinned in a bun at the back of her head. She had on a pair of beige pants with a striped shirt tucked in and a pair of white running shoes. She scooped up Ki-Moot into her arms as she came running by her feet. I stood by the steps while Dad got her packsack from the back of the truck. I saw Blink crawling over the driver's seat and sliding down to the ground. He'd been in the back seat and no one remembered to pull the seat forward for him to get out. That would really tick him off too. I waited for him to come around the truck, but Goom had finished enduring the puppy's licks to her face and set her down on the ground, saying, "Okay, who wants to kiss me with puppy spit all over my face?"

I ran and threw my arms around her. She held me for the longest time and then Mom was there beside me. All three of us were standing in a big hug when Blink spoke beside me. "Well, Grandma has doggie spit and pine beetle spit all over her face now."

Dad said, "Oh, you already had your hugs and kisses, get on with you! Bring Grandma's other bag into the house."

Goom laughed into my ear. "Pine beetle spit? You'll have to tell me this spit story later," and yelled over my shoulder at Blink, "I will kiss you in a blink again, if you don't watch out!" I hadn't realized that Blink had heard about the pine beetle story. I knew I was in for long teasing from him about that. Then we all filed into the house.

Dad finished his soup and bannock and had gone to put the last of the things into the boat and we were just about to clear the table when Maggie and Jane crashed through the door with Maggie yelling, "Grandma! Wow, I thought I might have missed you. We came as fast as we could after we put the baby to sleep."

She was hugging Goom as Mom set out two more bowls for them. I kept staring at her and Jane as I bit into the last piece of my bannock. They'd dyed their hair jet black and they'd braided it into tiny long spikes with multicoloured beads in them that scattered all over their heads. I glanced at Blink and he mouthed, "WOW," and spun a finger in a spiral at the side of his head. I smiled and watched Maggie's black-painted fingernails as she picked up a spoon for her bowl. Ever since our trip to Winnipeg, Blink had figured that I was the expert on city life and now he was treating me like I was superior to Maggie because he knew that she'd never left the reserve as long as he'd been alive.

Dad came in and lifted Goom's packsack to take it to my bedroom when she said, "Son, I don't need to unpack. Everything is there that I'll need to go blueberry camping with. Oh, I was getting so excited thinking about that on the plane. It seems that I've not thought about anything else besides Grandpa for the longest time." She paused and then added, looking at Mom, "Gilda thought this was the best idea you've ever had."

When Maggie and Jane were finished, they quickly cleaned up the dishes while I went and grabbed my jacket. Dad had finished loading up the boat and everything was ready. Maggie and Jane waved from the corner of the house as we got in the boat and pushed away from shore.

Ned and Alice were down by their boat, too, as Dad started the motor. Dad waved and away we went. Mom sat up at the front and Goom and I sat in the middle. Blink was beside Dad at the back. Ki-Moot settled herself on Goom's lap. It was a beautiful day! Seagulls flashed in the sun around the reef that jutted in a gentle slope out of the water. A few little trees stood at the very top of the rock pile. As we came around an island, we could see the bigger island with the sand beach surrounding it. That was the community blueberry-picking site. There had been a big fire there some years ago and now the island was loaded with huge blueberries. I smiled at Goom. It was sure nice to be near her again. I leaned my head against her shoulder and she kissed the top of my head.

As we came near the island, I could see Gish and Ching coming down to the water to meet us. They pulled the boat up and Gish was there to hold Goom's hand to steady her as she stepped out. In Ojibwe, I heard Ching say, "Easy, old man, she's way out of your league!" Everyone put their heads down to smile. None of them realized that Goom had understood every word they said. I giggled but said nothing.

I ran up with Goom along the path to the campsite with our packsacks.

The guys were unloading the boat and Mom had her own bags with her. There were four tents set around a firepit, where a huge stack of wood sat ready for the small fire that smouldered in the heat. The smoke racks were also already set up above the firepit. One tent would hold me, Goom, Blink, and Mom and Dad. The other one was for Linda, Mike, and David. There was one for Ned and Alice, and the smaller one was for Gish and Ching.

All the puppies were scurrying around Daish, who sat beside the entrance to Gish's tent. The boys soon had the puppies tied up before they ran off into the bush after a squirrel.

Goom looked around, heaved a big sigh, then walked to the fire and put another small log into it. I stopped beside her and she pulled me to her side, saying, "I've missed this. Your Choom and I always went picking berries in the summer, but you were probably too small to remember. When he got sick, we took to staying home. Oh, smell the air, child. Look around you and never forget the things you see and hear!"

I hugged her and said, "I've learned a lot already! From this time on, I'll remember you right here beside me saying what you've just said to me. Gish told me that."

She smiled, "That's a good girl. Keep learning and never forget! Now, which one is our tent?"

I nodded to the tent on the left and said, "Mom's gone off to get some spruce branches. We have to do that first, I think."

With that, we hurried to catch up to Mom, who was already heading out to a thick stand of spruce trees. She piled the boughs as she cut them and we struggled with them back to the tents. Some of the branches kept falling and, oh, they were so sharp, the needles punctured my arms right through my sweater. At one point, I saw Goom crash into the bush because she couldn't see around her bundle. We got into a hysterical fit of laughter just as Mom came by with her neatly stacked boughs which she held at the end of a protruding branch. She smiled, saying, "Oh, town folk! Come, best you two set up the boughs inside the tents and I'll carry back the rest."

Still laughing, I pulled Goom up and gathered up the scattered spruce boughs before I asked, "Set up boughs? What did she mean by that?"

Goom smiled and put her chin up. "That, I know how to do. Come on!"

We started with our tent and Goom was working faster than I could select and pile the boughs beside her. She marched the boughs across the floor of the tent and another row came up behind the first. With the three of us working, we were done in short order. At one point, we could hear the arrival of Ned and Alice, but when we came out of the tent there was no one around. So, we did Alice's tent next. By the time we finished with Gish and Ching's tent, we came out sweating hot. We'd just poured fresh tea into our mugs when I saw Alice come out of her tent, and I knew she was the one who got the cooking site set up, as well as the blueberry biscuits and tea. She stood with a big smile across her weathered face.

Goom walked over and shook her hand then leaned over and said softly in Ojibwe, "Oh, they look so delicious! Thank you so much!" Then she turned to me and said in English, "Let's get our bedding out and then we can go along the beach and see if we can find some special rocks." With a look over her shoulder at me, she added, "Oh, by the way, I brought you four silk kerchiefs. That's what's in the bag that I left at the house. I bought every kerchief they had in the store. All have flowers and they're red, blue, yellow, and purple along the borders. I know you'll love them!" I stole a quick glance at Alice and she was beaming fit to burst! I shrugged my shoulders and threw a hand over my mouth to indicate to Alice that no one in the group knew that Goom could speak Ojibwe yet!

I ducked into the tent behind her, saying, "Thanks! I can't wait to see them!" We picked a spot against the wall with me beside her. We heard a boat arriving as we finished setting up the bedding. When we came out, Mom, Alice, and Linda were looking at a tub full of fish. Mom smiled at Goom. "Well, Mom, what do you feel like eating for supper? Pickerel or sturgeon?"

Goom replied, "Pickerel for sure. I don't think sturgeon would like me very much."

I asked, "What do you mean?"

Goom said, "I mean that it may upset my stomach because if I remember correctly, it's rather rich, isn't it?"

Mom smiled and nudged me. "She means that she may be running to the toilet all night if she eats too much." Goom made a face at Mom and the conversation continued in Ojibwe between Linda, Alice, and Mom. I found it curious that everyone stopped speaking every time Mom said anything in English to Goom.

I walked behind Goom as we made our way to the shoreline and then we walked hand in hand down the beach. I asked, "Why don't you speak Ojibwe here?"

She shrugged. "I've always felt like I'm imitating a Nation's language when I speak Choom's language, so I normally don't speak in Ojibwe with Anishinawbeg. I also know that when Native people have to speak to me in English, I always feel some comfort that they would be more willing to excuse any cultural blunders I might make. But then, I've never gone camping with Anishinawbeg either. So maybe I'll find an opportunity to contribute to the conversation, eh?"

I asked, "What do you mean by cultural blunders?"

She replied, "Oh, things that Anishinawbe people would know that I wouldn't know. Just because I know how to speak the language doesn't mean I also know the beliefs and culture of the people."

I smiled. I could just imagine Gish's face when Goom started talking in Ojibwe. Just then, Blink came tearing along a boulder pile with David behind him, yelling in English, "Grandma, we saw a nigig and he had a pile of baby lobsters!"

She stopped and tilted her head to the side as she looked at the boys in puzzlement. I laughed and said in English, "He means they saw an otter with a pile of crayfish."

Blink came to a skidding halt and glared at me, saying, "So, now you're the expert?" in Ojibwe, then they were off down the beach toward the camp.

Goom looked at me with eyebrows raised. I pulled her forward, saying, "He's used to me not knowing anything and he was ticked that I translated for you."

As we walked along the beach, I spotted one of the smooth caramel-coloured stones that I liked. Next thing we knew, we'd taken our shoes off and were up to our knees in water picking up colourful rocks. Goom found one that was clear white. I found a round white rock that looked like it had a yellow golden yolk in the middle. I gave it to Goom to keep for me. We had our pockets full when we heard a whistle. It was a referee's silver whistle that someone was blowing to call everyone back to camp.

Our pockets clinked as we headed back to the campsite. We noticed that there were dark clouds headed our way. When we arrived, there was a large blue tarp already stretched over the campfire and eating area. "Rain is coming," Goom said as we sat down beside Mom. Everyone was around the fire and there was a large bowl of fried fish, wild rice, and bannock. Everyone laughed and talked as Alice dished out the meal. In broken English, Alice said, "Bunch of blueberries over there, over the rock pile. Many more past the swamp. Get big bucket full by lunch tomorrow."

Ching added, "There's also a bear there so you guys have to talk real loud and don't go too far by yourself. The tracks looked very fresh."

Mike added, "You have to watch the puppies too, boys. We can't leave them tied up here by themselves. So they'll have to come with us. We'll have to tie them beside the blueberry coolers in the shade somewhere."

The conversation continued to the next day's blueberry picking. Who was going where and who would have to come back to make lunch and stuff like that. I lost interest and concentrated on making sure I didn't swallow a bone. Alice didn't cut the bones out of her fish fillets.

We'd just finished supper when the first huge raindrops pelted the tarp overhead. Alice and Linda grabbed the leftover food and took it to Alice's tent. Goom and Mom hurried to wash the dishes and put them away. I ran for a pail of water and saw that there was no thunder or wind. Just a solid grey cloud that covered the sky.

The makeshift toilet was ready and I ran to it when I returned with the water. When I came out, I flung the door open and came face to face with Goom as she stood looking at her feet, saying, "How dumb am I? I didn't think to bring my boots! I just had images of sunny, warm days. I totally forgot that it sometimes rains here too!"

I laughed. "I'm sure someone has an extra pair of rain boots. If not, you can take Gish's boots and he wouldn't complain at all!"

She feigned a slap at my head. "Oh, you!" she said as she slipped by me. I waited for her while the rain started to fall heavily. When we entered our tent, Mom and Dad had lit the stove to ward off the moisture. Blink and David were on the blankets playing cards.

"That rain has woken up all the mosquitoes and now they're coming in by the dozens. I thought I'd wait to see if you had any allergies to the mosquito coil before I lit it," Dad said to Goom.

Goom replied, "You may light the coil. I already have a couple of mosquito bites on my face. I hope they don't swell up."

Blink giggled from where he sat. "Yeah, if they do you'll look like someone punched you in the eye!"

Goom said, "Well, then. I would have to borrow Ching's cool sunglasses, eh?" Everyone laughed because Ching always wore his wraparound sunglasses whenever the sun shone.

The noise and laughter gradually got louder at Ned and Alice's tent and we could hear Gish's voice and his rasping laughter. Dad ducked out and when he didn't come back, Mom also went. We could hear the laughter above the pelting rain on the tent. David and Blink were still playing cards by the door and Goom and I went to bed. She talked of Choom and how he was doing. It didn't sound good at all. Then she said, "I haven't seen you biting your sleeve or your scarf at all in the time I've been here." She was right, and I hadn't even noticed it! I sighed, then I told her about all the things that had happened since she'd left me here with Mom.

The smell of the fresh spruce needles along with the burning mosquito coil had a very calming effect on me. We talked way past the time that Blink went to bed, but I didn't hear when Mom and Dad came in. They must have been really late.

The next morning, everyone was up bright and early and the sun shone from a clear blue sky. There were two loons calling to each other right beside the island and the seagulls were congregating out on the reef. I could hear Alice by the cooking area with Linda, talking and laughing. Mom was talking to Goom about Choom when I slipped out. Dad had gone out with Ching and Mike to check the fishnet and look for ducks. I'd heard their motor taking off early that morning.

I ran to the outhouse and wandered back, looking around and checking things out. I hadn't done that the day before. There were some pink lady's slippers in the mossy patches beside the path. I ran my fingers over the flowers. They were so delicate and smooth. A chirp drew my attention to a squirrel that was upside down on a tree, looking at me.

Blink's voice startled me. "Stop hogging the path to the toilet! People are waiting for you to get back from there."

I took a big breath and headed back to the tents. What a pest! He stuck out his tongue as he marched by me.

I heard the boat coming in. That would be the guys. Everyone was by the cooking area when I arrived. Dad and Mike were coming up from the beach with the tub between them. Ching was laughing as he came up behind them, saying, "Mike was taking a fish out of the net and it squirted out of his hands and it hit John on the head. He had a mass of fish slime dripping down the side of his head!" Dad shook his head as he ducked inside the tent, shortly to emerge with shampoo in his hand. He headed down to the lake to wash his hair.

After breakfast it was time to head out to pick blueberries. Goom pulled a large collapsible straw hat out of her pack, jammed it on her head, and tied it under her chin. She looked funny and she stuck her tongue out at me for giggling. Talking excitedly, we went up the path that Ching used to get firewood and then we spread out when we came to the clearing. The hills were dotted with blackened trees and huge boulders that stood white in the glaring sunshine.

It was just before lunchtime when I stopped to eat some blueberries because I was getting hungry. Goom stood up and went around behind a boulder to get at a thick clump of huge berries. Suddenly, I heard her yell and she came stumbling back around the rock, yelling at me, "Go, run!" I didn't know if a bear was after her, but I stood frozen as she ran by me, flailing at her face. I remained rooted to the spot until I saw Gish appear in front of her. He grabbed the hat off her head and began spraying the insect repellent that he always carried with him. By the time I reached them, he had her head in a fog of repellent. That was when I noticed hornets buzzing around me, and Goom began babbling in Ojibwe.

"I stepped on a log and it flipped over and the branches smacked at the hornets' nest that I didn't even see. By the time I noticed that half of it had been smashed, the hornets were on me. Darn hat! They hovered around my face under the hat rim. I think I got stung on my eyelid!"

Gish stood still, wide-eyed and mouth hanging open, the spray can now dangling from his hand at his side. He'd lost his cap in the scramble and his hair was sticking up all over. Goom stopped and looked at him. "What's the matter? Gosh, you'd think you'd seen a ghost or something. I can feel my eye puffing up. Abby, I got stung on the eyelid, didn't I?"

Gish swallowed and I couldn't help laughing at how shocked he still looked. I picked up his cap and handed it to him before I took a good look at Goom. A big red puff was definitely forming on her right eyelid. "Yep, you got stung alright."

Suddenly, Gish got himself moving again and in a rather irritated voice, he said in Ojibwe to Goom, "Never occurred to me that you knew the language. Come with me quick. I know what I can put on it, but we have to put it on right away. Linda and Sophie should be at camp already." He put Goom's hat back on her head as he said to me, "Go pick up her bucket and follow us back."

I ran to get Goom's bucket. I was relieved to find it beside mine and not over by the hornets' nest. I ran to catch up as Gish went on and on in animated conversation with Goom.

I heard the camp whistle blast as we followed the path back to camp. The dogs were already there with the boys. Mom came running up when she saw Gish with his hand on Goom's arm. Mike and Ching were still not there, so lunch would have to wait until they arrived. Gish led Goom to sit by the fire while he went in search of his remedy for hornet stings. By the time Mike and Ching came up from the shoreline path, they had six partridge between them.

Gish emerged from the path by the swamp and he gave Goom a bark of some kind to put on the sting. Her eye was almost swollen shut and Blink said, "See, you shouldn't have joked about a swollen face yesterday. Now Ching will have to give you his sunglasses."

Goom laughed. "I think you're right." So, in a rather exaggerated gesture, Ching came up and put his sunglasses on her face. She did look funny and we all burst out laughing. The wraparound reflective lenses made her look like a huge dragonfly with a large straw hat on.

We'd just finished lunch when we heard a boat coming. We wondered who it could be. We weren't expecting anyone. Linda and Mom hurried to put the lunch stuff away and I was helping wash the dishes by the time the boat came to shore. Dad, Mike, and Ching went down and we could hear them talking to the fellow. Dad came up the path and we froze. The look on his face told all of us it was bad news. He came over directly to Goom and he held her as she sank to the ground. He spoke in a low voice, but we all heard clearly that Choom had passed away early that morning. Mom went to pack their things before she told Dad that she'd go with Goom and that she'd call us on Thursday.

Goom remained kneeling on the ground and Alice came and put Goom's jacket around her. I sat hugging Goom and we were both bawling. Finally, Mom was beside us and they were ready to take Goom to the boat.

At the shore, I hung on to Goom for one more big hug before Mom came to put her arms around me. I was still bawling and I became aware of the others who stood around us and then I was crushed to Dad's chest as the boat took off.

Dad, Maggie, Blink, and I flew out on Friday morning for the funeral on Saturday. When we arrived at Aunty Gilda's place, it was full of people I'd never seen before. They were Choom's relatives from the nearby reserve. He always went there to visit over the years, but I didn't remember all of his relatives. They had decided to give him a traditional Anishinawbe burial ceremony, which had finished before we arrived. Then there would be the church ceremony and burial on Saturday. The three of us endured the hugs and kisses as we were introduced from one person to another as Choom's grandchildren.

I looked around and noted that everything was as I remembered it in Aunty Gilda's house. Maggie and I discovered that Aunty Gilda's backroom office was empty, so I sat down on the small couch and she sat on the office chair facing me and we waited. She looked at me for a long time before I asked, "What?"

She sighed and said, "I was just thinking that I should have stayed home. I don't know those people and I don't know Gilda at all."

I became angry all of a sudden and shouted, "It's your grandfather we came here for! He's dead and we came to see him get buried! All you can think about is yourself!" My voice was breaking by the time I'd finished.

There was a sudden silence in the next room and then Maggie was beside me, putting her arm around me, whispering, "Sh, sh. I didn't mean that. I'm sorry! You got to know Granddad but I didn't, that's all. I felt like I was always left out while you got to live in town with Granddad and Grandma. Even when they came to Bear Creek, you were always there and they never bothered with me."

I began to calm down as this new information sank in. I turned and looked at her and said, "Why would you feel left out when you had Mom?"

She said, "I had Mom? Mom had John and Blink, and I had no one. That was one of the reasons why I decided to go and live with Aunt Lucy. I know she needs me, she appreciates me, and she's really a very nice person and I like it there."

We talked a bit more and I began to understand things from her point of view. I'd just thought she didn't like me. After another hour or so, Mom and Dad finally came into the room with Blink between them.

After we'd left Aunty Gilda's, I felt like a tour guide as I pointed out the restaurant and the Nibika Hotel, where we'd be staying. All the times I'd passed by the hotel over the years and I'd never have believed that one day I would be staying there as a visitor to Nibika. I tried calling Autumn several times but there was no one home. We were at the hotel for two nights as Goom and Choom had already sold the little white house and now Goom would be moving into an apartment nearby.

Maggie spent the time watching television in the hotel room. At one point I asked her if the kids were as mean to her as they were to me when she first arrived. She turned and smiled at me before she said, "Yeah. The very first one that said anything bad to me had a bloody nose at recess. Anytime something happened in class, someone always paid and it wasn't me. I wasn't afraid of anyone! Even the boys got bloody noses if they harassed me." That would explain that then.

"Do you still fight them?"

She shook her head. "Nope, no need to. Nobody bothers me."

I didn't know anything about defending myself. I never had to. I didn't even know what to say when the kids called me names. It was only after I got home from school that I'd think of what I should have said.

Blink figured out how to use the game machines in the lobby and I couldn't pry him away from them for very long. Mom was at Aunty Gilda's place the whole time with Goom. When we weren't at the hotel, we spent the time walking around the town with Dad or sitting crammed inside Aunty Gilda's little house.

On the second day, Mom took Blink with her right after breakfast when Aunty Gilda came to pick her up. I took Dad and Maggie to the little white house where I'd lived with Goom and Choom. We came down the street and there it was. But it had been painted brown! Whoever bought the house had fixed it all up. Even my upstairs window had shutters on each side. It didn't look the same anymore. I felt disappointed and sad, like I'd lost something special, as we retraced our steps down the street.

After that, Dad, Maggie, and I went shopping. Dad bought me a new jacket. It was even better than my old one. Maggie got a new pair of jeans and Dad bought a new fishing rod for Blink, and one for David too. Dad also bought spare parts for his truck and snow machine. We also bought Mom fancy aprons and sparkling hairpins and a really nice blouse. Finally, it was time for the funeral and Mom looked very tired. She said that Goom was holding up better than they'd expected.

We all sat at the front of the church, and before the service Maggie and I went up for one last look at Choom. He looked so peaceful, like he'd just gone to sleep. After the service, we piled into a vehicle that drove us to the cemetery. There, they buried Choom then all the relatives came back to Aunty Gilda's place again. While we were gone from the house, someone had come in to clean the place and now there were flowers everywhere and sandwiches were spread on trays around the room.

People chatted and laughed, remembering funny things about Choom. Maggie and I sat on the couch, slowly eating our sandwiches. Out through the backyard window, we could see that Blink had found a little boy his age to play with. They were pushing blocks of wood through the sand around the rose bushes.

Maggie turned to me. "I have to go to high school somewhere next year. Miss Tracy says that Winnipeg is a good place. She didn't know anything about Thunder Bay. Either way, I could live in a boarding home or live with a family. What's it like here? If I were to stay here with Goom and go to that high school up the hill, what would it be like?"

I almost choked on my sandwich. That possibility had never occurred to me. Maggie living with Goom? I felt a hot wave of anger, no, it was more like jealousy, shoot across my chest. I kept my eyes on the boys outside and forced my mind to keep moving as I wondered what to say about the high school. Finally, I said, "The kids in this high school are small-town kids. They're kids of people who work on the railway tracks or at the sawmill. I've never heard of any problems with them. Thunder Bay would be nice, though. You'd have your pick of high schools. There are many of them to choose from and you'd get to do things on the weekends, like go to the movies, shopping, or even skiing, if you liked." She smiled at me but didn't say anything. I think I gave myself away, being a bit too enthusiastic about life in the city.

Before we left for the airport, Aunty Gilda gave me a CD player and a stack of CDs and she gave Maggie a nice digital camera with a carrying case and a bag filled with stuff from her cosmetics case. Her parting gift to Blink was a real cowboy hat. I wondered where she'd got it from. It fit his head just right. Saying goodbye to Goom was really hard this time, but I knew now that she could come and see us anytime. We could also come visit her, too, when we had enough money for the plane ticket. I settled down in the plane seat behind Maggie with Ching's sunglasses in my pocket.

CHAPTER FIVE

Summer Camping

Blink's cowboy hat blew off his head one windy afternoon shortly after we got home from Nibika. I saw the hat fly off like a raven and a lone dog suddenly jumped up, grabbed it, and took off at high speed with its prize. Blink gave chase, screaming his head off at the dog. I followed, running as fast as I could. Other dogs came running and chased the dog with the black hat, and in no time flat, it was ripped to shreds and we found it in the slough by the baseball diamond. Poor Blink was so heartbroken and I was just bursting to laugh, but I didn't dare because Dad had caught up with us by then.

For the whole month of July, we stayed close to home and Dad and I went fishing a lot. I got really interested in the whole array of fishing lures that Dad had. I was getting really good at catching fish with Mom's fishing rod, so Dad decided to buy me my very own.

All that month Mom was a homebody, as Goom would say. She loved to sit and sew at her sewing machine, making skirts, shirts, and even a jean jacket for Blink. It looked really nice, like it was bought from a store. She was working on a quilt, as well.

Sometimes when Paulie was gone, Mom would lock the Band office and come home. There wasn't much going on when Paulie wasn't in the community. I kind of missed Paulie. She went on a long holiday in July and came home for a few days before she had to go to a conference somewhere again.

Mike had the boys most of the time. They took Blink with them several times when they went camping at a lake two portages down from our lake. Blink was getting really brown and I began teasing him about the white untanned mark around his eyelids. He looked a lot like the bird with the white stripe on its eyelids!

The one thing I was really excited about that summer were all the CDs Aunty Gilda had given me. When I'd find myself alone in the house, I'd play one CD after the other, or play the songs I liked over and over. Aunty Gilda had given me a large selection of all kinds of songs, from country to pop music. I'd never paid any attention to music before, but now it was like I'd discovered a whole new world.

One day, I was washing the lunch dishes after everyone had left and quite unconsciously I began humming and then started singing along with the singer on the CD. I was amazed that my voice actually blended right in! I sang the song so many times that by the time I heard the truck pull in, my throat was sore.

Summer holidays always go way too fast and before I knew it, it was August. On a hot, windy day near the end of the month, we set out to go berry picking one more time on the island at the far end of the lake. This was the same island that we'd gone to with Goom at the end of June. As we left our boat landing, we saw Mike and Ned coming back from the island. They'd left early that morning with the large canvas tents the community used when it put on an event.

Mike pulled up beside our boat as we floated in the waves, waiting for him to come up beside us. As Dad grabbed the front end of his boat, Mike yelled over the running motor, "The tents are all set up on the right side of the island between the sloping rock and the sand beach. I'm not quite sure how many people are arriving on the left side of the island, but we picked our old spot. Ching brought all the other groups' food supplies in his boat, and he's there at our campsite now, getting it ready."

Dad yelled back over the noise of the idling motor, "Lucy and Maggie have all the groceries packed in Ned's boat, so I guess you get to enjoy the company of the ladies in your boat!"

David was with us, sitting beside Blink. "Hey, Dad. I forgot my boat. Can you bring it? It's on my bed."

Mike laughed,. "That's bad. Big boy like you forgetting your boat on your bed! How are you ever going to get anywhere?"

They all laughed.

The boat that David was so worried about was a little wooden boat that I'd carved for him. He wanted one after he'd seen the one I carved for Blink. I'd discovered I liked making things, and Dad had bought me a real Swiss Army knife to use after he saw the spoon I'd carved out of wood using a kitchen knife. Mom also liked it and began using it right away in the kitchen to stir her soups. The week that Dad gave me the knife, I made a little boat with a motor at the back and I had cut little props from a pop can. They spun around on a nail that I had put at the end of the motor. Blink took it and lost it somewhere. I was not very happy about that! But Mom said that the person who took it would know that there was not another like it and if they were seen with it, people would know where it came from. Therefore, they could never play with it in public, whereas, I could just make another one. Like Blink's, David's had a carved motor attached with propellers that I had cut out of a milk can.

Finally, we headed out against the waves. I held Ki-Moot down at my feet as the waves lifted our boat up and down. Ki-Moot was my dog now. She always came to me for a cuddle. Even at night, she would curl up beside my bed. She was allowed inside in the summertime. The mosquitoes would eat her alive otherwise. She was very obedient and seemed to understand when I talked to her. I liked the way her head would turn from one side to the other as she listened to me. She even sang with me if she was in the house. She'd start howling when I sang. I could imagine what we would sound like from the outside if someone happened to come by!

As we reached the open water, I saw two other boats splash into the waves, heading in the same direction as we were. They were coming from the far side of the reserve. As our boat crashed through the waves, we entertained ourselves by yelling as each wave came up according to its size. A really huge wave would be a grandfather, a smaller one would be a grandmother, and then a father and mother, son and daughter, and a baby was the smallest wave.

Blink would yell, "Here comes a grandfather of a wave!" David would say, "And right behind it is a grandmother!"

I added, "That's a daughter behind it."

Blink said, "Behind her is a father."

David yelled, "No, that's not a father. It's a mother because the father's right behind her, see?"

Up and down the boat rocked as each wave family member rolled under the boat, only to send it splashing down on another wave. I soon lost interest in the boys' banter and turned my attention to the other boats keeping pace with us in the distance. Sometimes the boats would sink into the waves so deep that it looked like the people were riding on water. As another half-hour went by, the other boats were getting closer. I noticed then that the island was ahead of us. It looked like a green, bushy mound with many bald rocky spots and scraggly black hair sticking up all over the place. That would be the black burnt trees that were still standing. I spotted the tents just where Mike said they would be.

There were two large family tents and one small one. Without any discussion, it just came naturally that we would share one big tent with Mike and Linda, the other big one would house Ned and Alice, and the small tent would be occupied by Ching and Gish, and, oh yes, Daish.

I would share my bedding with Maggie. She said it was easier if we spread our sleeping bags flat, one on the ground and one for the cover. That summer Maggie had started coming by the house more often, and she'd shown me how to clean the fish if Mom hadn't cleaned them yet. She even told me she was proud of how much I'd learned in such a short amount of time on the reserve. Maggie was in Mike's boat somewhere behind us. I was surprised when she called to say that she was coming on the trip. Maybe it was because Jane had left on a holiday with her family. I was still happy she was coming.

We hit calm water as we neared the island. Soon we were at the shore with Ching pulling our boat in, saying, "Man, it's getting rough out there, eh? Not to be surprised if Gish needs to do a ceremony first before he gets into Ned's boat!"

Dad laughed as he held the boat steady for us to scramble out. Mom said, "Well, if Ned puts the old man at the front of the boat, Gish will bite his tongue off if he tries to talk in those crashing waves!"

Ching laughed. "Wouldn't that just be a blessing, eh?"

They were still talking as we ran up to the site. It was beautiful! The ground was smooth and level with small birch trees everywhere. It looked like a park around our campsite. With the wind blowing from the back of the island, it was calm on the side we were on. I noticed that Ching had already set up the temporary outhouse shelters in the bush away from the campsite. Wood was piled at the firepit that had also been cleared. The boys had already tied Ki-Moot to a tree beside our tent and they were playing beside the doorway.

Mom looked at me with raised eyebrows. I could tell she was testing me. I smiled. "Willow branches first for the firepit rack and spruce boughs for the tents and around the fire. And then, get a fire going, make tea, and lunch?"

She smiled and picked up her axe. Mom's axe was very sharp, and she used it for cutting spruce boughs, willow sticks, and setting up snares. She rarely went into the bush without it. She headed to the right, where we could see the willow bushes along the shoreline. She cut down six long, straight branches and about six more smaller ones. The long branches would be the frame of the smoke rack over the firepit and the smaller ones would make the racks. I hauled them to the firepit and began to peel the bark off the branches in long, wide strips. The bark would be used to tie the racks together and would become very strong as it dried and tightened. I had the bark laid out when Mom arrived with an armful of smaller branches. Dad and Ching had gone to get more wood since Dad had arrived with his bigger power saw. That's when I saw Ned, Alice, and Gish coming with their boat loaded with supplies and all the dogs! We helped them unload the stuff, and Ned left to investigate who else was camping on the other side of the island.

The dogs Wiener and Shingoos immediately went into a catch-me-if-you-can chase as they ran around and around the trees and crashed into the bushes before Alice yelled in a commanding voice for them to stop. They came to a screeching halt and she told them to sit down. I couldn't believe it, but they actually stopped and sat down with their ears flattened and tongues hanging out, panting. They looked so funny! Finally, the boys were able to tie them up beside Ki-Moot. Daish had settled herself beside her master's belongings outside the tent. The only dog missing was Mucko. Paulie was home and wanted to keep him in the house with her.

Mom, Alice, and I had the smoke rack up when we heard another motor coming. We could see the splash, splash, splash as the boat got closer. Blink and David were now at the sand beach catching minnows. I ran down to get a pail of water and saw that they had a large plastic pail with lots of minnows in it. Blink came running up with his wet shorts weighed down to around his hips and his belly stuck out as he tried to lift the bucket, saying, "Look, Abby! If you were a cat and ate all these guys, your guts would bust!"

I smiled. Trust Blink to come up with stuff like that! I peeked into the bucket again and said in English, "Yeah, that's quite a lot. At least five dozen."

He dropped the bucket and looked up at me. "How many is that?"

I replied, "Twelve is one dozen and add twelve five times."

He looked up at me for another few seconds and blinked a few times before he turned and ran down the beach toward the sloping rock. I went back up to find that Mom and Alice had a big pot of stew going, along with several fresh bannock. There stood the new white smoke rack and the firepit surrounded by fresh spruce boughs. Mom was just getting her pots and serving plates ready when we heard a boat pull up on shore. That would be Mike, Linda, and Maggie.

We met them at the beach as we pulled the boat in. When Maggie had all her stuff brought up, she grabbed my sleeve and we ran down to the lake to bring up the rest of the things that had been unloaded from the boat. Ching was carrying several packsacks followed by Mom carrying the box of pots and pans. After running back and forth with several more loads, Dad was the last, bringing up the rifle and his axe.

Maggie pulled my sleeve when she saw Mom heading into the stand of spruce trees on the right with her axe in hand, and we ran after her. I knew what needed to be done next. We'd get spruce boughs to cover the floors in the tents and some to set around the firepit. I picked up chunks of moss that I came across because I knew from when we went blueberry picking that Alice preferred to wipe her frying pans with moss. She said it was more absorbent than cloth, didn't need washing afterward, and it burnt in the fire faster.

Mom's axe rang out as she deftly chopped the lower branches of the spruce trees, and Maggie was piling them for carrying back to the tents. I was almost keeping pace with Maggie, until I tripped and crashed backward into a bed of moss so soft that I couldn't even lift myself up on my elbows! Mom and Maggie stood there bent over laughing until Maggie went into a coughing fit as I wriggled and wriggled around like a worm in the moss. Finally, Mom reached down and pulled me up.

Maggie and I carried back four bundles of spruce boughs that we deposited in our tent, and then Maggie ran back to get more while I started at the door and stuck the branches side by side flat on the ground, overlapping the layers. I marched the branches row after row as quickly as I could until my butt hit the back of the tent. I had just enough branches. Maggie knew exactly how much was needed for one tent. I heard her voice several times and I could hear another boat motor coming. I ran out of the tent, wiping the sweat off my face. Four more bundles stood inside the other tent. Mom was coming up from the bush with two more bundles. Those would go in the small tent.

Maggie grabbed my arm and was pulling me to go somewhere, but I brushed her off because I saw Blink come running and he grabbed my arm, hauling me down to the water and along the beach to the rock, where he stopped still. I looked down at the sloping rock and there, arranged in a neat line, were pebbles. Five rows of twelve pebbles each.

I giggled and said in English, "Yep, that's five dozen, Blink."

He looked up. "We got more minnows than that!" he said in Ojibwe. "You know why?" I shook my head and he said, "Because there's no such word as 'dozen' in Ojibwe!"

I smiled and asked, "Did you count them?"

He blinked and said, "You can't count them. What's the matter with you? They move around too much. That's like trying to count the flies at the bottom of the toilet hole!"

I gasped. "Blink! Yuck!"

He grabbed my hand as we walked along the beach, saying, "It may be yucky, but it's a good example. Did you notice the flies in the toilet hole are different than the flies around the cooking fire?"

I made a face. "No, I hadn't noticed that." And then I thought, I might as well ask. "How are they different?"

He stopped to kick at a stone, aiming for the water, and was satisfied with the "plop" as it made a splash. "The ones in the toilet hole are flashy greenish blue and the ones around the food are plain grey. And did you know the smaller ones that bite you are different ones altogether too?"

"No, I hadn't noticed that," I said.

He stopped to blink up at me and he dropped my hand, "You don't notice much, do you?"

"I do too!'"

Blink sure was a strange kid. He'd begun hanging around me more since our trip to Nibika for Choom's funeral. I wasn't sure why he'd changed, but I think he understood my loss when we were at the cemetery. While we were there, I caught him looking at Dad for a long time and then he moved over to me and took my hand. I was so upset at the time that I didn't really notice. I guess I'd changed a bit toward Blink too. Now, if I saw him sitting on the swing that Dad had put up on the tree that stood between our house and Ching's, I'd go over and push him until my arms felt like they were falling off!

We went back to the campsite and Maggie was already at work on the second tent. I sat down beside her and we raced as we worked the rows side by side. I began telling her about the CDs and the songs I liked. She wasn't interested in music, though. She told me about some of the watercolour paintings that she was working on. Mom had already finished the small tent for Ching and Gish before Maggie and I finished the second tent. With no breeze blowing through the tent, we came out sweating hot from our work.

When we got out of the tent, Maggie and I saw that Ned was laughing and Gish was standing by the fire with his hair sticking up. He looked like the wind had sucked at his head from all directions. Ned had a cup of tea in his hand as he said, "We hit a big wave and Gish was at the front. Well, the wind blew his cap off and into the water behind me somewhere. He starts yelling, 'Get my cap! Get my cap!' So I tried turning the boat around, but the waves were high and water started coming in and Alice is yelling, 'Don't turn the boat! Turn it to the front!' But I turned the boat around and then we couldn't find the cap. I figured it was so heavy from the years of sweat and dirt that it probably sank to the bottom right away. Alice was yelling, 'Never mind the darned thing! We'll buy him another one!' And Gish says, 'Dang it! That's my lucky cap!' and the boat is getting pounded by the waves and finally I ask Gish, 'Shall we leave or do you want to swim and keep lookin' for it?' He goes to say something and this huge big grandfather wave hit us and then Gish yells, 'Dang it! I've bitten my tongue!'"

Suddenly Ching, Mom, and Dad broke into a big fit of laughter and I too was laughing so hard because that was exactly what Mom had said would happen. Alice continued the story. "Well, we couldn't see anything in the waves, so we had to leave his cap behind."

After that, everyone scurried to their own duties and would be back again for supper.

Sometime in the afternoon, Ned came back to the campsite saying that there were six other families camped at the other end of the island. Ned explained that after we spent a week picking berries, we'd go to a central space between the two camps where a ceremonial area was being set up. After that, there would be ceremonies and a dance. The old Medicine Man would be there to name children and perform the marriage of two couples. After that, the couples would head back to the community to be married in a church. Mom said it was just a formality to record the marriage.

Mom turned to me and smiled. Now I understood why she'd made me the ceremonial dress of purple cotton with little pink flowers on it, with four stripes of pink ribbon at the hem and along the sleeves and collar. I didn't know what she was sewing until she asked me to try it on. I couldn't wait to put my dress on. We all had fried fish for supper that Dad and Ching had caught that afternoon.

I had never bedded down to sleep with another family in the room. I slept with Maggie at the back of the tent. She was against the wall, the boys slept beside me, and Mom and Dad were by the door. The grocery boxes stood against the other back wall and then Linda and Mike slept beside the little stove. There was a hole at the top of the canvas tent where the stove-pipe stuck out. At the front of the tent by Mom and Dad's feet was a stack of wood and our shoes and boots.

Linda began telling stories about the times she'd go camping with her parents when she was a child. As she talked, Maggie suddenly let out a scream. The flashlight went on with everyone asking, "What?" "What's the matter?"

Linda said, "Something landed on the tent wall above my head!"

By then, Maggie was babbling. "I think, I think it was a frog! It landed on my face! I flung it off!"

Linda jumped up from her bedding. "It's a frog! There is goes!" It landed on my Mom's bare feet because Dad had pulled up the blanket when he grabbed the flashlight. She let out a screech as it hopped up to her chest. She flung it off and it landed on David's mouth, which was open since he was howling with laughter. It was at this point that Blink grabbed it and held it up for all to see. It was a big frog, alright. Blink crawled over to the tent flap and threw it outside. He was so beaming proud of himself as he got back into bed.

The next morning we set out to pick berries. We had two big coolers where the berries were to be dumped. We picked highbush berries, saska-toons, and any other edible berries to be found that the birds and squirrels hadn't got to yet. Alice kept the fire going and prepared the meals, and Ned collected the berry buckets at central spots where we would bring them when our containers were full. I carried an ice cream container and set out with Maggie after a breakfast of porridge and bannock with blueberry jam.

About midmorning, I was at a bush loaded with huge saskatoons that bent the branches almost to the ground when I heard a crashing sound behind a bush. Thinking it was Maggie, I stood up and asked, "Why are you making all that noise?"

A huge black head popped up over the bush. It was a bear standing up to see who was talking. As soon as our eyes met, I didn't stop to look where I was. I just turned and ran as fast as I could. I didn't stop until I crashed into Ching, who had an armful of wood.

"Whoa, there. Stop! What's up?"

All I could spit out was, "Bear! Bear! He stood up and was looking at me! Bear!"

Ching dropped the wood and held an arm out and pulled me to him, saying, "Sh, sh, now. What do you think he did when he saw you, eh? He probably took off in the opposite direction just as fast as you took off, eh? I bet he ran faster than you too!"

I was shaking and I sat down on the log that he'd been sawing with a handsaw. He said once that he preferred the handsaw as it made less noise and you got to smell the wood more. After my heart stopped thumping, he asked, "Where's your blueberry bucket?"

I looked up and shrugged. "I have no idea."

He helped me retrace my steps for about half an hour but we couldn't find it. When we returned to the campsite loaded with wood minus the berry bucket, Blink was the first to meet us with, "Where's your pail? Did you lose it? How'd it get lost?"

I said with resignation, "While I was picking berries, I heard a noise and thought it was Maggie, but it was really a bear. As soon as I saw it and it saw me, we both took off in opposite directions. I guess I forgot to take my pail with me."

Blink blinked several times before he said, "Well, if I saw you out in the bush, I'd take off like the dickens if I ain't never seen you before either!"

"What do you mean by that?" I asked, getting irritated.

He said, "Look in the mirror, oops, don't have one. But if there was one, you'd see that your hair looks like something chewed your head and spat it out again and your lips are blue. Do you know what I think? I think you ate all your berries and decided to lose your pail because it was empty."

Mom said, "Blink, quiet. What would you do if you were in her place and came face to face with a bear? You're much smaller than Abby."

Blink blinked several times and said, "Probably the same as the bear did."

Mom added, "By the way, I wouldn't go criticizing Abby's hair. Yours doesn't look much better. It looks like the waves ground your head around into the sand beach."

We all laughed at that image and then decided that everyone would search for my pail the next day.

The next morning, however, I woke up and I could tell that it was going to rain. It was dark out and I could actually smell the rain coming. It was a damp, earthy smell. Sure enough, the rain started right after breakfast and it came down in a steady, foggy drizzle. It was the kind of mist that soaked through your clothes very quickly.

I was in the tent that we shared with Mike and Linda. Alice was there and Ned had also arrived. The adults sat around the doorway of the large tent, talking and laughing. The small stove was burning low and it gave a light warmth that kept the dampness at bay.

Alice picked up the deck of cards that the two boys had been playing with and selected two suits from the deck. The reds she put face down on the blanket and then she started shuffling the black suits. The boys moved closer to see what she was going to do next. Then she put down a card from the one black suit she held in her hand. It was a seven of spades. She said, "Each of you boys take turns and peek at a card on the blanket but don't turn it over. When you find a seven, you may turn the card over. The one who turns over the most cards by the end of the game wins."

The boys laughed at each other and Alice said, "The one to my right, you go first."

Blink looked at the scattered cards and peeked at one and replaced it face down. "No, not that one!"

Next David took a card and looked at it and replaced it, saying, "Not that one either."

On it went back and forth until David said, "Here it is! Seven of hearts!" The card was left face up and Alice put down another card. "Three of spades. Your turn, Blink."

I watched and realized that Blink had remembered where the cards were that he had already peeked at, while David still randomly took a peek at the face down cards. Very quickly, Blink turned the cards over after remembering where a particular card was. Blink was actually a really smart kid. Maybe that was why he noticed more things than I did. I wondered if he was smarter than me, or if I just needed to start paying more attention.

I looked away from the card game to the back of the tent, where Maggie and Linda were playing string games on their fingers. I watched as their fingers deftly spun the string as they passed it back and forth between each other. There was the crow foot piece that became a cradle and so on. Maggie had tried to teach me once how to do it, but every time I tried my string just kept collapsing.

When the rain finally stopped and we had already gone to bed, Dad came in laughing, saying that he had just seen Ching walking by without his shirt. Mom asked why and Dad said that Ching had gone to play some kind of traditional poker game where they gambled whatever they had on them. So, I guess he had lost the inner T-shirt he always wore and his outer shirt. I thought it was kind of cold to be walking around naked outside.

We spent Thursday picking berries and we heard from Ching that the people at the other end of the island were being harassed by a bear, so we tied our dogs closer to the tents. We always made sure that our food smells didn't hang around the campsite. Alice threw cedar branches into the fire and we periodically replaced the spruce boughs around the cooking area by the fire and burnt those in the evening too. Whatever food was left over would be fed to the dogs.

The next morning, just as we were gathering for breakfast, Gish came out of their tent and started throwing shirts, pants, coats, and all sorts of clothing out of his tent. Ching giggled and said, "Gish says that he doesn't want other people's dirty clothes in his tent." It appeared that all the clothes were his winnings from the night before.

Sometime during the afternoon, another high wind came up and blew hard for the rest of the day. It was wonderful to feel the cool wind out in the berry bushes. I walked toward the shore just before supper and came upon a boy standing on the high cliff between the campsites. He stood at the edge of the high rock pile by the shore and spun a large black button that was strung with string through the two holes. The button whirled and hummed a loud noise that brought Gish to the shore. He yelled, "Stop that! You're calling a mighty wind that will suck the pants off you!" The boy smiled when he saw me and then he took off running back to the opposite shore to his campsite.

I'd recognized the boy immediately. It was Abraham from my class at school. The last person I needed to see out here was him! That kind of dampened my spirits. His family must have been at the other campsite. I hoped he wouldn't be at my naming ceremony on Saturday

Gish was still standing there by the shore, saying, "Just you watch, the wind will start blowing very shortly. We don't want that kind of wind, do we? They're still out there setting the fishnets." Oh, yeah. Mom and Dad were out there and Mike and Linda had also gone fishing. Not even twenty minutes later, the wind picked up and kept blowing like there was no tomorrow. When Gish went to check his fishnet that evening, it also held a bad omen because he pulled up a sunfish. However, he was lucky that it was still alive, so he was able to untangle it and let it go.

I was still having trouble understanding bad omens. Just the day before, I was going to ask Gish a question and I pointed at a tree that looked like a giant had peeled a strip of bark off the whole length of it. Gish had yelled, "Don't point at lightning-struck trees! It will bring bad luck." Well, he'd answered my question anyway. I was just going to ask him what had caused the damage to the tree.

I turned around and wandered back to the camp. Ching's radio hung on a branch outside his tent, but it kept fading in and out. Maggie and I figured if we tied a stone to the end of a coil of copper snare wire and shot it from a slingshot to the top of a tree, we could hook it to the radio wire to get better reception. It was actually harder than we thought. The first time Maggie tried to shoot the wire off, I'd apparently stepped on the wire and the stone flew back and just missed my head! On the second attempt, the wire came off the stone and the stone sailed off into the sky. After several more times, Maggie handed me the slingshot. I stuck the wire-wrapped stone into the leather, pulled the slingshot hard, and let go. The wire snagged my finger and the stone whipped back and whacked the top of my hand so hard, I let out a scream. Maggie laughed so hard that Mom came to see what we were doing. After we explained the plan, she took the slingshot and took aim at the top of the tree. Much to our delight, the tethered stone shot to the top. The branch swayed where it hit and the wire stayed. Then we hooked it to the radio and we got music! When there was no one else around, Maggie and I danced to the music of the recent bands and some of the oldies.

When we weren't picking berries, Maggie and I helped the women pick bull rushes to make into mats to dry the berries. The pin cherries had to be made into jelly, though, because they were getting mushy. I was stirring a pot full of them as they simmered over the fire when Maggie came by and sniffed, saying, "It smells like stinky stocks!" I had to admit that they did smell like stinky feet. I thought Maggie was getting bored as she seemed to be wandering around by herself more and more. I couldn't think of a thing that we could do together either.

Saturday was the day of the ceremonies. Just before sunrise, Mom told me to go wash in the lake and I ran out and dove into the water. I didn't need to be told twice because I loved being in the water. I'd discovered that most of the young people in the community didn't swim. I was in the water every chance I got and I loved diving deep down to the bottom. After the initial sting of the water in my eyes, I found it very interesting to look around down there. It also became a challenge to see how long I could hold my breath. I remembered that I was quite small when I learned to swim. Goom and Choom used to take me to the beach in Nibika. Maggie didn't swim either. She said she had no wish to swim with the bloodsuckers.

When I came back up to camp, Mom had my ceremonial dress ready and she combed my hair and braided it. I was made to understand that this was a very sacred ceremony. I hadn't realized the significance when the Medicine Man had come to our house in the spring. Now I knew that the name that he would give me would be the name that the spirits would know me by. I wondered how on earth my mom had known the colours that would be mine and mine alone. The deerskin moccasins to match my ceremonial dress were also beaded in roses. They were so beautiful! Then, Mom opened a package and pulled out a shawl that would go over my dress. It was deep purple. I almost cried when I saw how beautiful it was! It was store-bought with inlaid roses surrounded by sheer fabric. I knew immediately that it was from Goom.

Alice came up and put her arms around me and somehow that brought me back to earth. I didn't know how she knew that I would need some strength at this moment. It reminded me of that time outside the Band office. She'd done the same thing for me then. I put my chin up and stood tall and they smiled at me.

Everyone had already gone to the ceremonies when Mom, Maggie, and I finally finished dressing, and we began the walk along the shoreline to the ceremonial site. Mom, Alice, and Linda had cooked all Friday evening for the feast that was to take place after the morning ceremonies. Now we all carried the last of the heated food in baskets and pots. Mom was dressed in a full traditional leather outfit loaded with beadwork and sashes. Maggie was wearing a blue cotton dress with blue and yellow ribbon trimmings and a blue shawl that had very long fringes that swayed when she walked. She also had a fully beaded belt and beaded hair clips that matched her outfit. She was also wearing a fully beaded pair of moccasins. I'd never seen anything like them! They were gorgeous! Even Blink had on cotton pants, a shirt trimmed with ribbons, and beaded moccasins. He and Dad had gone ahead with the rest of our group.

I felt like a princess as we walked along the beach to the place where the gathering would be. Mom also carried a blanket that we would sit on. As we walked, I asked Maggie if she also had a naming ceremony and why did I not hear about it? Mom laughed and said Maggie was named right before her wedding to John. I turned and asked Maggie, "So, what's your name then?"

She glanced at Mom and said, "You're not supposed to brag about it since the name is between you and—" She pointed upward. "But since you asked, I'm called Night Hawk Woman." There was nothing to say to that, really. Why would someone be called a night hawk woman I wondered.

I turned to Mom and asked, "Does that mean you also have an Anishinawbe name? And how come I don't know about that too?"

They laughed and then Mom said, "Well, I did get a name right beside Maggie that day before we got married. I was named Gentle Evening Breeze on Rushing Water."

Oh, I thought to myself, I wasn't even going to try to understand that one! I decided to stop asking questions before I started imagining what kind of name I was going to get.

The ceremonies were to begin just after sunrise and we were expected to all be gathered around the ceremonial site by that time. We walked along the shore, almost to the end of the island to where the boats converged in one spot. From there, we went up an embankment and we came to the level ceremonial area. I came to understand that this was where important events always took place. I wasn't prepared for what I saw.

There were spruce boughs spread like a big fan outward from the centre of the ceremonial site. The outer perimeter was marked off by rocks set in a circle and there was a central fire smouldering in the middle. I recognized the smell of sage and sweet grass from the Cultural Days at school when they'd brought Gish and some of the other elders in to talk about the teachings and taboos of our culture. The drums started just as we entered the area. I understood the language quite well now, so I was able to follow along without Mom having to explain things for me. From that point, I sat down and watched the ceremonies with nervous attention.

After some time, I suddenly focused on the fact that as the Medicine Man was speaking, he had turned to look in our direction. Then Mom and Dad stood up and I had to force my feet to move to the circle with them. My stomach began to feel weird when the elder was speaking to me. It was my naming ceremony! I forced myself to stand with my shoulders straight and my chin up as per Alice's last instructions.

In his rather authoritative voice, the Medicine Man turned and addressed all the people there and the spirits that be, that from that time on, my name was "White-Throated Sparrow." That is how I was introduced to all those in attendance and to the spirits of our ancestors as well. He explained that the white-throated sparrow is known as the "weather bird" to the Anishinawbe. If its birdsong notes went up, it was going to be a good day. If its notes went down, it would rain. And, it also applied to our human form as well.

I didn't remember what else he said because I was floored. I'd always felt kind of smug that I could predict if it was going to rain or snow, and here I was being given a name that meant that exact talent! How on earth could the Medicine Man have known? And what did he mean by "our human form as well?" Was I also supposed to be able to predict the bad and good in humans, as well as the weather? It was all very confusing to me.

I found out that Blink already had a name too. When the Medicine Man informed him what my name was, he addressed him as "Sandpiper." That would account for his bobbing head, I thought with a smile. Here I'd thought he was a partridge or some other kind of bird anyway! During the ceremony, there were seven other kids with me who also got their names.

After the naming ceremony, it was time for the feast. That was when I spotted Abraham. He was standing at the back of the crowd like he always did. I wasn't interested in who he would be talking to and making fun at me with. I turned and spotted Maggie in the crowd with some other women and I went to introduce myself. I met a lot of people I'd never seen before. There was one woman with a really beautiful face, I thought. She had a shawl that covered her hair and it went right over her shoulders too. She laughed when I told her I was ready to throw up on my moccasins when I walked up to the centre in front of the Medicine Man. She told me her name was Rebecca and that I was really beautiful in my outfit, and she particularly loved my shawl! That was when I spotted Abraham moving in our direction. I found an excuse and got out of there and went back to Mom and Alice, who had spread our blanket under a pine tree.

The potluck food was spread out in one location and you just had to go and pick whatever you wanted to eat. Our group became large when Ching's shirtless people began showing up to arrange a time to try to reclaim their possessions. Dad was with us at lunch but then disappeared until the drums started with the Grand Entry of the Powwow. My heart lurched when I spotted him in full regalia at the Grand Entry. He was in a traditional outfit with a fully beaded leather shirt and pants and feather headdress. Wow! He was very impressive indeed! I found myself swaying to his movements as he danced to the beat of the drums. I glanced at Mom and she was totally focused on him. When the next dance was called where everyone could join in, we all danced together. I'd been so embarrassed when the master of ceremonies reminded women who were on their monthlies not to enter the circle. I had asked Alice why and all she said was, "Women are very strong at that time." I, of course, had nothing to worry about. Then Mom told me we had to go in a clockwise direction when we were in the circle, and that if we were on the far side when the drums stopped, we would have to go all the way around to get back to our place. When the drums started, Maggie and I danced with Blink between us with Mom and Dad in front of us. At midafternoon, the marriage ceremony was conducted for the two couples and then another feast was held at supper-time. After that, the powwow would continue until midnight. Mom, Maggie, and I left right after the feast, along with Blink and David. Dad stayed with Mike and Linda for the powwow, and Ching was back with his group of friends somewhere behind the bushes, playing a gambling game. Gish sat with the elders and enjoyed the attention he was getting from the young women who doted on them. We walked along the sand beach rather slowly. It had been a long day and I was tired. The evening sun cast an orange glow against the clouds and the water was calm.

CHAPTER SIX

Fall Hunting

On the first day of school, Mom, Dad, and I arrived at the principal's office for our appointment. There I was informed that I would join the older class where Maggie had been. I was so happy about that! Maggie had left to go and live with Goom in Nibika the week before school started. Goom was now living in an apartment and Maggie called several days after she arrived to say that she really liked it there.

The entrance to my new classroom was on the other side of the building and I was a bit nervous when I walked down the hall. When I pushed the door open, there was Mr. Toms the math teacher! He gave me a big grin as he welcomed me into the classroom. The room was really huge and there were only eleven students there who were rather quiet. They turned to look at me when Mr. Toms introduced me before turning back to what they were doing. I took an empty desk at the back and surveyed the students. There were four girls who sat at the front and the rest were boys. There was one boy with a cap pulled down so low over his face that you couldn't see his eyes. One had a sweater with a hood that was pulled over his head and you couldn't see his face either. And so, I began my days in the grade eight class.

My next camping trip was the fall hunting around the end of September. All the kids at school were given two weeks off to spend with their parents on the fall hunt. It was part of the Cultural Days that were set aside during the year and there was another hunt in the spring. I was very excited to go on my first fall hunting trip. The school principal was also taking the teachers out camping for the weekend, but they were headed to the other end of the lake.

Goom sent Maggie home for the fall hunting camp too. She and Gilda had planned a holiday to England for two weeks right at the same time. So Maggie was with us again. Dad went to pick her up from the landing strip and brought her home for lunch and all she talked about was Nibika High School and how she liked the kids there. She went on and on about her first trip to Thunder Bay, the big movie theatre, and the shopping mall. I rolled my eyes and sighed and I was immediately given a stern look by Mom. Later, Dad dropped Maggie off at Aunt Lucy's place, which is where she wanted to stay. I was relieved.

I found out the next day that Maggie and Jane would be coming with Aunty Lucy and Uncle Joe. I hoped they did not go in our canoe or stay in our tent either. It felt kind of weird that Maggie and I seemed to have changed places. She was now just visiting and I was here to stay and Jane was still standoffish with me. As it turned out, they were already gone before we finally got ready to set out to the fall campsite.

We'd gone up one portage and over two rapids before we came around an island and saw a smoke-filled point across the lake. I'd never gone over portages before and now we were really far away from home. The fall hunting was a major camping trip. This was the trip where all the food was to be gathered to last the community for the whole winter.

"What are they burning?" I yelled over the noise of the five-horse motor.

"Well, I'm hoping it's the goose feathers singeing off the geese," Dad yelled back.

Mom glanced back from the front of the canoe and yelled, "Well, I say that it's probably the smoke pots from the leather tanning racks."

We were almost to the landing when we heard another boat motor coming up the channel behind us. We pulled up at the beach and were met by Aunt Lucy with her short light-brown permed curly hair and her husband, Joe with their crying baby in his arms. I picked up the baby to free Joe to help with unloading our canoe. The dogs were all there too. I walked up to the clearing to find four tents already standing. I saw Gish coming out of the last tent and heading toward us. The tents were the same canvas prospector type that everyone had used in July and August. They had a hole at the top for the stovepipes.

In the centre of the clearing was a large firepit with the smoke racks above it loaded with smoking sturgeon fillets. That was what the smoke was from!

The baby started fidgeting again and Gish indicated which tent was Lucy and Joe's. I found a flannel blanket and picked up a roll of rope by the boxes. I put the baby down on the blanket and strung two ropes between two trees. Goom used to make this type of hammock for my dolls. After I got the rope tied, Blink came running by and I got him to hold the baby while I threw the blanket over one rope and flipped it under to the other rope to form an overlapping fold-of-the-sheet hammock. I then stuck two sticks at each end of it to hold the hammock open. The hammock was ready for the baby, and so I turned to take her from Blink, but he practically threw her into my arms and decided to fling his own body into the hammock instead.

I kicked his bulging butt in the sagging blanket. "Get out of there! It's not for you!"

"Aw, come on! Please? Here, give me a push!" he said as he wriggled inside the fold.

"Get out of there!" I repeated.

"Naww, just count to a hundred, okay? And then I'll get out," he begged.

"One hundred!" I said in exasperation as Mom came up the path with her arms loaded with blankets.

"Mom! Blink won't get out of there!" I yelled.

Mom glanced at Blink and said, "Your new fishing rod is on the ground beside the canoe. Someone will step on it." In one leap, Blink was off and running down the path.

"Thanks." I smiled at Mom as I put the crying baby inside the hammock. After a couple of swings, she quietened down, enjoying the new sensation. In another minute she was fast asleep.

Aunt Lucy came by with a teapot and exclaimed softly, "Oh, I never thought to do that. Good girl!" I stood by the hammock until Lucy came out with some mosquito netting, which she draped over the slowly swinging baby.

Maggie and Jane came running from the bush, yelling, "Where's Ching? Where's Ching? There are partridge up there past the swamp!"

Just then, Ching emerged from the bush at the other end of the camp with a log over his shoulder that he deposited by the fire. The girls were pulling him to hurry with his .22 rifle to go kill the partridge.

Just then, there was a commotion down by the water. I ran down the path to see Alice and Ned getting out of their canoe. It appeared that the empty tent in camp was theirs. Being the two bachelors, Ching always stayed in Gish's tent on camping trips. I heard Lucy telling Alice and Ned that Mike and Linda had gone to set the net at the other end of the lake. David and Blink were over their knees in the water at the beach, using one of the baby's diapers to try to scoop up minnows that darted around their legs.

The sound of a rifle shot caused a pause in the conversation and then there was another. That would be the partridge. Then two more shots. Alice said, "Four partridge. That will be enough for partridge dumpling soup for lunch."

I walked with Alice, carrying a pot of water up to the campsite. "Where's your pretty blue kerchief?" I asked. I'd given her one of the silk kerchiefs that Goom had given me. I felt that I should give her something for helping me on the day of my naming ceremony.

She smiled at me. "Oh, I would never wear that here! I save it for special occasions like going to a feast, to church, the store, or the Band office."

I'd stopped chewing my kerchiefs, but I still caught my sleeve between my teeth sometimes. For awhile I'd taken to crunching on toothpicks or pieces of wood or grass, whatever I could reach at a given time. Now I no longer had the urge to bite into something when I was stressed. Instead, I memorized letters or codes that I would see like ISBN numbers on books, postal codes at the Band office, and bar code numbers on products in front of me.

Our tent was all set up beside Lucy and Joe's tent. Maggie and Jane were staying with them. I was sure glad they weren't staying in our tent! They looked after the baby most of the time, allowing Aunt Lucy to work around the campsite. Aunt Lucy and Linda were really good at cleaning meat and fish.

Alice was pleased with the racks of sturgeon fillets browning over the fire. She put some more wood at the edge and banked up the ashes. Mom came out of our tent with a bowl of bannock ready for frying over the open fire, and Alice prepared to clean and cook the partridge that Ching had just dropped beside her. Alice looked up at Ching and said, "Since you're so good with the rifle, when are you going to get a wife to clean and cook all the stuff for you?" I wasn't sure how Ching would react to that statement, but he put a most sorrowful expression on his face, put his hands over his heart, and said with full sincerity, "Why, Alice, you broke my heart so badly when you married Ned that I could never, ever, possibly look at another woman." I laughed and Alice said to Ching, "Oh, off with you!" and giggled as she began to pluck the feathers off the partridge.

Maggie and Jane arrived at the campsite, their arms loaded up with spruce branches, which they proceeded to lay around the firepit. They must have been stacking branches in the bush when they came across the partridge.

Suddenly Mom spoke. "Abby, why are you standing around? What is Alice going to need very shortly?"

I glanced at Alice, thinking, right! A bowl to wash the partridge in and a knife to cut them into pieces. The pot of water was already on the fire. I ran to the tent and grabbed the things that would be needed. I knew that the flour from Mom's bannock would be used for dumplings. When I'd put down the things for Alice, I saw that Mom would need a fork and a bowl for the bannock. That was my job. I was the gofer or the "go-for." Finally, I had a job to do!

When I went down to the lake for another pot of water, I saw Dad and Mike, who were constructing a fan out of spruce branches. In fact, they'd already finished one and were working on a second one. Maggie and Jane arrived with another bundle of branches. The large spruce fans would be tied to the front of the canoes to act as a camouflage or a blind. This would allow a canoe to get very close to the ducks, geese, and moose. Maggie dropped her load beside Dad and said, "I stepped on a log and there was a little salamander, a black one with orange dots, that darted away. That's the first time I've ever seen one!"

Mike said, "Tsk-tsk, that's a bad omen." I wondered what the bad omen was going to bring. I would just have to watch and wait. I wasn't quite sure whether I believed in bad omens or not, so I would just have to see what was going to happen first.

When I had finished with my gofer duties, I joined the boys, who had collected quite a few minnows in an ice cream bucket. They were going to use them as bait on their new fishing rods. I'd decided to see if I could carve some wooden minnows that Maggie could paint to look exactly like those. So, I'd laid out some of the minnows that David and Blink had caught beside me and tried to replicate them. Dad thought my first batch of carvings were really great. After that, I thought about maybe making a little birchbark canoe, complete with paddles.

Suddenly something whizzed by my face followed by a "plop" in the water. I yelled, "Gee, Blink! Be careful! You nearly got me in the face with that hook!"

Blink yelled back from the water, "Well, get your face out of the way of my hook!"

I walked back up the path to the campsite. Lunch was ready and Gish was telling a story. He always did whenever he sensed he had an audience. I sat down beside Mom and took a sip from her cup of tea. Gish paused as Linda and Mike and Blink and David joined us around the fire. Mom and Alice dished out the lunch for everyone.

Gish continued his story. "Well, it was that same fall when I was out hunting with Gilbert, Ottis, and Onik." I smiled as I silently translated "ottis" as "belly button" and "onik" as "arm" in Ojibwe.

Gish was saying, "Well, we had a huge blind propped up in front of the canoe as we slowly drifted around a point out into the bay down there. Sure enough, there was a moose standing by the shore munching away. He had his head down as we drifted closer. Ottis had the rifle ready in front of the canoe where he had parted the branches. I was at the back, slowly turning the paddle as we drifted closer. We were absolutely quiet. Onik, sitting in the middle, was slowly reaching for the bullet bag, when suddenly, he let out a very loud fart that brought the moose's head up sharply. We held our breath as the moose looked directly at us. It was at this point that I felt the canoe starting to shake from everyone trying not to laugh. Finally, the shot rang out as the moose turned to run. Down he went and the laughter exploded as Ottis pulled the blind down."

David and Blink rocked back in laughter and Gish grinned with pleasure.

Linda and Mike said that they'd met another hunting group from the community when they went to check out the fishing nets on the river. This group had already killed a moose. There were four community hunting groups that went out every spring and fall.

I found the first day of fall camping quite exciting and I was still proud that I was learning to do new things very quickly. Aunt Lucy and Linda worked very efficiently together and I was learning the quickest way to clean the fish. Aunt Lucy said that I was actually really good with the fillet knife. I also found out that Aunt Lucy was going to have another baby.

That evening, I decided to go with Gish to set the fishnet at another spot by the river that had huge rock cliffs. Gish pulled out his tobacco pouch and placed some of it on a small ledge on the rock face. I said nothing because I knew it was for the Memegwesiwug, the mystical beings who lived in the cliffs. Surprisingly, I had heard about these beings from Choom when I was a kid. I thought they were like the fairies often told about in English children's books. I took in a big sniff of air and said, "We're going to have rain. I smell rain." Gish glanced at the clear blue sky with little puffs of clouds drifting to the south and smiled back at me but said nothing.

We had just set the fishnet in the channel at the mouth of the river when we heard the thunder. We glanced up and noticed that huge thunderclouds had come up over the rock cliffs. Gish laughed and said, "I guess I should have listened to you, eh?"

In a very short time, lightning began to fill the narrow channel that we were travelling through. We hadn't gone more than half the distance when lightning began flashing above our heads on the rock cliffs. As the storm grew worse, the lightning flashes began to travel in long, spidery fingers across the water. Strangely, I wasn't scared because I was with Gish, but I realized that my hair was standing on end and that a strong smell of sulphur now filled my nostrils. We were caught between two high cliffs on each side and there was nowhere to pull in to shore. The rain came down and Gish wrinkled his nose at me. He looked funny with his soaking wet cap dripping in front of his face.

"We should have flashed a sharp knife, axe, or something. If you swish it back and forth, it keeps the Thunderbirds at bay and they could have gone around us," he said.

"What do you mean?" I asked.

"Well, they don't like sharp things, is all."

I'd noticed no one ever said anything when Gish talked like this, so I made no comment.

He cranked the old outboard motor on full blast and we continued across the lake, gradually leaving the storm behind us. Mom was by the shore when we made it back to camp. I could tell she was worried and, somehow, that made me happy.

The next day it was very windy. No one could go out on the lake so we got wood and did the laundry. The baby had soiled the white flannel blanket, and Maggie and Jane were by the beach washing it. I watched them wring it out into a long twisted sausage and then run up to the campsite where they were going to hang it on the clothesline directly in front of the smoke rack. The fire had been left to die out to keep the ashes from being blown about. That was a very lucky thing because before Mom could say anything, the girls flapped the flannel blanket open and a huge gust of wind immediately grabbed it like a sail and the girls were flung off their feet! Maggie went flying and crashed against Ching, who was sitting on the ground untangling the fishnet on a canvas sheet beyond the firepit. Jane landed on her butt right on top of the fishnet. The sheet draped itself over the smoke rack and it looked like a half-finished teepee. Mom and Aunt Lucy rushed to pull it off before the whole smoke rack was knocked to the ground. Now the white blanket was covered with streaks of black soot!

Oh, I laughed so hard my sides hurt! That was the funniest thing I'd ever seen. I liked it that even the know-it-alls could sometimes make mistakes.

I spent my time working with the women when I wasn't off doing my own thing, like whittling something or another. So far, I'd carved ten wooden minnows and a really nice tiny cedar canoe with paddles. I was thinking that I'd give a canoe to Paulie too. I still hadn't seen her since September, when she'd come out of her office while I was waiting for Mom to get off work.

She'd said, "Wow, look at you! You're brown! What a nice suntan. What did you do, lie around in the sun all summer?"

I smiled, saying, "No, the dogs did, though. We went camping several times." We had chatted a bit until Mom came out.

We heard an outboard motor coming and knew it must have been some of the men returning to camp. We weren't expecting them until around suppertime. Mike, Dad, and Joe had left early that morning to hunt for moose. Ned, Gish, and Ching had left in another canoe shortly after. In preparation for the moose meat, Alice had a pile of spruce boughs ready, and I had hauled water to fill all the containers that we had. It had taken the men this long to find moose tracks. Sure enough, when the canoe came in, I saw a large mound of black fur piled on top of it.

I yelled to Alice back at the camp, "They got one!" There were shouts of excitement from the women as they scurried to get the place ready where they would do the butchering. I was at the canoe and Dad jumped out from the front. I helped him pull the canoe in and then Joe yanked off the moose skin that covered the meat. I was shocked to see the red chunks of meat with blood drying on the surface and the white streaks of sinew and fat. My stomach lurched and I turned and ran back to the campsite. I met Alice, who handed me a roll of tarp, and I took off with it back to the canoe. I spread it on the sand just as Dad turned to find a place to put the moose meat. Joe and Mike began handing the chunks of meat to Dad, who put them on the tarp. At that point, the boys came tearing down the path. They'd been sent to bring more wood from the woodpile back in the bush.

I found an excuse to run back to the campsite and met the women coming back with more spruce boughs that they were spreading around the firepit. The first chunk of shoulder meat was brought up by Joe, who dropped it in front of Alice. The chunks of meat were brought up as fast as the women could work. They cut off huge chunks of roasts first that were deposited into the coolers. Then they began cutting the meat into thin sheets that Maggie, Jane, and I hung up on the smoke racks. We had to keep turning them over and make sure there was just enough fire to smoke and cook them slowly so that they would dry. That was the meat that would be turned into pemmican.

Alice had a big pot of meat boiling over the fire and also had roasting sticks hanging over the hot ashes. Oh, did it smell good!

Blink and David came running up the path, yelling, "They're coming! They got one too!" I glanced at Alice in alarm. How were they to clean two whole moose! She understood my questioning glance and indicated the men by the trees, and I saw that Dad and Mike had tied a log between two trees. That is where the second moose would be hung until they'd finished processing the first one.

The women worked into the dusk, trying to finish hanging up the rest of the meat and putting the bones into the hot ashes for the marrow to cook overnight. The boys were still running around, too, and at one point, Blink lit one of the roasting sticks at its end and kept swinging the burning tip around and around until Aunt Lucy and Linda said almost in unison, "Put that fire out or you'll pee in your bedding tonight!" Blink threw the stick into the fire so quickly that everyone laughed.

The next day at lunch, I was munching on a rather nice piece of jerky when Mom handed me a piece of moose fat on a piece of birchbark. I took it and placed it on my next bite. Oh, it was absolutely delicious! "Where did this come from?" I asked.

She said, "Bone marrow, from the jaw bone." I stopped mid-chew and then swallowed. But then I decided that, well, it was rather delicious. After that, I always went in search of moose fat or bone marrow to eat with moose jerky. It became my favourite food.

A week later, the women were just finishing turning the last of the dried meat into pemmican. Ching and Joe had taken the second batch of huge moose roasts to the community freezer several days after they'd killed the moose. This meat would be used for community celebrations. When they got back, they said that two of the huge freezers were full of moose meat and the other two had ducks and fish. There was also a freezer for the berries and sturgeon caviar. I peeked in there once and it had blueberries, raspberries, strawberries, chokecherries, highbush berries, and even a tubful of spring moss wild cranberries.

When the women had finished processing the meat, Joe took Aunt Lucy, the baby, and the girls back home. We said goodbye to Maggie because we probably wouldn't see her again this year, not unless she came home at Christmas, but we didn't know that yet. I gave her the ten minnows that I'd carved. She loved them and said that she would paint them and make a mobile with the minnows dangling from it and hang it from the ceiling in her room. I'd also wrapped the first little cedar canoe that I'd made, complete with little paddles, on a sheet of birchbark. That was for Goom. After another hug from Mom, Maggie hurried down to the canoe and they were gone.

My second little cedar canoe, the one for Paulie, was almost done. There were piles of cedar chippings by the fire from the paddle that Gish had made the day before that were just the right thickness for the carving. Dad and Mike had gone hunting for rabbits and partridge. Ned and Gish were taking a walk along the shoreline to see if there were moose tracks at the bay. Meanwhile, I sat by the fire by myself for quite awhile. I could hear Mom and Linda pounding away inside Alice's tent. They were making pemmican, and Alice's tent was the best place to do it because it was the cleanest and didn't have kids running in and out all the time. I was in charge of bringing the teapot when needed.

It was quiet there without the baby, and there were no more diapers hanging on the clothesline. I was left pretty much on my own, which left me to think about Goom, Maggie, and high school. Since I was in grade eight now, I still had two more years to go before I could go to Nibika for high school. I was starting to think I liked the idea of going to a high school in Thunder Bay, though. That would be really exciting! Mom had said that when Maggie went to college or university, I could go and live with Goom. But I thought I'd prefer going to Thunder Bay. I didn't know if I'd like living in an apartment in Nibika, even if it was with Goom. Autumn, my old friend from Nibika, lived in an apartment, and I always found the hallway a bit creepy because I knew different families lived behind each door. And besides, Goom was living with Maggie now instead of me and somehow I didn't know if I wanted to stay in Maggie's room even if she wasn't there anymore. I didn't understand why I was feeling angry at Goom, but I was. I threw a log into the fire and ashes shot up into the hanging meat.

David and Blink came tearing around the bush, chasing each other around and around the tents. Alice came out, saying, "Stop running around the tent! You should never run around and around a house or tent, or any-where where there are people inside!"

Blink skidded to a stop in front of her. "Why?"

Alice gave a big sigh before she replied, "Don't you know? You'll tie up everyone's lives who are inside the place, tie them into knots and they won't know if they're coming or going! It makes people all confused and mixed up inside! Oh, and in some instances, you could be winding up someone's life and making it shorter. Now, stop running around the dwelling. Go run along the beach or someplace else!"

I smiled at the look of total bewilderment on Blink's face. Thinking that he'd already got knots inside his head, I watched to see what he'd say, but without another word, he ran off down the path where David had disappeared.

Mike and Ned had left their big dogs behind at Bear Creek. Jane's dad was looking after them. Gish always brought Daish with him wherever he went. He even put her inside the tent at night. Ching brought his dog, Ozit, because he was a very good hunting dog. He fetched ducks where the canoe couldn't go amongst the rocks, and he fetched rabbits and partridge. The geese and ducks also just seemed to gravitate toward him when he ran along the shore. Gish said this was because Ozit was a beige-coloured dog, and that it was his colour that attracted them. At times during the trip when the weather kept the men from going hunting, they would train the young dogs. The dogs learned how to swim and fetch floating things in the water. From the time Ki-Moot was small, Dad always hid things for her to find. Blink liked playing hide and seek with her too. Gish had ordered eve-ryone to keep the puppies away from the other community dogs. He said that the other dogs would distract their training and that it would be harder to get them to pay attention.

Gish and Ned had just returned from their walk, and I watched Gish coming up the path from the lake with a partridge that he'd killed. He smiled at me as he sat down by the fire and I sat down beside him to watch him cut up the partridge. I watched as he dropped the pieces into the pot of rabbit stew! He stirred the pot over the fire. I knew that he knew that I knew there were still some rabbit pieces left in that pot, but I didn't say anything. As soon as Mom and Dad entered our tent, I followed Mom and whispered, "Gish put a partridge into the rabbit stew!"

Mom smiled and said, "I know. He always does that. To him, he's just adding more meat to the broth. He says, 'red meat to red meat or white meat to white meat.'"

"What does that mean?" I asked.

She laughed and said, "He means rabbits, partridge, moose, or any red meat can be cooked in the same pot. White meat? Well, I guess pickerel, jackfish, whitefish, or even sturgeon can be cooked together."

I made a gagging gesture with my finger in my mouth and she suddenly whirled around at me. By her expression, I expected her voice to come out loud and angry, but she whispered as she said, "You're never to do that! Never be disrespectful to anyone. If he offers you anything from his pot, you are to eat it! Understand?"

I was taken aback by her response, so I whispered back, "Why?"

She replied, "Because he'll be testing you. He'll want to know if you would be willing to do as he expects out of respect for him. You know that he wouldn't offer you something to eat that would make you sick"

I nodded my head and she continued. "Will you have it in you to do the right thing when you'd rather not? Do you understand?"

"Yes, Mom." Then I remembered something. "Mom, remember that time Gish gave some of the broth from his pot to Ki-Moot when she was a sick little puppy? You and Dad just smiled at each other. Was that why?"

She smiled and put her hand across my shoulder, saying, "Perhaps."

Near the end of the hunting trip, the last of the meat and fish had been packed up and left on the smoke rack. One night before we went home, I was instantly awoken by an eruption of sharp barking from Ozit, who was tied outside. Flashlights went on in the other tents and Dad crawled to the door with his flashlight shining out. Smiling, he poked his head back into the tent and said, "I just saw Ching come flying out of his tent headfirst!" Trying not to laugh, he continued, "I swear I saw his face shovelling the ground. His gun went flying out in front of him!"

We were quietly laughing now as Dad ducked his head back out. I could hear Ching saying, "Darn, I tripped on Gish's stinking shoes!" Gish could be heard laughing and by then, the guys were all standing around the campsite. All that night, the dogs would periodically burst into barking fits. The next morning, we found big bear tracks around the campsite. It was definitely time to go!

We'd just put our tent down when I pulled a rock out from where a rope had been tied around the tent pole and there was the strangest looking mouse I'd ever seen. It had pink paws that faced in opposite directions! Then, in a split second, it was gone! I thought it looked so cute. Gish was the first person I saw after that and I told him about the little mouse with the large pink paws. He remained very quiet for a long time but didn't say anything. It was later, when I had a chance to talk to Dad, that I found out the mouse I'd seen was a mole and that the mole was also a carrier of bad omen. After a few days, I got tired of waiting for something bad to happen and eventually forgot about it.

CHAPTER SEVEN

Mad Dog

It was very quiet and cold in the house when I awoke one Saturday morning. Thinking I was alone, I went into the kitchen. No one else seemed to be up yet. Well, that was strange, I thought. I made coffee and walked around the kitchen for a bit and decided that I would head outside to the porch to see how Ki-Moot was doing. I found her all curled up and cozy in her thick feather bed. I hooked up her leash and led her out to the path by the side of the house. From there, I could see the frozen lake. A lot of snow had fallen and it was very windy, and there, out in the middle of the lake, I saw one large snowy white figure marching across the lake with a smaller figure behind him. There were four other smaller snow spirals marching right behind them. I turned to see Dad coming around the corner of the house with an armful of wood and asked, "What's that?"

"Oh, that's North Wind, his wife, and their four children. Sometimes they have more children, sometimes less," he replied.

I smiled. It was nice to think of the north wind that way, as having a wife and children. Ki-Moot and I ran back inside the house where we met Mom by the stove. She said, "Whoa, hold on there. Ki-Moot can't stay inside too long. Get her a drink of water, but you have to feed her breakfast outside."

That was how most weekend days began, with me running outside to give Ki-Moot her morning run by the house and then tying her up again to wait until our breakfast was done, when she would be fed. After that, Dad usually took her out for a run somewhere. Sometimes they went to Gish or Mike's place to train the dogs, but most times he just took her for a jog along the shore. When Dad was done, Blink usually took her to the sledding hill or they just romped around in the snow out on the lake. I usually stayed inside with Mom and we'd draw patterns together and make more designs for the moccasins and mitts that the two sisters were beading for the tourist Experience.

After breakfast that particular day, Dad was sitting at the table drawing a pattern. I pulled up a chair and asked, "What are you doing?"

He smiled and said, "I had a dream last night and this is what I dreamt my mitts looked like. In my dream, I was taking off my mitts to tighten the laces on my snowshoes and this is what I saw." He held up a symbol of some sort. He'd also coloured it in with Blink's crayons.

"Are you going to make mitts and do beadwork on them too?" I asked in amazement.

I heard Mom snort from where she stood by the stove. "He's asking me to make them for him. I told him I'd do it for a price."

I laughed. "Oh, yeah? How much?"

Dad answered, "That hasn't been decided yet."

Then the phone rang. I ran and grabbed it, thinking it might be Goom since she usually called on Saturday mornings, but it was Mary! I'd talked to her a few times when I first arrived at Bear Creek, but we'd only really become friends that October, in grade eight. I'd been working on some math questions during our break one morning, when Mary came and stood beside my desk. She usually sat in the front of the class. I looked up and she said, "The other girls say you're good at math. Would you help me figure this one out?" She put her workbook on my desk, pulled up one of the chairs, and sat down beside me. I was really pleased and happy to help her. I explained each step to her and then her face lit up. She was just missing one step in the math calculation. After that, she moved her stuff over to the desk beside mine and we began hanging out at school together.

After that, she started calling me at home, and we'd arrange to meet somewhere. We usually hung out at the store or at the post office. Usually during our break at school, we'd run to the Band office to watch people coming and going and have some hot coffee or tea that Mom always had going in the waiting room.

That snowy morning, Mary was calling to ask me to come to her house because her mom was going to cut her hair and she wanted my opinion as to which one of the haircuts featured in a magazine would suit her better. I told her about the time Dad cut my hair after I first got to Bear Creek. She was still laughing when I hung up. I ran and grabbed my jacket, yelling over my shoulder to Mom that I was going to Mary's house.

Mary's house was just up the street from ours. Theirs was the only house on that block because most of the land was taken up by a large swamp. I ran up the path from the road and up the steps, then pushed the door open. Mary was at the table in front of the window, turning the pages of a magazine. I pulled off my coat and hung it behind a chair and sat down beside her. I could hear her mother in the living room talking to another woman. Mary glanced in that direction and said, "She's busy cutting someone else's hair right now. I might have to wait awhile." Mary's mother cut people's hair and they paid her whatever they had.

After flipping through the pages of the magazine for awhile, we finally settled on a hairstyle that was cut shorter at the back with the longer front hair swept forward. Mary's hair was jet black and her skin was darker than mine now that my suntan had totally disappeared. She got up and made some tea. Soon the woman who was getting her hair cut came out and she looked really nice. After she left, Mary's mom, Charlotte, came in.

"Hello, Abby. How is your mother today?"

I nodded. "My mom's fine. Dad says he wants her to make a pair of leather mitts for him."

She took down some cups from the shelf and put them down on the table, saying, "A pair of mitts, eh? You mean real beaded ones?" I nodded and she continued, "Oh, that's going to be a lot of work!"

After more chit-chat and a cup of tea, it was time for Mary's haircut. I stayed and watched Charlotte cut Mary's hair into the style that we'd picked and then she styled it with a curling iron. Wow! I couldn't believe it—it turned out really nice. I began thinking that I should get her to cut my hair too.

Later that afternoon, after I got home from Mary's, Dad came running into the house yelling, "Sophie! Sophie! Mad Dog just got off the plane. He's back!"

Mom came out from their bedroom saying, "Yeah? For good or just for a visit?"

Dad beamed. "Well, he's got boxes and Kitty is with him too. So I'd say he's come back to stay. Couldn't talk to him much; his family was there to pick them up. I told Mike. He's coming over later."

"Who's Mad Dog?" I asked.

Mom laughed, "He's the craziest guy you'll ever meet!"

Dad said, "Mad Dog, Mike, and I grew up together. We were buddies as far back as I can remember. Then I left to go to college, Mike stayed, and Mad Dog left when I came back. He's been living at his wife's community the whole time." Turning now to Mom, he added, "It was good to see him again. He nearly crushed my ribs. He grabbed me, lifted me off my feet, and spun me around, right there inside the airport waiting room!"

"Mad Dog must be a pretty strong guy," I said.

Dad said, "Just you wait until you hear stories about Mad Dog and then take a good look at him for yourself!"

Blink came running into the kitchen area with a hockey stick and whacked a puck across the floor right into my foot. As the pain registered, I howled, "Aow-wuy! He got me on the ankle!"

Dad yelled, "Blink, I told you! No hockey pucks inside the house!"

Before I could pick up the puck from under the table where it had ricocheted, he spun around me and shot it again. This time it shot toward his bedroom door and disappeared inside. He came running back into the room grinning. "Straight into the box, Dad!"

He had an empty box set up in the corner of his room that he shot the puck into. Quite proud of himself, he threw the stick on his bed and was now at the door yelling, "Can I go to David's house, Mom? I'll bring Ki-Moot." He grabbed his jacket off the hook by the door.

"Make sure she's on a leash and don't let her out of your sight!" Mom yelled. I rolled my eyes. Of course there were no consequences for the S.S.; he'd shot the puck into the box! Mom shot me a glance of her own. One that said, "Don't push the issue!" Well, it had taken me quite awhile, but I think I was finally getting into the swing of these non-verbal cues that everybody seemed to function on.

Ki-Moot's bed was still inside the porch. We brought her in when it was really cold outside, but Gish said that the dogs had to get used to living outdoors in order for them to grow their thick winter hair to protect them from the cold.

It was just after supper when Mike and Linda arrived with Blink and David. Linda went into Mom's bedroom to go over the bead patterns for the traditional Anishinawbe outfits that they'd be wearing once the tourist business got off the ground. David and Blink were in his room and I was at the table listening to Dad and Mike as they talked about Mad Dog. They used to call themselves the Three Northern Musketeers when they were young boys. Mike leaned back on his chair at the table and said to Dad, "Remember that time we got a bunch of chokecherries and were shooting the pits through the straws that my mom gave us with our pop?"

He turned to me and said, "Well, John here, shot one at Mad Dog and he turned to duck and John got him in the ear. I mean, the pit went right into his ear and the more he poked at it with his finger, the more he pushed it farther down."

"Well, how did he get it out?" I asked.

Mike said, grinning, "Well, he went to the nursing station. Can't remember what they did to get it out."

Dad took up the story. "Remember that time we were playing by the pile of old boards behind the old general store? Mad Dog slipped and fell on a slanted board and slid down to the ground screaming? There was blood on his pants, but he wouldn't let us look, so we walked him home. When we got there, his dad pulled his pants down right in front of us and there, in plain view, was a big huge sliver right on his butt!"

"How did he get it out?" I asked.

Mike giggled and said, "Well, he went to the nursing station." Both of them were now laughing hard.

Then Dad continued, "Remember his tree house?"

Mike wiped his eyes, saying, "Yeah, he'd built it to look like an airplane. He had a spot just behind the sandpit. We used to wonder where he'd got to every time we went to look for him"

Dad said, "Well, in the front of the plane was the control with dials and gauges made of pop bottle tops and snow machine panels and dials. It was neat! Then one day he was working on the tail end when he stepped through a very old piece of pressed board that he'd nailed on there. He crashed to the ground, right on top of his box of construction supplies full of paint and nails. Well, he got covered in yellow paint and got a nail deep in his thigh. As usual, he ended up having to go to the nursing station!"

Dad sat back in his chair, laughing. Then he said, "Remember that time he took his dad's fishing rod?"

Mike smiled at me, saying, "We found out later he wasn't supposed to touch it."

Dad continued, "Anyway, we went down to the lake with Mad Dog proudly holding out the fishing rod with its large, dangling silver hook.

Well, we got to the dock and with both hands on the handle, Mad Dog whipped the rod back over his head and flung his arms straight out in front of him and then, he screamed!"

As Dad laughed, Mike continued, "There he was with the big, shiny hook stuck to the back of his head!"

Dad picked up the story, "We tried to pull it out but he kept screaming in pain each time we touched it, so we decided to go for help. By then, there was blood running down his back. Mike was holding the rod out in front of him with Mad Dog shuffling in front sniffling and whimpering when we met his dad."

I drew in a breath and asked, "Did you guys get into trouble? What did he say?"

Dad said, "He just took the rod from Mike, and Mad Dog had to go to the nursing station."

Dad and Mike leaned back in their chairs and laughed so hard that Mom and Linda came back into the kitchen.

I asked, "Why do you call him Mad Dog?"

Mike answered, "Well, back then, he was a skinny little kid who was always getting beaten up by the brothers across the creek. Actually, he was always defending us and he always got it. Anyway, after he got beaten several times, his father decided to teach him some boxing techniques. That was all Micky needed. He started fighting back and soon he had those boys running. He'd growl each time like a mad dog when he went after them. So, he became Mad Dog, our hero!"

The stories about Mad Dog ended when Linda and Mom laid out their plans for the Anishinawbe Experience outfits and how many would be needed. Half of the stuff was already completed. The shelter at the Experience campsite would be one huge teepee where the guests and the guides would sleep. They would also have their meals there. It was now time to train the dogs and get the trial runs in motion. The Anishinawbe Experience would open for business next winter. That meant the puppy team had to be trained this winter so they could be mixed in with the adult dogs. Mad Dog was to be the dog trainer.

The next morning, just before lunch, Mom had just finished making a pot of partridge soup when we heard a noise that sounded like a snow machine pulling up to the door. Then there was a bang at the door, and suddenly Dad was in the arms of a huge man in a big beaver hat. It was Mad Dog! I stood by the bedroom door where I'd been with Blink stuffing a mink hide to train Ki-Moot with. Mom was by the door now as the two men did their weird swing and hug deal.

Finally, the man moved away from the door to allow a tiny woman to step inside. That was Kitty, Mad Dog's wife. Her eyes danced with mirth as she looked at me and then at Blink and then back at Mom. Mom laughed as she led her to the table, all the while giggling at the two men. Finally, Mad Dog pushed Dad back at arm's length and looked him up and down. "Oh, man! Are you a sight for sore eyes! Like I said yesterday at the airport, you being there waiting for me was the perfect homecoming, until I found out you were only there to pick up an oil drum for the schoolhouse!"

Dad laughed and said, "Heck, I didn't even know you were coming home! I was just so happy to see you. Hey, Mike was here last night talking about the crazy things you used to get into! Telling my daughter here all about you and our boyhood times together. So where are you living? Did you find a house yet?"

Mad Dog grinned and said, "John, my friend, I moved in right next door to you! Your old neighbours moved out the very morning we came in, and the house was still warm inside too!"

Mad Dog now focused his eyes on me. His eyes were very weird. They were light brown with an almost gold colour around the brown. He smiled and I saw that all of his four front teeth were gone. He whipped off his huge beaver hat to expose a bald head as he bowed to me and said, "Glad to meet you, young lady. I don't even know if your mom remembers this, but when I heard who John had married, I remembered that I did meet your mom once. I went to the college to look for John one day, and I met this girl in the office. She wanted to know who I was looking for, so I told her I was looking for John. Then she wants to know which John? So I tells her the John from Bear Creek Reserve. Then she says there's lots of Johns and she had no clue where they were from. So then I says that if she could just tell me where he was, I could find him myself. Then she says she couldn't go find him because he may not be in the building. Then I wants to know if he's not in the building, where would I find him? Then she says that if I were to tell her John's last name, she could tell me if he was in class or at a garage, airport, or office somewhere. So then I ask why would he be in a garage? Was he a truck or what? Then I could see that she's getting really ticked off, and I ask her what her name was. She tells me it was none of my business and that she would tell John Whatever that he has a nasty friend!"

I saw the look of astonishment on Mom's face. "That was you?"

Mad Dog laughed and pointed at Dad. "When I told him, he laughed and said that was the girl he'd been going out with for a long time."

I asked, "So, how did you find John?"

Dad laughed and said, "I'd just come out of class and was heading out when I came around the corner and saw Mad Dog by the office window, getting red in the face. He was talking to someone at the office window and I knew it was Sophie right away. So I just pulled him around, waved at Sophie, and we headed out the door."

Mom laughed, saying, "Oh, you make me sound like such an ogre!"

Dad smiled. "The problem was that you were so darned pretty, he couldn't for the life of him remember what my last name was!"

Mad Dog looked at Mom and said, "I did have a beard and long hair back then. That's probably why you don't remember it being me. To the woman who made a man out of our wayward John." He removed his beaver hat with a flourish as he bowed in front of Mom and added as he straightened up, "Did they ever tell you the tale of the Three Northern Musketeers?"

From then on, the noise at the kitchen table grew as stories continued through lunch and past into the supper hour when Mike and Linda arrived. I went to bed after Blink and David were fast asleep in David's bed.

I woke up early one cold November morning to hear the sound of Mom being sick in the bathroom. I ran to their bedroom, yelling, "Dad! Mom's throwing up!" I'd never known Mom to be sick. She'd had a cold once the previous spring but that was it.

Dad sat up, and propping himself on one elbow, said, "Sh, sh. I know. Sit here and wait until she gets back." I sat down at the edge of the bed and waited. Soon Mom came back into the room, but then she whirled around and ran back into the bathroom. Dad raised an eyebrow, saying, "Well, maybe you should get out of your pyjamas and get dressed. We'll see you at the table."

Blink was up blinking and rubbing his eyes when I passed his bedroom. He too had heard the commotion. Dad was making coffee when I came into the kitchen followed by Blink. We sat down at the table waiting for Mom. Finally she came out of the bathroom with a towel over her shoulder, wiping her face with one end of it. "I guess you're all lining up to use the bathroom?" She sounded weary.

Blink was the first to ask the question. "So, what's the matter with you?

Nurse says you throw up if you have a bug in your stomach. Have you got a bug?"

Mom and Dad glanced at each other as he handed her a cup of coffee. Then Mom said, looking first at Blink and then at me, "No, I don't have a bug in my tummy. I have a baby in there."

I sat stunned for a second before the information sank in. Meanwhile, Blink didn't miss a beat. "A baby! How long will it take before it comes out? Is it going to be a boy or a girl? I want a boy. I want a baby brother!"

I looked at him and said, "I want a sister." I couldn't imagine having another brother like him!

He turned and studied my face and then stuck his tongue out at me and said, "I don't want a sister. I already got you! I want a brother so he's got to be a boy!" It was kind of funny because I was thinking the exact same thing about him: I've already got you!

Mom looked at Dad and he started laughing. "Well, we're not going to know until he or she is born. So don't go making plans until you see him or her, eh?" He reached out and gave Blink a hug as Blink slipped off his chair and ran to the bathroom before it was occupied again.

I was still sitting there thinking, Wow! What would it be like to have a baby in the house? I could dress her and play with her and maybe I could make something for her. I could make a mobile for her like Maggie said she was going to do with the minnows.

Suddenly I remembered something. "Mom, you were making baby bonnets last month. I thought it was for the Experience. Were they for the baby? How long have you known?"

She smiled. "I just wanted to be sure before I told you all. The baby is due in July. Oh, what a hot month to be nine months pregnant!" She looked over at Dad and he said, "Oh, you can go float around by the dock to cool off all day long if you want."

After breakfast, I went to my room and stood looking out the window. This new turn of events could be good for me, I thought. I'd have my very own baby brother or sister in the house to look after.

Mom was calling me to come to the phone. She'd been talking to Goom for quite a while. I came back into the room just as she ran by me, heading for the bathroom again. I picked up the phone. "Hi, Goom!"

Goom's voice came across very softly, saying, "So, you're going to be a big sister and I'll be a grandma to another brand new baby, eh? How are you feeling about the news?"

I answered, "I love it! It'll be great to have our own little baby at home. Maybe Blink won't be such a baby if he becomes a big brother." I heard her coughing and I became immediately concerned. "Are you okay, Goom?"

Her voice came again. "Oh, I was just laughing and it got my cough going again. I have had a cold that won't go away. But I'm feeling better today. I'll be good as new in a couple of days. Listen, I have to call Gilda to tell her the news. Your mom had to go and throw up, she said. So I told her I'd call for her. I'll talk to you again soon, eh?"

I said, "Okay, Goom. Say hello to Gilda and Maggie for me too. Bye."

I knew Paulie was home, so I dialled the number and as soon as she picked up the phone, I said, "Mom's going to have a baby!"

There was excitement in her voice as she said, "Wow! Really? That's terrific news. When?"

I replied, "In July. She says it's going to be a hot month to be nine months pregnant." I could hear her laughing. We talked a bit more and then I hung up the phone. I listened to Mom retching in the bathroom and got a little worried.

I asked Mom through the door if she was okay. When she opened the door, she said, "You're going to have to ignore my throwing up for a few weeks until it passes." I gave her a hug and then she had to go back in. Finally she came out and lay down on the couch.

That day, I helped her sort out her bundle of sucker fish jawbones that she'd been collecting all summer. They were about an inch long and they'd been washed and dried and were now white and clean. She said that long ago, the bones used to be dyed and hung on the tikinagan, which is a baby cradleboard. They would hang from the handles and jingle when the tikinagan was rocked. She put a small bundle of the bones into some dye she'd bought at the store. There were pans of red, blue, green, and yellow dyes. I added my bundle to hers and we left them to soak that afternoon while we went to visit the sisters Minnie and Lizzy.

Last summer, Mom had told me she was collecting the sucker jawbones to dye and to see if we would need them for the Anishinawbe Experience. Now I asked, "Are we going to use the bones for the baby's tikinagan? Will Dad make one?"

She turned to look at me as we crossed the old wooden bridge. "Well, Lucy has the tikinagan that Blink used, so if she doesn't need it, she'll probably give it to us to use again. Normally, a tikinagan gets passed around in the family."

It was quite a walk to the sisters' log cabin. They lived in one of the old log cabins that were built before the Band got money to build more conventional houses. I'd seen the sisters occasionally at the store or at the Band office. They lived by themselves and had no other relatives in the community.

As we walked up the steps to their cabin, we could hear them laughing inside. We stomped on the porch to let them know that someone was arriving before Mom pushed the door open. When I first arrived at Bear Creek, I quickly discovered that people didn't knock on doors and wait to be let in to other people's houses. The sisters were sitting at the table with a tubful of rabbits between them. They were both tall and skinny and they had thin, dark eyebrows. Lizzy's eyes danced so merrily that her whole face seemed to light up when she smiled. Minnie was the quieter one, but she also smiled a lot. Both women had grey hair at the front that faded to a solid black colour toward the back. Lizzy's hair was braided and pinned into a circle at the back of her head. Minnie's hair was braided too, but her braids hung down on each side of her shoulders. Both sisters wore green sweaters over full-length flowery print dresses. Brown stockings and brightly beaded moccasins were visible under the table.

They were about to begin skinning the dozen rabbits that had accumulated over the week. People would just drop the frozen rabbits into a covered tub that sat on top of the woodpile in their porch. It was tradition, Mom had informed me, that people would drop rabbits or partridge at old people's homes as a gift of wild food. But the sisters were also collecting the rabbit skins to make things for the Experience. Just then, I noticed two cats on the bench behind the stove. They were Siamese cats! I went over and ran my hand over the head of one of them, but her paw came up and swatted my hand away. So I decided to leave them alone and sat down at the table beside Mom.

The rabbits were thawed out now and we pitched in, pulling the rabbit skins off. We started at the bottom and pulled the hide to the head inside out like a stocking. Then the women cut around and around the tubed skin about an inch wide, leaving long strips of rabbit fur. The sisters would stretch the strips, which would contract to form a kind of long furry yarn. It was my job to hang the strands of fur outside on the wooden beam that was tied between two trees. The strands would freeze-dry and all the loose hair would blow off. About a week later, the sisters would finger weave the long furry yarn to make hats, mitts, or jackets for the Experience.

Lizzy gave me some rabbit front feet and showed me how to turn them inside out, pull out the bones, and cut them off. I was left with rabbit puff paws. These would be strung together and left to dry. Children's toys! I would need to create another box for these at Paulie's house. I'd never seen anything like them. The rabbit paws would be gathered to hang with the partridge rattles that I'd saved from the fall. The partridge rattles were the throat sacks that held the stones and pine needles that the partridge ate. They had been blown up like balloons and left to dry. They would become rattles to entertain small children. Minnie and Lizzy said that they'd played with these kinds of toys when they were children.

By then it was time to go home for supper, and we left the sisters' house with four rabbits in our basket. As Mom and I walked back, we decided we'd fry them instead of making rabbit stew. We walked hand in hand down the street that had become a snow machine road during the winter, since most of the vehicles now sat frozen in the yards, covered in a foot of snow.

Mom suddenly said, "The pine cones. There's a big tub of pine cones behind the shed. We need to boil them for the fishnet that Alice has just finished. She insists on using the traditional method to dye it." She made a face at me and whispered, "We should just buy a rusty coloured dye from the store and mix it up instead. You think she would notice?"

I shrugged my shoulders and asked, "How do you make dye from pine cones?"

Mom sighed and said, "We'll have to put the cones into water and boil them until the colour becomes thick. Then we strain the cones and pour the coloured water out into another tub. Alice will then boil the water again and use it to dye her net."

Mom pulled my hand deeper into her hand and said, "Red willow bark is also a really good dye to use on fishnets. The colour blends into the water so the fish don't see it."

I remembered the question I hadn't had a chance to ask when we were at Paulie's place the day before. "What was that rolled-up yellowish white rope that Gish had soaking in the tub that he brought to the sisters' house? They seemed very happy to see it."

Mom said, "It's good that you don't interrupt to ask questions. That was sinew. It's the traditional thread that was used long ago and it's strong like nylon thread. You can split and peel it apart to however thick you want it to be. Depending on what you're sewing, of course. That sinew came off the whole back length of one of the moose the men shot, along the spine. Shorter pieces come from the heel of the animal up to the back of the knee. Gish only left it soaking so the women could pull it apart to the desired thickness themselves. If it dried whole, it would be rock-hard and not much good for anything, other than a doorstop, maybe."

I laughed and looked down the road toward the Band office as we walked by and said, "I had no idea that all this preparation for the Experience would take so long! Dad and Ned got the two handmade toboggans done last week and the other sleighs with the runners are also done. The dog harnesses are done. Most of the clothes are done. The snowshoes are done. Ned says the dogs are ready. What else needs to be done? When are they going to be done? Why don't they just get the Experience up and going, already?"

Mom giggled and pushed me with her elbow. "Patience! Remember that Gish would say that the best things take time to make and the best time to do something is when the time is right!" I snorted because I knew that's exactly what he would say.

Mom sighed. "Well, there's a big meeting at Chief Paulie's house tonight. The Real Anishinawbe Experience group is going to decide when they'll do the official trial run of a full-week tourist adventure. But before that, after supper tonight we have to meet the sisters at Paulie's place to finish the last fitting for Mad Dog's outfit. I haven't seen it all together yet."

At supper that night Dad said, "Ned said that Mad Dog had trouble with Mucko and got so fed up with the dog that he threatened to kick him off the dog team. After another big fight with Wiener, Ned hauled Mucko off the dog harness and tied him outside Mad Dog's house until the dog team came back from another run to the tourist tent spot." He glanced at me. "That canvas tent will be converted to a huge birchbark teepee structure when the actual tourists arrive for the real thing." I tried to imagine what the birchbark teepee would look like. Again, my mind conjured up the pictures from early history textbooks on the "Indians" of North America.

He continued, "When Mad Dog came back, he put Mucko on a leash and pulled him back to the chief's house. Chief Paulie wasn't there, so Mad Dog then hauled the dog to the Band office. Mucko kept putting on his brakes and growled at every dog that ran by, so that by the time Mad Dog got to the Band office, he was sweating hot, and he flung the door open and marched across the room. Dragging the dog behind him, he flung the

Chief's office door open, bellowing, 'Paulie, here's your darned dog! You keep him away from us and you make sure he never goes anywhere near the team dogs again!'"

Mom laughed and said, "Paulie was on a teleconference call and apparently everyone in the city boardroom thought this was so funny. I had to pull the dog out of there and shove him outside."

That evening, Mom and I went to Chief Paulie's place to add some more things to the team members' growing number of traditional outfits. Chief Paulie's house really had become the costume department! I was in the fitting room hanging Mad Dog's outfit ready for him when he and Kitty arrived for the big man's fitting of a coat that the sisters had made especially for him. It completed the finished pants, mukluks, and mitts they had already made. I slipped out as Mad Dog whipped his beaver hat off his bald head and threw off his black and red ski jacket.

Mom had sorted the new moccasins, and I'd just finished labelling the sizes on the moccasins in the living room area when we heard Kitty laughing in the fitting room, which was actually one of the bedrooms. Kitty came out and gestured for us to come and look at the new outfit. A shock went clear through to my toes when Mad Dog flung himself out of the room into the brightly lit hallway and stood there facing us. Mom drew in a breath and I stepped on her toes as she grabbed me around the shoulders. Mad Dog had a big grin on his face and since his front teeth were missing, only his canines showed. He widened his light brown eyes, which accentuated his terrifying appearance. He slowly turned around and the lights highlighted the rippling, moving mass of his huge bearskin coat.

The coat hung down to his knees and when he turned to face us again, I saw that each of the sleeves was one whole piece that started at the collar and joined another section that flowed from the massive chest. He looked, for all the world, like a huge bear standing up! On his head, however, was a hood that was made of dark brown wolverine skin that ran up and over the top of his head. The lighter burnt shade flowed back from each side of his head. There were golden strips that edged around his face that now took on a fierce look as he rolled his eyes at us. Now he looked like a massive wolverine! My eyes fell to his feet and saw that his legs were covered with a lighter shade of gold fur on top, and I recognized the beadwork on the top of the moose leather vamps on the mukluks. They were one of the designs that I'd drawn. "What's the leg fur made of?" I asked Mom in a whisper.

"Fox," she said.

I looked at Mad Dog as he raised his eyebrows for my opinion and all I could say was, "Wow!"

Kitty sighed. "The sisters have outdone themselves, I think, eh?"

Mad Dog said, "I think I should maybe put a streak of black ash or something across my cheeks when the tourists come. That will cement the image in their brains, eh?"

Mom laughed. "We don't want to scare them to death, now!"

It was just then that we heard Chief Paulie's voice at the porch and her stomping feet as she kicked off her boots. The door flung open and Mucko ran inside first, wagging his tail at me and Mom as he ran by. He was on his way to greet Kitty when he caught sight of Mad Dog.

In one split second, Mucko whirled around to face Mad Dog. Then he gave a horrific scream and with frantic scrapes on the linoleum floor—his feet ran on the same spot for a few seconds before he got some traction— he crashed against the far wall by the door, before he turned toward the open door that had just then been blocked by Paulie coming into the room. In one mad scramble, Mucko threw himself out into the porch, where we could hear him trying to crash through the closed porch door. Paulie's face was still in shock as she came into the room, so thoroughly puzzled that all we could do was point to the giant monster that still stood in the brightly lit hallway. Mad Dog hadn't moved throughout the whole commotion and now Chief Paulie drew in a sharp breath when her eyes came into view of the big man. Their eyes locked and I saw Mad Dog drop his gaze as Paulie slowly made her way toward him, checking him over from head to foot. She made a motion with her finger that made him slowly turn one full circle. Mad Dog flexed his arms. Paulie glanced back at us with a wide grin on her face and said, "What magnificent work the sisters have done!"

Mucko had now grown quiet. I went to the door and peeked into the porch. He was sitting hunched over with his nose to the door, and I could see his shoulders shaking. I went out and whispered, "Mucko, it's okay, dog. It's okay." Gently, I put my hand on his back and he jumped and trembled under my hand as I continued to talk to him. Gradually, he began to relax as I stroked him from his head to his back. Then he started to pant like he was very hot. I talked to him until he finally lay down. I could hear Paulie laughing now and all four of them were talking and exclaiming at the effect that the three items of clothing had made on Mad Dog's body.

Then I heard Paulie's excited voice saying, "You must have a new name.

You can't be called Mad Dog for the tourists. What shall it be?"

Mucko's breathing was now almost normal. I knew he was also listening to the voices inside and he must have been thinking that his beloved master wouldn't be laughing and happy if there was indeed a monster inside. I did worry, though, about how he was going to come out of this shock. I came back into the room and they were still standing there looking at Mad Dog and then Mom said, "*Kwingo-aggeh*. That sounds powerful and certainly fits the man, don't you think?"

Kitty smiled in approval. "I think that's good!"

Paulie had to practice the word several times before she started nodding. "Yes, yes, that does sound perfect! What does it mean?" Paulie wasn't good at speaking Ojibwe.

Kitty answered, "Wolverine."

With that, Mad Dog thumped his chest with a fur-covered hand and said, "My name is *Kwingo-aggeh*!" They all laughed and I realized I'd totally overlooked the bearskin mitts that fit neatly under his sleeve cuffs.

I cleared my throat and said to the big man, "You almost scared Mucko to death. What are the other dogs going to do when they see you? I don't want you scaring Ki-Moot to death too!"

He stopped as he was heading into the change room and pulled his hat back. "Whew, it's getting very hot in this. Good question, though. They'll either attack me and tear me to pieces or they'll take off and leave me to sweat my buns off walking back to civilization!"

We waited until he came back out, holding the outfit in his arms. He said, "I'll have to introduce the outfit slowly. Maybe I can hold it like this until they get used to the smell. Then I'll hang it on the clothesline where they can get used to seeing it—out of their reach, of course. Then I'll put on the pants and mukluks first. After that, the coat. And pretty soon, they'll get used to seeing me in the whole outfit. Good plan?"

Just then, a snow machine pulled up beside the house and Mom and Kitty hurried to put the stuff away. The Real Anishinawbe Experience group meeting was about to take place. We were just getting things off the long table when Mike, Dad, and Blink came in. I heard Mom ask Chief Paulie, "Have you even eaten yet? I brought some fried rabbit and wild rice for you in the kitchen. Go and eat before the others arrive."

Chief Paulie glanced at the guys as they came in, saying, "Remember now, we have to agree on a final name for the Experience tonight," and she went into the kitchen to eat.

Dad looked at me and asked, "What do you think? Got a name picked out?"

I shrugged into my coat, saying, "Well, you're using a dog team and the place would have a lot of dog tracks, so I would suggest 'Dog Tracks.'"

Mike grinned and Dad nodded. "That sounds good actually, Abby!"

As Mom and I walked home, with Blink hopping along ahead of us, Mom asked, "You know, Abby? Something's just occurred to me. Remember when the Medicine Man gave you the name White-Throated Sparrow, he said that besides predicting the weather that you would also have the ability to apply your skills to humans? Do you think that has anything to do with you coming up with those suggestions for Dog Tracks?"

I almost stopped walking as I paused and thought about what Mom had said. I was of course aware that when I made the suggestions that had not been thought of before, at least not voiced out loud, that I had somehow accomplished something or thought of something new. It suddenly hit me that this was perhaps just what the Medicine Man had meant.

The next evening, on Sunday, there was a potluck supper at our place and Ned, Alice, Mike, Linda, Mad Dog, Kitty, Gish, Ching, and David filled up our house. The group gave a toast to me for thinking up the name Dog Tracks, which everybody had apparently loved. I was rather embarrassed. Paulie had flown to a meeting in the city and wouldn't be back until Monday, at which time the first tourist trial run was to take place. The fake tourists would arrive in the morning at Mad Dog's place, where he would get them prepared over lunch and then take out in the afternoon. They would arrive at the tent in the late afternoon, have supper, and settle in for the night. I hadn't been to the tourist campsite yet, but I understood that the place was at least a half-hour ride by snow machine from the Band office.

As part of the tourist package, Tuesday would be ice fishing day. Everyone had decided that the traditional fishing method was a real pain and that since the tourists were supposed to be transported back into the early fur trade era, they opted for using two-inch baited hooks. The traditional string also wasn't feasible for freezing and thawing, so rolls of it would be left hanging in the tent for show. They would use cotton trolling line instead. On Wednesday the tourists would be snowshoeing and rabbit snaring, Thursday there would be partridge hunting, and on Friday the tourists would return. The volunteer tourists would be the two kindergarten teachers, Miss Karen and Miss Sherry, who were always keen on volunteering at community events, as well as Chief Paulie and Reverend Roberts.

Monday morning came and I went off to school. Mom went to work at the Band office, and Dad went in search of the tourist gang. Ching had already taken Ned, Alice, and Kitty by snow machine to the tourist tent that morning with all the needed supplies to wait for the tourists to arrive. Mad Dog would drive the first dog team, with Daish at the lead of course, and Mike's dogs, Bingo and Bannock, and the young dogs, Mucko and Shingoos. Then, according to the plan, Mad Dog would come back with the dog team on Wednesday and change dogs, with Ki-Moot in the lead, along with Ozit, Chippy, Samson, and Wiener. With the tourists safely stowed at the large birchbark teepee, they were to take Gish out there for the long story-telling evening. Ching would be the emergency transportation system with his use of the Band's snow machine. Dad couldn't leave in case something went wrong at the Band office, school, or nursing station. Mike was the emergency backup personnel, and he and Dad would man the emergency satellite phone at all times. The tourist gang would carry the other phone with them wherever they went.

I got so engrossed with all this planning that I had not even had time to hang out with Mary at all. I'd been corresponding with my old friend Autumn all through the fall though. It was Autumn who first told me that Maggie was being a bad girl at Nibika even before we got the call from Aunty Gilda.

After Mom hung up the phone with Aunty Gilda that day, I wanted to know exactly what was happening. She told me Maggie had started hanging out with a group of teenagers and wasn't coming home some nights. Goom and Gilda would have to go out looking for her. Then Maggie had begun getting rides from friends to Thunder Bay without asking permission. Goom was furious about it all. Aunty Gilda was also mad and said she wasn't willing to be responsible for Maggie either. It didn't sound good at all. So Mom had a long talk with Maggie on the phone that afternoon. Goom said she was going to send her home if she didn't smarten up. I felt so bad for Goom. What was Maggie thinking?

I was enjoying the times when I was alone in the house. I'd started turning down the volume very low on my boom box when I'd sing the songs out loud. One evening, I was totally into it when I turned and saw Mary standing at my bedroom door. All she said was, "I thought I was listening to a singer! Sing that again! Wow! Your voice is absolutely wonderful!"

In music class at school I'd been learning about musical notes and measures and had to memorize some of the famous European and American musicians and the kinds of music they made. We didn't have any instruments to play until I found some old flutes in the music cupboard. Then Miss Tish, the music teacher, announced that she had to come up with a Christmas concert every year at the community centre. That caught my attention! She was trying to put a choir together to sing some of the Christmas songs. So we started practicing. She even got some of the younger girls from the lower grades to join in. I was dreading actually singing in public, but it was rather exciting too!

The sun came up on a clear blue sky Wednesday morning. As Mom and I got ready to go out the door, the emergency satellite phone rang and Dad spoke with Ned. So far, everything was going fine with the trial run. Mad Dog would arrive that night to change the dog team. At lunch, clouds began rolling in from the north and I helped Mom take a big pot of moose stew over to Chief Paulie's house for Mad Dog to take back to the tourist tent with him. When we got there, Gish came out of the dressing room in a beaded moosehide coat with a rabbit hood and mitts. His feet were encased in fully beaded mukluks. The sisters grinned as they sat on the couch, sipping tea.

Mom said, "How warm are you going to be in that?" Gish grinned and pulled back the flaps of his hood and we could see that it was lined with a rabbit skin. Genius! I thought he looked like a beaded inside-out toad myself, but I didn't say anything.

By evening, as we sat down to supper, there was still no reply on the emergency satellite phone that Mike had tried to call several times. Mike, Linda, and David were having supper with us while we waited for Mad Dog to arrive. A storm began to blow as we sat down to eat. By the time we'd finished, we couldn't see a thing outside, the snow was coming down so thick. Quite late in the evening, they went home and Dad went with them to check out Mad Dog's place and visit Ching and Gish across the way. Gish was staying at Ching's place that night so he could just go next door when Mad Dog arrived back in town. I could tell everyone was getting very worried.

I'd just dozed off that night when I heard the phone ring. I came running into the kitchen to hear Mom talking on the phone where it sat beside the window. She put the phone down and dialled a number. Then I heard her say, "Mike? John just called from Ching's house. He said he was on his way home when he heard the dogs coming. They pulled up in front of Ned's house. They came home on their own. They had the toboggan tied behind. John went back to get Ching. Check if the emergency box is tied inside the canvas wrap on the toboggan . . . okay."

She hung up and we looked at each other across the silent room. What could have happened?

The emergency box was a plastic container with a lid that held the satellite phone, a first aid kit, and the survival pack.

It snowed all that night and turned into a fierce storm early in the morning and into the afternoon on Thursday. There was no way that Ching could venture out into the storm alone. So, by late afternoon, when the snow had slowed down, Dad and Mike decided to take Chief Paulie's snow machine and follow behind Ching on his machine as he picked out the trail to the tourist tent that was marked with little pine trees stuck on each side. This was the traditional way of marking a trail. They carried a satellite phone with them while the other one sat on our kitchen counter.

Dad called late that night. Gish was snoring on the couch beside the stove when the satellite phone rang. He reached the phone before Mom got there, and he sat down by the table after he put the phone down. I came into the room with Mom and we sat down at the table as Gish poured another cup of tea. He looked very worried as he said, "They arrived safe at the tourist tent. Everyone is there except the Reverend. It seems they all went ice fishing yesterday. After they'd gotten back from ice fishing with the dog team, the dogs were restless so the Reverend decided to take them for a quick run to tire them out, saying he'd be back about the time the fish were finished cooking. Mad Dog yelled at the Reverend that he wasn't to touch the dog team, but with a wave, Reverend Roberts was gone. With Bingo in the lead, Mad Dog says the toboggan practically flew down the trail and onto the lake! That was the last time they saw him. They searched on snowshoes all day yesterday as far as they could go, hoping that the Reverend was in the community. Since then, they've just been waiting for somebody to come."

Gish sat there in silence for awhile. Then he shook his head and said, "That's not good! But the Reverend's been around here for a long time, so he should know what to do to stay alive."

The next morning, the satellite phone rang again. Gish had already gone back to Ching's house and Mom talked to Dad. They were just leaving the tourist camp to try to find the Reverend and Dad said that he'd call back before he left to come home. Ching would bring back the two teachers and the Chief by noon on her snow machine.

In the afternoon, I'd just come through the door from school for lunch when I saw Ching coming to a stop beside our house. He came in behind me. Mom was inside with Blink at the table. She got up and Ching sat down for lunch that Mom dished out for him. Ching had just finished delivering the Chief to her house and had dropped the teachers off at their cabins. He looked very tired. Just then, the satellite phone rang and I saw Ching's spoon stop midair on the way to his mouth. He sat very still as Mom said into the phone, "You're leaving now? You found him! Is he okay? I'll call her . . . okay."

She put the phone down. "They found the Reverend. At the far point about a kilometre to the right . . . he'd finally managed to light a fire and they saw the smoke. He's alright, but he's sick. They should be here before supper. He says to call the Chief and make sure the plane waits until they get here. The Reverend needs to get to a hospital quick."

There was a big sigh of relief that the Reverend was alive! Ching leaned back in his chair, saying, "Whew, that could have easily ended in a huge tragedy. I think it's a lesson learned, all around."

Ching called Chief Paulie and relayed the message. After a quick nod of thanks, he was out the door. The phone rang and I picked it up. It was Goom! "Hi, Goom. How are you doing? Are you feeling better?"

Her voice sounded weary, but she said, "I'm fine, Little One. I'm just calling to see if everyone was alright." I told her about the Reverend and the trial run that nearly ended in disaster. She told me that Maggie was grounded for a week but that she was getting better. After a few more minutes, I handed the phone to Mom when she came into the room. I heard someone coming into the porch and when the door opened, Mary came in with a bag of books. It was time to head back to school.

That afternoon when I got back from school, a snow machine came to a halt at the door and took off again. Dad walked in and sat down. He looked very tired as he sat down for a late lunch. Blink was all over him, checking him to make sure he was alright, and then he squeezed right in beside him while Dad ate. When Dad finished, we sat down at the table to hear the story.

Dad began, "It seemed that after he took off with the dog team, the Reverend had come careening around the point on the island, being unable to slow down the dog team, and then the dogs had started barking and yipping. That was when he noticed that a pack of wolves had emerged around the island, and they stopped when they saw the dogs. He'd looked back to see if the wolves were following when the toboggan hit a bump and he lost his footing. As soon as his heel hit the ground, it spun him around and he landed in the snow beside the trail. By then, it had started snowing, coming down thick, and when he yelled after the dogs there was no way they could hear him, since they were still loudly yipping and barking, and soon they faded into the distance. He'd walked for a while, thinking the dogs would be sitting somewhere in the middle of the lake, but then decided that he'd better turn around and find land. But he says he has no idea when he left the trail and ended up walking knee-deep in snow trying to find land. Sometime during the night, he realized that he was on shore when his ankle twisted over jutting rock under the snow. So that's where he holed up in a thick pine-branch shelter that he'd managed to put up. Unfortunately, he couldn't start a fire.

"Mad Dog said that the Reverend had developed a bad cold on the second day and that was why he was sick. Probably has pneumonia. It wasn't until this morning when the snow slowed down a little that he managed to burn the pine branches. Lucky he had a lighter in his pocket instead of matches! He left no tracks because the snow quickly filled them in and the wind wiped them out."

Mom said, "Chief Paulie says that they'll be waiting for him at the airstrip. They're probably there now. They'll just have time to change his clothes and put him on the plane."

I asked, "How bad is pneumonia? Is he really sick?"

Dad replied, "Yeah, it's pretty bad, especially with an old person like the Reverend. But he's a tough old man; he'll be fine."

Just then, Mike, Linda, and David came in. Mom and Linda were preparing supper when Mad Dog and Kitty arrived. Mary came in right after them and we hurried to finish our homework in my bedroom. Dad, Mike, and Mad Dog had a map spread over the kitchen table. I could hear David and Blink buzzing with their wooden snow machines in his bedroom. I had carved them for the boys. They even had black handlebars that I'd made from a piece of black plastic. Mary called home to ask if she could stay for supper and she came back into the bedroom, beaming, "Yes! She said I could."

We'd just finished our last page of math when Mom called for everyone to come for supper. We all fit around the large table and I noticed that everyone always sat in the same place. After supper, the men headed back out. When the dishes were done, Mary ran back home as it was getting dark. I sat down with the women at the table. Kitty was talking about how bad it was trying to cook anything over the stove in the tent. It was so hot, the flap would have to be left open, which dampened everything toward the back. She was wondering how much worse it would be to try to cook in a firepit in the middle of the tourist teepee!

The teachers had also been so busy trying to learn how to skin a rabbit that one of them cut her finger rather badly because she had a finger stuck inside the pelt while cutting off a rabbit's ear. Kitty said, "She didn't say anything until I noticed a trail of blood coming out of the rabbit pelt! I pulled it off her hand and the pelt was covered in blood. I had to go into that white box with the red cross on it to get a bandage to put on the cut. Which reminds me, there should be somebody there who can fix people who hurt themselves. I don't want to have to bandage anyone when I'm not trained to do that."

Everyone at the table agreed that there should be a designate who was at least certified in first aid. Then everyone looked over at Linda. She sat upright and said, "But I've never been part of the plan to be out there. What would I do?"

Kitty smiled. "You could talk English to the people who would be pestering me to tell them how to do things while you helped me with the preparation of food. I would do all the cooking."

Mom added, "I could look after David here with Blink. And there's a first aid course starting next month at the community centre."

Linda sat back and sighed. "I guess I've been conscripted. Okay, I think I'd love to be out there anyway."

Kitty smiled. "If I had a choice of someone else working with me, I'd pick you."

Mad Dog, Mike, and Dad came back in when they'd finished checking the dogs. Over their cups of tea, they began to laugh. Dad threw his head back and said, "Wow! What a terrifically bad start for Dog Tracks. We lost the Reverend and he nearly froze to death!"

Mike said, "We need to space the pine tree trail markers a little closer. The Rev. veered off between two of them without realizing it."

Dad added, "And we need another satellite phone. One on the toboggan and one at the tent."

Mike pointed out, "We also need backup transportation at the campsite. We can't have both dog teams sitting at the site, so we should have a snow machine for emergencies."

Dad sipped his tea. "No sick people going out to the tent and bushing it."

Mom looked at Linda. "And we definitely need a certified first aid person out there."

Mike smiled and nodded at his wife, saying, "I wondered when you were going to volunteer to do something." The women laughed before Kitty said, "She said I con . . . conscripted her."

When the laughter died down, Mad Dog sat up and announced, "No one's allowed near the dog team except me or Ching! The tourists need to be instructed that we're the only ones allowed to handle the dogs."

Ned asked, "What's with that darned Mucko anyway? You get near him he just puts his tail between his legs and tucks his nose in the snow! I had to nudge him to his place to leash him into the dog team."

Mike laughed. "Yeah. I saw small Shingoos shove big Mucko out of the way with his shoulder and he ate up Mucko's bowl of stew. Mucko just put his ears down and turned away. Before that, he would have rolled Shingoos in the snow and taken a chunk off his ear or something."

Mad Dog said, "I think it was from the time that I near scared him to death that he became a coward. Remember that?"

Alice laughed. "Best thing that happened to that dog. He was getting to be a big pain! I was feeding them one time and he near knocked the pot out of my hand because he wanted all the food by himself! Good thing Ned came out and yanked his chain back and made him wait until every dog was served first."

Ned shook his head. "Yeah, now he just sits there and patiently waits for me to fill his bowl. You know, I kind of miss the old miserable mean Mucko."

CHAPTER EIGHT

Holidays

We had our last math assignment a week before the school break for Christmas. Mr. Toms had asked us to map out the community and indicate how many people were at each house and so on. He gave each of the students different sections of the reserve to map out. I was in a group with Josie and Tommy, and our section covered Mike's house straight north, up to the two sisters' cabin and west to the lakeshore. One evening, I'd been hard at work on getting all the houses down on all the streets in the whole place and was in the process of trying to figure out how many people were in each household when Gish came for a visit. I proudly showed him my project and told him that all the kids in my class were doing the same thing.

Old Man Gish took one look at all the houses on my map along the curving streets and finally he said, "That's a nice map, Abby. But you can't count the people. You'll jinx the population and people will die and not enough babies will be born to replace them. So you can't count the exact number of people in the community." I knew better than to question Gish, so I counted all the dogs in the community too and added them to the total population so that I didn't end up with the exact number of people.

The next day, I met Mary at the grocery store and we were checking out cake mixes when a woman spoke behind me. "Abby! I haven't seen you since the summer. How are you doing? How is your mother?" It was the beautiful woman that I'd seen at my naming ceremony.

I couldn't remember her name, but I replied, "Hi. Oh, I'm fine and my mom is going to have a baby in July." She seemed really pleased to hear this and after a few more comments she moved on.

I turned to Mary. "Do you know her? I forgot her name."

She glanced back and said, "That's Rebecca." I told Mom when I got home that Rebecca from the naming ceremony had asked after her and that I'd told her that we were going to have a baby. She raised her eyebrows but didn't say anything.

The next week, we were over at Mad Dog's place to see the young dogs pull the sleigh by themselves. Mad Dog had devised a harness for them. He'd discovered that the smaller dogs in between the big ones caused problems with the harness. Shingoos had apparently kept pulling his head out of the adult collar that he'd been wearing and Wiener kept getting his back feet lifted by the bigger dog behind him. So Mad Dog had them strapped in according to size. Ned offered an opinion that they should be laced according to disposition, but Mad Dog suggested that he should first see what each dog was like. So he had them lined up to size with Shingoos first as the lead dog, followed by Wiener, Mucko, and Ki-Moot at the end. For better traction, they'd pull the sleigh along the snow machine paths that circled around the bay. When all was ready, Mad Dog and Ned asked Chief Paulie and Father Bailey, who happened to be in the Band office at the time, to be the fake tourists and get the royal puppy treatment.

Mad Dog had no sooner laced the dogs in place, got Chief Paulie settled in at the front, and was about to seat Father Bailey at the back of the sleigh, when Shingoos got distracted by a female dog that ran by along the road. Before anyone knew what was happening, Shingoos took off, followed by an enthusiastic yelp from an undisciplined Wiener and Mucko, and Ki-Moot was dragged along behind against her will.

Off went the sleigh at full speed down the road with Paulie hollering at the top of her lungs and Mad Dog running as fast as he could, trying to catch the rope that was dangling behind the sleigh. I ran with Mike and Dad as we chased the team down the road. The dogs made a sharp left and then a right at the corner. A truck veered out of the way as the dogs sped through the intersection, made a left turn in front of the senior citizens' home, and made another left turn. This time, a truck came sliding sideways trying to avoid the sleigh as it went by with Father Bailey hanging on backwards. He had twisted around somehow and now had one leg dragging as he hung on to the back ropes for dear life. Chief Paulie had hold of his parka hood, and Father Bailey had managed to wrap the ropes across his chest but his butt was dragging on the ground.

Down the hill went the toboggan toward the Band office and over a hump, with the arms and legs of the fake tourists flailing all over the place. The flapping limbs caught the attention of some stray dogs, who joined in the chase with many humans yelling and running flat out to try to catch the dogs and the sleigh. When the original troublemaker, that female stray dog, finally decided to turn toward the Band office driveway, the team of sled dogs was brought to a halt by a snow machine that came careening to a stop in front of it. Out jumped Ching, who had just finished dropping a load of wood off in the woodshed behind the Band office. By then, Father Bailey's pants were hanging around his knees, full of snow. As for Chief Paulie, her jacket had filled with snow while she tried to hang on to Father Bailey's jacket hood.

Everyone skidded to a halt and pushed their way forward to see the fake tourists sprawled on the ground. Slowly, they both got up. Father Bailey shook the snow out of his old underwear before he pulled up his pants, and the Chief shook her top before she pulled her jacket down. After a few shakes and stomps to rid the snow from their clothes, a few hesitant laughs from the people gathered around the two tourists turned into uproarious laughter when Chief Paulie and Father Bailey, too, began to laugh. The whole crowd pushed to get into the Band office behind the dishevelled couple to get the full story.

The dogs were unlaced and Mad Dog prepared to take them back to the dog houses. That was it for the trial run that day. One thing was for sure. It was decided then that Shingoos would never see a clear view in front of him again. Meanwhile, Mucko looked very humble as Mad Dog yanked at his leash to get him to come along. Poor Ki-Moot looked so embarrassed, she kept her head down and her ears flat against her head. I reached out to pet her, but Mad Dog was already walking away with the dogs on their leashes trailing behind him.

The next day, I was at Paulie's place and she was surprised to discover that I was rather fluent in both dialects (southern and northern Ojibwe) now. Although she could understand Ojibwe, she didn't speak it very well because she said that her parents always insisted that she learn English, only because they wanted her to live in the city. She motioned me over to the window, where we took up pretending to imagine what the stray dogs outside were saying to each other. Paulie said the stray dogs had started calling me Cheap Spit Speaks Two Tongues in their conversations. That was really funny, until we saw a dog run up to the others and Paulie pretended to have it say, "Hey you, Skinny Ribs, did you hear Cheap Spit Speaks Two Tongues met her future mother-in-law at the grocery store last week?"

I turned to her with a puzzled look and asked, "What's that dog talking about?"

Paulie burst out laughing and said, "Everybody tells me what goes on around here, didn't you know that? Rebecca came into the Band office the other day and mentioned that she'd seen you at the grocery store. She said that her son Abraham had been quite smitten with you when you first arrived, and that he was apparently pretty sad when you were moved to the higher grade class in September." Then she added, "Close your mouth, Abby."

I could feel my face burning, but I couldn't think of a response so I blurted out, "I hate him! He was always making fun of me in class every day! How can such a miserable excuse of a person have a mother like her?"

Paulie let out a squealing laugh. "It's not funny!" I said. Then she wrestled me to the couch, where she began tickling me and wouldn't let go until I started laughing.

We got our community assignments back on the last day of school before the Christmas break. Mr. Toms had pieced all of the maps together to come up with a map of the whole community. I asked if I could take the map home to show my family and Mr. Toms agreed, if I was careful and brought it back the next day. Gish came in after supper and I proudly laid out the project for him to see. "Very nice," he said as he examined the map. I leaned over the map, commenting, "I found out that the rest of the kids also counted people who had moved away or were just here visiting, or they also included dogs like I did. Some even counted cats. Did you know that the two sisters have two cats? I saw them when Mom and I went there one time. They're really cool!"

Gish raised his bushy eyebrows at me. "Yeah? Two cats? Why have I never seen them?"

"Well, they're beige with black markings. They're called Siamese cats and they keep them in a cage when they take them outside. Otherwise, they're not allowed to go outside because the dogs would tear them to pieces."

Gish turned the map around and around, saying, "Hmm, smart ladies. You're missing some houses over here, you know?"

I leaned over. "But they're empty. There's no one living there and they're about to cave in."

He shrugged, "Well, they're still houses."

I smiled, asking, "Did you know that the old man who lives here . . . " I pointed my finger to the house on the map and continued, "has an owl living in the shed? Josie, one of the girls in class, said that the old man found it lying on the road. He brought it home and he fixed it and fed it and when it grew big, he opened the door for it to fly out. It did, but it kept coming back. Now it just lives in the shed and it comes and goes whenever it feels like it. Anyway, Josie said she counted the owl too."

Gish gave another "humph" and said, "See this shed here? There are four stray dogs living there. They've been there for a couple of years anyway. You missed those too." But then he gave me a big grin and said, "I'd say you kids did a very good job, though! I wonder what Mr. Toms thought of all those numbers of people when he added all your population reports together. Do you think he believes there are that many people?"

I shrugged. "I don't know. He only mumbled something about minnows in a bucket."

Saying this reminded me of Blink. I yelled, "Mom? Where's Blink? Somebody said that there were kids around the thin ice area by the Band office dock!" Mom came into the kitchen area and dialled a number on the phone. No, he wasn't at Linda's place. She dialled another number and I could see her body relaxing and I could tell she was speaking to Alice. They were obviously playing games on her television again. That reminded me of something else. So I asked, "Gish, when Mary and I were at the store yesterday, there was an old man there who yelled at some kids who were winding their forearms around and around. The old man just stopped in his tracks and pointed a finger at them all and shook it at them as he said, 'Never, ever, do that. You're unwinding your mothers' lives. You're making their lives shorter every time your arms go around!'" I smiled and waited to see what Gish would say to that.

He smiled back at me and winked. "Well, he's right, you know." I remembered then what Alice had said about the boys running around the tent last summer. Maybe it meant the same thing. Then again, maybe not.

Dad came into the Band office when I was there the next day, so I hopped on the back of his snow machine and we dropped in at Mad Dog's place on the way home. There was Mad Dog, sitting by the table with piles of dog harnesses. He was humming along to a song playing on his CD player. Dad and Mad Dog talked and I sat with Kitty as she drew flowers and designs for the beadwork that would be done for the mitts and moccasins that the sisters were making. The Dog Tracks group had decided to sell souvenirs of traditional objects for the tourists to take home. So they needed as much stuff in stock as they could get. Mad Dog kept replaying the same song over and over again on his CD player. It must have played four times before we got out of there. I told Mom that if I heard that song on the radio, I was going to turn it off!

I realized that I didn't miss the television at all anymore. I read a lot more now, and I liked reading books. Goom sent me a big box of them the week before to read over the holidays. She always thought about things like that. I remembered seeing the box at the Band office when I ran in to see Mom. Then they brought the box home when Dad went to pick up Mom after work. It had apparently arrived on the morning flight. I didn't even know that the box was for me! I called Goom to thank her for the books. We found out that Maggie had decided to behave herself and the frantic calls from Aunty Gilda had stopped. Now, when she called, it was to say hello and exchange a bit of news.

The box of books from Goom included mystery stories, horse stories, dog stories, and a lot more. I even found some books written by Anishinawbe authors in there. Right after supper that day, and every day after that, I curled up in bed and read. Sometimes Blink came in to find out what the story was about, but he never stayed long. He was always on the go. I'd see him running around outside and I'd see him bobbing his head, checking out one thing or another. I was rather disappointed my friend Mary didn't like reading as much as I did. I'd tried to give her some of the books that I really liked, but there was no point since she didn't read them anyway. After the map project, I got to know my classmate Josie a little better. She was one of the girls who sat at the front of the class. The other two girls hung out together and never talked to me. They were really shy.

The next morning as I stood with Ki-Moot outside, the snow was shimmering in the bright sun. Dogs were barking down the street and a snow machine went by across the lake.

A raven squawked as it flew by overhead and the blue jay was back at the pail on top of the woodpile where Dad threw the fish guts. The blue jay was so beautiful, I wondered if I could find beads just that shade of blue in

Mom's bead box. She had a fishing tackle box where she kept her beads and I was always running my fingers through them. The beadwork on Dad's mitts was almost done. Mom worked on them during the weekends when she had time.

I could hear Mom and Dad laughing in the kitchen. The smell of frying bacon reached me as I pulled Ki-Moot around and into the porch. I pushed the door open and took a deep breath as I entered. Mom was making pancakes with bacon. Oh, I was so hungry!

Blink was finally up and he was at the table in a short time. He'd even brushed his hair without being asked. Funny how the smell of bacon got everyone up to a happy start. I smiled at Blink and he smiled back. Dad and Mom were also beaming at each other like they had a secret or something. I guess it had been a long time since we hadn't been worrying about one thing or another. Mom had stopped throwing up and Maggie had stopped going crazy in town. Goom was now somewhat back to normal. We found out later from Aunty Gilda that it had taken Goom quite awhile to get over her grief at Choom's death and begin some kind of a routine without him. I realized now why Gilda was trying to distract her by taking her to Vancouver and then to England for a holiday.

After breakfast, Mom and Dad decided to take us to mush the adult dogs to a fishing spot at the next lake past the portages where the fall hunting area was. Mom, Blink, and I were on the sleigh and Dad was standing on the back runners. The sky was still clear blue with not a cloud to be seen. I watched the snow go by like many sparkling diamonds. We had all five of the adult dogs: Bingo, Bannock, Ozit, and Chippy, with Daish in the lead. Gish was looking after Ki-Moot at his cabin.

It was very quiet with just the sound of the runners going over the crispy snow accompanied by the breathing of the dogs. When we got to the portage, the shadows of the trees marched across the path as we sped over the dips and bumps. Blink kept digging his skinny sharp knees against my back. Little S.S.! I'd have bet he was doing it on purpose! It was only at times when he irritated me now that I mentally called him S.S.

Out on to the lake again, Dad slowed the team down at a point of land where one tree was leaning over into the snow. I remembered this place from last summer. We'd reached the spot. Mom and I picked pine branches to sit on at each fishing hole Dad was cutting on the ice. Dad and Blink had the dogs tied up and the ice-fishing holes cut by the time Mom and I had finished setting up the pine branches. We settled down to a day of fishing.

We used sticks with our lines wrapped around at the tips, and we baited our hooks with some bacon rind.

I had my very own fishing hole, Dad and Blink shared one, and Mom was leaning back on the packsack that Dad had brought to carry the lunch stuff. Soon, the smell of woodsmoke reached me. Mom was making lunch and I'd just been daydreaming about singing a solo in public! I often dreamed about singing onstage with lights shining on my face and the noise of people in the darkness who were watching and listening to me. Suddenly, I felt a huge tug at the end of my line. I yelled and ran back with the line and I could feel the fish pulling. Then Dad was there and he pulled a huge pike out of the hole for me. My heart was thumping when I saw the fish flapping on the ice. Wow! My first ice-fishing catch! I didn't catch another one that day, but Blink got a really big pickerel.

After a lunch of hot dogs and tea over the fire, we had eight fish to take home. First, though, Dad wanted to try out the wooden minnows that Ching had carved and Ned had fastened to a three-pronged metal spear at the end of a stick. That was his fish spear. Ching's wooden minnows had large, thick nails inside them so they would sink. Dad had to widen his ice-fishing hole with the chisel and then had to lie down on his belly on a bed of pine boughs. He lowered the brightly stained orange and yellow minnow into the hole and waited. I sat down beside him for the longest time while Blink was running around with the dogs on the ice. Mom had let them loose while she packed the sleigh.

Suddenly Dad whispered, "There's one. He's circling around the minnow. Coming to investigate." He picked up and held the spear ready for quite a while when he suddenly plunged it down. It came back up empty. He smiled at me and got up on his elbows, saying, "I was sure I'd touched the fish, but the prongs didn't seem to grab it. Maybe the prongs aren't on right. I'll have to give it back to Ned to see if he can change the design a bit."

As Dad was strapping the dogs back into the harness, Blink wanted to know how Dad told the dogs to go left, right, stop, or go. Dad said, "Well, we use commands that we've taught the dogs. When I say, 'Hup,' it means go, and when I say 'Oooo,' it means stop. I give a short whistle when I want them to go left and a long whistle when I want them to go right. Ned says he used to just drag a pole on the snow when he wanted them to turn right. Everyone has their own way, I guess."

I'd never have thought to ask that question. I also never paid attention to see how the dogs knew what Dad wanted to do. I'd have to pay closer attention to things. Mom sat on top of the box with our food and fish in it and I settled down on top of the sleigh in front of her. Blink was wedged in between my legs. Dad ran with the sleigh until the dogs got to a pretty brisk pace and then he stood on the back runners. I watched the shoreline go by in the bright sunlight. The only noise was the swishing of the runners on the snow, the dog's panting breath, and Dad and Mom periodically talking about something. It was a wonderful day.

That evening, Mom and I had just returned home from the Band office when Linda and Aunt Lucy arrived with a list of things that needed to be done for the next day's holiday festivities at the community hall. Aunt Lucy's belly was really huge now. Mom made some tea and I sliced up a bannock from the shelf and put it on the table with some butter and jam.

During the conversation, I discovered that there would be several feasts and socials planned for the holidays. There was a community Christmas dinner that needed to be organized and a social entertainment of some sort that evening. That was when the school choir would sing the four Christmas songs we'd been practicing. Then there was the New Year's feast and social. Other women were looking after the gifts and another group was doing all the cooking. Some of the teenagers who were involved in the drum group were looking after the music. There would also be country music, Anishinawbe music, and the three drum groups that would serve at the ceremony before and after the feast.

During a lull in the conversation, I asked, "So, what are you ladies going to be responsible for?"

Lucy laughed, saying, "I'm getting to that. Sophie hasn't told you what you have to do?"

I shook my head and Aunt Lucy said, "We're in charge of decorations. Do you have any ideas?"

Mom laughed. "Well, so far we have a Christmas tree in the corner of the community hall. That's where the kids, including you, Abby, come in. You'll decorate the tree. Tomorrow, we have to go and get some spruce boughs and weave them into wreaths and you get to decorate those as well. Now, the question is what kinds of decorations do we have to work with?"

Linda went through the list that she'd brought with her. The storage room in the community centre held all the decorations. For some reason, I thought if only Aunty Gilda were here, she'd have known exactly what to do. Without thinking, I stuck out my lips and said, "Well, we should have bright red and white tablecloths, green leafy placemats, something red and round for berries . . . "

I became aware that everyone was quiet around the table and that they were glancing at each other, and then Mom burst out laughing and said, "That's her! Gilda to the letter! And that's just exactly what she would have said."

I laughed. "Sorry, I don't know. Well, when I was at the Band office yesterday waiting for you, I looked through the Christmas catalogue that's on the table and I remember seeing pictures of wreaths with ribbons, little bulbs, and pine cones with snow on them."

Everyone looked at each other and Mom said, "Now, I never would have thought of that! Well, we have ribbons, but they're the real ones. What we need is the wrapping plastic kind and I remember seeing fake snow spray cans at the store . . . "

Aunt Lucy added, "There's a couple of broken mini-Christmas trees that we had put on the tables several years ago, remember those? Oh, they were a pain and people had to crane their necks around to talk to the person opposite them. People started requesting that we remove them from the tables. Whose idea was that anyway?"

Linda giggled. "Lucy, that was your idea! Remember, you had gone to town and you saw one on a table at the hotel lobby?"

Aunt Lucy sighed. "Right! Anyway, they have small bulbs on them that could be glued on the wreaths. There are several glue guns and glue sticks in a box beside the tape rolls."

I had a question. "Where are we going to get pine cones? They're all under the snow. Would the cones from the jack pines work? We could use the branches from the wood piles across the lake. I could get a ride from Ching to go over and pick the cones off them."

Aunt Lucy said, "Wow, that's great! Joe has rolls of leftover fishing line that we can use to tie the boughs into wreaths. Now, how many will we need to make? Twelve big ones?"

Suddenly the enormity of the work sank in. I would need a huge wash bucket of pine cones! I wondered if Mary or Josie would help round up enough pine cones with me. I kicked my foot under the table. Mom jumped, saying, "Aww, why did you kick me?"

I hunched my shoulders, saying, "Oops. I was just kicking myself for making the suggestion in the first place!"

Blink came running in as the ladies broke into laughter. "Whath'tho funny?" We turned to see a Band-Aid stuck to his obviously swollen upper lip.

Mom went to him, asking, "What happened to you?"

He pulled off his coat, saying, "I thot the puck and it bounthed off the wall and hit me in the mouth! There wath blood all ober the plaith. I went to the nurthing stathion and they put a band-aith on it. It didn't need a stith though. Hey, they called and thew wath no ansther. Whaw wew you?"

I left the table and went into my bedroom to laugh into my pillow. Oh, he looked so funny! He looked like a duck with a Band-Aid stuck to the tip of his beak!

The next morning, Dad came into the house. "Abby, I brought a jack pine branch with a load of cones on it." I grabbed a serving plate, threw on my coat, and ran outside. Although the cones were frozen, they were still very hard to take off. I had to twist them around and around before they broke off. By the time I had a plateful, my fingers hurt. These cones weren't open like the cones in the catalogue.

When I went inside the house, I got out the fake snow spray and began spraying the cones on one side. That way, I thought I would just glue them to the wreaths. The cones were kind of long and skinny and I'd arranged them in rows on the plate when Blink came running in. He stopped at the table and said, "What's with the frozen dog turds?" I looked at the plate, picked it up, threw the cones up in the air, and left the table.

I lay on my bed remembering the Christmas decorations that Goom had in the little white house at Nibika. There was always a real tree in the living room and we would wrap strings of shiny red, blue, green, and yellow around and around the tree. They reflected the sunshine from the window and the tree would sparkle and twinkle like magic. I especially remembered the warmth and happiness with just the three of us sitting in the living room, with me pigging out on candies. Here, the only Christmas thing going on in the house was that Mom had hung four cedar wreaths around the main room. That was it. The main decorations were at the community centre, where we had to make up the wreaths and table centrepieces and set up all the Christmas decorations that we could find in the storage room.

The school choir was getting better and better. The smaller kids in the choir had been practicing separately from us bigger kids, but one day they came into the music room and we got to sing all together. The first attempt was a riot! I laughed so hard my face hurt by the time I came home. I began practicing singing at home with Mom as my audience and it wasn't too bad. I'd started with Mary and then Mom and then sometimes both of them would sit and face me while I sang in the kitchen. I still wouldn't sing in front of Dad, though, or Blink either!

Miss Tish, the music teacher, had discovered that I had a good singing voice, so there was a section in one of the songs that I was to sing alone. I was very nervous at first, but once I got going at the practice, I got this tingling shock that went clear to my toes and I forgot everyone else and sang my heart out. After the practice, the teachers stopped me to say that I sang really well. Meanwhile, the girls never said anything and the boys just giggled.

Finally, the day of the community Christmas dinner arrived and the school choir songs were to begin right after the plates had been cleared. I couldn't eat every much, I was so nervous. The large room was really packed full. People were coughing, laughing, talking, and children ran around between the rows of tables. There was a clearing at one end of the room where a stage had been constructed that was about two feet higher than the floor. Then, there was Miss Tish, making her way to the microphone that stood in front of the stage. That was our cue to get onstage. I saw Mary, Josie, and the rest of my class moving to the stage and I stood up on wobbly knees. I threw a glance at Mom in panic, and she smiled and whispered, "Just keep your eyes on me and ignore the rest. You'll be fine."

When we'd all assembled on the stage, Miss Tish introduced us and the audience grew quiet, waiting for us to begin. We concentrated on the song sheets that we each held and the songs began. The first three songs went really well, and finally the last song started. Right on cue, I heard my voice singing alone and then the other voices joined mine. I'd done it! I was shaking a bit when we finally got offstage. Dad was beaming with pride when I got back to the table and Mom squeezed my hand.

When we got home, Blink gave me a high-five, saying that I'd done good. He even grinned at me and said, "Yo, best singer yet, everyone says!" I just rolled my eyes, thinking, yeah right! Still, I was really happy to hear him say that.

The next day, Goom called to say that she was sending Maggie home. Apparently, Maggie had got into trouble again and Goom had had enough. Dad went and picked her up at the airport in the afternoon, but he arrived back home alone. It seemed that Maggie had wanted to go to Aunt Lucy's place first and that she would come over to visit later.

Maggie came in after supper and sat down at the table with Mom and Dad. Mom asked me to leave when she came in, so I grabbed my coat and went to visit Mary. I never found out what she'd done this time. Mom just told me to mind my own business and that Maggie would be sent to Thunder Bay for high school in September. After that, Maggie and Jane seemed to pick up where they'd left off back at Aunt Lucy's house again.

Then, it was Christmas.

The mitts Dad had thought up in a dream were now a real-life pair and they turned out very nice. Mom finally finished them just in time for Christmas. He was so happy, he picked Mom up and carried her around the room while we all laughed. Maggie spent the day with us too. Mom had made a nice dress for each of us. Mine was blue and Maggie's was green.

I'd carved a small wooden bowl with a butterfly design on the side and a little wooden spoon to go with it. I gave it to Mom thinking she could use it for jam, but she was so pleased when she opened the package, she said, "It's perfect for the baby! It'll be his or her first bowl!" I gave Dad a leather knife sheath that I'd made in art class. The leather was thick and smooth and I had great fun pounding neat designs on it with the leather-working tools at school. For Blink, I'd made a wooden flute that I later regretted because of the noise he was making afterward, walking around and blowing a screeching whistle. I sat down with him and showed him how to actually find notes on it and blow a tune. Once he found out he had to work on it to play a tune, he seemed to lose interest.

Goom sent us all gifts too. I received a set of beautifully carved bookends, and Mom got a silk blouse. Dad's face lit up when he opened his package from Goom. It was a big coffee mug from England. When Maggie opened up her package, she pulled out a pair of black leather gloves. I got a book from Maggie, which was really nice, and I gave her a decorated leather hair clip. I pulled her hair back and anchored the leather strip with the smooth stick that went through the holes at each end to hold it in place. Maggie gave Mom and Dad picture frames that she'd bought in Thunder Bay. For Blink, she'd bought a slingshot. From Dad, all three of us got thick woollen socks from the store. He gave Mom a bright pink toque with a huge pompom dangling from the top. She swung her head around and the pompom whacked him across the face as he was leaning over, laughing into her face. That was funny! We spent the day baking cakes and cookies.

After the holidays, when school began again, Miss Tish gave me more songs to practice for school concerts and I continued to sing the songs from my CDs. Then Aunt Lucy had her new baby around the end of February, so we didn't see much of Maggie after that. It was a little girl whom they named Cindy, and Maggie always carried her around like she was her own. Aunt Lucy and Uncle Joe's older girl, Betty, had been sick a lot lately. She was in and out of the hospital so many times over the months that I didn't know if she was at home or not. Usually, when Betty was in the hospital, Maggie would hang out at our place. But when Cindy arrived, Maggie and Jane were so happy. The baby was like another toy for them to play with. It was odd, but we hardly ever saw Jane while Maggie was in Nibika. Not even at the post office or the Band office. Mary and I had run into her once at the store, and all she said was "hi" in response to my greeting. Now she was at our house whenever Maggie came over. I still didn't like her too much, so I'd go over to Mary's house to visit just to avoid her.

The Dog Tracks group was still training the young dog team, and the dogs were getting better at obeying the commands. At those times, Ki-Moot would be at her dog house outside Mad Dog's place. Ching and Mike sometimes went out on weekends to go ice fishing, but Dad was staying close to home to keep Mom company. However, that meant frequent visits from Mad Dog, who liked to crank up the volume whenever his favourite song came on the radio.

I hitched a ride with Ching a couple of times when he went off to get wood across the lake. After he finished loading up the sled, I'd go with him to find some partridge. We arrived early one Sunday morning across the lake by the woodpile and he stopped and pointed to holes in the snow and whispered, "Tell me what those are."

Well, they looked like someone had thrown snowballs and they landed in the snow. Then I noticed some brush marks beside them and figured out that something with wings had gone in or come out of the holes. I glanced at him and he said, "The partridge land in the snow and burrow deep down into it where they sleep the night. When morning comes, they fly out and hang out in the trees and branches again. You can't get near them when they're in the snow. The snow echoes like a big drum. When you move toward them, your footsteps sound like you're coming through a very loud metal pipe. They fly off before you even know they're there. So when you see these holes, you know there are partridge around."

I smiled and asked, "How do you know what it sounds like under the snow?"

He laughed and said, "Here, pull that kerchief over your ear and lay your head flat down in the snow and I'll come back down the path." He walked back down the path a ways and when he was far enough away, he turned and I got down on the path and lay my ear to the snow and, sure enough, I heard the crunch and heavy steps coming closer! It sounded like elephant steps echoing through the snow.

I came home with partridge several weekends in a row when Dad finally said that he'd take me hunting because Blink and David were at the skating rink that Mike had made on the ice in front of his house. After that, I went with Dad every chance I got when Mike was busy with David and Blink. I absolutely loved walking through the bush in my snowshoes, brushing branches aside with my arm and always scanning the land in front of me, or just stopping to breathe in the fresh, crispy cold air.

CHAPTER NINE

My Second Spring

It was almost the end of May and I was looking at Mom on a Saturday morning and realized just how huge her belly was getting! She groaned and puffed when she rolled off the bed onto her knees on the floor from where she pushed herself up to her feet. She always grinned to make out that she was just using the sound effects to make us smile. Dad wouldn't let her go to work, now, so she kind of just shuffled around the house in Dad's thick grey work socks. Over her shoulders was the pink and blue crocheted spread that Goom had sent her for the rocking chair that she had sent by plane last week. Since Mom could no longer bend over, Dad insisted that he wash, comb, and braid her long hair every morning before he went off to work.

The sisters Minnie and Lizzy would most often come over to sit and sew at our house to keep Mom company when we left to go to school. Sometimes they even came on weekends. One Saturday, they arrived just after breakfast and they were sewing more mitts and moccasins for Dog Tracks. Lizzy began showing me how to make a pair of mitts. I carefully followed her instructions and started sewing. I sewed each stitch as evenly as I could and I'd just finished the thumb piece when Lizzy reached over and picked up my mitt. She lifted the thumb and I could see that it was way too long. I'd continued sewing right past the thumb and into the palm piece, which resulted in a very long thumb. It was just at that point that the door flew open and Blink walked in, threw off his coat, kicked off his boots, and was right at the table, saying, "Ohwa! A mitt for E.T.!" That did it; everyone burst out laughing. And that was the extent of my attempt at sewing.

Dad had got the truck going again while there was still a bit of snow on the road. The solid ice on the lake had blown to the other side and our shoreline was left with floating ice blocks. Before lunch, the sisters went home and Dad helped Mom into the truck and we headed out to Gish's house. When we arrived, there was a "tap, tap, tap" noise by the shore. When we came around the house, Ned was there at the cleaning table by the lake. He'd just finished cleaning muskrats and Gish was stretching the skins onto the stretch boards. The boards were flat and tapered at the top, and Gish was pulling the skins onto the boards like socks, with the head ends of the skins at the top, then tacking the bottom of the skins with small nails. This was where the tapping sound was coming from. Gish turned and dropped several pairs of muskrat paws into my hands and pointed to the lake. My hands closed around the paws and I glanced at Mom in confusion.

She held out her hand to me, and as we walked to the lake, she said, "The youngest person in the group always gets to do this. Children are always told that muskrat helped Wesakechak to create land after the great flood. Muskrat was the only one that was able to dive the deepest into the water to grab some of the mud below, which was all Wesakechak needed to create land. The bit of mud that the muskrat held in his paws became the land that we stand on now. So now, we return the paws to the water so that the muskrat may return again whenever we need him. When you throw the paws back, he can live again. So, thank the muskrat for letting us catch him and may he come again, just as you throw the paws as far out as you can."

I walked out to the shore by myself and said what Mom told me to say as I threw the paws out as far as I could. I saw them plop into the water. I wondered how many years the Anishinawbeg had been doing this. It seemed the right thing to do, and I was glad that I happened to be the youngest one there that day.

There were big chunks of ice floating around along the shore and some had jostled their way to the rocks. I noticed that the branches of the tree beside Gish's canoe were hung with many animal skulls. I remembered asking Dad about them once when I'd first noticed them last spring. His answer was that putting them up high kept the bones off the ground and would keep the dogs from gnawing on them or dragging them around disrespectfully. It would offend the animals if this happened. Dad usually took his animal skulls out into the bush when he went to check his traps or get a load of wood.

When we went back up to where the guys stood, Aunt Lucy had just arrived with David and Blink following the smell of the carrot cake that she'd brought over to Gish's house. The adults all sat around the table talking and, as always, I pulled my feet up on the couch in the living room and listened to what everyone was saying.

My Ojibwe was very fluent now and I was also getting really good at picking up and understanding the non-verbal stuff too. Gish was describing how Bear Creek looked before it became a settlement. He was saying that a trader's post used to stand where the Band office now was. He remembered that, as a child, there would be many ceremonies that took place on the grounds by the clearing where the store now stood. I glanced at him, trying to imagine what he would have looked like as a child and realized that I had a big smile on my face just when he was talking about a sickness that had come through, and that many people had died, including both his parents. I quickly glanced away and hoped he hadn't noticed me.

After about an hour, I decided to see where the boys had gone. I knew that Gish had set the dogs free to run under the boys' "watchful eyes." Rolling my eyes at the thought, I went out the back door to check on them when I saw the dogs come toward me chasing each other, with the boys running behind them up the path all out of breath. Blink ran right by me, but David paused to sputter, "Mucko, he wouldn't jump over!"

I grabbed his sleeve and yelled, "What?" He stopped and said, "A big iceberg floated by and we got on it at the rocks and the dogs jumped on right behind us. Me, Blink, Mucko, Ki-Moot, Wiener, and Shingoos. When it started to tip over and float away, we jumped onto the hard ice that is still jutting out at the point, but Mucko was scared. He just kept whimpering and whining and wouldn't jump over! He was floating away when we decided to run for help!"

I knew the ice would quickly melt once it floated out into the open water, and Mucko could drown! I ran down to the lake only to be followed by the other dogs, who continued to chase each other around me. I ran along the shore, yelling, "Mucko! Mucko!" I didn't see anything black swimming in the water. There were blocks of slowly drifting ice but no sign of Mucko. I ran, searching the shoreline and was just about to run back when I saw some movement in the dry bushes and grass to my right. There he was! He was on his back, rolling around and around on the ground before he jumped up and shook the rest of the water off his fur. He was still soaking wet and when he saw me, he ran up with his tail high up in the air, swinging his head like he was so proud of himself.

I yelled, "Mucko! Good boy! Such a brave boy!"

He began to shake again then jumped up to my chest, and I gave him a good scratch behind his ears. Then the other dogs were on us. Ki-Moot growled jealously at Mucko, but Mucko growled back and shouldered her out of the way before he took off to the sound of Gish's voice yelling, "Mucko! Come here, boy!" I stood there looking after him. He was back! Mucko had got his courage back. He was his old bold and masculine self. Watch out, Bannock!

I took off at a run, back along the shoreline with the dogs out in front of me, wrestling and jostling as they ran. I got back just in time to see Mucko swipe his nose against Gish's hand, side-swipe Dad's legs, and head straight for Bannock. Bannock never even saw it coming. He was rolling around under Mucko by the time we all ran to them and then Bannock managed to wriggle away with his tail between his legs and flop down in submission as Mucko stood over him, his teeth bared and growling. The rest of the dogs, Wiener, Ki-Moot, and Shingoos, were quick to get down in submission while Mucko strode around stiff-legged but tail still slightly wagging as he looked up at Dad, Ned, and Gish, who began to laugh. Gish stopped laughing long enough to say, "Welcome back, boy!" Mucko went over to Gish and shoved his head under his hand to have his ears scratched.

It was from that time on that every time the group took him home to Chief Paulie, Mucko always came back to Gish's place. Paulie kept him tied up most of the time, but whenever he got loose, that's where he'd head. I happened to be working in Paulie's living room one day and I'd let Mucko inside the porch. I saw Paulie coming and I heard her pull the door open and exclaim, "Shoot! There he goes!" I saw a black streak cross the window as Mucko headed down the road to Gish's. She came in, saying, "What am I going to do with that dog?"

I smiled and said, "Go take his bowl and his bed to Gish."

She stopped and looked at me and said, "You know, that's a perfectly good idea! I've dragged him home so many times that, well, he can just stay there!" So she took Mucko's bed and food bowls over to Gish. After that, Mucko spent his time stretched out on Gish's living room floor or kept watch outside. Daish didn't seem to mind him, and Mucko began taking a personal interest in not allowing any other dogs to come near Daish. He'd stand like a sentry by the corner of the house. He either welcomed or challenged people coming near the house, depending on whether or not he knew them. One day when Gish heard Mucko barking and growling by the path from the road, he'd gone to investigate and found Reverend Roberts standing there, waiting for him to call off his watch dog. Gish thought that was funny. The Reverend had recovered from his harrowing ordeal during the Dog Tracks trial run without any complications, but he never volunteered to be a fake tourist again. Neither did Father Bailey for that matter!

It was the day before my fourteenth birthday when I awoke to feel something sticky between my legs. I reached down and my fingers came away covered in blood! Mom had told me what to expect and I had pads ready inside the drawer of my side table. My heart was pounding when I went to the bathroom to clean up. I was glad to see that I didn't get any blood on my bedding. I washed my underwear and a bit of my nightgown, which I put into my laundry bag. Mom was standing at the table when I came into the kitchen, and I went over and whispered to her that my periods had started. She gave me a hug, kissed my forehead, and said, "You must call Goom and tell her."

I realized that my eyes were level to the top of her head and I said, "Did you shrink?"

She laughed. "Did I shrink! You just shot up like a little tree this winter. I had to let down the hem of your pants again. You should wear your skirts during this time now." Wearing skirts wasn't a bad idea, especially for the next few days. I was sure everyone would see the pad I was wearing if I wore pants. Already it felt like trying to walk around with a pillow between my legs!

Mom was on the phone talking to Goom already, telling her that my periods had started. Then she handed the phone to me. I laughed when Goom told me that when Mom started hers, they'd been in the city having supper in a fancy restaurant. Goom said, "Sophie suddenly put her fork down and had a strange expression on her face and then she jumped up and ran to the washroom. I sent Gilda after her to see what was the matter. When she came back, she said that Sophie wanted to see me and was insisting that she was dying! 'Dial 911! Dial 911!' She'd screamed at her sister. So I went to the washroom and found her sitting on the toilet seat just shaking! I had to remind her about our previous conversations where I had told her what she was to expect any day, but apparently she'd forgotten about it. Gilda called her '911' for a long time!"

We talked a bit more and when I hung up the phone, I sat down beside Mom at the table and said, "So, 911, what are we doing today?"

Her eyes popped open and she exclaimed, "No! She didn't tell you that story, did she? Oh, don't tell anyone. That was the most embarrassing moment of my life!"

I smiled. "No, I won't tell anyone." So now I shared a secret with Mom that I'd guard forever.

On my birthday, Goom called to wish me happy birthday. I'd received her gift a few days before with a note that said I wasn't to open it until she called. So now I was holding the receiver against my shoulder as I unwrapped the gift. I opened it and said, "Wow! This is beautiful! Where did you get it?"

Goom replied, "All the way from England. I saved it for your birthday!" I turned the beautifully decorated box of English cookies around in my hands. There was also a large package of English toffee. After I hung up, Mom and I had a toffee in our mouths when Mike called to say that we were invited to come to their place for supper because he'd finally got the gas barbeque that he'd ordered from the catalogue. I passed the cookies and toffee around the table when Blink and Dad came in. We were very excited as we piled into the truck. Mom made wild rice salad and bannock and I made a cake. It was the first cake I'd ever made and it turned out really nice. I had to slap Blink's hand away several times before I could get it into a cardboard box so that it wouldn't break before we got there.

When we arrived, Ned and Alice were already there with Gish and Ching. Just as we finished unpacking our food, Aunt Lucy, Uncle Joe, Maggie, and baby Cindy arrived with the sisters Lizzy and Minnie. Maggie had grown a lot over the winter so that she was now almost the same height as Mom. Her hair was reddish brown with blond streaks in it. She no longer had long fake red fingernails. Aunt Lucy and Uncle Joe's older daughter, Betty, was in the hospital again. Linda was still running around setting up the tables and chairs on the deck in front of the house where the silver barbeque stood ready. The propane tank was attached at the bottom and the lid sat open, waiting for the chef. We were all inside around the kitchen table when we noticed that Mad Dog and Kitty had arrived.

I got the tea and coffee going on the stove and had just turned around to see David slipping in through the window from the deck. Before anyone could say anything, Gish bellowed, "You, go back the way you came in! Only dead bodies are taken in and out of windows to confuse the dead so they don't hang around the house. Now, get back out there!"

After all the time that I'd been here, I was still surprised at how many things I hadn't heard about. Dad looked at Gish and said, "It was after the funeral that the dead person's goods and personal belongings were also distributed. I never knew what happened to half of my brother's things. The few possessions I got were things he'd given me before he died. Then they moved all the furniture around and put everything everywhere else. I couldn't find anything for the longest time!"

Gish laughed and said, "Oh, long ago they used to burn the whole house with everything in it. That was to make sure the dead person's spirit didn't come back to the home and bother the people in there, if he or she couldn't accept that he or she was dead."

Mom smiled. "I heard it a bit differently why someone should go back the way they came in. It had something to do with . . . " Suddenly, a huge explosion shook the house. We all jumped up from the table and ran out to the deck in time to see Mad Dog running around with a cloud of smoke billowing behind him. Mike lunged and hit Mad Dog's fur cap off his head and stomped on it to put the fire out. Then Ned grabbed it and threw it over the deck railing, where the dogs grabbed it and ran off with it, chasing each other down the road. Someone started giggling and then everyone burst out laughing. Mad Dog had apparently left the propane on too long before he lit the match. The exploding fire had set his fur hat on fire.

After awhile, Mad Dog came in, rubbing his bald head and looking pretty sad, and Lizzy said, "It was time we made you another cap anyway. What kind would you like?"

Mad Dog perked up and gave a toothless grin at the ladies and said, "A wolverine cap?"

Minnie smiled. "Yes, I do believe we have enough wolverine fur to make a new cap for you." That settled, Mad Dog looked pretty pleased. I never could understand how he didn't get too hot wearing that old beaver cap during the summer anyway!

Linda had packages of hot dogs and frozen hamburgers, which Mike and Dad got set to barbeque. Alice, however, didn't like the store-bought buns, so Mom was making small bannock rolls in the oven. Mom was very happy that she didn't have to sit by a hot open campfire to roast the hot dogs and fry the hamburgers.

Gish had brought four traditional bows and arrows that he'd made. There were two large bows for the adults and two smaller ones for the boys. They were wonderful! Gish's bows and arrows were so beautifully made that people who saw them wanted to buy them right then and there. He said that when he took them to the Band office to show Chief Paulie, he had to fight off the young guys. He'd brought them here so everyone could practice and target shoot at balloons that were attached to some bushes along the far side of the yard. Some of the arrows were even tipped with fluorescent bluish-green mallard feathers. Alice told me that long ago, women were forbidden to touch men's tools or weapons during their moon time. When I asked her why, she said, "because women are very strong at this time and they could compromise the male spiritual strength or energy contained in the men's belongings." She went on to describe how there were special huts that the women stayed in away from their homes until their periods were done. I thought that must have been like a break from everything.

After a rather loud meal with everyone talking and laughing, my cake was brought out and some gifts appeared on the table. I was surprised since I hadn't seen any gift packages brought in by the group. I got something from everyone. Gish gave me a wonderful chunk of dry straight-grained cedar for carving. Ching took out a carrying bag from his pocket that he'd made from moosehide and gave it to me; Ned and Alice gave me a beautiful birchbark basket; and Lizzy and Minnie gave me a big bag of beads. Mike and Linda gave me a bag of different coloured embroidery thread. The thread was silky and bright, although I couldn't see myself making anything with it. I thought to myself that I'd have to learn. Then Joe and Lucy gave me a large envelope of assorted needles. I hadn't a clue what most of the funny-shaped needles were for, but I guess I'd find out. Maggie gave me a package of assorted hair bands, and I got another skirt from Mom and Dad. It was blue with tiny yellow flowers. Nothing had been wrapped, which was nice because everyone got to see the wonderful stuff I got.

People gradually moved to the grass off the back deck as Mom, Maggie, and Linda washed the dishes. Mad Dog was helping put the barbeque things away. They'd ushered me out, saying it was my day off from cleaning up. Just then, Paulie came around the corner of the house and yelled, "Birthday girl! Come here, I've got something for you!" I ran down the steps and she handed me a package, saying, "I got an invitation to join the party, but I've got a plane to catch. Here, this is for you and happy birthday!" She kissed my forehead and said, "I'll call you when I get back." She waved at the others who had gathered around the deck, saying, "See you next week!" and then she was gone.

Everyone gathered around me as I pulled the package open and a black and white dog head popped out! I ripped off the paper and examined the stuffed black and white toy dog. Blink asked, "Why did she give you a toy?" Then I saw a button just under its collar and I pressed it and suddenly it said, "Hi, my name is Yappi. Would you like to play?" I burst out laughing. That was just great!

I turned to Mom and said, "It's a talking dog!" Gish looked baffled but didn't offer an opinion.

I sat down on the deck with the toy dog on my lap when suddenly Gish threw a ball that was made of pine branches tightly tied into a ball. After that came a looped stick with meshing inside the loop. When the dishes were done, Maggie came down to join in the game and she landed flat out, arms outstretched and face in the muddy ground at Blink's feet as he deftly flicked the ball up over her head and into Ned's open hands. I sat and laughed with Lizzy and Minnie and watched the game. For the first time, I felt like I was someone else sitting there, looking at a game like I was a mature woman.

It was sometime later when Linda and Mom came out onto the deck with a large square cake loaded with sparkling candles. The crowd burst out hooting and clapping as Mom, Linda, and the cake made their way to the tables by the barbeque. I hadn't seen the cake so I'd assumed that I wasn't getting one. I was near to tears when everyone sang "Happy Birthday," ending the second half in Ojibwe. Dad rescued me from bawling by planting a big kiss on my forehead and then Gish was there with a huge hunting knife in his hand to cut the cake. After many puffs of air, I managed to blow out the spaced-out candles, and Gish cut the cake into many pieces so everyone got one.

Just as I finished my piece of cake, a large flock of geese flew overhead and everyone was so happy to see them, they burst out into many imitation honks and hoots! The geese were headed north and soon the hunters would be out to get some for the spring ceremonies. It had been my best birthday ever.

CHAPTER TEN

Family Time

I t was a beautiful day near the end of May and we were all at Gish's house where we met Mike and Linda. Gish had gone to the hospital in Thunder Bay and had been away for awhile, but he was back home now. Everyone was sitting around the table telling their hunting stories to him. I sat in the living room part of the house that faced the road and watched Blink and David collecting rocks for the new slingshots that Gish had made for them. I tuned in to the story behind me. Mike was saying, "The ducks and geese had arrived by then and the last of the ice had gone from the mouth of the river where we usually go hunting. So off we went that morning."

Dad said, "You know that area where we usually park the truck and then we canoe to the bay, just before the rapids?"

Gish nodded and took a sip of his tea. Dad continued, "It has sandy soil with low cedar trees. It's a perfect home for skunks as we discovered."

Mike said, "We took Wiener since he's becoming a good duck hunting dog. We had just crawled over a high bank from the bush to the shoreline and we were watching the ducks, still too far to shoot. But they were really interested in Wiener's antics along the shoreline. The mallards were laughing and the grebes flittered back and forth with glee at the spectacle on the shoreline. Wiener was running back and forth and jumping over a washed-up log each time he ran by."

Mike began laughing and Dad continued, "Finally, just as we put our guns up to our shoulders to aim, Wiener suddenly whirled around and took off after something that had caught his eye behind him. After a short chase into the bush, the smell of skunk wafted up to us. We had to tie Wiener downwind from us and we continued to hunt the ducks without him."

Mike said, "When we'd chased all the ducks away, having killed only six mallards, we began wondering what to do with Wiener. Going back would be difficult because we had to paddle back in a canoe to the landing where we'd left the truck. So we decided to try to wash him first."

Gish made a sputtering sound and his shoulders shook as he laughed. Dad continued, "Well, we took off our pants, socks, and boots and waded into the cold water with Wiener in tow. We tried not to breathe through the nose as Mike held him by the leash and I rubbed the dog with sand and cedar branches. That darned dog! Each time we got him wet, he'd shake and shake the water off, spraying both of us with stinky sand and water. By then, wet skunk smell covered all three of us." Gish was laughing even harder now.

Mike said, "When we realized that the smell was only getting stronger, we decided to put Wiener into the packsack that the ducks were in. So we dumped the ducks into the canoe and stuffed skunky Wiener into the packsack with just his stinking head sticking out. We lifted him into the canoe where he kept toppling over and his head got scrunched to the side of the canoe when we got in. I had to prop him up again as we pushed the canoe off into the water." We were all laughing now.

Dad sat back and said, "His head stank so bad that Mike said he was the most humiliated and dejected-looking dog ever! When we got to the landing, we dumped Wiener out of the packsack, but now the packsack stank so much, we had to leave it hanging on a branch by the truck. Wiener rode the rest of the way home in the back of the truck with the gas cans and tool box."

I remembered when Dad arrived home—as soon as he came through the door, Mom hollered, "Out! Get outside!" Later, he said he was thrown out of the house so fast he never even got a whiff of the coffee simmering on the stove. Mike said he had to take his clothes off outside and get dressed in clean clothes before Linda would let him in. Wiener stank up his doghouse and was fed and watered from a distance for some days. The inside of the truck stank for quite awhile too.

After this story, we all went home, leaving Gish to rest. Mom said that she had to get supper done early that night and there was a big rainstorm coming. I already knew that! I was getting very good at predicting when a rainstorm was moving in. There was a very distinct smell in the air. I could tell when it was going to be a very hot, sunny day too. There was no dampness to the heat in the air.

The next weekend, Dad and Mike took Ki-Moot hunting because Ozit had been taken by Ching and his buddies to go duck hunting, Wiener still stank, and there just wasn't another beige dog around. Well, that morning you couldn't have seen a happier dog, so excited to have been picked to go with the hunters. She ran around and around the truck barking, and at the first opportunity, she was inside the truck and into the back seat, wedged between the jackets and packsacks. So off she went with Dad and Mike.

When they returned that evening, Ki-Moot was the first one off the truck in a flurry of excitement. Mom was by the truck now helping Dad and Mike, pulling their stuff out of the truck, sorting out ducks and their belongings before Dad got back into the truck to drive Mike home.

Mom had just dumped the ducks into the tub in the back porch when Dad arrived back home. He came stomping in, saying, "I'll have to take off my socks in here. My boots got flooded this afternoon. That dumb dog! I was so ticked off with that dumb dog today!"

Mom and I glanced at each other. As Dad pulled off one sock by the stove, he said, "You know what ol' Gish always says? You need a beige dog to go duck hunting? Anyway, as you know, we had only little Ki-Moot this morning. So when we got there, we sent her off to the beach to attract all those ducks and geese to shore. When they saw her running back and forth barking at them, they just stood back and laughed at her. They were quacking and heckling like she was the funniest thing they'd ever seen! They wouldn't come any closer. Then Mike had the bright idea that if I put my beige long johns on her, they would surely think that she was a beige dog. Remember this morning when Mike came in, I came out and told him I was just putting on my beige long johns? Well, that's how he knew I was wearing beige long johns. Anyway . . . "

Dad adjusted his seat on the chair to pull off his other sock. "Well, we'd been throwing all the meat we had for her over to the beach to keep her running around. But by late afternoon, like around four, we still had no ducks. They were just hanging back laughing at Ki-Moot. Well, I called Ki-Moot over to our pine branch blind along the shoreline. I fed her a piece of meat from my sandwich and Mike grabbed her and we put the long johns on her that I had taken off. Mike came up with some safety pins that Linda had used to pin his overall suspenders onto his pants, so we put the dog's legs through my underwear legs and arm sleeves and we just kind of folded and bunched all the rest of the excess material up with Mike's safety pins. I had no idea the man had so many safety pins on him!"

By then, Mom had a dishtowel over her mouth stifling her laughter, as Dad threw his socks over the wire line behind the stove. "Anyway, after we had Ki-Moot into my long johns, Mike threw the last bit of his moose meat sandwich way out onto the sand beach. Well, Ki-Moot went sailing over the embankment onto the beach and the ducks just went nuts! You should have heard them! They began to gather around to watch Ki-Moot. We couldn't believe it! She actually pranced with her tail up in the air as she trotted up and down the beach, but then it became very clear that something was happening. We'd fed her so much that afternoon that, well . . . now she needed to go to the bathroom! Just then, the whole bunch of ducks and geese shot forward toward the beach and the next thing we knew, there they were, all within shooting range and we let go with our guns going off at the same time. In the chaos of gunshots, the squawking of the ducks, and Ki-Moot barking her head off in panic and us yelling that the ducks were down—suddenly we stood quiet and we watched Ki-Moot taking her slow, sweet time having a crap inside my long johns! Mike was the first to start into a giggling fit as he said, 'You fed her too much, John, my man!' Well, we had to catch her and she kept running around trying to lose the contents in her pants. We finally caught her and then we had to remove all those safety pins and, boy, the stink! Anyway, we took off the long johns and washed Ki-Moot at the beach. After all that, I just threw the long johns over a branch. We picked up the ducks and I decided to leave the darned thing hanging there."

"You left your long johns hanging on a branch?" Mom asked.

Dad laughed. "Why, did you want me to bring them home for you to wash?"

Mom got up, still laughing. "No."

All I could think was, yuck!

One evening, several days later, Mike arrived with Mad Dog. The men sat around the table planning their next hunting trip. I was still doing my homework on my bed. When I finished, I came into the kitchen area just as Mom put the coffee pot on the table.

Mike was saying, "Well, we could plan to stay several days and bring one of the tents. We'll camp by the mouth of the river or over by Long John Bay."

Mom giggled. That was what they called the bay where Dad's now weathered long johns still hung. The planning went on for several more minutes when the phone rang and Mom talked on the phone for quite awhile. I turned my attention to what she was saying. "Yeah, sure. I think he'd like that, especially if David is there. Yeah, okay."

She came back to the table and sat down with her cup of coffee and said, "That was Linda. She was talking to Alice and Alice has offered to look after David and Blink so that Linda, the girls, and I can go pick the marsh berries. We'll stay overnight by the portage. She says Ned told her that the berries are ripe and huge."

Wow! I was so happy to be going somewhere. We hadn't gone any-where since the fall hunting trip. So it was settled. The guys were going hunting and we were going berry picking. Blink threw a fit when he heard about the plans and he refused to come out from under his bed until he heard David would be at Alice's as well. Alice also had brand new games for the television. That was all it took to convince Blink. He packed up his little backpack and was gone the next morning before we even finished loading up the boat. We were using our boat and picking up Linda on the way.

Uncle Joe dropped Maggie off early that morning on his way to work. The guys had left very early in the morning. As Mom started the outboard motor, we could see Alice waving to us from her house with David and Blink beside her. We waved back and the twenty-horsepower motor took off along the shore to Linda and Mike's house. Linda was already at the shore waiting for us. The boat was packed full when we finally started out for the portage at the far end of the lake. It was a good day with just a little chop on the water.

When we reached the portage, the blackflies descended on us with a vengeance. Mom pulled out two spray cans of mosquito repellent and we sprayed every exposed part of our bodies before we did anything else. Mom and Linda put up the canvas tent, while Maggie and I brought the food and bedding up to the site. It was a well-used campsite with poles already lean-ing against a tree. The canvas tent was smaller than the large prospector tents with the stovepipe holes that we'd used in the fall when we went hunt-ing. This one just had two flaps at the front with one pole along the roof centred on two crossed poles at each end. The sides were anchored with three ropes.

Maggie ran up the portage trail but she came right back, yelling, "Mom, there's a bear out there! I was just coming around the bend when I saw it. I don't think he even saw me."

Linda looked at Mom and said, "The sucker fish are running, maybe?" There was a creek that ran along the portage path. A shock had gone through me as soon as Maggie said "bear."

Mom snorted, "Probably, or maybe we're the suckers for forgetting they're running. Well, we'll just have to bank on having company tonight."

Linda said, "Well, we could go across to the island and have our supper there. What did you bring?"

Mom said, "I have bannock and a chunk of bologna for lunch. As for supper, I was hoping to catch some fish or shoot a partridge or something. I did bring the .22 rifle."

Linda smiled, "Okay, let's get our bedding ready and we'll go set some rabbit snares across the bay and look for partridge."

Maggie piped up, "I heard one thumping over there on the other side of that small island."

Linda replied, "Well, that would be a good place to have our lunch and supper."

Mom added, "Actually, that could be a good place to sleep too. If we're going to eat there, why don't we just move our tent to the small island?"

We all looked at each other and smiled. No more was said as we pulled the tent down and loaded the stuff back into the boat, including the poles, and headed out to the small island in the bay. There we quickly set up camp again. It was much better when some wind picked up to blow the flies away. There was no more fear of bears wandering into our campsite when we just had enough room for a tent space, the swampy space to pull the boat in, some spruce trees to the back, and a smooth sloping rock in front. It was perfect!

As we ate our lunch of fried bologna and bannock, sure enough, we heard a partridge thumping in the bush across the bay. It sounded like a slow slap to the thighs and it gradually went faster and then it would stop. That was the sound of the partridge flapping its wings to its body during its mating call. Mom and Linda left to set up the rabbit snares and hunt down the partridge, while Maggie and I got the campsite ready. We got the bedding down, created a cooking area on top of the smooth rock, and gathered wood from the surrounding windfallen trees. We worked silently for the most part, except for exchanging a few comments about the berries and the blackflies that would probably be really bad in the swamp.

When we were done, we picked up the two fishing rods. I took the one that had a red and white spoon hook on it. With my first cast, I immediately caught a snag. I could actually see my hook caught between two rocks. That was the first time I'd attempted to cast from shore. Feeling like an idiot, I was debating with myself if I should wade out there in the cold water to get it when Maggie said, "The first thing you should do is see where the rocks are before you throw your hook out. Mom will get it out when they come back."

With that, she walked down the shore and cast way out into the lake. She had a yellow feathered jig on her rod. Her first cast caught a pickerel, which she dragged to shore. I made sure it wasn't going to get back into the water by throwing it into the bushes. After I removed the hook, she hopped back onto the rock and cast way out into the deep again. It was then that we heard two shots from the .22 rifle. After several more casts, she caught another pickerel and then a huge northern pike. By that time, Linda and Mom came back with two partridge. They were very pleased with Maggie's catch and they were able to retrieve my snag.

Looking at Maggie, I noticed for the first time that she looked nothing like Mom, whom I took after. I guessed she must have taken after our Dad then, although I'd never seen a picture of him. Suddenly, I realized how important she was to me.

Maggie grinned at me with her curved-up smile and said, "Do you know how to clean a pike so there are no bones left in it?"

I said, "Absolutely not!"

She picked up the knife and said, "Come, I'll show you." I followed her to the shore, while Mom and Linda prepared supper. I watched her knife deftly sever each side fillet of the pike and then she sliced off each side of the ribs. To take off the Y-shaped bones that ran along the back of the fish, her knife slipped along the top side of the Y-shaped bones down to the tail. Then she sliced along beneath the Y-bones and pulled off one tube-shaped piece of flesh that contained the bones. Quite impressed, I smiled at her.

Then Mom yelled, "Come on, girls. Bring the fish." Maggie quickly removed the skin from the fish and we ran back. We had fried fish that evening, and I went to bed very happily sandwiched between Maggie and Mom. Linda was by the front flap beside Mom.

About halfway through the night, I was awakened by urgent whispering between Mom and Linda, and I said, "What?" Mom answered, "Sh, sh, sh, listen." We all heard the distinct "chik, chik, chik" sound of nails over the smooth rock out front. A bear? Bear claws on the rock? Did the bear swim across to us? I felt very hot and my heart was thumping in my chest as we waited. Finally, Linda couldn't stand it anymore, so she took the flashlight, flipped open the tent flaps, and shone the light out to the shore. Suddenly there was a loud splash followed by a definite slap on the water.

Mom breathed a sigh of relief and lay back down. "A beaver. It was only a beaver. Go back to sleep." I stared into the darkness of the tent and said, "What do you think the beaver is thinking? He just saw a flash of light go over his body and maybe into his eyes in the middle of the night." After a two-second silence, everyone burst into giggling fits. I wasn't trying to be funny, but I guess it was a funny thing to say.

The next morning, we had fried eggs and bacon that Linda had brought along with Mom's delicious fried bannock. We laughed and talked and I discovered a very funny and bright older sister whom I never knew I had. Then I realized what seemed so new about her. It was like she was all grown up now. At one point when the question came up as to how we would store the berries outside without having to come back to the boat all the time, Maggie suggested that we hang our berry buckets on a tree until our containers were used up. Everyone thought that was a very good idea.

I noticed that Mom came between Maggie and me to give us a hug at every opportunity. I'd never seen her so happy. After breakfast, Mom and Linda went to remove the snares, while Maggie and I packed the tent and bedding. We were finished by the time they arrived with four rabbits. We left our gear on the island but took the partridge and rabbits in the cooler with us to the marshy area of the bay, thinking that they would be safer in the boat. We got out our ice cream buckets and prepared the two coolers where we were going to dump the berries once our buckets were filled. We waded into the spongy moss with our boots on and proceeded to pick the juicy red berries.

The marsh berries were like cranberries, only they were all juicy inside. I took my time for the first three bucketfuls until I realized that Maggie was already ahead of me by two buckets. So I took off and practically ran from one berry bush to another until I'd filled up my bucket so fast I couldn't believe it! Then I stood up. I saw no one around me. I heard nothing. I looked back to where I thought I'd come from. There were no tracks. The moss I was in was the kind that when you stepped on it, it came right back up, so there were no footprints. I was lost and had no idea which direction I'd come from. I stood there with my full bucket and was debating which way I should turn when I heard a shot from the .22. But the sound echoed so quickly around the poplar trees that surrounded the swamp that I didn't know which direction the shot had come from. Another shot rang out that bounced around, but by then another shot was fired. I was able to figure out the direction it came from and I ran toward the sound. I came out of the bush at a full run to discover that Maggie had just finished cleaning the four partridge that Linda had just killed. Mom and Linda were on their way to the lake to pour the last of the berries into the now-full coolers.

I walked up to Maggie like I was taking my time and even picked a few more berries along the way. Maggie glanced at me and said, "One more minute and I was having to go look for you. You're sweating buckets and you look like a ghost just walked over you. You got lost, didn't you? Didn't Mom tell you not to wander? I knew you'd wandered off when I lifted my head and you weren't in sight. You don't ever go off unless you know where everyone is and you let everyone know where you are. Why did you take off like that?" It hurt to hear her give me heck, and I felt like I was going to cry any minute.

I stood with my head down in front of her and pointed at my full bucket. "I wanted you to be proud of me. That I could pick the berries as fast as you. I'm sorry."

She pulled me into her arms and whispered into my ear, "You're never to try to prove anything to me, you hear? You're my sister. No matter what, you'll always be my baby sister!"

I cried then, as I hung on to her. I thought, though, that it was more out of relief at making it back from the swamp than anything else. But then she started to cry too and I realized that her reaction had nothing to do with me at all. I felt rather shocked at this turn of events. I let her cry against me and I just held her.

Finally, she stood back and said, "Sorry. But I have to tell you something. As soon as I got to Nibika, I looked up our dad's family and I found a sister of his. I talked to her for awhile and she told me that our dad was actually driving to Thunder Bay to get us when he got into that accident. His parents blamed us because if it weren't for us, he'd still be alive."

That sent a shock through me and I asked, "Does Mom know this?"

She shrugged. "Yeah, I told them that night when I got back, but Mom said not to tell you because it might upset you. But I thought you should know." Somehow, this information left me with a calming feeling that our own dad had loved us after all. I think I understood now why Maggie went into that spiral spin in the fall.

"What's Dad's sister's name?" I asked.

"Margaret," she said. Between our snotty-nosed sniffling, we vowed that nothing would stand between us again. She linked her little finger with mine and whispered, "Sisters forever!"

We walked back to the lake, hand in hand. We had a lunch of fried partridge before we headed for home. It was such a wonderful day that Maggie decided to spend the night with us. Linda, David, and Kitty came over that evening and we played cards, and the rest of the cookies and candies from England disappeared. The next morning after a breakfast of pancakes, Mom, Blink, Maggie, and I had a lot of fun making a big batch of the berries into jam. Linda had taken the rest to the community freezer. The elders liked the berries served over the geese and ducks at the community feasts.

That evening Maggie was still there when Dad, Mike, and Mad Dog arrived back from duck hunting. Instead of dropping each one off as he normally did, Dad brought them all home. When they arrived at our house, Mom had to call Kitty next door to help her with supper, and Linda arrived just in time to help too. Kitty finished frying the fish and Linda dished out the supper, while Mom sorted out the ducks at the back of the truck. By the time she came in, everyone was seated at the table and along the couch and the story began about their weekend hunting trip.

The first story came from Mad Dog, who laughed out loud so long before he could tell the story. Finally he began, "Mike, he shoots, bang, bang, bang, at the ducks. John drives over where the ducks fall; Mike grabs them and throws them into the boat. One, two, three, four, then off we go again. Except, one of them was only stunned and it comes to life just when Mike is trying to stuff them into his packsack. Oh, man! The duck starts beating its wings, left, right, smacking Mike across the face and it starts kicking, thump, thump, thump, on Mike's belly and then, and then, it clamps its beak right on Mike's nose, in the meantime whacking both his ears with its wings!"

Mike pipes in, "I tried hanging on to one leg but nevermind, that's when it clamped its beak on my nose!"

Mad Dog continued, "That's when John shoots this huge goose that nearly lands inside our canoe just when Mike's duck makes a getaway and off it goes, planting one leaping kick on top of John's head!"

Dad adds, "Well, after that, the wind picked up and the water got really choppy. We were in the bay then and the waves can get quite high pretty fast. Anyway, we came across some ducks at the edge of the bay so we decided to head right at them at full speed and try shooting them on the fly. Well, the canoe was going up and down at the front in the waves where Mad Dog sat. He got a bead on several ducks flying low and suddenly they swerved toward him and he pulled the trigger—just when the canoe front popped up on one big wave and, bang, he blew a hole in the front of the canoe!"

A gasp came from the women, and I was trying hard not to blow my mouthful of bannock. Finally Kitty managed to ask, "You shot a hole in the canoe?"

Mad Dog grinned at his wife, saying "Oh, just nicked the tip off."

Everyone laughed as the stories went on, including our story about the fright we got when we heard the beaver claws on the rock in the middle of the night, not to mention how scared the poor beaver must have been, looking into a bright beam of light from heaven one spring night.

We were all very tired when we finally headed for bed. Dad drove everyone home and Blink was already asleep with his bag of homemade chocolate chip cookies that they'd baked at Kitty's place. Maggie was curled up beside me, while I lay listening to Mom getting ready for bed as she waited for the truck to pull up at the door.

CHAPTER ELEVEN

Back to the Blueberries

I came into class one morning and I knew something was wrong. There was tension in the classroom. Mr. Toms was at the front of the room, stacking a pile of geography books, so I went over to him. The students were all there except Josie and Mary. I whispered, "What's wrong?"

Mr. Toms' head came up and he responded in a low voice. "Mary and Josie had a big fight and Mary yanked a handful of hair off Josie's head, so she ran out. She's probably gone home and Mary is in the principal's office at the moment."

I whispered again, "What was it about?" He shrugged and indicated that I should go and sit down, and then class began. Finally, at our break time, I ran to the principal's office, but there was no one there. Then I ran to the Band office and called Mary from there. She was at home and she answered the phone.

I asked, "What happened? You had a fight with Josie?"

She said, "Yeah, now I can't go to school for a couple of days."

I asked, "What was it about?"

She replied, "It doesn't matter. I don't ever want to talk to her again!" Realizing I wasn't going to get anything out of her right then, I told her that I'd drop by after school.

When I popped in at Mary's house after school, there were people waiting to get their hair cut in the living room, so Mary pulled me into her bedroom. She shut the door and said, "I struck out at Josie because she said something about you and I got real angry."

I stopped still. "About me? What was it she said about me?"

Then she looked right at me and said, "I'm not going to tell you that. Just don't pay attention to her and don't say anything to her at all! Okay?"

I shrugged. "I guess." Suddenly, Paulie popped into my head. I bet she'd know what was going on. She always did.

That evening, I ran to Paulie's house because I knew she was home. I bounded up the steps and pushed the door open. She was on the phone in the kitchen, so I yelled, "Yo, it's me!" to let her know that I was there.

She yelled back, "Come and get some hot chocolate." I went in and poured myself a cup while she finished her conversation and hung up the phone.

I sat down at the table beside her and right away she said, "I hear there was a little scuffle at school today." I knew Paulie would know all about it!

I asked, "Do you know what it was about? Mary wouldn't tell me."

She smiled. "You should ask the dogs. I bet they'd know."

I cried, "What? You're not going to tell me either? That sucks!"

She broke into laughter and said, "Josie was following Abraham around and he apparently told her something that threw her into a fit. That's all I know. Honest!"

Abraham? That was so stupid! I hadn't seen Abraham since the Christmas dinner at the community centre. I sighed and leaned back in my chair and took a sip of hot chocolate.

It was the end of June and the last day of school. Summer came quickly and then it was just one more week and we'd be going to the blueberry-picking island again. Mom insisted on going as long as the two sisters were with us. She didn't want to fly out to the hospital and was intent on having the baby at home, or at the summer camp if the baby came before the expected date. Dad seemed very nervous, but Sara, the nurse at the nursing station, had assured them that there was no reason to expect trouble. She'd been doing checkups on Mom all winter. Mom sat with the fan blowing in her face as she sewed the last flower on the little embroidered gown she was making for the baby.

I was learning to embroider, but finding it very tedious. I was using the embroidery thread that I got for my birthday and large hoops that Mom said would make the sewing easier. Huh! The white cloth was sandwiched between the inside and outside hoops and pulled tight. I'd drawn a nice flower in the centre of it as my pattern, but it was now covered with blood stains. Mom had been very patient with me, but I kept pricking my fingers. I just didn't know where the needle would pop out on the other side of the hoop when I pushed it in. Almost always, it ended up being right into my finger! Still, I liked embroidering much better than beading. I'd figured out how to make little flowers, and I'd sewn quite a few on my shirts.

Just then Dad and Mike came into the house laughing. Mom lifted her head from her sewing and asked, "What's so funny?" Mike sat down and smiled at Mom, knowing that she was still waiting for him to tell the story. She pretended to throw her sewing bag at him.

Dad turned from the counter with two cups of coffee, set one down for Mike, and said, "We stopped by at Gish's house and remember when he said he was going out to get some wood yesterday? Well, he did. He'd gone out in his canoe to the other end of the lake and loaded it up with dry wood. The logs were about eight feet long and he'd stuck them in like a bunch of matchsticks sticking out the front of the canoe. There was only one still left on the ground when he finished and there was no room for it with the others, so he figured he could just balance it on top of the other logs. Once he got it in place, he started paddling toward home.

"The wind came up about halfway across the lake and the waves started rocking the canoe. He managed to balance the canoe all the way toward his boat landing. But he was still out about fifty feet when the loose log slipped off the pile and the bottom end wedged itself in the middle rung of the canoe. Gish tried to balance it, but a wave hit the canoe and over it went! He found himself floundering around amongst the floating logs and he tried to grab on to them, but they kept rolling and slipping away.

"As you know, Gish doesn't swim. Well, down he went again and just when he was getting tired, his feet hit the bottom of the lake and he kicked. His head popped up well away from the floating logs and the overturned canoe. Then he thought, 'The logs float, so make like a log.' He straightened his body and kicked his feet up. He noticed that his old workboots were gone. His legs stayed up, but then his head went down a couple more times as he flailed his arms around. Finally, he said, he held his arms very straight at his sides, and suddenly his face cleared the water. He breathed and breathed and floated. He tried turning his head to see the shoreline, but he couldn't find it. When he started moving his hands, flapping them in the water, he realized he was moving. Then he flapped the left hand only, and he turned to the right. When he flapped his right hand, he turned to the left. He tried his right hand several times and he could see that the logs were moving toward his head and suddenly the treetops came into view. Now with both hands flapping, and his feet kicking up and down, he was a floating log speeding toward shore! He says he was moving pretty fast when suddenly his head crashed into a rock! As he was moaning and his hands grabbed his head, his body bent and suddenly his bum hit the sandy bottom of the lake. He was on shore! He was right at the rock that sits where he normally pulls up his canoe. He said that was when he broke into a loud laugh as he sat there rubbing his head. He watched as both his overturned canoe and all the logs floated to shore. He was able to collect them with the canoe after that."

Mom had stopped sewing and she sat there shaking her head, "*Anina*, to think that he could have drowned out there and no one around to see him."

Mike said, "Yeah, he's the only one home down at that shoreline too. The other three houses are empty right now. Summer holidays. Where did your sister go, John?"

Dad said, "Joe's taken Lucy and the girls to his family's place in a small tourist town in southern Ontario somewhere. They own a tourist gift shop there. They get overrun with tourists in the summer and it's practically a ghost town in the winter, he says."

Since Joe and Lucy had left on their holidays, Maggie had moved home and we were sharing a bedroom. There always seemed to be lots of people in the house now, which made it hard for me to practice my songs. Miss Tish, the music teacher, had taken an interest in my singing after the school choir's performance at the community centre at Christmas. She brought an electronic keyboard into class that she used to teach me different notes. It was easier than I thought. I'd already learned something about musical notes at school in Nibika the year before I left. Now I was learning how the notes were strung together in measures and how they became songs. Miss Tish had started giving me music sheets of songs with the words on them. Now I could sing a song even if I'd never heard it before, just by looking at the notes on the staff. Miss Tish would call me to come and sing whenever the teachers had one of their get-togethers. I'd sing while she played the keyboard. I was nervous each time, but once I began singing, I was totally oblivious to the people around me.

Mom came home from work one day and said that a woman had come into the office to ask her if I could sing at her wedding. She wanted to change some words to a song to make it more personal. She gave me a CD with the song on it. I played it and went into a giggling fit! It was a real sappy love song and I couldn't imagine standing up in public and singing something like this. But, after some discussion with Mom about the wording, I figured I could do it. After changing this and that, I decided I could get over my embarrassment. I called the woman, who was named Sandra, to check the wording with her and she loved it. I told her I didn't play an instrument, but she said she knew just the right person to play the guitar for me.

I would be singing at the wedding reception at the community centre that coming Saturday for the couple. It was on Wednesday at lunch when the phone rang and Sandra, the bride-to-be, said that "guitar boy" would be at the centre that evening to practice the song. So right after supper, I went to the centre with the song sheet in hand. I pushed the door open and there were people there decorating the room for the wedding reception. A woman came toward me and said, "Abby! I'm Sandra and over there is the guitar boy." I turned and saw Abraham standing there with a guitar resting on his foot! His hair was jet black and he had a sweatshirt and jeans on. He was taller than the last time I saw him. For some reason, I got very flustered and tried to ignore my pounding heart, thinking, dang! Why did it have to be him! But I smiled and took a deep breath and walked toward Abraham.

I stopped in front of him and he said, "Hi."

I answered, "Hi." I looked at my music sheet and couldn't think of anything more to say.

He said, "There's a room back there." I nodded and followed him as he made his way around some boxes to the large storage room. He found a box to sit on and I sat down on an overturned wash bucket.

"Have you been practicing?" I asked. He nodded and began strumming the opening chords. He was really quite good!

I began singing softly to the music and he said, "Louder." Suddenly, he was in control of the practice session. He even had me repeat the places where I'd changed the wording. It wasn't too bad. I began to relax and we repeated the song several more times before I sang all the way through it without corrections. Later, Mom and Dad laughed when I told them who "guitar boy" turned out to be.

I asked Mom if I could get my hair cut by Mary's mom for the wedding reception. She got up and rummaged around her dresser before she came back and handed me a ten-dollar bill. Suddenly I felt very guilty that I was going to waste ten dollars on a haircut. I shook my head. "No, that's okay. It was a crazy idea."

She smiled. "No, it was a good idea. A nice haircut would be good." So I grabbed my coat and ran out and down the street to Mary's house. When I got there, her mom, Charlotte, wasn't in, so Mary and I went through the hairstyle magazines and picked out one that had the hair layered and flowing back in gentle waves. Yeah, that would look nice on me. My bangs had grown to the end of my chin by then.

When Charlotte came in, I gave her the money and went into the living room. She had plastic on the floor with a chair sitting in the middle. I sat down on the chair and she came in with a comb and scissors. She glanced at the hairstyle I'd picked and I heard the scissors snipping their way across my head. Then she styled my hair with a curling iron and mist from her water spray. I went over to the mirror apprehensively, but I was very happy when I saw my reflection. Mary exclaimed, "Wow, that turned out great!"

When I got home, Dad and Mom were sitting at the table. They smiled in approval and Dad said, "Wow! What a pretty face!" I felt immediately embarrassed and hurried to my room.

When Saturday came, I put on one of my nice dresses from Goom. I picked the soft blue one with the fancy lacing at the front and Mom took a picture of me. This was my singing debut. She said she was going to frame one picture and send another copy to Goom. Mary was coming with me and bringing a tape recorder. She was going to record the song for Mom and Dad to listen to when I got home. When we walked into the community centre, Mary nudged me and I turned and saw Abraham already at the podium on the stage. He wore a freshly pressed black shirt and pants. All of a sudden, I felt nervous. I'd actually have to stand up there and sing! People had just arrived from the wedding ceremony at the church and they were milling around, finding seats. There would be an announcement, then I would sing the song while the new couple danced to it on the stage. After that, the reception would begin and there was already a feast laid out on the tables.

I went over to Abraham while Mary set up the tape recorder by the speakers. I whispered to him, "I didn't think we'd be on the stage. I thought we'd be sitting down." I noticed he had really long black eyelashes.

He leaned closer and whispered, "Don't worry. Just focus on the newlyweds. They'll be dancing while you're singing and all eyes will be on them." I nodded. Then the master of ceremonies walked to the microphone and made the announcements. I didn't pay attention to what he was saying, my heart was beating so hard. I wished I could get over this nervousness. I took a big breath and then Abraham nudged my foot. It was time. The guitar started softly, then gradually grew louder and right on cue, my voice came out loud and clear and then I calmed down. The couple moved to the stage and began to dance. The groom wore a tuxedo and the bride was in a white wedding gown. They were so beautiful! Then it was the last verse and the song ended. Claps and hoots erupted from the audience and Abraham and I also clapped for the couple.

When Abraham and I stepped off the stage, the bride's maid of honour came over to us and gave each of us an envelope. I thanked her and locked eyes with Abraham because I hadn't a clue that we were going to get anything. He shrugged and grinned at me before he leaned over and whispered, "Well done, White-Throated Sparrow!" I was taken aback and didn't know what to say, and then Mary was there with the tape recorder and we hurried out the door.

When we got outside, the sun was just setting and I waited until we got to the shortcut trail to our house over the rock outcrop before I opened the envelope. It held money! Mary and I ran all the way home and everyone was at the table when we came running in. I put the envelope on the table and Mom was the first to reach out and open it. She closed it again and put it back on the table with her eyes on Dad. Dad reached over and opened it, counted the money, and said, "One hundred dollars!"

Mary asked, "What are you going to buy with it?"

Dad looked at me and said, "Let's talk about this later." He picked up the envelope and gave it to Mom and she went and put it in the top dresser drawer where she kept important papers.

When she came back in, she said, "Okay, let's listen to that tape recorder. We've just been bursting to hear it!" Mary pushed the rewind button, and I held my breath as she pushed "play." The gentle guitar music started and I sat down on a chair and closed my eyes, reliving the moment.

When it was done, and the clapping and hoots erupted on the tape, Dad said, "Wow, it sounds like they really, really liked you guys!"

I said, "No, we were clapping for the newlyweds who had finished dancing too. I didn't think it was for us."

Mary said, "No way! They were all looking at you and Abraham! The applause was for you guys!" I was thinking that it was a good thing that I didn't know it was for us because otherwise I might have cried or something embarrassing like that.

Mom said, "I called Goom but she wasn't home. I wanted to know if she was coming on Monday. If she is, let's wait until she gets here and we can play the song for her. It'll be so much better than playing it for her over the phone." That decided, Mary and I ran to my bedroom, where we went through some more songs to see which one I could sing next.

On Sunday, Dad dropped me and Mom off at the sisters' place to pick up some more finished mukluks in a cardboard box. While we were there, we dropped off another bag of beaded moccasin vamps—those were the tops of the moccasins—and mitt cuffs when the rain started. Another thunderstorm! We'd just got into the sisters' house when the rain came down and the Thunderbirds rumbled above us.

"Cover the mirror quick!" Minnie said urgently. "Don't forget the tub outside, sister!"

Lizzy turned to me. "Cover anything that's shiny. Cover up all shiny things quick!" I spun around in the middle of the room. Cover everything shiny? What for? I ran to put a towel over the mirror that hung over the wash basin by the door. Mom sat down at the table and watched us all scurrying around.

"Why? Why do you need to cover up shiny things?" I asked Minnie as Lizzy went running by with a kerchief that she put over her head as she dashed outside to throw the old porch rug over the shiny galvanized washtub that lay overturned beside the door.

Minnie smiled. "Because if you don't, the Thunderbirds will see their reflections and think the lighting is coming back at them and then they'll strike back!" she said as she left the room.

Lizzy came back inside the house and added, "Don't you know that electricity comes up from the ground and the Thunderbirds connect with it? That's how lightning strikes. They think something else is shooting lightning at them. Every time lightning flashes in the sky, it's actually the eyes of a Thunderbird opening and sending out a lightning bolt."

Just then, Minnie came back into the kitchen and sat down at the table with us and lit her pipe, just like Gish would often do. Mom poured more tea into the cups from the teapot that sat in the middle of the table. It looked funny because it had a furry toque over it to keep the pot warm. This was the first time that I'd been around the women during a thunderstorm. I was still learning and now I realized that I'd seen Mom put a towel over the bathroom mirror during storms. We sat in silence while the thunder boomed overhead. I was petting one of the cats that didn't seem to mind me touching her. Then Lizzy began telling a story about the time there had been a horrific storm when they were young girls.

I started thinking about the thunderstorms out there when we were camping. They seemed louder and closer then, and you could feel each boom vibrate right through you as the ground shook. Well, that could have been because we weren't inside an insulated house. We had just the canvas over our heads. The women laughed and I realized that I'd missed the whole story.

After the storm, I went out to hang up the soaked porch rug and saw a massive rainbow arched across the sky over the island out in the channel. The air was filled with the smell of moist earth and the mosquitoes were out in full force, rejuvenated and mighty hungry after the rain.

Minnie's tobacco smoke had dissipated by the time I came back in and we were all at the table again. Minnie took off her black kerchief that had big red flower designs on it and folded it into a triangle. When she knew I was watching carefully, she began to roll the wide end. I watched her hands carefully roll the cloth and then suddenly a solid body emerged and in one pull, a head popped up and then she separated the two corners at the tip and they became big, long ears. It was a rabbit!

Lizzy laughed at the look on my face and said to her sister, "You were supposed to tell a story while you were doing your folding!"

Minnie replied, "You know I can't talk and fold at the same time!"

Lizzy gave her kerchief to her sister, saying, "Make a frog and we'll tell the story." I watched Minnie roll up both ends of the square cloth, and Lizzy began telling a story about a frog that lived in the swamp behind their house. Then she asked me, "What's the frog's name?"

Without thinking, I said, "Finnias." So Finnias the Frog began his adventure as we took turns continuing the story. After that, the frog kerchief was turned into a partridge and it actually had wings! Suddenly, a truck pulled up the driveway and we realized that we'd been there for so long that it was almost suppertime! Dad was there to pick us up. Minnie said that there were many more folded birds and animals that could be made and I promised to come back and learn them.

When we got home, Dad said that he was taking the boys to go hunting for partridge after supper. I sighed that he didn't pick me to go with him because he knew I didn't like going if the boys were coming. They were annoying and I liked hunting with Dad by myself.

The phone rang while I was still sitting at the table sulking. Mom answered it and turned to wink at me. Goom was coming to the blueberry-picking camp! I was so excited that I ran to clean up my room for her.

Goom's plane came in the next day, which happened to be very windy. I was feeling sorry for her, since a bumpy flight is the worst thing for motion sickness. I went with Dad alone since Blink was off playing somewhere. The landing strip had a little shack that served as the airport. We sat down on a bench beside the building and waited for the plane to arrive. Finally we could hear it coming. When it came to a stop beside the building, I had to put my kerchief over my face as the sand swirled and blew from the airplane propellers. Then the door was pulled open and people began to descend the stairs, and there was Goom. I could tell right away that she wasn't feeling well. Her skirt billowed up when she stepped to the ground and Dad went and helped her to the truck. All she did was plant a kiss on my forehead as she settled into the passenger seat.

"Go, before I puke on my lap," she said as Dad got in after throwing her bags into the back of the truck. I settled down on the seat behind her. I reached around and patted her shoulder and Dad tore off down the street with the old tires stirring a cloud of sand behind us on the gravel road.

When we arrived, Mom was at the door and she came to help Goom off the truck. Once inside, she lay down on the bed that Mom had made up for her in her sewing room at the back of the house. This would be the baby's room when it came. We found ourselves whispering in the kitchen as Mom went about making supper. About an hour later, Mom had thawed and sliced moose meat into the frying pan and I was preparing the vegetables when the door flung open and Maggie and Jane came in, giggling and laughing. Mom immediately put her finger up to her lips to get them to be quiet, but the door was flung open again and Blink ran inside, yelling, "Where's Grandma? Where is she?"

Before Mom could tell him to be quiet, Goom yelled from her room, "I'm okay now, come here!" Blink tore off down the hallway. We could hear them giggling and talking. Several minutes later, they both entered the kitchen just as Mom turned the last piece of meat over in the pan.

Goom smiled. "The smell of moose meat cooking will bring me to my feet anytime!"

Blink added, "As long as you're not dead at the time!"

Shocked, Mom opened her mouth to reproach him, but we all burst out laughing and Mom said, "Now, look at what you've done. I'll never ever fry another piece of moose meat without thinking of Grandma as a zombie, walking in at the smell of it!" Goom was still laughing as we sat down and began our first meal with her at the table.

The next day, after a visit to the period-clothing room at Chief Paulie's house, Goom decided to show me how to sew pants for the kids. As she said, "You can't just have grown-ups running around by themselves. After all, where did *they* come from?" Paulie just smiled and Mom and I laughed. Chief Paulie had bought another sewing machine to handle the thicker leather pieces that needed to be sewn, saving the ladies many hours of hand sewing. When we got home, Goom pulled out a thick woolen material that Mom had and cut out the first pair of pants for me to sew. I decided to try sewing them together as a surprise when she went off with Mom to the Band office. Well, it seemed simple enough. I sewed one of the leg pieces together and up around the arching crotch, straight up to the waist. I was just about to start up the other leg when they arrived home with Blink running in front of them. I was so excited to show off my work that I shook the piece and held it out for all to see. There was something wrong! I held it up at the waist, but the bottom half was a large flat piece with a pointy thing sticking straight out at the crotch! Goom and Mom doubled up into a laughing fit and Blink was clapping in glee. He said, "Why does Abby keep making pointy tubes? Remember her mitts that looked like E.T.'s thumb? Now, what is that pointy thing between the legs supposed to be for?"

I threw the material on top of the sewing machine, went off to my room and closed the door, thinking, "I'll never, ever sew anything ever again in my whole life!" I flung open my window and breathed in the fresh air as I lay down on the bed. I could hear them talking in the kitchen and then I heard the click, click of the sewing machine. That was probably Goom fixing the pants. I must have sewn the same leg front pieces together. I began to smile. Yeah, I guess that was pretty funny!

We were sitting around at the table when I asked Goom if she'd like to listen to my first taped song. That was when Mom remembered the hundred dollars in the envelope. I ran and got the envelope for her and put it on the table. Dad said, "She got one hundred dollars for that wedding reception song that she sang."

Goom arched her eyebrows and smiled. "Wow! A hundred dollars for one song?"

Dad looked at Mom and said, "We can't let Abby have it. What I mean to say is, we can't take that amount of money."

Goom looked puzzled and said, "They appreciated Abby's voice and that was their thanks to her. I think she should be allowed to keep it. It's her money." I glanced at Goom and silently thanked her, although I didn't know what I'd do with the money.

Finally, Dad looked at Mom and said, "Maybe Grandma's right. She does have a gift and she should share it. If people are willing to pay for her time and effort, I guess that would be okay."

So I could keep it!

I stood there looking at the envelope and asked, "What am I going to do with it? Where will I put it?"

Goom said, "Well, I could open a bank account for you in town and deposit it there. Every time you get some money for your singing, you could send it to me and I'll put it into your account each time. That way, when you're ready to come to high school, you'll have extra money sitting there waiting for you."

Dad looked at Mom and she smiled. "That's a very good idea, Mom." And so it was settled. Goom took the money and put it into her purse and shoved it under the bed. Then she pushed the "play" button on the tape recorder. She really loved the song too!

On the Monday, everyone piled into their boats and we headed out to the blueberry-picking island. Maggie was back at Aunt Lucy's place and didn't want to come with us. That was a relief to me because I didn't want Jane there either, and I was looking forward to quality time with Goom all to myself. It was a beautiful calm day and the boat ride was much appreciated as the wind blew against our faces, cooling us off. We quickly set up our campsite and everyone headed off doing their thing. Mom and Goom were in the tent setting up the bedding with moss, just in case the baby arrived while we were out here.

I wandered off by myself down the beach. I was feeling left out for some reason. Everything and everyone was focused on Mom now. Goom was busy with the planning and preparation for the baby's arrival. Mom was constantly surrounded by the women as they helped her move about. With everything being on the ground, she needed help getting up and even putting her shoes on, and I felt like I was just getting in the way.

The camp was humming with noise as the sun settled down to the treetops. I stood down the beach by the rock cliff and listened to the echoes of dogs barking, the boys laughing, an axe on wood, seagulls and birds, and the occasional cry of a loon that filled the air. It was very peaceful. As I slowly wandered back to camp and brushed flies away from my face, I realized that everyone was already around the fire and I sat down to our evening meal.

A few days later, there was a lull in the berry picking. Mom and Goom had gone along the shoreline to the point where the sisters were smoking the two moosehides that they'd brought with them. Everyone else had gone to fish or hunt. Ching had wood to cut for the fire and Gish had gone off to pick some herbs and root medicines with his birchbark basket. I decided to head along in the opposite direction, thinking I'd see if I could find some partridge for Ching.

As I walked along, I checked every bush and branch but there was no movement anywhere. It was very hot and muggy in the bush and the horseflies were continually buzzing around my head. I came toward the shoreline at the rocky point and saw someone sitting on the highest ledge. I knew from the back of his head that it was Abraham.

I approached the shoreline from below the rock and stepped out onto the sand beach. He turned and said, "I heard you coming from a long way. You make a lot of noise, you know."

I snorted, "I guess that explains why I never saw a thing in the bush!" He laughed and I said, "You know, that's exactly where you were the first time I saw you here on the island. You were twirling that big button and making that whirring noise that got Gish all upset with you, remember?"

He laughed. "Did the high winds ever come that day?"

I shrugged. "I don't know. I can't remember."

He said, "Why don't you climb up here?"

I looked at the loose rock ledge and decided that climbing up there in a skirt would be a tough scramble. I shook my head, sat down on the sand and said, "Why don't you come down here?" I heard the cascading rocks behind me before he flopped down at my side. I asked, "Could you teach me how to play guitar?"

He turned toward me. "Why? If I taught you to play then you wouldn't need me anymore."

I smiled. "Well, two guitars would sound better. Why don't you sing? Sing backup for me. That would be nice."

He laughed. "I used to sing but then my voice started changing and I still never know when I am going to croak!"

I laughed and suddenly he turned and dumped a handful of sand on my lap, saying, "Don't you laugh!" Suddenly I heard the camp whistle. What was that for? I knew it was far too early for supper, so it must have been an emergency.

I jumped up and dumped the sand off my skirt onto his head before I turned to run, saying, "Camp whistle. Gotta go!" I turned to look back and he was gone.

When I ran up the trail to camp, Ching was putting on his gloves beside the woodpile and there was no one else around. He turned to look at me just as Goom came around the path. She stopped beside me by the smouldering campfire and I noticed Gish coming from the bush with his basket. So I guess it was Ching who had blown the whistle. Gish settled down beside the campfire and I handed him the washing bowl with water that he normally used to clean the roots and leaves that he had in his basket. Finally Goom said in Ojibwe, "So what has brought us all here?"

Gish lifted his head and asked, "Did someone call a meeting? I didn't hear anything."

Ching picked up the power saw and said to Goom, "Ask her where she's been."

Then he turned and walked into the bush. Goom was looking at me with raised eyebrows, waiting. I sat down beside Gish and said, "I saw Abraham by the shoreline when I was in the bush looking for a partridge, so I went to the shore and sat down on the sand beach and he came and sat down beside me. Then I heard the whistle."

Goom said, "So Ching blew the whistle because he saw you with Abraham?"

I looked at Gish and said, "Remember that time last summer, there was that boy up on the rocks with the whirling button? That was Abraham. That's what we were talking about."

Gish dropped a pile of roots into the washing bowl and said, "Yes, Abraham. I met him once, out in the swamp, after that. He had three rabbits tied to his belt and he had a .22. I've never seen a kid shoot rabbits like that. Just to see rabbits in the summer is something, let alone get close enough to shoot them."

He began scraping the bark off and cutting off the tiny shoots in the root that he held in his hands. I felt proud for Abraham, hearing about his hunting skill, and I also silently thanked Gish for supporting me. Goom reached for my arm, saying, "Come, we'd better go tell your mother what the whistle was about."

When we got to the smoking hides, Mom was leaning against a tree in the shade and asked me, "Where have you been?"

Goom nudged me. "That's what the whistle was about." Mom raised her eyebrows at me, so I repeated the story about Abraham.

Mom turned to Goom and wondered out loud, "Why would Ching blow the whistle?"

The two sisters were just coming back from the lake with buckets of water. When they were filled in on the story, Lizzy said, "You spent a lot of time with Ching this winter, didn't you?"

Minnie added, "Ching might just be overprotective. I think he may be overcompensating for the fact that he doesn't have children of his own."

Goom reached up to pin up the hair that kept escaping from the bun on top of her head and said, "So I was right then. He thought it unseemly for a young woman to be with a young man unchaperoned. Ha! I figured as much."

I asked, "Why did he do that anyway? He looked at me like I did something wrong."

Lizzy smiled. "Ching is an old body who still believes in the old ways of doing things, that's all."

I was still feeling hurt that Ching thought I had done something wrong. I sat down on the blanket beside the Siamese cats, who were out in the open but leashed to their cage. I scratched one behind the ear and it started to purr. I was lucky that it turned out to be the friendly one; the other one would have scratched me. I could never tell them apart.

The next day, the sun came up on a clear blue sky and after breakfast, when he noticed me hanging around the shoreline by myself again, Dad asked if I'd like to go fishing with him. Some time later, Dad had the motor running as slowly as he could as we trolled along the shoreline. I'd just thrown my first perfect cast when I noticed a snake right beside the boat in the water. I grabbed my paddle and backstroked, yelling, "Dad, there's a snake right beside me! Is he going to get inside the boat? There it is! Hit it! Hit it! Let's take off!"

Dad turned the boat around and since the motor was running, we reeled in our lines. He turned the motor on full blast and we raced straight across the lake. He said, "That was a garter snake. He wouldn't have hurt you."

I answered, "Yeah, but I just don't like snakes and I've never seen one in the water either!"

Dad decided to turn the boat up a creek and chug through the weeds to get into another small lake. We had to stop in the middle of the creek to pull the motor up. It was thick with weeds and we paddled the rest of the way. Coming back to camp was harder. Dad said from behind me, "Since the beavers built that dam up ahead, it'll get pretty dry here quickly. It was easier coming up, but I think we'll have to get out and pull the boat over."

As I put my shoulders into the paddle, another snake came right toward me in the water. I pushed it away, but it kept coming and I yelled at Dad, "It's another snake! Dad, go! Go!" The snake went by me and now Dad was splashing it with his paddle, but still it kept coming! I saw it dive under when Dad splashed his paddle on it. I was so shaken that I refused to get out of the boat when Dad pulled the boat over the dam. I hated snakes! And it was even creepier that they could swim and dive in the water.

That evening, when we sat around the fire, I told Gish about the two swimming snakes we'd seen that day. He seemed alarmed and kept looking over at Mom and Dad with a meaningful expression on his face. Finally, I could no longer stand the suspense. "What? What does it mean to see snakes in the water?"

Gish took a deep breath and said, "Well, swimming snakes are a bad sign. It generally means that they're there to tell you that there's some bad news coming your way—like someone's going to die. So they're trying to warn you to prepare yourself that someone close to you will be going off on the journey to the other world." I heaved a big sigh. I was really beginning to hate bad omens, all those "bad news" birds and creatures! The snakes had been really weird, though. Even though I didn't want to believe any of this stuff, I'd worry for the longest time, until I'd eventually stop waiting for the bad things to happen.

It was very early the next morning when I smelled woodsmoke. No, it was more like moss smoke. I could hear Mom and Dad talking. I turned to see that Goom, Mom, and Dad had already gone out of the tent. Only Blink still lay sprawled out on his bedding. I jumped up and hurriedly pulled my clothes and shoes on and went out. Everyone was standing around the campfire and there was thick smoke everywhere. It hung over the lake, almost like a thick fog. The trees were also filled with smoke. The wind howled over the treetops and out onto the lake. That would mean that the waves were very high at the community shoreline.

I picked up the plate that Mom held out to me. I guessrd everyone else had already eaten. I must have slept in. I picked up the plate and sat down beside the campfire. The adults stood around with their coffee cups until Gish came up from the path to the shore. "I see people coming from the campsites at the other end," he said.

All the guys headed to shore to meet the other men, whom we could see walking on the sand beach toward our camp. There were four men. They stopped where our guys met them by the boats and they stood there chatting for awhile before the four men headed back to their camp.

Dad came up with Mike, while Ned and Ching went out to retrieve the fishnets from where they'd set them the previous evening.

Dad said, "They got a call on the satellite phone from the Band office. We're being told to come home immediately. Apparently, there's a huge forest fire coming our way very quickly."

The sisters glanced at each other and ran into their tent to pack. Goom and I also quickly went into our tent to pack our things, and so did Alice. Mom started cleaning up the food, and Gish began taking the tents down before we even finished packing. I saw Dad whip the sheet out from under Blink, who was still sleeping. He rolled over and came up howling in protest, which made everyone laugh. David came running into camp, all excited, and both he and Blink took off to find Wiener and Shingoos, who had apparently taken off in full pursuit of something straight into the bush.

"Who untied those dogs? Go find them. We can't leave without them!" Mike was yelling. I found myself standing in one spot with a growing pile of camp gear beside me, slowly turning around and observing the absolute chaos around me.

Gish came to a stop beside me and said, "Go take that pile beside you to the shore. Ned and Ching are coming back and those fish need to be cleaned before we go."

I grabbed some bags and ran down to the lake in time to see Ching jump out and pull the boat in. I ran back up to grab the large bowl and a knife, only to find that the camp food stuff had already been packed. I looked around at the boxes, trying to figure out where the bowl and knife could possibly be when I caught sight of Gish looking at me. I stopped and glanced at the birchbark basket on top of the woodpile. It had the knife sticking out of it. Gish came up to stand in front of me and softly said, "Take a deep breath and calm down. Things will go smoothly if you pay attention to what you're doing. Everything is always fine. There's no reason to panic."

I smiled and said, "I don't seem to be all here, that's all. I've never seen everyone move so fast at the same time." He let out a rasping laugh and looked around. I couldn't believe it, but everything was pretty much all packed and the tents were neatly folded in a pile. All that remained was to load the boats, and I still had fish to clean! I turned and ran down to the lake and saw two boats from the other campsite already heading home.

I'd just finished cleaning the fish and laying the fillets inside the basket when Alice, Ned, and the sisters took off in the boat. Ching and Gish's boat was loaded with the dogs, bedding, food, and tents. I just had time to wash my hands when I got into the boat with Dad, Goom, and Mom. Mike and Linda took the boys and the last of the stuff into their boat and together we headed back to the community. I wondered what would happen if the fire came to the community. Could it burn the whole place down?

There were two more boats coming up behind us from the other camp. Ned's and Ching's boats were out in front of us and I soon realized why they'd hung back in front of us when the waves began to get higher and higher. Soon the waves were topped with whitecaps and Mom had to lean back on the sleeping bags as the boat pitched and rolled and landed on the back of another wave. Dad had to speed up a bit because the waves were washing over the back of the boat and water started to come in. The two boats in front were pushing the waves down for us, but I could see that they were having the same trouble. We began going faster and faster and I could see their propellers clearing the water at times.

Finally we could see the water splashing on the rocks at the shore, and we headed to our landing as the other boats veered off to their own landing sites. Dad headed right to shore and a wave pushed us all the way onto land. Goom, at the front, just stepped out and Dad stepped into the water to keep the boat from getting swept sideways. We helped Mom get out of the boat last, but there was clearly something wrong by the way she held the side of her huge belly. Goom stood beside her, while Dad pulled the boat in. Then he picked up Mom and carried her to the house.

Mom was protesting, but Goom was already out in front to get the door open. I ran up with whatever I could grab from the boat and began running back and forth with the rest of the stuff that I could carry up to the house.

When I finally got in the house, Mom was resting on the couch beside the stove and Goom had got the stove going. I asked, "Where's Dad?" Goom turned from the stove, saying, "He ran off to get the nurse. Her water has broken and the baby is knocking."

I stood there for a second, saying, "Water? The baby is knocking? You mean the baby is coming?"

I ran to Mom and she smiled from her propped-up position and said, "Yep, the baby is coming. As babies normally take their time, it may not be until tomorrow before we see him or her."

I glanced at Goom and she smiled. "It's okay. Everything will be fine." Why did people keep saying that to me all day? Just then I noticed a familiar crunch, crunch, crunch noise echoing inside my head and I froze. I had a corner of my kerchief in my mouth and I'd already neatly sliced three holes through it with my teeth. My beautiful purple silk kerchief! I stopped and turned to the kitchen table. I looked at the boxes and bags and wondered what needed to be unpacked first. Where was Maggie? Just then, the door flew open and Maggie ran in with her hair all dishevelled. "Evacuation! They're evacuating everyone!"

CHAPTER TWELVE

A New Arrival
Amidst Chaos

Evacuation! Goom froze where she had just put a large pot of water on the stove. Mom lay looking at her belly and I whispered, "No!" Just then an airplane roared overhead and I could tell that it was the float plane coming in for a landing. I asked Maggie, "Are they also using the float plane to evacuate us? What about the landing strip?"

Maggie flopped down on the kitchen chair and said, "Well, the scheduled plane has already come and gone and isn't due to arrive until tomorrow morning again, but there will be one coming in this afternoon for the elders and sick children or people with asthma . . . Mom? What's wrong?"

Mom had let out a groan and Maggie was there in a second. I sank down on the kitchen chair and twiddled my thumbs on my lap. Goom was still busy laying out a bedding place beside the stove and then Maggie grabbed the phone. I heard her say, "Are the sisters still there? Yeah, Alice. There's an evacuation. You heard? Send the sisters over; the nurses are busy with the sick elders and children that are being flown out right now. Okay."

Why didn't I think to do that? Meanwhile, Goom didn't seem to be too concerned. Mom was giggling from the couch when Maggie said that she'd seen Dad go tearing across the green grass from the nursing station, heading for the Band office. That was how she knew we'd returned home.

I'd managed to get myself going again and made a pot of tea and began preparing some bannock that I fried on the stove. Next, I made some blueberry jam from the two coolers full of blueberries that we'd brought with us in our boat. We'd just settled around the kitchen table when the sisters arrived with their cats in their cage. After they checked Mom over, changed her dress, and got her settled on the bedding on the floor that Goom had made, they declared that Mom couldn't be moved. They didn't want to take the chance of her having the baby on the plane. So they settled down to making lunch with the fish that I'd hastily cleaned at camp.

It was a noisy, excited chatter that Dad walked into just when lunch was being served. He stopped at the door and he was visibly relieved as he let out a huge sigh. Mom was at the table and she smiled, saying, "Come, you're just in time for lunch." Dad kicked off his shoes, strode to the table, and took his seat beside Mom. He told us about the commotion in the community and how people were scrambling, trying to arrange rides to the airport and loading people on the float plane. There had been a quick emergency meeting of the Chief and council and now everyone knew what they were responsible for. Dad, it seemed, had volunteered to stay behind and look after the pets that had been left behind and to keep an eye on residences that had been vacated.

A group of firefighters had been gathered and they'd already gone out to see if they could head off the fire with a firebreak. The forest fire was still coming straight toward the community. Answering my questioning glance, Dad explained that a firebreak was usually a trench to stop the fire on the ground, or they would burn a section of underbrush to burn anything that could catch on fire.

All that afternoon airplanes flew over the community, coming and going. We sat in the house, playing cards and telling stories. The sisters made themselves at home in my bedroom, and Linda called to say that Blink would be staying at their place. So far, there hadn't been a call for a general evacuation of all the residents.

Mad Dog and Kitty arrived just before supper and shared their stories of having to get Kitty's visiting parents onto the float plane to head to the nearest town. There was also a boy getting on the plane who wouldn't let go of his puppy and the evacuation organizers had to pull the dog from his arms. There were no pets allowed on the plane. I saw Minnie and Lizzy glance at their cats and the same stubborn set of their chins made it clear there was no way they were going to be separated from their pets. I smiled. I knew I'd feel the same way if I didn't have Dad to look after Ki-Moot.

All that evening Dad periodically appeared to check on Mom and then he was off again. They were monitoring the fire and the councillors were on call all the time. Ned and Alice came in from time to time to see if there was anything the ladies needed. Linda was on the phone with Mom almost every half-hour. Mike was still busy at the Band office somewhere. Just before midnight, Goom told me and Maggie to go to bed, while the other ladies sat in the living room waiting and trying to keep Mom comfortable. Mom would moan from time to time but otherwise appeared in good spirits.

The next morning I awoke to thick smoke in my bedroom. Maggie had already left the bed and I hurried down the hall and found the women softly whispering from the table, where they sat drinking coffee and eating their breakfast. I didn't even smell the pancakes and bacon that sat on the table; everything smelled of forest fire! Mom was now lying on her side, beads of sweat glistening on her forehead as I knelt beside her. I wrung out the cloth that was in the sink and wiped her face. She looked very tired. "Did you get any sleep at all?" I asked.

She smiled and took my hand, kissing my fingers. "Sleep? Oh, there's no sleep with this little one." Just then, I almost freaked when I saw a huge bump rise up and cross the middle of her belly to the other side. She sighed, "A foot, maybe?" I must have gone pale because she was now handing me the cloth. I wiped my own face, thinking that I could possibly keel over right that minute. I got up and went to the washroom to brush my teeth and wash my face. I combed my hair nicely before I came out. After I'd got dressed, Goom had my food dished out on a plate and they sat talking as I ate. Dad had apparently arrived after midnight and had left again early that morning after four hours of sleep.

I'd just finished my breakfast when the guys arrived. Dad and Mike had a quick breakfast and were gone again. Ching hadn't slept the previous night and he looked exhausted. The women had sat him down and heaped his plate full of food when they realized he hadn't eaten since camp the morning before. Right after he finished eating, they told him to lie down on the couch for a few minutes. He no sooner put his feet up and he was sound asleep. Right around that time, we noticed that the wind had suddenly changed and the air cleared. We went around opening all the windows in the house to let the fresh air in.

Suddenly, the women went into a flurry of activity just before lunch. Mom was groaning and they were all around her, with Lizzy standing over her with a piece of cardboard she was using for a fan. She swung it slowly back and forth over Mom's drenched face. The door opened and Dad came in with the nurse, Sara Jones. She came and knelt beside Mom, and Minnie moved aside from where she had been at Mom's feet. Goom was behind Mom, propping her up and helping her push. Sara washed her hands and examined Mom and her face stretched into a big smile. "Sophie, you're almost there!" Suddenly, a snort and loud snoring erupted from the couch. We'd forgotten that Ching was lying there still asleep!

Dad just smiled and put a finger to his lips and whispered, "Let's see if he can sleep through this."

The phone rang and Dad had to go, but he said that he would be right back. He'd just gone out the door when right at that moment, Mom had another contraction and I knew that the baby was coming. I went into my bedroom and found Maggie lying in bed. I hadn't realized she'd left the living room.

We lay there talking for awhile. What would we name the baby if it was a boy? What if it was a girl? Wouldn't it be nice if we had a girl? Then we heard the baby's cries! I went to jump up, but Maggie grabbed my arm and we both lay there until I heard Sara say, "Grandma Beth! Come see!" I was about to jump up again, but Maggie still held me down.

"What? I want to see!" I said as I pulled my arm away.

She looked at me and said, "The afterbirth still has to come out and they still have to wash the baby, and two more bodies getting in the way isn't going to be appreciated!" I looked at her blankly. I had no idea what she was talking about. I turned and hurried down the hall and came into the room in time to see Goom reaching out to the blood-ringed, white-plastered little body that lay draped over Mom's stomach! I stood shocked at the scene and then I noticed that Goom was smoothing down the thick blond hair on the baby's head!

I retreated down the hall, ran into my room and stretched out on the bed beside Maggie again. She whispered, "So?"

I smiled as I looked up at the ceiling. "Goom's name is Beth! And the baby has blond hair!"

Maggie poppped up onto her elbow and looked down at me. "BLOND HAIR? Did you say blond hair?" I nodded and smiled.

She lay back down and said, "You must be mistaken. I know there's lots of white gooey stuff on babies when they're born. That's probably what you saw."

I lay there still smiling and said, "Goom's name is Beth and the baby's hair is definitely blond."

She propped herself up on her elbow again and looked down at me. "Why do you keep saying that Grandma's name is Beth. Of course her name is Beth. Didn't you know that?"

I shook my head. "Nope, I never knew or maybe I forgot. I've always called her Goom and everyone else called her Grandma."

She lay down with a sigh and said, "Chee, you are dumb sometimes. I was wanting to know if it was a boy or girl!"

I turned my head and said, "I don't know. The baby was lying on Mom's belly, facing her." Suddenly, the women burst out laughing and after some commotion, we heard Ching's voice. He must have woken up to the sight of the baby on the other side of the stove! We started giggling.

We heard someone dialling the phone and Goom talking. Then she appeared with the baby wrapped in one of the little blankets that Mom had so carefully embroidered along the seams. The baby had been washed clean and the soft blond hair lay wet on her little head. Goom placed her on the bed between us, saying, "Say hello to your little sister."

We each got up on our elbows and examined the little face. Her eyes were clamped shut and her tiny lips made sucking motions. We unwrapped her just enough to pull out her hands and they were so tiny and each little fingernail was so neatly shaped.

After a bit of time, we heard the door open and Dad's voice was coming down the hallway and then he was standing there looking down on us. He tipped his head as he examined the little one, then he reached down to pick her up. He held her up and suddenly her eyes opened and we saw them looking at each other and then Dad whispered, "Hello, my little one. Your daddy's here."

We jumped up and I exclaimed, "Her eyes aren't blue, are they? That's the colour of Goom's eyes!"

Dad answered, "I don't think so. I think all babies arrive with that colour in their eyes and then after awhile, they darken. The same thing with the hair. It may become light brown like yours, Maggie, later on. But right now, she's a blondie like her grandma!" He carried her off down the hallway and we followed. Ching was nowhere in sight when we came into the room.

Minnie and Lizzy had just finished cleaning up the bedding on the floor and Mom was back up on the couch. In a short time, nothing of the birthing place was in sight and the baby was passed around before Mom got to breast-feed her. So far, the baby hadn't cried since that initial shock when air must have hit her little body.

We noticed then that it was getting dark outside. Ching came in, saying, "There's a big storm coming. This is the first time I've been so happy to see rain! You can even see it coming halfway across the lake now." We all ran outside and, sure enough, there were huge, billowing clouds and the horizon was now barely visible with rain rather than smoke. By the time we sat down to supper, our overcrowded house was happy with noise and laughter. As anticipated, the focus of the story at the table was Ching waking up to find that a baby had been born just on the other side of the stove while he lay snoring!

Nurse Sara had stayed for supper and she was the last to leave. Ching took the sisters home with their cats right after supper and Linda and Mike had arrived with the boys to see the new baby. If Blink was disappointed at not having a brother, I couldn't tell. He was definitely pleased to see a blond-haired sister. Ned and Alice were busy with family, but they'd called to say that they'd come to see the baby tomorrow.

While Maggie and I were washing the dishes, Goom came up to us to say that she'd need one more gift. She'd brought only two gifts for the sisters for helping deliver the baby. She'd not counted on Nurse Sara being here too, so she was wondering what to give to the nurse from the store. Maggie immediately said, "There's nothing in the store for gifts!" I agreed. Then I remembered my hoard of beautiful silk kerchiefs that Goom had sent me. I'd only worn two. I gave one to Alice that time. I still had one left—the yellow one.

I smiled and said, "Grandma Beth, I do have one silk kerchief left. The yellow one. It would be a perfect gift for Nurse Sara. She wears yellow all the time!"

Grandma Beth looked at me and smiled. "You're a lifesaver, Abigail. I'll find you an especially special gift the next time I go to Vancouver." That settled, I ran to fetch the neatly wrapped kerchief that I'd stashed in the corner of my closet.

All the excitement and chaos of the fire was over now and things were back to normal. I was coming back from the Band office the next day when I met the sisters on the road. They were heading to the Chief's house with another bag of finished outfits. Lizzy suddenly pointed up to the sky and asked, "Do you see that?" I looked up and it was some time before I noticed what she was pointing at. A bird was flying around and around and gradually getting farther and farther away.

Minnie said, "The old woman is fishing again."

I looked at her and asked, "What old woman?"

Lizzy answered, "There's an old woman that lives up in the sky above the clouds and she fishes from a hole there and every once in awhile, she catches a bird and that little bird will just keep going in a circle round and round until it disappears up there."

Then Minnie said, "Now, if we had a knife, all we would have to do is swing it in a cutting motion and the bird would be able to fly free." I smiled and reached into my pants pocket under my skirt waist and pulled out my pocket knife. I flicked the blade up and gave it to Lizzy.

She took it and said, "Are you ready? Keep an eye on the bird." She made a slashing motion in the air with the knife. I saw the bird still going around and around, but then suddenly it flew free! It flew off into the treeline and the women looked at me, smiling. I took the knife back and giggled as I turned off the road to our house. I couldn't believe it!

Several weeks after the baby's birth, a decision still hadn't been made about what to name her. According to tradition, the naming of the baby depended on events that were happening at the time and who or what showed up at the point of birth or shortly after. After some debate among our family and the other four families of our group, it was decided that since Grandma had been there all the time, as had Nurse Sara and the two sisters, the only ones that shouldn't have been there were Ching, the two cats, the forest fire, and the storm afterwards. After some translation possibilities, everyone settled on the name Charlisse for Ching (Charlie). As for the middle name, the words "forest fire," "storm," and "cat" were too long for translation into Ojibwe, so we settled on the English version of "Fire-cat." So it came to be that my little sister was named Charlisse Firecat.

Ching had been busy with hauling the logs for the construction of the Dog Tracks office when the baby's name was picked, so we decided to throw a surprise potluck supper at our place that evening. The Dog Tracks group told him that he was to come over to our house because Dad wanted him to pick up something to hang on the name post of the new building. When Ching's ATV pulled up to our house that evening at supper-time, everyone was there.

Gish was there with his gift for Ching—a hot water bottle covered in rabbit fur made by the sisters to help him sleep. He got gifts from the others as well. Mike and Linda gave him a shiny new thermos bottle for coffee to help keep him awake when he needed to be; Ned and Alice gave him a new pair of fully beaded moosehide gloves; the sisters gave him a goose down quilt to go with the hot water bottle; Mad Dog and Kitty gave him a big bag of bullets and shells; we gave him a brand new bright red camp whistle; and Goom gave him a fancy pair of expensive sunglasses. The last gift, of course, was the baby's name.

Up to this time, Ching was totally confused and didn't understand what all the gifts were about, then he heard about his last gift. The poor man began to tremble, and everyone looked away to focus on something else as they continued the conversation. I glanced up to see that much as he was struggling to remain composed, tears had begun rolling down his face. Charlisse suddenly let out a wail and a screech and Mom handed over the squirming bundle to Ching and said, "Here, Namesake, hold her while I get her diaper ready for changing!"

Everyone laughed then, and Ching took the baby and held her in his arms like she was the most precious bundle he'd ever held in his whole life. On impulse, I went over and put my arms around him. He reached and touched my face briefly before Maggie came and took the baby away for changing. After that, there was eating and laughter and more storytelling about the strange circumstances of Charlisse's birth.

Mom and Dad decided that the Medicine Man would be called to include Charlisse in the Walking Out Ceremony later in the spring with the rest of the little children in the community who would just be learning to walk. That's when the Medicine Man would be free to give her her Anishinawbe name, if he could, at which time it would be announced to the whole community. I didn't care what Anishinawbe name she got, I just thought Charlisse Firecat was so cool!

The next day, Chief Paulie came into the house yelling, "Hey, girl! I have a message for you." I came out of my room to see her cross the kitchen to peek into the baby's cradle that stood by the window behind the table. Mom was sitting there sewing.

The baby was asleep, so she lowered her voice. "Joe the fireman wants to send a love song to his special nurse on Friday night's community radio hour at eight o'clock." She pulled out a tape. "Here's the song he wants you to sing, except he wants you to insert the words 'lovely Nora' in there somewhere."

I made a face. Not another sappy love song! Before I could ask, she said "I gave a copy of the tape to Abraham too. He said he'd do it if you were willing. You can practice at the Band office tomorrow afternoon if you'd like."

I nodded. "Sure." I picked up the tape recorder, slipped the tape in, and pressed "play," dreading what I was about to hear. I was pleasantly surprised to hear a very soft gentle song with light guitar in the background. Listening to the song, I immediately picked up on where I could add in "lovely Nora."

I said, "Whew, that's a relief! This is an easy one."

The next afternoon, I met Abraham at the Band office. There weren't very many people around. Emily, Mom's replacement secretary, sat at the desk and leaned back to listen to us. I'd sat listening to the tape the day before and had set the words to paper. By the time I was done, I'd memorized the whole song. Abraham wanted me to sing the song first and then he would join in with the guitar. After the fourth try, we had the guitar and words down and the song went perfectly from beginning to end.

After a few more practices with Abraham, it was Friday evening and Dad drove both of us to the community radio station, which was far from walking distance at the other end of the community. When we arrived, I discovered that the radio station was just a little shack lit by one light inside. There was a small porch with a row of pegs along one wall on which you could hang your coat, and then off to the right was a small room where the DJ sat in front of a microphone and a panel of buttons against the wall. That was it. The room was so small that the DJ would have to leave to make room for Abraham and me to broadcast our song. While Dad waited for us outside, Abraham and I heard a truck pull in as we waited in the porch. Soon after, a man stuck his head through the porch door and said, "Hi, I'm Joe, the fireman."

We said hello back and then we heard the DJ introduce us. "And now for your listening pleasure, we have a song coming up live from our little radio station. It's by special request from our friendly neighbourhood fireman, who is dedicating this song to his special lady. So now, here's Abby and Abe!"

Abraham and I crowded in front of the microphone. His guitar started softly and then my voice blended right in. I closed my eyes and let the song flow through me and then I was singing the last line, the guitar fading with my voice. It was over. Clapping, the DJ slipped back into the room and we left so he could sit down again.

Once we stepped out of the cramped little room, Joe, with a big grin on his face, said, "That was just beautiful! Thank you so much!" He reached out to shake our hands and then shoved some rolled-up money in my hand and did the same with Abraham. Dad was beaming with pride and said that it was indeed a beautiful song. We drove Abraham back to his house, which was quite a ways from ours.

After we'd dropped him off, Dad asked, "So how much money did Joe give you for that performance?" I pulled the money out of my pocket where I'd shoved it and came up with fifty dollars. He smiled. "Send that to Grandma and now you have one hundred and fifty!"

That evening Blink came running in, yelling, "Abby! Everyone heard you sing and now everybody's talking about Abby and Abe!"

Dad said, "Blink, you're late. Where have you been? I was just about to go looking for you!"

Blink replied, "We were at the community centre and the radio was on full blast and everyone got to hear the song!"

Mom said from the couch behind the stove, where she was dropping soiled diapers into a bucket to soak overnight, "The community centre? It's bingo night tonight, isn't it? What were you doing in there? Weren't you supposed to be with David?"

Blink sat down at the table looking deflated. "David left to go home early and then I ran into Tommy and we had to go and get his basketball by the community centre because he forgot it there. We were going to walk home together when we heard the music coming from the community centre, so we ran inside to listen. That was all!" He stomped out of the kitchen and into his bedroom.

We went camping for just one weekend before school started. Amidst protests from Dad, Mom refused to be left behind. She had Charlisse safe and warm in the new tikinagan, the wooden cradleboard that Dad had made especially for her instead of using the one that was normally passed around the family. We headed out to the fall hunting campsite by the river where we normally went. Every one of our group came along, including the two sisters. Most of the group would camp for the full two weeks, or however long it took to process the moose that were killed, but Dad insisted that we would be going home after the weekend.

Only Grandma Beth wasn't along on the camping trip. She'd already gone back home to Nibika. She'd stayed with us for over a month, until Aunty Gilda had called to tell her that she should come home as she had a doctor's appointment coming up.

The house certainly felt empty after Grandma Beth left. The last thing she said to me was, "Take care of your baby sister." I was the big sister now and no longer the child I was when I lived at her house. I'd also stopped calling her Goom because to my mind she was now Grandma Beth.

When she was gone, we settled into some kind of routine for taking care of the baby. When Charlisse's umbilical cord stump fell off her belly button, Mom kept it and slipped it into a beaded disk of leather that she had made. It now hung on the looped front *tikinagan* handle, while on the other handle swung a bundle of red, blue, green, and yellow sucker bones. The leg support frame of the *tikinagan* was covered in brightly beaded leather with laces that went up to the middle front of the board. Another strip of leather was used to lace the covering over Charlisse's arms. The top sheet that was spread around the pillow at the head of the *tikinagan* was full of embroidered flowers of all colours and the edges were trimmed with lace. Lying in her tikinagan, Charlisse looked very pretty!

It was the second day at camp and the campfire smoke drifted over me as I sat under the tarp beside the fire. There had been a steady drizzle all day. It was the kind that came down in tiny droplets that penetrated even the thickest jacket and sweater. Even the dogs seemed to be soaked through. Ki-Moot had been curled up beside the stove inside the tent all morning. The pine trees dripped with the rain, and the remaining leaves in the bushes were bent, laden with moisture. Mom, Maggie, and the sisters were laughing inside our tent, while Alice, Linda, and Kitty were inside their tent working on something. For some reason, I had no interest in joining the ladies. I wished Grandma Beth were here.

For the rest of that weekend, I worked hard at camp and pretty much kept to myself. I cleaned the fish and cooked the meat or dried it over the smoke rack. The men had killed a moose that morning and I was happy just to work quietly with Alice and Kitty. On Sunday our family packed up our things and left the others at camp. Maggie sat in the middle of the canoe with the baby in her arms, Mom was back up front, and I was on the seat with Blink in front of Dad.

Maggie had been home with us now most of the time since Charlisse was born, but it was soon time for her to head out with six other teenagers from the community to attend high school in Thunder Bay, where they would board with other families.

On the very first day of school, I looked at the class lists posted on the front door of the school building and I saw that I'd be in Miss Tish's class. Lucky me! Maybe now I could learn to play a musical instrument! There were several new kids in the room and I was dismayed to find that Mary wasn't in my class, but neither was Josie, and thank goodness. Before class started, Mr. Toms popped his head into our classroom and nodded to me, so I got up to see what he wanted. He just whispered, "You sing from the heart and you've got soul! You rock, girl!" He winked and then he was gone. I turned back to face the kids but no one was paying attention to me. I'd found a desk at the back of the class and settled in. Besides music, Miss Tish also taught art. There were masks hanging on the walls of the classroom and hands and feet in clay. I examined the artwork on the wall and wondered how on earth I was going to learn how to do that. Aside from carving, any other attempt I'd made at artsy stuff really sucked.

At the end of the second week of school, I came home at lunch to find no one home. I made some soup and Blink came running in, looked around, ate quickly, and ran out of the house. He said he'd go find Mom and Dad. I waited around as long as I could for someone to return. Just as I got my coat on to go back to school, Dad's truck pulled in. He came in with Mom holding Charlisse, and I could tell that they'd both been crying. I froze in my tracks and waited for what had to be the bad news. Dad took the baby as Mom made her way over to me, gave me a hug, and softly said, "Little Betty passed away at the hospital."

I stood there, stunned. I knew Aunt Lucy had taken the little girl to the hospital several days ago, I never thought she might die. Then I remembered Maggie! "Has anyone called Maggie?" Maggie had looked after Betty from the day she was born.

Mom said, "I don't know what to do. I'll have to call Mom first." She dialled the phone and after a short conversation with Grandma Beth, she hung up and said, "She says that the Band could probably send Maggie home to attend the funeral. I'll have to let Paulie know." After a few more conversations on the phone, she said that Maggie would be home the next day.

Dad said, "Lucy is coming home tomorrow from the hospital. My parents are flying in this afternoon, so Maggie will probably stay here tomorrow or my parents will be staying here. We don't know yet." I took my coat off and made some tea. They sat down at the table and I dished out some soup and sliced some bannock to put on the table. Dad insisted that Mom eat and they slowly munched on their lunch and we waited.

"Did you see Blink?" I asked.

Mom nodded. "We saw him with David outside the school and I waved to him and he ran in when the bell rang." The bell rang? I'd almost forgotten I was supposed to be back at school!

I jumped up, but Dad put his hand on my arm and said, "It's okay. I'll call the school. Keep your mother company in case I have to go to the airport."

I didn't know what we were waiting for, but it sure felt like we were waiting for something. Then the phone rang. Dad picked it up and spoke in Ojibwe and I could tell he was speaking to one of his parents. I'd met them before, but I was too young to remember what they looked like. Dad usually just hopped on the plane to see them when they wanted him for something. They lived at Ashiganish, the neighbouring reserve. I glanced at Mom. She was just sitting there with the baby in her arms, slowing stroking Charlisse's blond hair back. A little girl had just died and her own baby was still very young. She seemed so concerned that I suddenly wanted to call Grandma Beth very badly.

When Dad hung up the phone, he said, "I'm to pick them up at the airport around three o'clock, but they're going to stay at Lucy's place. If Maggie wants to stay there too, when she gets in, I'll make sure that Jane is there as well."

With that, he gave Mom a light kiss on the forehead and he left. We sat in silence for awhile until I got up and dialled Grandma Beth's number and handed the receiver to Mom. With a touch of a smile she picked it up and I could hear Grandma's voice at the other end. I picked up Charlisse. She was still asleep, so I put her in the little bassinet that Dad had made. It rocked and it had beaded flower designs on the leather ends that were laced to the frame. I remembered how Dad had taken so long to carefully sand and bend the wooden frame so that it would rock. I let Mom talk to Grandma as I cleared the table and washed the dishes.

Dad returned an hour later. He said that his parents had decided to come in the morning. They wanted Maggie to look after little Cindy and they would see us in the morning at Aunty Lucy's place. We were to go to Lucy's when she got off the plane with Betty's body. Mom looked at him for a full minute but didn't say anything. Then I realized Dad's parents still hadn't seen their new baby granddaughter.

I went into Charlisse's room to prepare the bed and pick up the dirty diapers. I set out her bedtime bathtub and a clean gown. It was one of the routine things that I did every evening now. I heard the door slam and stomping feet told me that Blink had just arrived. I could hear him babbling on about his Grandma and Grandpa. I guessed he was really excited to see them again.

The next morning, I came into the kitchen just as Dad was going out the door. He glanced at me and said, "I'm going to Joe's place to be with my parents and wait there until the airplane comes in. Then Joe and I will pick up Aunt Lucy at the airport." Tears filled my eyes when I saw how much he was hurting. I went to the window and watched the truck pull out.

Dad called around noon and apparently Maggie and everyone had arrived at Aunt Lucy's house. Lucy's plane hadn't arrived yet and Dad was heading back to the airport again. Mom puttered around the kitchen and finally stopped, looked at me, and said, "I think we should go by boat to Aunt Lucy's place, pick up Maggie and Jane, and go and have a picnic at the island for lunch. By the time we come back, all the stuff will have been sorted out and we don't have to be involved in the chaos. Apparently, Joe's parents are angry about something and they came in at the same time as Dad's parents."

I raised my eyebrows, thinking, "Oh, really!" I'd never met Joe's parents. All I knew was that they were white people who owned a tourist gift shop somewhere in southern Ontario. I decided the picnic was a great idea, and I ran around getting the baby's diaper bag and bottle thermos ready as I heard Mom talking to Linda about keeping Blink with David for the day. Then we packed up the boat and Mom got the motor going. As we pulled up at Joe's landing, Charlisse started crying, so Mom couldn't go up but she said to me, "Go tell Maggie and Jane to come down her. Joe's mom can look after little Cindy until Aunt Lucy comes home. No arguments!"

I ran up the path and went through the back door. I saw an old woman with a scarf over her head sitting in an armchair. There was no one else in the room with her except Maggie and Cindy on the couch. I could hear a conversation going on in the front kitchen. There was no sign of Jane. I looked at Maggie and said in English, "Mom's waiting at the boat. She wants you and Jane to come down there and we'll have a picnic somewhere until all the stuff is settled. Then we'll go back to our house and wait for whatever arrangements have been made. Call Jane!"

Maggie glanced at me and put Cindy down in the crib that stood beside the television in the living room. The old woman now fixed her gaze on me and said in Ojibwe, "Is that the other one? Is that your mother's other child?" I saw Maggie duck into a room at the back that I knew she shared with Jane. After Maggie emerged with Jane in tow, we ran down to the boat where Mom had just finished breast-feeding Charlisse.

Mom started the motor and we took off to the far island with the soft sand beach facing away from the community. I'd never felt so relieved in my whole life! I knew we'd just escaped from something very bad. Maggie and Jane began laughing when we got to shore and they continued their belly laugh while Mom and I unloaded the lunch and campfire supplies. I was just busting to find out what they thought was so funny, but Mom frowned at me that it was best that I didn't know. Shucks! Double shucks! I knew the "no gossiping" rule was in effect.

It was a very nice Indian summer day and we sat by the shore and made tea over an open fire. Mom made ham sandwiches and she'd even brought half of a blueberry pie from the day before. We enjoyed ourselves as much as we could have that afternoon. We romped around the beach, wove some wreaths from cedar branches, and even found some high bush berries that the birds hadn't knocked down yet. They would make very nice decorations for Christmas if we froze them immediately. We stayed later than we should have, but the girls didn't want to go back to the house and be with Dad's parents, so Mom finally agreed that Maggie and Jane could stay with us for the night. Then, quite to my relief, Jane said that she was just going to head home for the night, which was next door to Aunt Lucy's house. So we dropped her off and then headed home to our place to wait there.

When we arrived, Dad was just pulling into the driveway with his truck. He came down to the landing to pull the boat in and picked up baby Charlisse in the tikinagan. He kissed Mom on the forehead and said, "Smart woman! I'm so proud of you. I just don't get how you know exactly what must be done at a given time. Wow! You should have seen my mom getting irritated when Cindy started to cry! Then Joe's mom comes into the room and picks up the baby and asks where the nannies were that Joe had been telling them about! Then my mom starts yelling for Maggie and Jane and they were gone!"

He pulled Maggie into a hug and said something to her that we couldn't hear, but she nodded her head when she stood back from him. Mom put her arm around me and Jane and we hugged each other with Charlisse between us.

When we were once again around the supper table, Dad told us that the funeral would be held early the next morning, since the plane would be leaving before nine to take Joe's parents home. Dad's parents would stay until the afternoon to catch the next flight back to Ashiganish. The church service and funeral came and went with us just standing by the sidelines. Dad's parents didn't come up to speak to us, and Mom refused to go to Aunt Lucy's place after the funeral. Maggie told me that Dad's parents didn't like the fact that their son had married a woman who already had two children. Meanwhile, Aunt Lucy didn't want Joe's parents to meet her mother, because her mother was very displeased that she hadn't married someone from within the community. And then there were Joe's parents, who were furious that they weren't notified of the seriousness of Betty's condition until her death. They also didn't like Aunt Lucy's parents.

I checked out Joe's parents at the funeral. They wore city clothes, but Joe's dad's shiny shoes were now covered in mud and I saw that Joe's mom had lost one of her high heels. Just then Mom nudged me for staring.

A large swirl of fallen leaves suddenly came up and blew all around us where we stood. It was like a huge blowing machine had twirled them around us and then the wind was gone. People who noticed it had turned to look at us.

That evening, we all sat around our table for supper after everyone else had gone. There was Aunt Lucy, Joe, baby Cindy, Maggie, Jane, and us. It had been a sad day topped up with the stress of fighting in-laws and their many levels of distrust and bitterness. So perhaps it was out of relief when Joe suddenly reached out to the people on either side of him to hold hands and we all joined in. Even the baby girls had their little arms stretched out to the people beside them. We all smiled and laughed at our newly recognized little family circle.

CHAPTER THIRTEEN

Work at Camp

The call of the loons out in the middle of the lake awakened me one morning. It was the first week of October. I was wedged between the canvas wall on my left and Maggie on my right. Mom and the high school had decided to let Maggie come with us for the fall hunting trip. The death of little Betty had really hit Maggie hard, and Mom had told me not to leave her alone too long because she had a tendency to start crying.

I lifted my head to see Ki-Moot curled up beside the little heat stove. The fire had gone out during the night and it was a bit cold inside the tent. Everyone was still asleep. Blink was on his back between Mom and Maggie, his elbows sticking out of the blankets and his hands tucked under his head. His sand-covered wet socks were still draped over the woodpile beside the stove. Mom had asked him to hang them outside the night before after he'd pulled off his boots and showered the blankets with sand. Dad was stretched out on his back beside the entrance and baby Charlisse was in her bassinet beside him with the mosquito netting over it.

I sat up, carefully slipped my shoes on, and picked out an exit route, being extra careful not to step on anyone. The sun was just coming up over the horizon. Ki-Moot lifted her head as I pulled on my nylon jacket and stood up. She was by the door wagging her tail even before I got there.

Dad lifted his head as I stepped around his feet and whispered, "Start the fire outside before you come in." I noticed that Charlisse was watching me and her arms came out waving under the netting. I smiled and pointed at her hands to Dad. Then I grabbed the box of matches from the stack of wood and went outside. The fresh smell of damp earth and rotting leaves filled my nostrils. The leaves were turning yellow and many more brown ones already carpeted the ground. The air was crisp as I headed out to our makeshift outhouse. I loved the early morning fall smell.

Ki-Moot met me when I came back and I grabbed the pail and headed down to the shore for water. Mist hung over the bay and I could see the loon that was creating such a racket. Then I saw another loon, and another, and I soon realized that there were more than twenty of them out there. I'd heard Gish say the day before that they were rather late heading south. The water was calm as I dipped the pail into it. Ki-Moot was wagging her tail like crazy and pouncing on something in the water. I got up and walked to where she was. It was a frog that she'd chased into the water. I giggled as I lifted the pail and headed back up to camp. There were four tents standing in the same place, just as they were when I first saw them last fall. I couldn't believe that more than one whole year had gone by, and now it seemed like I'd always been here.

I gave no thought to what must be done; I just did stuff automatically. I really loved it out in the bush. It was so peaceful and away from the community. It was like taking a break from everyday life and work.

School was a lot better this year. The kids in the room got along better than the ones last year and they were always laughing and teasing each other. By the time we left for the hunting break, some people in the class had been given nicknames. It began with Jim's hair, which always stuck up at the top of his head no matter how hard he tried to keep it down. Everyone began calling him *Kishkimunsi*, which is the name of the kingfisher bird in Ojibwe. Then there was Andy, who was known as *Pinungosi*, which meant "loose one," because he always slouched and his arms swung like they were just dangling off his shoulders when he walked. Jenny was called Ribbons because she always wore ribbons in her hair. Elijah was Gum Boots because he'd always say that he was "gumboot'n" somewhere. As for me, I was called PS (postscript) because I always had a tendency to add something else to what I'd just finished saying.

Just then Ching came out of the bush to my right with four rabbits in his hand. He must have left before I got up but I never even heard him. He smiled as I put the pail down and together we started a fire without saying a word. He set about cleaning the rabbits, while I put the coffee pot on to boil. The tent flap to the right opened and out stepped Alice. I could hear Ned still snoring inside. She smiled at us as she headed out to the woods. Then Gish came out of the tent that he shared with Ching and raised his eyebrows at Ching in pleasant anticipation of a good breakfast. Mike came out next from their tent to the left. I could hear Linda talking to David inside. By then there was some activity inside our tent with the sound of Maggie hissing at Blink about stealing her socks. I smiled when Blink's wet socks came flying out of the tent. So much for a quiet morning. Gish went off to the bush after carefully putting on his socks and boots outside and met up with Alice on the path, which left them laughing after a short exchange that I couldn't hear.

At the breakfast fire, Alice got to work getting the rabbits cooked and Mom had the bannock done before long and then we all prepared for the day's work. We'd been here for only three days and already there was a whole moose that had been cleaned, and there was still quite a bit of meat that hung on the smoking rack, ready to be made into pemmican. There were also six large sturgeon tied by the shore that would have to be smoked. Right now, they were tethered by a long rope through the mouth and tied to a tree along the shoreline. They would swim around out there until someone was free to start processing them. Mike and Dad came up the path.

Mom smiled. "I was just about to call you. Where are the boys?"

The men glanced at each other and then Ching said, "I sent them to start digging another hole. We need a girls' outhouse and a boys' outhouse, they said."

Now I understood the comment that passed between Alice and Gish. Everyone had been so busy, they only had time to dig up one outhouse before chores needed to be done elsewhere.

Mike said, "That's good. That'll keep them out of trouble for awhile." Ned yelled for the boys and they were by the fire in under a minute. I smiled. They were all covered in sand and dirt, but Mom didn't seem to notice.

As they sat down to eat, Dad said, "I believe today is the day that we'd told the two sisters we would come and get them and bring them out here to smoke the moosehides. So you women will have to decide which things we need to take back for the freezer."

Alice was quick to respond. "Take all the smoked meat back and put it into the freezer. We don't have time right now to pound it into pemmican. There are the sturgeon that need to be cleaned and dried, and we need to get this morning's fish into the freezer too."

Ned added, "I need to clean the fish from the nets this morning first and they'll need to be packed in the moss."

Mike said, "Why don't we just clean the sturgeon and pack them whole and freeze them whole too? The elders really liked the whole fish in the spring." They all nodded. My mind was quickly going through the contents of the baskets stacked inside our tent.

I added, "Don't forget the late berries we have in the baskets in there. And you may as well take the coiled pine roots with you too. We need the baskets."

They nodded and suddenly I felt very self-conscious. Maggie smiled at me as she chewed at a piece of bannock. "That leaves, what? Abby's been dying to try to do some beadwork again. She has this really nice design that she wants to sew on a pair of moccasins."

Mom's eyebrows went up and she said, "That's good, Abby! I've been wondering when you were going to get tired of just drawing your designs and not doing anything else with them. Now is a good time to try to learn how to do beadwork and select your own colours too!"

I was surprised at what Mom had said. I hadn't realized she was waiting for me to begin making moccasins. My last attempt at it had been a disaster. I concentrated on my piece of fried rabbit and bannock. Alice poured another cup of coffee for Ned and he smiled at Dad, and Mike saying, "While you guys are gone, we should have the fur all cut off the moosehide that's still floating in the water out there and have it on the stretch rack by the time you come back." Alice winked at Linda and Mom, but they didn't say anything.

Then Blink piped up. "Hey, where are the sisters going to sleep?"

Alice was quick with an answer. "Why, Ned will move in with Ching and Gish and the sisters will be staying with me." Ned quickly swallowed his mouthful of coffee while Mike and Dad giggled into their cups. Gish and Ching were going moose hunting and had already packed a large lunch to take with them.

The activity began rather smoothly with canoes taking off and another coming in while we hurried to get everything done. By midmorning, we had a large pot of sturgeon heads, giblets, and caviar sitting by the fire. The dried moose meat had been packed in large canvas bags, and the baskets of roots and berries were already safely stowed in the canoe. Two large tubs of sturgeon and fish were both packed in thick moss to keep them fresh. With that, the canoe was loaded and Mike and Dad were off. Ching and Gish had also gone on their way to go moose hunting and we figured that they would all be back by suppertime.

The boys were back to digging the outhouse hole and Maggie and I had long since finished cleaning up the campfire area. I looked at the mass of caviar. It was a mound of clear membrane packages of little grey balls with yellowish white veins of fat running through them. If I had seen this last fall, I thought to myself, I surely would have puked! Now I knew that half of the caviar would be fried in oil with dried gooseberries or high bush berries and the other half would be made into caviar bannock. The bannock would turn a bluish grey but it would be very fluffy, like a cake. After all, caviar were merely little eggs. It would be like adding a half-dozen chicken eggs into the flour mixture. Funny, too, that they had no fishy taste at all.

"Hey, are you ready? Come get Charlisse." Maggie came out of the tent with a blue flannel sheet that she used to hold her sewing stuff. I went into the tent and carefully picked up the bassinet. Charlisse was still asleep. I walked with Maggie to a spot along the shore where she handed me the blanket that she'd draped over her shoulder. I spread the blanket on a piece of flat, leaf-covered ground overlooking the lake.

Ned had dragged the moosehide to a place far to the right of the camp, but we could still see where they had spread a sheet of canvas. That was where they were now spreading the moosehide. Cutting the hair off was a messy business. Ned had his job cut out for him just sharpening the knives that didn't keep their edge for very long. It was the women who did the actual cutting. Using sharp, deft swings of their knives, they would cut the hair off right to the skin. Ned once said that the mark of a woman's skill was when she left the moosehide like a clean-shaven man's chin. That had brought a quick grunt from Alice, indicating Ned's constantly grizzled-looking face.

My hands kept cramping as I clumsily tried to hold the string of beads firmly while sewing them down with the other hand. I looked up once to see Maggie looking back at me with her tongue sticking out of the corner of her mouth, imitating me. Then she said, "It's time to go give them something to drink." How time flew! The boys were still hacking away out in the bush. This time, they sounded like they were actually nailing on the frame of the outhouse. They'd sworn that they would make theirs look exactly like the one Ching had made.

I got up and nearly toppled over. My foot had fallen asleep! I could hear Maggie laughing behind me as I made my way back to the fire, picked up the pot of hot tea, and poured in some canned milk. Not one of the moosehide shavers took any sugar. I stirred the pot, picked up their cups, and walked back down to the shore. The wind was blowing slightly and clouds periodically covered the sun. The weather was very nice.

They were laughing as I approached and Ned said, "Oh, look who has brought over some tea!" They smiled as I handed over the pot and cups to Ned.

I asked, "What shall we make for lunch?"

Alice said, "There's a trout in the birchbark basket under the pile of spruce branches beside the fire. Just boil that. There's enough of your mother's bannock left over to feed us all."

Mom put her knife aside and asked, "Is the baby still asleep? What are the boys doing? Can you hear them?" Wisps of her hair had escaped the elastic from the ponytail on top of her head.

I said, "Charlisse is still asleep. Yeah, the boys seem to be nailing the beams on now. Haven't gone up to see what it looks like yet, though. Not sure I want to."

Ned laughed. "Have faith now! They seem to be getting better at building things. Remember the doghouse they built for Mucko last fall? It's actually still standing!" They all laughed at that. The boys had been concentrating so hard on making the sides and the roof of the doghouse that it wasn't until they had finished that they realized it had no door. They'd built a square box with a slanted lid nailed on top of it.

When I got back to the campsite, I told Maggie that we were having trout and bannock, and somehow, she knew when to begin boiling the water for the trout. By now, she just watched while I cleaned and cut up the trout and put it into the pot. No comments from her meant that I was doing a good job. By the time we called everyone for lunch, I'd finished beading one flower petal on one moccasin vamp. In that same time, Maggie had finished all the petals of her flower plus the stem for one vamp. She just had the other one to do. I was disappointed with my effort. My neck hurt, and my hand muscles hurt, and my fingers hurt where I'd pricked them with the needle so many times! Finally, Charlisse was waving her arms around and Maggie was immediately beside her, lifting her out of the bassinet.

Mom glanced at my work and said, "Your hands need to do something else for awhile. There are still the *amungs* to make." Those were the flat wooden needles with the hole in the middle that would be needed for the snowshoe mesh work. One would be smaller for the top and bottom mesh and one would be larger for the middle mesh work ,where the foot would go. I glanced at the slivered pieces of cedar that had been set aside beside the woodpile for that very purpose. Yeah, I would love to carve for awhile. I was really good with the carving now. Mom just asked me to make wooden things that would be needed, like the wooden needles. I'd also made a bundle of fishnet spindles and crossbars. The spindle held the thick nylon thread used in making the fishnet, and the size of the crossbar determined the size of the holes in the fishnet. I'd also made a mobile for Charlisse with flying wooden birds. It turned out really nice.

It was well on in the afternoon when Maggie called me from the shore. I sat on a large flat rock beside the lake where I'd piled the cedar shavings that would go into the fire-starter birchbark basket beside the fire. I had a pile of *amungs* beside me already—in both sizes. Mom and Alice had long since finished stretching the moosehide onto the large frame that Ned had made. It stood against a tall poplar tree beside the shore. I picked up my bundle of carved needles and the shavings and made my way through the boulders to the sandy beach that led to the path to the campsite. The boys were playing pickup stones. They would throw one stone up and pick up another before the stone came falling down and catch it before it hit the ground. They had stones of many colours but all were about the same size. I asked, "What's the purpose of the game?"

David answered, "The one who has the most wins!"

Blink glanced at me and said, "The new outhouse is the boys' toilet. No girls allowed!"

I smiled. "Good. Might be afraid to fall in otherwise!"

Mom glanced at me as Blink sat up and yelled, "You're just jealous because you don't get to use it! And besides, we left the back toilet seat part open so that boys can just pee without peeing on the toilet seat, see?"

I made a face, thinking how disgusting that was. I made no comment, though. I was still learning not to answer back so that I didn't start a fight or create an argument with Blink, but Mom just needed to remind me once in awhile now. I got to the tent and went inside and found out why Maggie had called me. She'd finished my flower! I stood there looking down at the vamp that she held out to me. "Thanks. But I wanted to do it myself . . . you know?"

She put it down and glanced up at me. "Sorry. Hey, you still have the other one to do. I won't help you with that one. But at the rate you were going, I'd have finished both my moccasins and you'd just be finishing one vamp."

I smiled. "Yeah, I guess so. Okay, now we can start the other foot together."

Then she said, "I've been thinking. Instead of making moccasins, let's turn them into mukluks. That way, we get to wear our own stuff when the others wear all the other outfits for Dog Tracks!"

I looked at her. "You mean you want us to make our own pants—or is it dresses? Plus coats, hats, mitts, and stuff?"

She smiled, all excited now. "Yeah! We have furs of all kinds! We could design our own winter outfits and make them all just the way we want them!"

I wasn't sure about this. I'd never made a single thing in my whole life! Remembering my embarrassing pants with the spike at the crotch and my mitt with the super long thumb, I sank down to my knees. Well, it never hurt to dream, so I said, "I want a fox fur trim on my muskrat skin hat. And, and . . . fox fur trim on my mitts—no beads on my mitts! And . . . I want a muskrat skin coat with fox fur pompoms hanging off the collar . . ."

Maggie's eyes twinkled as she laughed. She looked so happy and excited, like she'd just discovered something really special. Maybe she had. I wasn't sure, though. I still had no idea where I was going to begin. It was just so nice to see Maggie laughing again. The sisters said that this camping trip was the best thing for her right now.

Suddenly there was a yell from the boys. "I hear the motor! They're coming!" We scrambled up and I waited for Maggie to pack the sewing stuff away before we ran out of the tent. There they were for sure. Just halfway across the lake and supper was just about done. Talk about good timing! Alice was by the fire frying fish and Mom had just set aside the pot of boiling potatoes. A thick caviar bannock was already in the birchbark serving plate. Ned added a few more pieces of wood under Alice's frying pan. He had already moved his stuff out of their tent and a space awaited the two sisters, Lizzy and Minnie.

We were all by the lake when the canoe pulled in. The first thing that was unloaded was the cage that held the two Siamese cats. That was going to be fun, I thought, as Ki-Moot made a lunge at the strange-looking animals inside! I grabbed her and pulled her up to camp, where I tied her to her leash as the boys caught and tied up the rest of the dogs. The only dog loose was Gish's dog, Daish, who glanced at the cage, checked out the cats, and decided that if they'd come with the women, then they were okay. I wondered if she remembered them. The cage was brought into the tent and the women went in to deposit their packsacks. They emerged as everyone gathered around the fire for the evening meal.

Alice dished out the meal for everyone. There was still no sign of Ching and Gish. The stories around the fire were just updates to let the two sisters know what had been happening around the camp since our arrival. They were most interested in the moosehide on the frame leaning against the tree by the shore. They'd brought six moosehides, already softened and prepared for smoking. Each hide had been sewn into sacks with canvas skirts attached at the bottom. Each hide would be suspended from a pole and the canvas skirt would fit over a pot filled with punky dried wood that would be stoked to smoulder into thick smoke. The smoke would turn the hide to a light tanned colour and it also acted as a preservative.

Dad and Mike kept glancing at each other and smiling. Finally Ned said, "You're just busting to tell a story, eh? Well, you just wait until the others are back!"

We finished the meal and Maggie and I washed the dishes by the shore. After everything else was put away, we settled around the fire again for some tea. Just then, Ned came up to the fire, sat down beside Alice, and said to Mike and Dad at the other end of the firepit, "I've just tried the new 'boys only' outhouse. As soon as I sat down, it kind of started sagging backwards and then I couldn't get up, being off-balance like, so I ended up in a lounging position on the frame over the toilet hole!"

Everyone burst out laughing, including the boys, as Ned imitated his attempts at trying to get up out of that contraption.

He ended by saying, "I was yelling and yelling for the boys when one pole finally broke and it just kind of dumped me out. Only then was I able to pull my pants up!"

It was while everyone was laughing that we heard the motor coming. That would be Gish and Ching. The evening sun was now close to touching the treetops across the lake. We scrambled to get ready for what they could be bringing home and we also heated up their portion of the supper that had been set aside.

Mike and Dad had gone to the shore to pull the canoe in and I heard Dad yell, "Get the pan ready for the hunters' kill—heart, liver, and kidneys!" That was the moose meat that hunters always brought back first. Along with the heart, liver and kidneys, the hunters also brought the nose and tongue—delicacies that would go to the eldest female or male. As Ching and Gish came up, it was Gish who carried the basket with the nose and tongue. This he put between the two sisters with a nod and a smile. The women glanced at each other and giggled. Alice began slicing the heart, liver and kidneys, and I set about getting the teapot refilled and boiling again as quick as I could.

When Gish and Ching finished cleaning up, the contents of Alice's frying pan were now in a birchbark basket. Gish and Ching took a piece of the fried heart, liver and kidneys first before the rest of it was passed around to everyone else. We all gathered around the fire again to hear the story of the hunt. The teapot needed to be refilled again too, so I missed the part about how they killed the moose. By the time I came back to sit and listen, Mike and Dad were now talking about their trip into the community. At the mention of Mad Dog, Dad burst into sudden laughter and nearly sprayed out his mouthful of tea before he caught himself.

Mike told the story. "John and I went to the store to get more matches and there we saw Mad Dog with a huge bandage on his hand. He was supposed to be guiding at the tourist camp, then there he was, so I asked, 'What happened to you?' He said that he was coming home on Sunday to bring Kitty to the lodge and that he'd stopped to fish at the mouth of the river when this huge grandfather of a jackfish grabbed his hook. He said he fought it for over half an hour before he figured he had it tired out enough to try to get his hook out. He got the huge fish right up to the side of the boat and was reaching down to grab it behind the head when it suddenly shot forward, twisted, and clamped its huge jaws right over his right hand. Well, he couldn't grab it with his other hand since it was still holding his rod at the time. So he broke the line and the fish started swinging its head and there was blood all over the place by then. He grabbed the fish under its gills and pulled it into the boat. Still, the fish wouldn't let go of his hand, and he said he was afraid that it would slash the veins off the top of his hand if it kept swinging its head side to side like that. So he reached for the knife on his belt and stabbed the fish beneath its jaws, but it still wouldn't let go! He ended up cutting off the fish's head and by now, there was really a lot of blood everywhere. So he finally started the engine and took off at full speed across the lake. He said he pulled up at the dock and by now he was feeling dizzy . . ."

While he paused to laugh, I dared to ask, "Did he go to the nursing station?"

Dad started laughing even harder and said, "Mad Dog said when he walked into the nursing station, there were people sitting in the chairs waiting their turn, but there was no question who should go in next when Nurse Sara saw him with the hand stuck inside the fish's head dripping blood all over the floor!

Dad was laughing so hard, he couldn't speak, so Mike picked up the story. "He says he'll never forget the expression on everyone's face in the waiting room when he came out of the doctor's office. They all tried to avoid looking at him, but each one of them looked like they were about to burst into laughter. So Mad Dog says out loud, 'Whew! That fish nearly caught me!' That did it, he says. There was an explosion of hysterical laughter as he walked out the door."

During a lull in the conversation, Ching had gotten up and gone down the bush path. Ned said, "Oops, I forgot to tell him about the state of the new outhouse."

There was a bit of laughter as Ching returned shortly and walked over to the boys, saying, "Meeting at the construction site first thing in the morning, eh?" Blink and David grinned sheepishly at each other.

The next morning, I rolled over and felt the damp on top of my blanket. It was raining outside and the tarp over the fire popped as it flapped in the wind. Dad was at the stove getting the fire going. I was aware of voices by the campfire and realized that Mom had already left the tent. Maggie was still lying beside me rubbing her eyes, and I saw that Blink had rolled into a ball in the mound of blankets that had been vacated by Mom and Dad. Charlisse was also still asleep. She sure slept a lot for a tiny little person, I thought. Then I heard the sound of the small motor on the canoe coming in. Someone probably went to get the fishnets that had been set at the channel last evening.

Maggie and I waited until the tent filled with warmth from the roaring little stove. There was a burst of laughter from the campfire. It was Mike, probably laughing at something Ching had said. Not wanting to miss out on anything funny, I threw the blanket off and Maggie grabbed her sweatshirt from under her pillow along with the dress that she pulled over her black stretchy pants. I pulled on my jeans. We dressed quickly and ran to the outhouse together. By the time we got back to the campfire, talk had started as to what needed to be done first that day. Everyone was concerned about the wind. The butchering crew would need to get to the moose quickly before the waves got worse. The waves might get too high for a loaded canoe. They decided to go immediately, grabbing only some bannock and some leftover food from last evening's supper. After a quick cup of coffee, Dad, Mike, and Linda took off in our canoe, and Ned, Alice, and Ching left in the other.

Those of us who were left behind had a leisurely breakfast around the fire. Gish had to hang a piece of canvas in the direction of the wind to shade the fire while the two sisters made breakfast. Later, Gish and Mom cleaned the fish that were piled in a big tub, while Maggie and I hung the fishnets over a pole tied between two trees. Minnie and Lizzy decided to go around the bay, away from the wind, to smoke the moosehides. Maggie and I would keep the teapot and the fire going. Mom settled down inside our warm tent to sew thick cotton bags for the pemmican that we would make from the pile of dried meat that had been left on top of the smoke rack. The boys had had their conference with Ching about the "boys only" outhouse, which they were supposed to get back up after getting more firewood. So far, they were still at the beach, hooting and hollering as they jumped over the white-capped waves rolling in.

Maggie decided to do some more beadwork, but I wasn't in the mood for tiny little beads. I watched Mom and Maggie as they talked with the sewing basket between them. They were discussing which furs could be sewn together and which furs didn't work well together. Charlisse was fast asleep in her *tikinagan* with the mosquito netting draped across it. I quickly lost interest in Mom and Maggie's discussion as I sat on top of the woodpile and began wondering what I could make from bones. I already had a big bundle of sucker bones that I'd cleaned and tied together. Those were the same kind of bones that Mom and I had dyed and tied to Charlisse's *tikinagan* handle. Maybe I could dye the bones I'd collected into different colours and make a fish-bone mobile. That would be pretty. I also had eight partridge pine needle pouches that I'd blown up like balloons. They hung from the centre beam of the tent. I could add those to my inventory list for Paulie too. She was really pleased with the stacks of things that had been made for the Dog Tracks tourist venture, especially now that everything was neatly labelled and organized. The problem was that the stacks had taken over her house. She was already working on an answer to that problem, though. She'd recently ordered lumber and supplies to have a proper building for the Dog Tracks office built outside the Band office.

I snapped out of my daydreaming when I heard Maggie giggling. Mom was looking at me. "What?" I asked.

Mom smiled. "Tea for Minnie and Lizzy?" she said. Oh, I'd forgotten! I ran out and got the teapot and cups ready. The rain had stopped but it was still overcast as I followed the path that led to the bay. There was no let-up in the wind, but it was relatively calm when I reached the bay and I could smell the smoke that rose from the small point of land.

I noticed some rabbit scat by the path that looked very green and fresh. I decided to come back and set a snare there when the sisters were finished with their tea. They were talking softly when I approached. Without a word to me, they threw down a bundle of spruce boughs for me to sit on as I set the pot and cups beside them. The two moosehides had been sewn into tubes that were suspended over the smouldering pots. Some old cotton fabric was sewn at the bottom of the tubes that covered the smouldering pots so that the women had to reach in to drop more short twigs into the pots without having to pull the up skirtings. The tethered cats lay lounging on a blanket in the shade. I poured the tea into the cups and sat back to listen. The sisters were talking about their grandmother.

Minnie and Lizzy had been just young girls when they were given their first moosehide to tan. Minnie had been put in charge of periodically checking how dark the leather was getting and Lizzy had to pull up the skirt around the pot to put more sticks in the fire. When she did this, a gust of wind blew the pot into flames. The sticks had caught like a bonfire and their leather became pinched and puckered. They'd failed miserably at their first try at tanning. "It was nearly a year before we were given another piece of leather to tan." Lizzy ended the story with laughter.

They talked of times gone by and who used to do what and mentioned their aunts and uncles. After awhile, I began trying to find the right time to make my exit. When the teapot was emptied, I stood up and said, "You wouldn't know it here, but the wind hasn't died down yet. The boys were still jumping over the waves by the shore."

They looked at each other and Lizzy said, "The wind will be behind them, then. It must have changed since they left this morning. They'll get home fine."

I smiled and made my way back down the path. I thought about how much I still didn't notice, like the wind having changed direction.

I'd just put the teapot and cups back by the fire when I heard a motor out on the lake. It was them already? I yelled, "Mom? I hear a canoe coming!" She came out with Maggie behind her and they stood listening. I ran to the shore and searched the direction where the guys had killed the moose. I couldn't see anything.

Maggie stopped beside me and said, "There's the canoe. Wow, look at how it's splashing through the water. Someone's going to be soaked!" I looked down the lake from the portage and there was the canoe riding sideways across the waves.

Mom came up behind us, saying, "Better get the campfire going higher. They'll need to dry off. I suspect it's Mad Dog and Kitty. If he hurt his hand, he'll not be working for awhile."

Sure enough, as the canoe got closer, we could hear Kitty shouting something at Mad Dog. When they finally reached the shore, Mom was there to pull the canoe in and Kitty was laughing. "I told him to put his raincoat on, but you can't tell him anything!"

Mad Dog grinned, his bald head glistening with water. "The other canoes are gone. Have the guys killed a moose?" he asked. His coat and pants were totally drenched, but he and Kitty had put canvas over the contents of their canoe. Kitty, who had been at the front, was totally dry.

Mom replied, "Yes, they left this morning to get the butchering done before the waves got too high. It was blowing from the north this morning, but now it's coming straight from the west."

Kitty laughed. "We thought we were safe from the waves when we headed out this morning, but the wind changed while we were going through the portage and next thing we knew, the waves were hitting the side of the canoe."

The boys arrived to help Mad Dog unload the canoe and they carried the contents quickly up to the camp area. Mad Dog shook himself by the fire and hung up his coat to dry while steam rose from his pants. He'd protected his new wolverine hat from getting wet by shoving it into his pants! Kitty had already dumped their tent out from a drenched cardboard box. They would put it up in the empty spot beside Gish and Ching's tent. Maggie and I ran to cut some spruce boughs for their floor. When we arrived back with two large bundles, lunch was ready. The sisters were also there and we all sat around the fire to hear Mad Dog tell a few stories. He still had a bandage over his hand but seemed to be using it fine.

We'd just finished cleaning up the lunch stuff when we heard the canoes coming. They sounded close since the wind was blowing from the direction they were coming from. Mad Dog and Kitty's tent was already up and the floor had a new carpet of branches. I was busy getting another pot of tea going and Mom was heating up the boiled trout in the pot when the first canoe came in. We could hear Ned hooting and Alice laughing. Gish came by, dropping a half-dozen large roasting sticks. I smiled, knowing that he was looking forward to roasting moose ribs over the fire. The sisters had another bundle of boughs spread beneath another tarp overhead in case it rained some more. That was where the first load of moose meat was deposited. The animal had been cut up into manageable chunks, and there were Gish's moose ribs being carried up to camp by Ned.

The fish tub had been washed and filled with water and that was where Ned dropped the ribs. Gish was there, swishing them around in the water to wash off the leaves that were stuck to them. I ran to give him one of the roasting sticks from the fire. I helped him with the other rack of ribs while everyone else scurried to make room for the second load of meat from Dad and Mike's canoe, which had just come in. Linda was laughing at something by the shore. I noticed that Mom had already gone down to the canoe. I finished helping Gish and ran to dump the tub of bloody water. I would need to refill it quickly. Grabbing a pail, I ran to the water. When I got to the shore, Mad Dog was up to his knees in the water and his butt looked very wet. Maggie was there with another pail of water and I asked, "Why is Mad Dog in the water?"

She said in a low voice, "He went to pull the canoe in and a huge wave suddenly pushed it forward. He had to back up and he tripped over that rock in the water and went down. He actually sat down in the water in slow motion!" I laughed as I lugged my full pail back up to camp.

The rest of the afternoon was quite noisy with laughter as everyone talked at once during the flurry of activity. Another black cloud went by in the sky, dumping more water that puddled and poured off the tarps. At one point I saw Gish duck under the tarp to get his teacup and just as he pulled back, the tarp tipped and poured water down the back of his neck! I couldn't help it; I burst into a giggling fit!

Just as the meat for supper had finished cooking, the rain came down in a solid downpour and it became impossible for us to sit around and eat by the campfire. So Alice put the food in trays that were then brought into each tent. I wanted some of Gish's moose ribs, so I went and sat beside him in his tent. He loaded up the birchbark serving tray and set it down between us, along with some lard from his food box. This he spread on each rib until the melted lard ran down into the tray. Ned and Ching were filling their faces with fried moose meat sandwiched in fresh bannock that they were dunking into the pan grease. A pot of tea sat simmering on top of their little stove.

After supper, I ran back to our tent in the pouring rain. Everyone had finished eating when I got there. Maggie had pulled out her beading again and Mom and Dad lay talking on the rolled-up bedding. Blink was in David's tent. We went to bed early since there wasn't much we could do. There was no let-up in the rain, and the wind was whipping the tarps into such a noisy racket that Ching had to take them down.

It was dark when I awoke to the sound of voices. The women were still talking and giggling in Alice's tent. Then I heard Gish's voice from outside by the flickering campfire. "If anyone's still awake, come have a look at the northern lights. They're really going crazy tonight."

I sat up and Maggie turned her small flashlight on. We quickly located our shoes and crawled to the door. Mom and Dad pulled their feet up out of the way to let us through. When we got out, all the other women were there, as well as Ching and Gish. Ned was snoring in the guys' tent. Wow! The sky had cleared and the lights were dancing frantically across the dark sky, all bright shades of colours, weaving, swerving, and dipping as though dancing to a heavenly tune that we couldn't hear. Minnie spoke from behind me, "Sometimes you can hear their rustling skirts as they dance by."

Gish said, "Those are the souls of dead people from the beginning of time. Never whistle at them either or you'll excite them and they'll dance faster and faster. If you continue, they'll get so excited that they'll dip right down to the ground and snatch your soul!"

He suddenly grabbed my arm and I drew in my breath as I jumped about a foot high!

Minnie hissed, "Sh, sh, you'll give her nightmares, now!"

Alice giggled and said, "Some say that you can smell their stink like old dead bones if they come too close." That was enough for me. I pulled Maggie along with me as we crept back into bed. I lay listening to the talk outside a bit longer and then, finally, everything was quiet. I pulled my blanket over my shoulders thinking that I'd never again look up with such innocence and admiration at the northern lights that rose and blended in a brilliant display of colour in motion!

The next morning, we'd just finished breakfast when another layer of black clouds came up over the horizon. I quickly ran down the path to where I'd seen the rabbit scat and set a snare where a section of the rabbit path was clearly used often. When I got back, Mad Dog, Mike, and Dad were getting ready to leave in the canoe. They still had to pick up the moosehide and antlers from the butcher site. The sisters also wanted the moose head. Gish had the moose leg bones roasting in the ashes. He loved eating the marrow with pemmican. The boys had finally finished the boys' outhouse to Ching's satisfaction and were inside Gish's tent wrestling among the blankets. Ned was by the fire carving a new paddle when I heard the canoe take off. Alice, Linda, and Mom were in our tent making pemmican. Maggie, Lizzy, and Minnie were in Alice's tent sewing on the fabric bottoms to another two moosehides for smoking. I stopped to watch Ned for a few minutes and then decided to go for a walk along the shoreline.

I picked up some nice rocks among the pebbles and thought about Grandma Beth. She seemed to be back to herself since Choom's death, with even a bit more independence. She'd really taken to travelling lately. Even if Aunty Gilda wasn't able to go with her, she'd head off on a trip on her own. She'd be in Vancouver now. After Vancouver she was going to Toronto to see a musical.

I'd just gone around a rock pile when Ching stepped out from the bush with a .22 rifle in his arms. "Oh, you startled me," I said as I walked up to where he'd stopped.

"I didn't expect anyone to be walking around here. What if I'd shot at something in this direction?" he said.

I hunched up my shoulders. "Oops, I didn't know you were here either." He stopped at a boulder and sat down. I sat down on the boulder beside him and checked out his gun. Finally, I asked, "How does the gun work?" He laid it on his lap and named each part and explained its function. Then he pointed to a spot along the shore where a tree lay half in the water with one branch sticking out. "See that branch? Would you like to take a shot?" My heart started pounding. He explained a bit more about how I should hold the gun and why. He spoke slowly and took his time and finally, I held the gun to my shoulder, held my breath, lined up the sight, and pulled the trigger. I saw the branch splinter and fall into the water!

I gave him back the gun like it was made of gold, then suddenly I started skipping around, yelling, "Yes! Yes! Yes!" Ching sat there laughing at me. I loved it, I loved it, I loved it! Ching let me take several more shots and I hit the mark each time. I could tell he was really surprised and pleased that I was such a good shot for a beginner.

As we headed back to camp, he talked about gun safety and safe storage of guns and bullets. I repeated each sentence in my head so I wouldn't forget. We'd just reached the canoe landing area when we heard the canoe coming back.

I hurried up to the campsite while Ching decided to stop and wait for the canoe coming in. As soon as he was within hearing distance, Mad Dog was yelling, "We got another one! Hurry, go get your stuff!"

Ching ran up and left his gun in his tent and then he was off to find Ned. After that, there was another flurry of activity, eating supper fast, and then Mom was off with Dad and Mike, and Linda went with Ned and Ching. Mad Dog and Kitty were in charge of getting the other meat off the smoke rack to make room for more.

The next morning, I awoke to the sound of steady drizzle on the tent roof. It was another rainy day, but it was nice and warm inside the tent as I listened to the little stove make its popping sounds. After a week of steady work, everyone was exhausted. I decided to get up and start the campfire. But no matter how early I tried to get up, someone was always up before me. Gish was coming up the path from the lake. "Heavy fog out there," he said. I stopped and looked out on the lake and saw nothing. It seemed like we were on a floating island to nowhere. I smiled and took off to the outhouse.

When I got back, the campfire was already billowing smoke from the damp wood. I picked up the water pail and headed down to the lake with Ki-Moot trotting beside me. She followed me everywhere I went. She'd look up at the branches of every tree we passed, always looking for squirrels. Whenever she spotted one, she'd bark and jump at the tree. She hadn't figured out that there was no way she was ever going to reach the squirrel. All she did was entertain the squirrel as it whirled around with its head down and scolded her. It was so funny to watch.

The loons were quiet this morning. There was total silence as I stood by the shoreline until Ki-Moot started slurping at the water. After I deposited the water pail beside the fire, I decided to run and check my rabbit snare. With Ki-Moot bounding beside me, I ran down the path and saw that my snare was exactly where I'd put it. No rabbit. I removed the wire and raced Ki-Moot back to camp.

I sat down beside the fire and waited for the coffee pot to boil. One by one, people emerged from their tents. Ned looked funny. He had bed head and his hair looked like a mop left to dry out on the floor. Minnie and Lizzy were very energetic when they came out of their tent. They always seemed to be in great spirits, just raring to get going on the next moosehide. Gish sat by the fire beside me with his bag of fresh pemmican, which he was dipping into with a glob of bone marrow. He had carefully split the bones and piled the marrow into a birchbark basket last evening. He seemed happiest when he sat by the fire eating moose meat. Suddenly, the silence was broken by a gaggle of geese by the bay, and more activity erupted as Ching came running by with Mad Dog at his heels, each of them carrying a gun.

There were several shots and then after some silence, the men came back up the path, laughing. They got into the canoe to fetch the four geese that they'd killed. I knew what I would be doing fairly soon—plucking feathers.

After breakfast, it was decided that Mike and Ned would make another trip to the community freezer with a load of fresh moose meat. Maggie came out of our tent with a packed bag. It was time for her to go back to school. When Maggie, Ned, and Mike were gone, everyone else got busy with everthing that needed to be done. I was still sitting beside Gish when I saw Ching walk by with his gun. I jumped up. "Wait, I'll come with you!" I ran and grabbed my jacket and slipped on my rubber boots. Mom raised her eyebrows at me but said nothing as I rushed pass her.

I followed Ching into the bush and walked as quietly as I could behind him. He seemed to scan every bush in front of him. He stopped once in awhile and listened. I stopped breathing at times when he seemed to have heard something. Suddenly, he stopped and pointed. I stepped closer and stopped. I didn't see anything, and then the partridge moved. He handed me the gun and I remembered to release the safety clip and slip a bullet into the chamber. The partridge walked a few steps. I aimed until I saw the sight on its head and pulled the trigger. The partridge fell and then Ching whispered, "Wait. There will be another one nearby. There." I saw it. It was now moving forward into the open. I fired another shot and it went down. I gave the gun back to Ching with a big smile on my face.

I danced around, saying, "Yes! Yes! Yes!" before I grabbed the partridge and started plucking the feathers off while he stood there laughing at me. When I was finished, I wrapped the partridge in moss and stuffed one of them in each of my pockets.

We'd just gone over a hill when it began to rain, so we went back around to the campsite. As we got near, there was a sudden explosion that sounded like firecrackers from the campsite. Ching pulled me back until the noise stopped. I ran into the campsite to see what was happening. Mad Dog stood up from behind the woodpile and Dad came out from the embankment to the shore. Ching stopped behind me, asking, "What happened?" By then everyone else was there asking the same question.

Mad Dog stood there looking sheepish and said, "I was shaking the rain off my coat over the fire, trying to dry it, like . . ."

He started laughing and Dad said, "He was shaking his coat upside down over the flames and then I noticed some little things falling into the fire and I looked at him. '.22 bullets?' I asked. Then he goes, 'Oh, geez!' That's when we dove for cover and shortly after, the bullets exploded!"

Dad started laughing and pointed at Mad Dog's head. "Your wolverine hat is smoking!"

Mad Dog whipped off his hat and stomped it into the wet sand, saying, "Geez! There were hot ashes shooting off everywhere. One must have landed on top of my hat! Darn!"

By then, the sisters and Gish were doubled over in laughter. Mad Dog whipped his hat across his thigh to get the sand off and examined it. There was a singed spot on the top of it. Shaking his head, he jammed it back on top of his bald head. When the laughter subsided, I took my two partridge out of my pockets, washed them, and skewered them on one of Gish's roasting sticks. Ching looked so proud when he said, "She shot and killed her first partridge this morning. She's a pretty good shot."

Mom stopped midsentence in her conversation with Minnie, and Dad raised an eyebrow, but then Mom smiled. "Really? Where have you been practicing?" I was just bursting with pride, totally happy with my new-found skill.

CHAPTER FOURTEEN

Dog Tracks

During the first week in November, Dad came into the house saying that the funeral would start at two in the afternoon that day. It was for the Medicine Man who had given me my name. I'd heard that the old man had died when I was at the Band office waiting for Dad several days before. Somebody said that he was eighty-six. There had been a full traditional funeral ceremony for him already at the community centre. The whole family went and I met up with Mary there. There was thick smoke from the smudge bowls, and the drums beat as people shuffled by where the body lay. Mary and I decided to hang back and we didn't go through the procession around the body. Linda, Alice, Kitty, Aunt Lucy, and Mom, along with several other women, had been busy with the wake and feast that followed. He was a very important person in the community so everyone would be at the funeral.

Dad pulled up in the truck around noon, saying that he'd have to pick up several people so we would have to walk to the church on the hill. It was all Mom could do to get Blink and David out of the house and up the path to the church on time. They absolutely didn't want to go. When we got there, all the dogs had followed their owners to the location, and, as we walked up the steps to the church, a dogfight erupted. We had to step aside as some men dashed outside to chase the dogs away. I looked around the room. There were so many people I didn't know and many others I knew I'd never even seen before. It was the first time I'd seen the inside of the church too. The casket was sitting sideways at the front. There were many plastic flowers of all colours everywhere. Some were woven into an archway that led to the pulpit.

There were many people who didn't go to any church and I knew that Dad and Lucy's family didn't go. Neither did Mary's family. Actually, I don't think any members of the Dog Tracks venture were churchgoing people.

When the service began, people stopped shuffling in their seats and an Aboriginal minister began the service in Ojibwe. When the service was over, people went up to talk about the Medicine Man. Some stories were funny; others were testimonials of his skill as a healer. Charlisse started crying, so I had to take her outside to the lobby. I decided to stay there until people started to come out. When Dad appeared, we moved out of the way until Mom came to join us with Blink and David beside her. The funeral procession began forming a line but we were waiting for Linda and Mike. When they came out from the crowd, we headed to our place for supper. Along the way, Alice and Ned also joined us. Gish was included in the group of elders from the community in some official ceremony at the gravesite, and Ching was driving the elders to where they needed to be.

We'd received a call from Maggie in Thunder Bay and she talked about the house she lived in with four other girls in the basement recreation room. Their landlord and landlady had ten-year-old twin boys and they were pests. The man worked at the local mill and his wife stayed home. They went up for meals and helped clean the dishes but that was it. They had a bathroom with a shower in the basement, a television, a pool table, and a wall-to-wall bookshelf that was full of books of all kinds. She also said that Grandma Beth came down to see her every weekend and that they always did things together on Saturdays. I felt a tug in my heart when she told me that. I still missed being with Grandma Beth.

My music lessons at school were coming along really well. Miss Tish came into class one afternoon with a beaming smile and announced, "Look what Chief Paulie has bought us!" She held out a really expensive-looking guitar. I knew that I was going to try my best to learn how to play that thing.

After that community radio dedication love song we did, Abraham and I became known as "Abby and Abe." People started calling us to come and sing songs for them right away, but we just didn't have any prepared. That was when we decided that we should record some and play them over the phone and have people pick the ones they wanted us to sing. That would make it easier for us. We had done another song just the week before for a young woman's birthday party. A boyfriend she had broken up with asked us to sing a song at her birthday party. He'd given the song to Abraham, so I hadn't heard it yet when we met at Paulie's house after supper. Paulie was there, of course, and we sat down in the living room with the tape recorder on the coffee table.

Abraham put the tape in and once the song started playing I couldn't believe what I was listening to! It was so really, really, bad! I remembered a lyric that went, "The holes in my shoes, that I wore out in the hall, kicking the wall over you, are the size of the hole that you put in my heart, that is killing me every day!" Paulie was just wailing and I watched Abraham as he burst into laughter so hard, he had tears running down the corners of his eyes before he could take a breath in. That whole time, I think I just had my mouth wide open. It would have been hilarious if someone had videotaped our reactions. Paulie was on the floor before the chorus began again and she stretched her arm out to the machine and hit the "stop" button. It was a good fifteen minutes before we could stop laughing long enough to say anything. I finally managed, "Uh, uh, no way!" So that was the end of the practice session. Paulie wanted to know what she could do for us, anything at all.

Abraham said, "More CDs and blank tapes would be nice."

I added, "Music sheets of contemporary songs would be nice."

She clapped her hands and said, "Done! I'm off to the music store after the meeting in Toronto on Friday!"

Abraham went back to the guy and gave him some options, and the guy picked a happy birthday love song instead. We were able to sing that song at the birthday party as a special birthday present. We didn't tell the birthday girl who had sent us because he'd given us fifty dollars each to sing it to her and not say who it was from. We walked back to the Band office since the girl only lived about four blocks away. On the way, I was looking at the ground when I asked Abraham, "You were so mean to me when I first got here. What did you say to those boys about me that made them giggle and laugh at me?"

He actually stopped and I didn't notice until he wasn't walking beside me anymore. I had to stop and turn around and he just stood there looking at me. I walked back to him, looked up at his face, and asked rather loudly, "What? You can't remember?"

He went around me and continued walking. I turned and kept pace with him for a few minutes and then he said, "I used to look at you from the back of the room and I'd say to whoever was beside me, 'See that girl? She's going to be my wife someday.' Then they'd look at you and laugh at me and say, 'No way! City girl like her? What would she want with you?' Sometimes they'd say, 'She's got a rich white grandmother who probably has a rich white boy lined up to marry her!' And on and on it would go. I'm sorry that you thought I was saying anything bad about you."

My heart was beating fast and I couldn't think of anything to say. Here, all that spring, I'd hated him, thinking he was so mean to cause me so much hurt. After a dozen steps or so, I reached over and tugged a corner of his jacket and let go. I couldn't bring myself to actually say anything.

I took off my good pink dress and hung it up on the hook. I only wore my good dresses from Grandma Beth when I went to sing for people. Afterward I'd put on my reserve dresses or my jeans. After supper, I went to Paulie's house to start boxing the outfits that would have to be moved to the new Dog Tracks office building. I did have a shock when I came into the dressing room to put some more mitts into the boxes. I turned and came face to face with myself in the full-length mirror. I looked exactly like Maggie did when I first saw her after moving to Bear Creek. When she wasn't wearing jeans, she wore the same kind of clothes that I was now wearing. I remembered feeling embarrassed for her and had stopped myself from giggling just in time. Well, now here I was. I had on a pair of boots that stuck out beneath the hem of my cotton skirt. I still wore stretchy black pants underneath my skirts since I didn't want to wear stockings. I had my blue ski jacket on and a blue scarf pulled tightly over my head. I looked like one of the old Northern Indian women I used to see in town at Nibika or even in Thunder Bay. "When did this happen?" I thought as I blinked at my reflection. I looked like the rest of the women in my community now.

Maggie would have shed these clothes in Thunder Bay to put on jeans and sweatshirts and ski jackets and long coats. She would probably wear a toque or one of those fancy hats that women wore in the city. Black leather gloves, a fancy scarf around her neck, and high-heeled boots. Yeah, I could see her in high-heeled boots! I looked down at my own boots. Well, you couldn't avoid the mud. There was mud everywhere—on the gravel roads, the paths, the playground outside the school, and at everyone's front door.

Alice came in and noticed me examining my reflection. She was dressed just like me too. She raised her eyebrows, tilted her head, nodded her approval, smiled, and took my hand as we headed out of the Chief's house.

Several weeks later, there was some commotion from some of the Band members about the construction of the Dog Tracks tourist building right beside the Band office. After some discussion, the Chief called a meeting of all those involved with Dog Tracks. We all arrived at the appointed time the next evening in the Band office meeting room with all the councillors present. Chief Paulie announced that we should put on a demonstration of the Dog Tracks tourist venture for the community. She was suggesting that we get into our period garb and demonstrate some of the activities that would take place at the 1800s-era Dog Tracks Anishinabe campsite. What had started out as a small community project had become what could be a huge tourist attraction, We needed the full support of the whole community to continue.

After two hours of brainstorming, the Dog Tracks members and the Chief and council decided that we would put on a half-hour presentation. When? It would be held at the end of the fall festival at the community centre. We all turned to look at the calendar. Four weeks away! I was to sing a song with Abraham around a campfire in front of the platform that would serve as the stage. The only music would come from the youth drum group providing soft background drumming.

I was just bursting with the news, so I dashed into the Band office and called Abraham on the phone. I ended my excited blabber at him with, "Oh, by the way, you're going to be a hunter in the presentation."

All he had time to say was, "Wait, wait, a what? A hunter?"

I said, "Yeah, come as yourself! I'll meet you tomorrow!"

After my initial excitement about the presentation, I became concerned about finding an Aboriginal song that Abraham and I could do. I'd have to go see Miss Tish and find out if there was anything in her collection that we could use. The next day, notices were put up announcing the event, and the radio station announced it as well.

Everything was pretty much complete at the Dog Tracks campsite, with the outhouse and a huge teepee where everyone would be sleeping. The construction of the Dog Tracks tourist building was now almost complete, with help from additional hands from the community. There had been a moment of anxiety when Chief Paulie decided to videotape the presentation to use as a promotional video. The sisters balked at the idea, and Gish didn't want to be seen walking and talking on videotape long after he was dead. In any case, Chief Paulie assured them that it would be a good show-off for the outfits and that the presentation would highlight the daily life adventures of the 1800s Anishinawbe camp for the other community members whose support we needed. They were assured that their permission would be requested if the tape was going to be used for anything else. Finally, everything was set and everyone was satisfied with their role. The presentation began to take shape.

A big snowstorm hit the following week and the snow kept coming down for three whole days. By the time it blew over, there was a lot of snow shovelling that needed to be done at the construction site where the tarps had fallen in, laden with snow. Work was quickly restored and the roof was on, along with the floor, by the end of the week. Miss Tish found a song that Abraham and I could sing without music and we practiced with her help. I discovered that Abraham had a wonderful voice when his croaking finally disappeared. He and I sang the chorus with Miss Tish in the room and she said that we sounded wonderful together. Abraham was still very uncertain about his voice. "What if I suddenly croak when it's my turn?" he asked. "They'll call me Abe the Frog!"

We started practicing with the youth drum group, but we soon discovered that all eight of them could never be there at the same time. There was always one missing! After some frustrating practices, Miss Tish tape-recorded us singing and then gave the tape to the group. A week later, the drum group told us that they didn't like having to play background music for us because it wasn't what they were meant to do. Wondering why they hadn't just said so in the first place, Miss Tish said she knew how to play the flute, so she recorded a soft flute tune that could go with the song. When she gave us the tape, we put it on and after the fifth beat, we began to sing. By the time we were done, Miss Tish was jumping up and down. It was perfect. Whew! Abraham and I celebrated our achievement by going hunting together for the first time—with Ching.

Finally, the day arrived. We were at the community centre at nine in the morning to do one rehearsal. That was all everyone could handle. We all went in through the back door to a curtained-off area and up three steps through a curtain to where we emerged from the half-wigwam. In front of us was a stage area just high enough so people could see us from their seats. The bare plywood stage was covered with sheets of white cotton batting to make it look like there was snow on the ground. There were piles of spruce boughs stacked at the sides of the doorway. They were to be used to cover the floor at the entrance.

We went through our paces but didn't actually sing or say what we would end up saying during the presentation. Even the dogs were brought in. Ki-Moot, Mucko, Shingoos, and Wiener were dragged in through the curtain by Ned onto the stage in the empty room, where they stood around with their tails between their legs and their ears plastered to their heads, milling around Ned, looking totally bewildered. After that, they were hauled out again. On and on the practice went with, Ching and Gish crashing into each other at the entrance. Yeah, I guess we all got the basic idea!

After the practice, we all left to get ready for the presentation. Sooner or later, we ended up at Chief Paulie's place to pick up our outfits. It was a good thing that Linda and Aunt Lucy had thought to bring a big tray of food for us because no one thought that we'd have any time to eat before we had to appear onstage. There was much laughter and jostling as we got dressed. At one point, Gish couldn't find his rabbit hat, until someone noticed that it was hanging out of Ned's big muskrat pants!

Abraham looked handsome in his leather outfit. He rather looked like one of those fake Indians from an old Western movie. His black hair was swept back and his tanned face and dark eyelashes really accentuated the typical Hollywood Indian look. Alice called him a handsome young Tonto. His leather shirt was beaded in symmetrical designs across the shoulders that swung down across the chest, and from the fringed leather shoulders, the beaded symmetrical designs flowed down the sleeves. The bottom part of the shirt was beaded and fringed as well. The pants were just as spectacular. There was beaded trim that ran down the side of his leg. Below that, he wore beaded moccasins that disappeared beneath his fringed pants. The vamps of the moccasins were clearly visible, however, and I experienced a shock of recognition that the beaded pattern on them was one of several that I'd designed for the sisters!

I wore a full-length leather dress with a beaded belt across my waist. There was a beaded collar around my neck that spilled out over my chest. The sleeves of my dress were fringed and came down to my elbows. The bottom of the dress had a trailing vine of beadwork that went around the hem. I also had beaded moccasins on. My hair was tied back with a beaded hair clip. I felt good in my outfit and received many compliments.

So then it was on with the show. We arrived just when the tables were cleared at the back of the community centre to make room for the view of the stage. The final stage set-up required a man to throw down four pieces of wood, crossed at the ends, for the campfire and put in one of those Halloween fan-blown pieces of white cloth set against orange light that looked like fake flames coming out. He set that inside the crossed logs and it certainly looked like flames coming out between the logs! Then the show began when the overhead spotlights went out. The only lights on in the room were the flickering lights from the fake campfire on the stage.

I grabbed Abraham's hand as we pushed our way past the wigwam curtain. We walked onstage and sat beside the flickering fire. Then the flute music started very softly, which was my cue to start singing. We kept our eyes on each other as I began softly and let my voice lift to the pretend stars. At the chorus, Abraham's voice joined mine and much to my relief, we sang on key with the flute. When the song was over, there were resounding whistles, hoots, and clapping from the audience. Then he extended his hand and held mine as I got up and we withdrew to the side of the wigwam. Not only was my heart pounding from the exhilaration of the performance, but the touch of Abraham's hand on mine sent shivers up my spine and left my knees feeling weak.

Then the light changed and the youth drum group began to sing a song as the women—Alice, Kitty, Minnie, and Lizzy in full traditional outfits— walked in with clothing and hides draped over their arms. As the drumming continued, they hung the beaded leather outfits on poles and put the birchbark contents of mitts and mukluks along the edge of the stage. Everyone sat down around the edge of the wigwam except Alice. She made her way back to the entrance and shook her butt in a wiggle before she stepped back inside the wigwam. The audience laughed and cheered!

Linda and Mom were next to come out, dressed in their outfits, with Charlisse in the fancy tikinagan. Behind them were David and Blink. They came in to a loud quick note from the drummers as they found a place on the other side of the wigwam. Then Gish stepped out, his smaller form decked out in a rabbit-skin semi-white outfit. He kind of looked like a small Big Foot character, I thought, or perhaps a mottled snowball that had rolled in the dirt along the baseball diamond slough. His skinny legs were tightly encased in leather with fringes that disappeared into huge white rabbit-skin mukluks. I felt Abraham shaking with suppressed laughter beside me and I pinched his arm. I'd never actually seen Gish in this particular outfit either. He'd traded in his beaded leather jacket for the woven rabbit-skin one. The rabbit skins weren't all white either. Some of them were darker summer skins. I did remember the sisters trying to discourage him from wearing the rabbit-skin coat with the leather pants. Oh well, I thought. You couldn't ever tell Gish anything! We did hear sporadic snickering and giggling after he finished his turn on the stage before he sat down at the other side of the entrance to the wigwam.

The giggles were just subsiding and the drumming had slowed down a bit when suddenly the drums picked up tempo and with a loud crash, *Kwingo-aggeh* flung himself through the doorway of the wigwam. There was a loud gasp from the audience and children screamed and rushed away from the stage when he came pouncing to its edge, growling, hissing, and careening around the open space, flexing his arms and completely showing off his shimmering, monstrous fur. His face was painted black, and his broken nose accentuated his two white canine teeth. He gave one monstrous hooting growl and jumped clear off the stage and then back up and into the wigwam. There were many hoots and claps when he disappeared.

Just when the song ended, another began, slower this time, and then Ki-Moot, Bannock, Shingoos, and Wiener pranced through the doorway to the wigwam with their tails up and ears at full attention, followed by Ned in a full leather trapper's outfit. The dogs stopped in the middle of the stage, uncertain of where they were. Their ears and tails went down and we could hear Ned talking to them. He ran them around the stage on their leashes several times and then they ducked back into the wigwam. Ned did a really good job with the dogs. Everyone clapped and hooted. Then Dad and Mike emerged in traditional men's clothing, each holding a bundle of ducks and rabbits that they deposited beside the fire.

Suddenly, the lights went out and the drums stopped. Then the drummers hit a loud, resounding boom in unison and a figure hurled out of the wigwam. He had a mask on that totally covered his face and he began to dance a very crazy wild dance, jerking and flowing to and fro. He had on a bearskin that flowed with his movements and his body was encased in leather so as to look like he was totally naked under the cloak! His head was horrible to behold. His mask showed grotesque bear teeth, horrible painted eyes that glistened, and wild hair that hung down in chunks around his face. He was also wearing a huge headdress that looked like ears with horns. He pranced about and gave a wild guttural roar at the end of the dance. Then he disappeared back into the wigwam. Ching? Yes, that was Ching! The audience exploded into hysterical whistles and hooting.

After Ching's dance, the youth drum group were given time to do their own song while the rest of the people standing backstage got ready to come back in. When the song ended, Mad Dog and Ching came back onstage together to the sound of resounding clapping and hooting, and then Ned and Alice came onstage with the baskets of gifts that would be distributed to the kids, just like they would be at the end of a feast.

The lights came on and we all lined up around the stage while Chief Paulie introduced the Dog Tracks team. After that, people came rushing up and everyone was very excited to touch the clothes and ask questions while Chief Paulie asked some of the students to run around and pass out the gifts of goodies for the kids. I was so relieved that the whole thing was over and that we'd pulled it off perfectly!

The presentation turned out to be a very good idea indeed. Dog Tracks received all the support that it could ever want from the community, including some expertise on traditional trapping methods from several of the older hunters. The sisters also discovered there were two other women in the community who processed hides the way they did.

The excitement was high, right up to the day when the first official tourists were set to arrive, and then anxiety began to set in. Ned got sick with the flu and we had to pull in one of the new trappers to take over for him. The new man, Jim, was a trapper from up the hill by the airport road who turned out to be a very nice man. It also turned out that he worked very well with the dogs. Kitty was prepared to replace Alice for the weekend while she stayed home to nurse Ned back to health. The Dog Tracks office was open now with its fully stocked rooms of period clothing and supplies, along with a gift shop run by students from the college off-campus business program. Everything was set to go.

Finally, it was the first day of business. The chartered flight came in on a ski plane at the Band office dock and Chief Paulie was there to welcome her friends from the south. Five people got off the plane, two women and three men. Dad was there when they were introduced and he came home to tell us that they were all Chiefs of different First Nations from southern Ontario. There were movie cameras and people to accompany the first expedition to the 1800s Dog Tracks Aboriginal camp. Chief Paulie had enlisted and flown in a friend and his camera crew to make the initial promotional video.

I sat with Charlisse at home while Dad and Mom joined the group at the Band office to complete the details on who was going on which snow machine. Even Blink would be going to the campsite with David. I couldn't go because Abraham and I were scheduled for practice tomorrow for the school Christmas pageant. Grandma Beth had already put more than three hundred dollars into my bank account. That didn't even include the money I got from Paulie for the stockroom work at her house. That money I gave to Mom for her little hoard that Dad teased her about sometimes. She saved every bit of money from her pay and put it into a jar. Whenever she had enough accumulated for airfare, she'd plan a trip for all of us somewhere. It was money from the jar that had paid for our trip to Winnipeg for my thirteenth birthday.

After our practice, I told Abraham that I was banking my money for when I headed out for high school. It would be my spending money for whatever I would need. I asked Abraham what he was going to do with his money. He said he was saving up to buy a snow machine so he could go hunting farther away. He said that he could make more than three times the money on pelts than what we made singing songs if he could go out farther to get them. We were now singing together most of the time and had started making up songs by ourselves. He had a soft voice that complemented mine very well. I think he was gradually getting over worrying that his voice would suddenly croak. Our songs were in Ojibwe and sometimes we made up songs that didn't require a musical instrument at all. It was a lot of fun singing in Ojibwe. All of a sudden, we were getting feedback from parents, grandparents, and even our Native language teachers. We sang one of our Ojibwe songs on the community radio station just as a lark to see what would happen. It was amazing the outpouring of community support that we received.

After a very successful first week out at the 1800s campsite, there was a feast and celebration to honour the first Dog Tracks tourists. The tourists went home early the next morning. Several nights later, all of us, including Abraham, of course, assembled at Mad Dog and Kitty's place, since they had the clearest satellite and largest television screen. When the news broadcast came on the television to announce the latest business venture of a Northern community, we saw the footage about the new tourist camp up north called Dog Tracks, complete with footage about the heroic rescue of a moose that had fallen through the thin ice in the river. The cameras had captured our group, with help from the tourists, rescuing the poor animal. The last segment of the footage showed the moose slowly wandering away and then picking up speed toward some underbrush well away from the river. Then there was Ki-Moot, Mucko, Shingoos, and Wiener pulling two of the tourists in one sled and right behind them, Daish, Bingo, Bannock, Ozit, Chippy, and Samson with the rest of the five tourists, fading into the sunset across the lake.

We all clapped and hooted, "Yeah! Yeah! Well done!"

When we finally left the house, we headed back home, all of us rather quiet and thoughtful. I thought about how far I'd travelled to becoming a member of this community. But then, looking into my future, I knew that I'd be flipped out of it again when I left to complete high school in the city, just like that stone in the river that Chief Paulie had told me about when I first came to Bear Creek. I'd have to ask her how this little stone would fare when I left. After all, she seemed to know everything. Suddenly, Blink landed flat on his back in front of me and I nearly tripped over him. He'd insisted on wearing moccasins and he'd stepped on a sheet of ice on the road. Ice on snow-covered moccasins was indeed very slippery.

About Fifth House

Fifth House Publishers, a Fitzhenry & Whiteside company, is a proudly western-Canadian press. Our publishing specialty is non-fiction as we believe that every community must possess a positive understanding of its worth and place if it is to remain vital and progressive. Fifth House is committed to "bringing the West to the rest" by publishing books about the land and people who make this region unique. Our books are selected for their quality and contribution to the understanding of western-Canadian (and Canadian) history, culture, and environment.

Look for *Silent Words*, another book by Ruby Slipperjack, at your local bookstore.

"Ruby Slipperjack is one of the strongest Native voices in Canadian literature."
Thomas King

SILENT WORDS

A NOVEL BY
RUBY SLIPPERJACK

Silent Words
a novel by Ruby Slipperjack

Set in northwestern Ontario in the 1960s, *Silent Words* tells the story of a young Native boy and his journey of self-discovery. When Danny runs away from his violent and abusive home, he learns about himself and the world he lives in. *Silent Words* offers an intimate view of Native communities and their values: being nonjudgmental, open and accepting, sharing with others, and respecting elders.

The *Keepers* Series

These bestselling books have been long-time favourites with educators for their innovative approach to teaching children about Native cultures and the environment. Each book, co-authored by Joseph Bruchac and Michael J. Caduto, combines Native legends with information and activities about the natural world. Books in the *Keepers* series are recommended by educational journals across North America for children aged five to twelve.

"Gives a wonderful overview of the rich diversity of cultures that flourished on this continent before colonization."
—*The Indigenous Times*

Look for the following titles in the *Keepers* series in your local bookstore, or call 1-800-387-9776.

Keepers of Life

Discovering Plants through Native Stories and Earth Activities for Children

Keepers of the Animals

*Native Stories and Wildlife
Activities for Children*

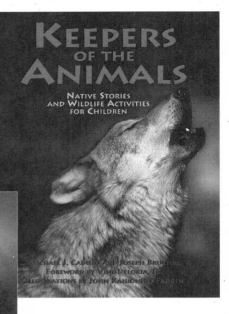

Keepers of the Night

*Native Stories and
Nocturnal Activities
for Children*

Keepers of the Earth

*Native Stories and Environmental
Activities for Children*

The Land is Our Storybook

The Land is Our Storybook is a series of books about the diverse lands and cultures of Canada's Northwest Territories. In the books, storytellers, Elders, and cultural leaders in the territory share real stories of everyday life in the North today. The books are illustrated by the striking images of northern photographer Tessa Macintosh. Series writer Mindy Willett, an educator in Yellowknife, helped bring the storytellers' words into book format.

Look for the following books in *The Land is Our Storybook* series at your local bookstore, or call 1-800-387-9776.

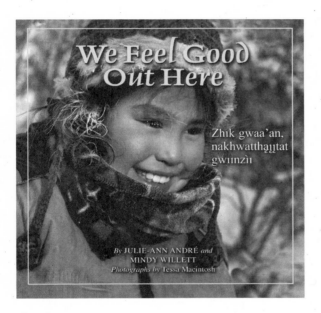

We Feel Good Out Here

by Julie-Ann André and Mindy Willett

"*We Feel Good Out Here* makes me feel good about the future of Aboriginal people in the North."

— CATHERINE PIGOTT, CBC NORTH RADIO

The Delta is My Home

by Tom McLeod and Mindy Willett

"Tom's story is a call to action for all of us to conserve invaluable places and ways of life."

—DR. RICK WISHART,
DIRECTOR OF EDUCATION,
DUCKS UNLIMITED CANADA

Dreaming Mountain

by Therese Zoe, Philip Zoe, and Mindy Willett

"This book is a celebration of our inheritance as Tlicho people, and I am grateful for its sweet medicine! What a treasure! *Mahsi cho*!"

—RICHARD VAN CAMP, AUTHOR
THE LESSER BLESSED AND
A MAN CALLED RAVEN

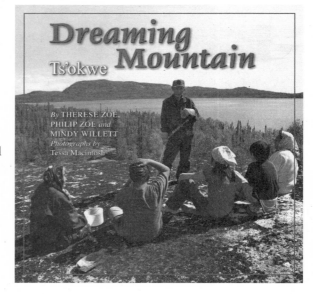